Righting the Hourglass

Righting *the* Hourglass

Lisa Blumberg

FERNFIELD IMPRINTS

WEST HARTFORD, CONNECTICUT

Published by Fernfield Imprints
West Hartford, Connecticut
© 2019 by Lisa Blumberg
All rights reserved

ISBN: 978-0-578-48916-2

Cover design by Katherine B. Kimball. Photograph 185335 © Dana Rothstein | Dreamstime. com. Typeset in ITC Galliard by Passumpsic Publishing.

Manufactured in the United States of America

To the four generations of my family,

with love and appreciation

Contents

Acknowledgments

It may take a village to raise a child, but it also takes a village to enable someone to write a novel, especially if it is a debut novel.

Thanks go first to my sister-in-law Jane Blumberg and niece Gwen Blumberg, who on an August night in 2008 at our summer house in Vermont listened as I recounted a lengthy plotline I wanted to turn into a story. It was late and they wanted to go sleep, but still they listened as I droned on and on. "Stephen was eaten?" Gwen asked in surprise at one point. "No, Stephen went to Eton," Jane replied. With their encouragement, I felt I should start typing.

I also thank Jane, as well as my great college friend Carolyn Wood, for reading the entire first draft in installments and giving me valuable comments on what didn't work. What's more, they each had saved enough of the installments that when my computer crashed with my two-thirds-done manuscript gone forever, I could reconstruct everything except for sixty pages that I hadn't sent them. Jane and Carolyn truly saved the bacon.

My gratitude to my late aunt Holly Mitchell Kimball for telling me a little-known family story about a friendship my mother Janet Mitchell Blumberg had during the Second World War with a man named Louis who was in New York City buying supplies for the French Resistance. He became the inspiration for the book's fleeting references to Louis the Buyer.

Thanks to Susan Leon for her editorial advice. She caused me to think critically on both characterization and plot. If one can't get an MFA in writing, Susan is the next best thing. Thanks to my friend, former colleague in the insurance world, and novelist Deborah Hauer Schwartz, who connected me with Susan and shared her knowledge of publishing.

I am grateful to my cousin-in-law Kathy Kimball, book designer par excellence who connected me to Ann Brash who connected me to Glenn Novak. Without the three of them, there would be no book. My thanks go as well to Doug Tifft of Redwing Book Services who also provided invaluable guidance.

My techie friend Victor Pina set me up on a new PC after the crash and taught me how to digitally store documents. Andrew DeVito, my personal trainer, frequently asked how the story was coming, thus encouraging me to keep on when my enthusiasm flagged, just as he does in other contexts. My friend Jan Perry suggested books to read on raj orphans that contributed to my historical insight, although Amelia did not come close to being a raj orphan.

Then there is my friend Hope Seeley, who was instrumental in saving my life on *two* occasions during the ten years I was intermittently working on my story. Although she didn't know about my project, it never would have been completed without her help. Thank you, Hope!

Lastly, I would like to give a nod to the best advice I read about writing fiction. It was that instead of writing about what you know, you should tell the story you need to tell. This allowed me to write about places I've never been to, experiences I've never had, and create families not my own while still remaining myself.

Righting the Hourglass

CHAPTER I

War!

West Coast of Devon, 1943–1945

MY FIRST MEMORY is of Devon and of our rented house where the morning sun came through the bay windows of the sitting room and made patterns on the rug. I was probably three, so that would make it 1943. My five-year-old brother Stephen and I were sitting on the floor in a crisscrossed oval of light, playing with our alphabet blocks. Stephen was trying to build a castle with his share. I was making designs with mine. My mother was at her writing desk. She was wearing her tweed skirt, a white blouse, and perhaps her beige cardigan. Our tan cocker spaniel, Folly, was lying in the wing chair as was increasingly her habit, even though she wasn't supposed to, but my mother said she had more to think about than a dog sleeping in a chair. This was war.

Folly sat up and gave two yips as we heard a soft thump at the front door. My mother said, "Why, thank you, Folly, for heralding the post" and then went to the hall to collect our letters. She came back and stood while she opened a thin blue envelope that was on the top of the stack. She read the front page and then the back page to herself. Biting her lip a little, she reread the letter. Then she said in her important news voice, "Stephen! Amelia! Your father sends you his love."

"Love," I repeated, liking the way my tongue moved as I said the word.

My mother smiled briefly and nodded. She read the letter a third time before sitting down and turning to the rest of the post.

My first memory may have details from different days. It may be reconstructed, although I have read that all memory is. This was before time was linear, when it swirled and ebbed and flowed, so all I know for double sure is that the scene or variations on it had happened before and would happen again in a repeating pattern. My mother would never read us any portion of our father's letters, but she would tell us that he sent us his love or that he gave us his love or he assured us of his love.

[1]

Once, Stephen asked, "When is Daddy finally coming home forever?"

"When we win the war, which we shall," my mother replied. "But really, Stephen, I've explained it to you often, and I don't see how I can explain it better. I'd prefer it if you didn't ask again." Then her voice softened. "We don't want to worry Amelia, do we? She's so small."

I wasn't worried. My mother and Jenny, the older girl who lived with us, were always making plans. My mother told her that if we ever needed to hurry to the basement of the church in the middle of the night, she would grab me, and Jenny should help Stephen. They would just have to trust Folly to follow.

"Should we take a second to get some of your silver items, Mrs. Ord?" Jenny had asked. "You said they've been in your family for generations. I can carry a satchel in one hand and still help Stephen run."

My mother had look startled. "Oh no, Jenny," she said. "If the siren sounds, our only goal is to get to shelter with the children."

"Of course, Mrs. Ord," Jenny had said.

Stephen and I were getting bigger all the time. When Stephen looked for his gray sweater, my mother told him that he had outgrown it and she had given it to another boy. She handed him his blue sweater.

My mother was a very busy person. Often in the mornings, she rode her bicycle into the village to roll bandages at the council hall or to read and write letters for blind Mrs. Lathrop, whose son was in the Royal Navy, or to check on the vegetables that Mrs. Lathrop let us grow in her greenhouse in exchange. Sometimes, too, my mother met with her ladies' group.

Once when Jenny had the day off, the ladies' group came to our house. Stephen opened the door, and I passed out the teaspoons, even though there was no sugar for the tea. There were only four ladies, but they crowded the sitting room. The ladies in their Sunday dresses were happy, though, and clapped and cheered when my mother, whom they called Olivia, told them that Louis the Buyer had been in New York and he had sent word through his London contact that the woman and the boy had gotten to Switzerland. They had helped save two. Two, they had helped saved. Two! Two! I held up two fingers for two, and the ladies clapped and cheered again. They all wanted to help save more. My mother said, "I think Louis knows that we are like Barkis. We are willing."

I whispered to Folly, "Barkis," and she licked my nose.

My mother sang "tea for two, and two for tea" as she poured the tea, and everyone joined in. My mother said that this was such a grand day that she would like to open a tin of biscuits she had been holding back, but she felt that she should keep it for Stephen's and my birthdays because she would not be able to manage even small cakes this year. The ladies all told Olivia that she was doing the right thing. Children must have treats on their birthdays, even in wartime.

My mother was always with Stephen and me in the afternoons, and so after rest time, except when it was pouring, we went walking. We would cross the road in front of our house and be on the moor. The moor has paths for us to choose, but it was really a great garden of silvery green grass with rises and swells, stretching on and on under the sky. Laced into the grass was heather in all shades of purple, from light lavender to nearly a dark blue. Mingling with the heather were bright wildflowers, as well as the proper flowers that people, including ourselves, had planted. Through October, when we had begun to wear our woolens, there was a bloom, with the white asters hanging on to the last. We walked this way and that, and even in winter, looking at moss and twigs and into crevices, we remarked on things we had not noticed before.

In high summer and at other times when the weather was very fair, we walked in the other direction, down a trail lined with roses, to the beach. As grass changed into sand, the smell of salt would rise, and gulls circled overhead. We would watch the waves of the ocean, called the Atlantic, come in with a whoosh and out with whoosh, surf and spray bouncing towards the gulls and then sailing to our feet. Folly yipped when the tide was high, and we pretended that the tide heard her and went back in the sea, only to come in again. Stephen and I looked for shells or played in the rock pools where the water, warmed by the sun, stayed contained but always rippled.

My mother, taking snaps of us with her box camera, said we should pretend we were on holiday, although, of course, we could not go on a real holiday until after the war. Once she added with a faint smile that when we did go on holiday, maybe we would come to Devon, or at least stop in Devon on our way down to Cornwall.

Our afternoons would end when my mother said we had to go home so she could listen to the BBC, but we knew there would be another afternoon the next day. My mother called it our routine.

[3]

There came an afternoon, though after I had turned four, when we did not go out walking, although it was not even cloudy. Jenny came into our room after rest time and said that we must change into our best clothes because we had a very special visitor.

"Where's Mummy?" I asked.

"She's with the visitor, of course! Now, no more questions. He is waiting very eagerly." Jenny's eyes sparkled.

"Who is it?" Stephen asked.

"Didn't I say no more questions?"

Stephen got into his dark blue knee pants, his dress socks, and a white shirt. Jenny tied his striped bow tie for him, saying "I used to do this for my brother when he went out with his girl on Saturday nights. I need to write to him." I put on my pink velvet party dress with the smocking in front and the puff sleeves, and Jenny buttoned it up the back. She buckled my patent leather shoes and undid the yarn that gathered in my pigtails.

"Your mother said that you are to wear your organdy hair ribbons. Where might they be?" I pointed to the bureau, and Jenny got them, separated my pigtails again, and tied the ribbons around them. She told me I was pretty. This was a compliment, so I said "thank you."

Jenny went down the stairs with us, but we went to the entrance of the sitting room by ourselves. My mother was standing by the bay windows, and the sun still coming through made glints in her hair. She was wearing a lemon silk dress, a silver bracelet, and her pearls. There was a scent of jasmine about her. My mother often gave Stephen and me bits of smiles, but now she was glowing. Next to her was a large sturdy man in a blue-gray uniform. He had sandy hair like Stephen, only shorter, and my hazel eyes. We had his picture on the mantel.

"Daddy," Stephen whispered breathlessly. "Daddy!"

"Craig," my mother said joyously. "May I present Stephen and Amelia." She made a little flourish.

The man's look had been expectant as we came in, but now he gazed at us in silent wonder.

So this was Daddy. I had seen him once when I was a baby but didn't remember him.

We just stood there, and then Stephen took a step forward, put out hand and said, "Hello, sir."

"Hello, Stephen, hello!" the man said, taking Stephen's arm and pulling him to him. "You've grown to be quite a chap. And Amelia, come here, no need to hang back."

Mummy said, "It's all right," so I went to him, and he scooped me up. His arms were quite big.

I sat on the man's lap and looked at all the badges on his jacket, while Stephen showed him his coin collection. "We'll have fun working on this after the war," the man told Stephen. "I'll be able to get us coins from all over—Africa, the Arab states, Siam, India."

"Here are some Swiss coins Mummy gave me," Stephen said.

Daddy asked what my interests were. My mother brought me my dried-flower book, and I turned the rustling pages for the man. "Wax paper is crinkly," I explained.

"In London, we can get cellophane," he answered.

We got to the last page, and I said, "These are the asters. Mummy says they are hardy."

"And luckily, no relation to the other Astors," my mother added, and they both laughed.

"Did you hear about what Churchill said to Nancy?" the man asked her.

"I did," my mother said, and she giggled in a way that was different from her usual laugh.

Daddy turned back to me, and he said he knew I liked to sing. I nodded and sang "Do you know the muffin man" for him twice and "Ba ba black sheep" once.

"R-A-F," I read on one of his badges, and he seemed impressed.

Next, we went outside so that we could show him what a clever dog Folly was. She would roll over when asked. She could fetch a ball. When Stephen held a stick, she jumped over it and then turned around and jumped over it again. I took her front paws and said, "Folly, will you dance with me? Will you dance with me?" Moving her paws back and forth, I started swaying, and Folly danced. Daddy laughed.

He said to my mother, "They take so much pleasure in the dog. I'm glad we have her, even though I said at the time it was folly."

"Yes," my mother said, "we thought she would be our substitute for children, and now she is our children's substitute for playmates and toys."

"Do they know it won't always be like this?" He sounded concerned.

"I tell them, but I don't know if they can imagine. Although last

Christmas, when their main gift was an ancient rocking horse that it took hours of scavenging through the village to find, I said that after the war Santa would go back to doing his shopping at Harrods, and Stephen's eyes did light up."

My mother had told me who Harrods was, but I could not remember. I was glad though that she had told the man about our rocking horse. Santa Claus had gotten it from another family, and my mother and Jenny had repainted it a sparkling white with green and red stars, while we slept. We kept its Christmas bow on it so that it would look even livelier. Stephen and I were always riding it during rest time.

We went back inside, and Stephen and I sat on each side of the man on the sofa. He said to us, "Your father loves you."

"I know," Stephen said, and leaned against him.

I sat straight up, but I also said "I know," and of course, we did. My father wrote my mother once or twice a week to say just that.

He pulled out two small paper bags and gave one to us each. Inside were two sticks of peppermint, one solid white and one with pink swirls, and something wrapped in foil.

Daddy said that the candy was a very small token of all the good things to come when this terrible war was over and we were all living the lives we had expected to live. The peppermint was English, of course, but a friend of his who was a Yank had given him the chocolate. It had come from a place called Pennsylvania.

"Pennsylvania," I said.

He said, "Yes, that's right."

He talked to us a little more about our future until Jenny came in, because it was time for Stephen and me to eat. The last thing Daddy said to us after kissing us each was "Keep close to your mother."

It was a meatless day, so Jenny gave us cheese over toast, and sliced tomatoes with slivers of a hardboiled egg. I waited until she had sat down and then said, "He mentioned my father, but I thought Daddy was my father."

"He was referring to himself," Jenny said.

"That's right, you silly, you dummy," Stephen exclaimed. He started to throw his napkin at me, but Jenny caught it and told him to behave.

At the end of supper we had a bit of the peppermint candy, sharing it with Jenny and saving some for the next day.

Jenny put us to bed that night. "Where's Mummy?" I asked.

"She's still with Captain Ord. He has only an eighteen-hour leave. Do you begrudge them the time?"

I didn't know what "begrudge" meant, but it sounded like a wrong thing to do, so I said no.

Jenny read us our Babar book, although she told us she was not the reader my mother was, and she was right. She read some words slowly and did not use special voices for the elephants as Mummy did, but we fell into the drift of the story even so. Then she lined up our shoes by our beds in case we had to get to the church, and said good night.

Sleep pictures of waving grasses by water were coming before my eyes when our door opened and the shadowy forms of my mother and my father came into the room. "Mummy," I murmured.

"Shh, darling," she whispered. "Please do not speak. Please don't wake up. We just want to sit here for a while."

There was only one chair in our room, so my father sat in it, and my mother got on the floor and put her head against his knee, and he put his arm around her shoulder. I don't know how long they stayed there.

In the morning, the man who was Daddy was gone. I loved both the peppermint and the chocolate, but the peppermint was more familiar.

Stephen and I tried to follow our father's advice to keep close to our mother, insofar as we could. In the mornings when Jenny took us out to play, we ran helter-skelter, but on our afternoon walks, I held my mother's hand, and Stephen walked next to her on her other side. Even Folly would take short running leaps ahead and then race right back to her feet. We walked on the moor amid the purple heather. Even if we walked as far as the giant tors, the heather was before us.

I suddenly was five, and Stephen was seven, old enough to learn school subjects. Every evening after we ate, my mother did words and numbers with him. Then they did geography while I and sometimes Jenny watched. They moved pins around on a map of Europe that we had in the kitchen. First, the pins were only in France and Italy. Some evenings, the pins stayed where they were. Then there were a run of evenings where my mother and Stephen moved them quickly. The pins were in Belgium. They were in Holland. One night, my mother told Stephen to move them all to the edge of Germany.

"That means—"my mother said, and then she hesitated.

"The Nazis' goose is cooked," Jenny suddenly suggested.

"Quite right, Jenny!" my mother replied, and they both clapped.

My mother explained that there were, in fact, other pins that she had omitted from our map to keep things simple, but perhaps children, sitting with their mothers in far away Russia, were moving them in from the east, and when our pins and their pins met in the center of Germany, the war in Europe would be over.

Then one evening, without even waiting for us to have supper, my mother came from listening to the wireless and breathlessly told Stephen to move the pins to Berlin, in the center of Germany. "I know where Germany is," I said, and I did, for I had learned what Stephen had learned. "Then, help him, Amelia!" my mother replied. She beckoned Jenny too, and the four of us moved the pins into the center of Germany together.

"Hooray for England!" Stephen shouted. "Hooray for Daddy!'

We all cried "Hooray! Hooray!" We clapped, we cheered. Folly yipped. Stephen made the victory sign, and my mother kissed him. She kissed me, and she and Jenny shook hands, and then they hugged.

The world has the hope of being safe again," she told Jenny. My eyes widened. We lived in the world. "Haven't we been safe?" I asked.

Stephen gave me a look of disdain, but my mother put her hand up. She bent down and kissed me again. "Of course, darling, we've been safe. That's why we've been in Devon all these years, yes?"

She went on to say that now *all* of England would be safe, and Europe as well, and Daddy would hurry home as fast as he could so he could take up being Stephen's and my father.

"I know," Stephen exulted. "I know." My mother turned and kissed him, so the kisses she had given us would be equal. I danced with Folly and my mother, and Jenny laughed. We heard church bells ringing in the village.

That night, a while after my mother had read to Stephen and me about Christopher Robin and tucked each of us in, I heard her coming back up the stairs with Jenny. They were talking in a quite regretful way about people they had known who were no longer here.

A few evenings later, we went down to the beach to see the bonfires and the fireworks. The whole village was there, and although it was after dark, Mrs. Lathrop, who was still nearly blind, said it was as bright as day. Boys shouted and ran about waving the union jack, old men made speeches, a woman played a flute, and everyone sang. There was suddenly somber silence as they talked about Caleb and George who had once played on this very beach. We finished bowing our heads, and then the cheer of noise started again. It would not subside. My mother told Stephen and me that we would remember the V-E celebration in our part of Devon all our lives (and we have).

Things kept happening now. My mother said she needed to take the train up to London. She told Jenny that her uncle had assured her there was no damage to our house, but she had to see for herself and arrange to have it opened up. She wanted to have "a settled household, up and running" by the time her husband returned. If it was all right with Jenny, she would leave early in the morning and be back by noon the next day.

She asked Jenny to keep us occupied, because we weren't use to having her gone overnight. "Certainly, Mrs. Ord," Jenny replied. "I'll plan a day of games."

"Wonderful, Jenny!" my mother said.

Right after breakfast on the morning that my mother left, Jenny, Stephen, and I climbed the knoll with Folly to explore the castle ruins. We scrambled over the scattered bricks and swung around pillars that for a hundred years had held up nothing. Jenny buried pennies in the earth, and we dug them up so we would have spending money. Stephen climbed up on the wall that stood around part of the ruins, and with Jenny's hand on my back, I made it up, too, even though the wall was about as high as I was. When we turned one way, we saw the moor with its spreading heather and the May flowers of gold, blue, and pink just starting to peep through. When we turned another, there was the beach with its crescent of sand and the foamy, rolling blue sea beyond.

Stephen opened his arms and said, "I am a king, and this is my kingdom."

I kept my hands at my sides but said, "I am a princess, and my mother loves me!"

"Surely she does, surely she does!" Jenny responded, lifting me off the wall. She twirled me around until the colors on the moor swirled into the beach and the sea and everything blended with the sky and the sun. I laughed and shouted because I was in a living kaleidoscope.

"She loves the king, too," Stephen said, and jumped down.

"Well, of course, of course," Jenny answered.

We joined hands and went around in a circle singing "The farmer in the dell." We tried to keep Folly in the center of the circle, but she escaped and raced in her own circles, yipping for joy.

Jenny had packed a picnic, so we ate lunch on the knoll, and then, skipping our rest time, we went down to the beach. We took off our shoes, and all afternoon we played on the sand and by the rock pools. We made little boats out of bits of driftwood and sailed them. We threw sticks for Folly, and we had a game of "Simon Says," the waves lapping at our feet. It was only when the shadows appeared and then lengthened that we started for home, our pockets laden with shells.

Suddenly, I sank down into the grass. I said, "I'm so tired I can't walk another step."

Stephen bent down to pick me up but could hardly budge me.

Jenny said, "Oh, sweetheart, she's too heavy for you. Let me do it."

She swung me onto her shoulders and anchored my feet with one of her hands. Her other hand took Stephen's hand, and that was the way we went home, companionable like.

It had been such nice day, but when we walked through the door, we became sad because my mother was not at her writing desk, nor was she anywhere in the house. Jenny was sad as well. She sighed as she had us put away the picnic things. She sighed again as she fixed us supper. She missed my mother too.

At bedtime, Jenny read us a chapter from Mary Poppins, pausing a bit when she read words like "amaze-mint."

As she was shutting the book, I said, "I want Mummy."

"The silly wants Mummy. She always wants Mummy," Stephen said. He thought a moment and said, "I want Mummy."

"I want her now!" I said, almost crying.

Jenny ran her tongue over her teeth. For a second, she looked dismayed. "I can—I can read another chapter!" Her voice had a note of amazement.

I said "all right," so she did.

At the end, she said, "Whew! I've never read so much at one time, but sometime you just need to plow right through, no turning back. I'll tell this one to Mrs. Ord."

Jenny told us that the fastest way for tomorrow to get here was for us to go to sleep now, but we could leave our door open. If we called out during the night, she would hear us, and she would come.

My mother was home the next day, as she had promised, and that afternoon we walked to the tors. While we sat together on the biggest one, my mother said she had gotten three train tickets to London for the beginning of June—one for me, one for Stephen, and one for her. Folly could ride in a wicker basket. She asked Stephen if he remembered anything about the trip down to Devon.

"There were boys and girls with tags around the necks," he answered.

"Yes, wasn't that heartbreaking? I was grateful that we could do better."

"I wanted a tag," Stephen said.

My mother opened her mouth but then didn't say anything.

"Jenny needs a ticket," I said.

My mother said that we were Londoners but Jenny was a Devon girl. She would go to her parents' home in Biddeford and wait for her friend Davey to return. Jenny had to get on with her life, just as we had to get on with ours.

"I didn't know that," Stephen said. He looked at the ground.

My mother, with a little quaver in her voice, said our house in London was quite nice. It had radiators that turned on in the winter. Stephen and I each had our own rooms. Above the porch was a balcony where we could play on summer evenings. In a few months, our father would be with us.

I slid closer to my mother, and she patted my shoulder. This made me remember that no matter what else happened, she and I would always be together. It was because I was her daughter. That was the main thing.

We got up to go home. The heather was all around us. My mother said that our moor was not Dartmoor, but it was still glorious. Did we agree? We said we did.

Every morning now right after breakfast, Mummy and I looked at how the sun came through the bay windows of the sitting room and made patterns on the rug. I was over five now and so understood when she said there were some things that we needed to fix in our minds so that they would stay there, no matter how much time passed.

On the day that we left Devon, Jenny walked with us to the train, a lorry having picked up our things earlier. My mother, who had given

Jenny her bicycle and a silver dish, thanked her six times: three times on behalf of herself, twice on behalf of Stephen and me, and once on behalf of my father.

"It was my gain," Jenny said, "all my gain."

When we got to the station, we sat on the bench, and then Stephen and I gave Jenny our presents, an American nickel from his coin collection and rose petals in wax paper from me. "Oh, my!" Jenny said.

After that, everyone was quiet. We were so sad to part from Jenny, but unfortunately, we all had to get on with our lives.

The train, all steaming black and steel, came in roaring and clanging and stopped abruptly. My mother put Folly, who looked surprised, into the wicker basket. With Jenny's help, she fastened down one flap but said she would leave the other flap open. It would be Stephen's and my job to make sure Folly stayed calm and happy.

The conductor said, "All passengers with tickets, board now!"

"Well, Jenny, this is it," my mother said. "I'll write you. You will always be in our hearts."

"Likewise!" Jenny replied. They smiled at each other.

I took my mother's hand, and she held her purse and the wicker basket with Folly in it in her other hand. Stephen held our satchel. "Keep very close to me, Stephen," my mother said. We got on the train.

CHAPTER 2

A Family of Four Who Lived Together Every Day

London, 1945–1947

IN LONDON, EVERYTHING was hustle and bustle, with lorries and buses and even some cars going by our house at all hours. The first night, neither Stephen nor I could sleep, and my mother had to come into our rooms several times. Finally, we all ended up out on the balcony at midnight watching the city, including Folly, who had been barking. My mother said we weren't doing this again, though. That was for double sure.

London was so large that different parts had different names. Our part was called Belgravia. There was no grass in front of our house, but we had a back garden and a side porch with glass double doors. Folly could no longer lie on wing chairs because now it was not war, and our furniture was better, besides. She could race in circles in the back garden, but whenever we went elsewhere, she had to be on a leash. The first few times we put her leash on, Folly thought we were trying to play a game and pulled back, gaily yipping. It took several days for her to remember how to be a proper city dog.

There were streets where the buildings had been damaged, with gaping holes in their sides, and some had even been totally knocked down by something terrible called the blitz. Yet all up and down the blocks near us and in the square, families were moving into their houses. They opened their windows, newly hung curtains blowing in the breeze. They walked on the sidewalk. My mother said these happenings were like signs of spring, although by now it was summer, and we had petunias and phlox blooming off our side porch and geraniums on the balcony.

One day when we were at the playground that we called the little park because it was not Hyde Park, a woman wearing trousers, a long blouse, and two sparkly necklaces came rushing up to my mother. The woman, who had two boys and a girl with freckles trying to keep pace, shouted, "I come here with my ducklings, and who do I find but my friend Olivia with former baby Stephen and, uh, Folly—how's that for recall?—and even a chick to play with my chick."

"Valerie!" my mother cried as they hugged.

"We really aren't ducks, and I'm not a chicken," the girl said. "Mum knows it, too!"

"The cubs are so literal," the woman said.

These people were the Cooksons. Ian was a little older than Stephen, and Jon was a little younger. Christa was my age. Mrs. Cookson told my mother that they had all wedged into her parents' postage-stamp house out beyond Blenheim during the war. Her prissy sister and her bawling tykes had been there, too, and the main edict had been no painting on the walls, even where there was no wallpaper. There had been lots and lots of rows, but it was over, and Don had come back unscathed, and the juices were flowing again in more ways than one. She was doing a mural of a bowl of fruit in the hall, and one of sunset in the kitchen, so if my mother didn't see her on the social scene that was why.

My mother laughed and said, "Val, you haven't changed much! We sheltered in Devon. I acclimated."

"Needs must when the devil drives," Mrs. Cookson said. "And don't you have a French cousin? Did she make it through all right?"

"Céline," my mother said. "She was in the underground, hid people. I was in touch with her but only through another."

"Louis the Buyer," I murmured. Mummy looked at me, quite surprised.

Stephen, Jon, and Ian were already on the slides, but Christa and I were still standing with our mothers.

Christa said "Folly has nice ears." She reached for my hand, and after my mother nodded, we went to the swings together.

Christa had bobbed hair like her mother, and she wore shorts like her brothers. She could play hopscotch better than anyone I ever saw and was also good at jacks. She knew all the letters of the alphabet and could read several words, although not as many as I could. By the end of the week, Christa had played with me at my house, and then I played over at hers. That was what friends did.

My father returned in late July. We thought he might have to leave again, but in August the Americans used a big new weapon that no one had known about—my father said it would change the world Stephen and I would live in—and my father was able to stay with us for good. Perhaps it is strange that although I remember meeting the Cooksons in the little park vividly, I can recall so little about my father's arrival or of the days that his presence must have seemed new. In my mind, London, our home, life, and my father swirl together like colors in kaleidoscope, just as the moor had blended into the beach and the sea the time that Jenny had twirled me. My father had always been my father, just as he had always been Stephen's father, and so there was no start, no beginning. It was just the way it was meant to be.

I do remember, though, Stephen jumping sky high when my father opened the door, and the bit of caviar on a cracker that our parents gave each of us after they toasted my father's arrival with champagne.

There is one other thing that stands out. At the end of the summer, my father decided we should get a present to celebrate that we were a family of four (plus dog) who now lived together every day. We went to Harrods.

I knew now it was where everyone in London, including Santa Claus, did their best shopping, and it was now being restocked. It took a while of walking up and down the aisles to find the perfect thing. It could not be the bow and arrows that Stephen wanted and would probably get for his next birthday, nor could it be the stuffed panda I looked at for a time. It had to be something that would provide a family activity. We finally picked a badminton set.

"Manufactured in 1939," Mummy whispered to my father as she lifted the box.

"Of course," he said. "They must have found it in a back closet. They haven't gone back to making things like this yet."

When we unpacked the set at the home, the first thing we did was to each choose a racquet, and then my mother labeled it with the right name, so that everyone would know which racquet was whose. She wrote in capital letters in indelible black India ink on the dark blue handles—MUMMY, DADDY, STEPHEN, AMELIA.

The frames of the racquets were made of wood so light that my mother said the racquets felt almost buoyant. I turned my racquet in my hand and liked the way I could grip it. Stephen got a shuttlecock over the net on the first try, and my father said "good one, Amelia!"

whenever I got a hit. Folly, of course, raced around among us as we played. If a shuttlecock landed in the bushes, she retrieved it.

We played whenever we could in the evenings and on weekends, my father and I on one side and Mummy and Stephen on the other, just to mix things up. "Isn't this enchantment?" my father said, as we finished one of our games in our back garden. We nodded because that particular evening was so warm and soft and the crickets were making their happy sound. My mother kissed him and said, "Enchantment, forever!"

On Saturdays, we went on excursions. My father took Stephen and me to see the changing of the guard at Buckingham Palace. He took us to the Tower of London to see jewels and told us not to worry about all the other things that had gone on there because it had been a long time ago. We went to the British Museum, where the treasures of Greece and Egypt were, along with a document called the Magna Carta, which my father said was England's greatest treasure. We took boat rides up the Thames. We did not do all these things the first summer, but over time we did them.

Then on Sunday afternoons, the whole family, including Folly, would go to Hyde Park, where we would walk and play, and Stephen would fly his kite, and we would say hello to anyone we saw whom we knew. Always before we went home, we would go round by the Speakers' Corner to see who was speaking, and each time, my father said that in England people could say what they pleased, and it stemmed from the same Magna Carta that was in the British Museum.

In the fall, something else was added to our routine. Stephen and I started in at Regency Day School, which was three blocks away from our house. Stephen had to take a test to show what he had learned in Devon so he could be in the class for children turning eight. I wanted to take the test, too, so I could be in the same class as he. My mother said I would probably pass the test, given the chance. She had seen me taking it all in, when she had taught Stephen. She had most certainly noticed it. It would be preferable socially, though, if I was in the beginning class with my age group. Christa would be there, she reminded me. Perhaps we could have desks next to each other.

On the first day of school, some children cried for their mothers, and one boy named Teddy even wanted his nanny to stay. They did not care about the bright numbers on the blackboard or the cutouts of the apples and zebras or that our teacher, pretty Miss Taylor, said, "You're going to learn so much this year." They would not even glance at the bubbling aquarium. They missed home. I looked at Christa, and Christa, who had to wear a dress in this situation, smiled back. Our mothers had told us that they would be waiting for us in the school-yard in the afternoon, and in my case, Folly would be there, too. There was no need to worry.

Miss Taylor asked if anyone could count to twenty. I raised my hand, which was what you did in school if you knew an answer. She said, "Yes, Amelia, show us how it's done," so I did.

At recess, Teddy was still looking distressed. My mother had said I should be helpful to other children who might not be as confident as me, so I said, "Teddy, we will all be home again soon. What's wrong?"

He said he was supposed to learn to tie his shoes before he got to school. Everyone at his house told him that he could not ask the teacher. That was not her job. But he had only learned how to cross the laces, and he could not do the loops. He did not know what he would do if his shoes became untied in school. He might trip and cut open his chin and bleed all over, and then his shoes would still be un-tied but with blood on them until he got home. Tears were coming into his eyes again.

I had learned to tie my shoes in Devon, so I said, "Teddy, I can do loops. You can just ask me."

"I can?" he asked.

"Absolutely," I said.

He looked puzzled, and I remembered a talk my mother and Mrs. Cookson had had in the little park about boys tending to run young for their age—Mrs. Cookson had said even when they were thirty-eight they ran young—so I said, "Yes, Teddy, absolutely means yes!"

Teddy was so glad he wanted to kiss me, but I would not let him, for fear of germs.

The system worked well. I only tied Teddy's shoelaces a few times, each time telling him how I made the loops, just as my mother and Jenny had told me when they were doing it for me, and then Teddy tried it himself and was successful. Miss Taylor saw and said she was pleased with him and pleased with me.

My father walked with Stephen and me to school every morning because it was on his way to work at the Colonial Office, where he had been before the war and where it turned out he was a very important man. Stephen would hold my father's hand, and I skipped alongside. My father, who now wore a suit and tie, said that he was glad that we could have this extra time to talk, and he told us many things. He discussed the birds in London, old city and new city architecture, the importance of roads and bridges to a nation, and the difference between empire and commonwealth: one would dwindle as it should, and the other would last forever.

Sometimes Stephen wanted to know what my father did in the war, and my father got very serious then, as if he preferred my questions about the costumes of the palace guards better. He said that he had supervised a group of men who had flown planes and went on missions.

Stephen asked, "Is supervising the same as commanding? That's what Ray's father did."

My father paused and then said, "Yes, in the military, it has to be the same thing."

"What type of missions?" Stephen asked.

"I'd prefer not to go into detail. We had not expected to be in these circumstances, but we did what was needed to win the war." He turned to me and said, "Love, hold my other hand as we cross the road. Gracious, it seems that with every week that goes by, there is more traffic. The light is in our favor. All right, let's cross."

As we neared school, we usually met Ian, Jon, and Christa with Mr. Cookson coming down from their street. The fathers would say goodbye to us, and as we headed into school, they would go on to work together. Often, I heard them laughing about how they had become family men. My father said it was like waving a magic wand. "Can you beat it?" Mr. Cookson replied. That made them laugh even more, because, as they said to each other, they had used rather different expressions in their military existence.

We all quite liked London now. The only thing I had misgivings about was that my parents had what my mother called a "social life again." This meant that sometimes at night my parents went out or had people over for grown-up dinners. Once in a while, too, my mother had a luncheon or meeting that ran into the afternoon, and then it would be Alice waiting for us in the schoolyard.

Alice was boney and pale with flat hair. She said, "Yes, Mrs. Ord," or "All right, Mrs. Ord," or "I'll take the dog for an extra walk, Mrs.

Ord," but she didn't smile or give compliments the way Jenny always had. She came to our house in the mornings and left before supper, except when she stayed with Stephen and me into the evening while my parents were having a social life again, in which case she got paid extra. I knew the last bit, because Alice told it to the nannies. Alice was not a nanny herself, of course. She was with us only when my mother was unavailable, and she did other things for my mother besides. She sat with the nannies, though, when she "had to" take us to the little park. It was probably because she was not a mother and so couldn't sit with them.

She would point to Stephen on the seesaw with Jon and say, "This one is a real mummy's boy. Whenever his mother's in the room, he's right near her." Pointing at me swinging, she said, "That one is even worse. She wants to talk to her mother a hundred times a day. Everything is Mummy, Mummy."

I didn't know why Alice talked like this. Our mother was our mother. That meant she was everything to us. Why wouldn't we want to be near her? Why wouldn't we want to talk to her? I decided it was best just to ignore Alice, but I couldn't always.

Once, Teddy was swinging standing up. I thought I would try it. I put one foot on the swing, tested my balance, and was about to bring my other foot up when Alice was suddenly there with her hands on my waist.

"Just what do you think you're doing?" she asked angrily. "Are you so careless of yourself that you would like to crack your head on cement?"

I said no.

"Then, sit down, if you want to swing."

As I sat down on the swing, Teddy's nanny called over from her bench, "Teddy, now that I think of it, maybe you'd better sit down, too."

Alice went back to her seat and started talking again as if nothing had happened. She had never seen children who were coddled more than Stephen and I were. All our parents did was plan things for our enjoyment. She told the nannies that my mother had even dressed me up and taken me to the ballet. "Can you imagine that?" she asked the nannies.

Alice was really very strange. When my mother and father were out, she sat with us at supper, but she would spend the time reading magazines to herself. Then, at bedtime, she was supposed to read out loud to us, but she found fault with every book we gave her. Stephen brought her *Black Beauty* and showed her where my mother had left off, and she said, "I don't like books about animals." I brought her *Five Children and the It*, and she said, "I don't like books about children."

Most of the interesting books in the world were either about animals or children or both, but, as a last resort, I was going to get *Romeo and Juliet* from the sitting room when she said, "Look, your mother asked me to put you to bed, and that is what I'm trying to do. I don't see where reading comes into it. Reading to you is not my department."

The next day I asked Stephen whom he liked better, Alice or Jenny. He said, "Jenny, dummy."

As we walked home from school with my mother later, Stephen asked her, "Does Alice know Amelia's proper name? She calls her 'this one.'"

"No," I said. "She calls Stephen 'this one' and me 'that one,' and she call Folly 'the dog.'" Folly heard her name and looked up at me.

My mother coughed a few times and then said, "I hear a lot of 'she's' from you two, but of course, Alice knows your names. She uses them all the time."

I said, "We prefer Jenny. Mummy, can you ask Jenny to come to us in London?"

My mother said she had gotten a letter from Jenny that very day. She was going to show it to us as soon as we got home. Jenny had married her Davey. They were moving up north to Langley Mill in Notts, where they would help his cousin run a grocery store. Jenny had sent us a snap. She looked lovely in her wedding dress. Jenny had her own life now. She could not be with us.

"During the war, people who would have never met otherwise became very close," my mother explained. "Things needed to be different."

Almost as if she was talking to herself, my mother told us about a friend of hers who had expected to be a librarian at St. Hilda's College all her life, coming home to a bedsitter flat every evening. Now she was gone to the States and married to a coach for a baseball team called the Yankees. With surprise in her voice, my mother said, "She lives in a ranch house in a place called West Orange, New Jersey. I think though that ranch refers to a style of house. I don't believe they have cattle ranches in that part of the States."

"Mummy, is that near Pennsylvania where the candy came from?" I asked.

"Why, Amelia, sometimes you amaze even me!" my mother said. "Yes, if I remember the map of the States correctly, Pennsylvania is on the far side of New Jersey. On the other side of New Jersey, there's the Atlantic Ocean, and that's what is between the States and our country."

There was a crack in the sidewalk, and I jumped over it. We had had the Atlantic Ocean in Devon!

Stephen, going back to our original subject, said, "Jenny could play games. Alice doesn't do anything."

My mother said that we should always be glad that we had known Jenny, but if we expected everyone we met to be like Jenny, we would be sadly disappointed in life. That was for double sure. She added that Alice was a good employee; she did her best. We needed to be kind and friendly to Alice. There were things we didn't know about Alice.

"Do you understand, Stephen?" she asked.

"All right," Stephen said.

"And you, Amelia?"

"Yes, Mummy, I will," I answered.

I remembered what my mother had told us, so the next time my parents had a social life again and Alice was trying to put Stephen and me to bed, I said, "Alice, watch this! Daddy taught me the polka, and I taught Folly." I took Folly's front paws and said, "Folly, will you dance with me? Will you dance with me?" I started the steps with Folly.

Alice said, "Are you trying to put off going to bed? Stop being silly and get into your night things. Stephen, go to your room and do the same." Folly and I slowed and then stopped dancing.

Stephen told her, "My sister was not being silly. She was trying to entertain you."

"I'm not in the mood to be entertained. No one was entertained during the war."

"Do you know that the war is over? My father helped win it." Stephen said. I laughed because everyone in my class, including Teddy, knew that the war was over, but maybe Alice didn't.

Alice raised her arm and then dropped it to her side just as Stephen jumped back. She looked away for a moment and then said quite slowly, "I am going downstairs. I'm taking the dog with me. I will come back up in fifteen minutes. You better both be in bed. I am warning you."

We did what Alice said, but I was still awake when my parents got home. I heard the talk in the hall. My mother said it had fortunately been a very early night. Alice said she had been short with us. She was very sorry. It was a bad day for her, an anniversary. My parents replied that they felt terrible for her. They wished there was something they could do.

After that, my mother rearranged her schedule so that she could almost always meet us after school, and if my parents needed to go out at night, my mother read to us in the early evening, or else my father did, while Mummy was getting ready. Alice did the vacuuming. She peeled potatoes. She picked up the dry cleaning. She took Folly for midmorning walks.

I asked Stephen what were the things we didn't know about Alice. "She has three warts on her stomach," he suggested. Then, he said, "Maybe she's a witch!"

Stephen was joking, of course. There were no such things as witches, and even if there had been, my mother would have avoided letting any of them into the house. He was probably right though about the warts. Alice's eyes were so dull.

By this time, it was winter. Our radiators came on with a hiss. We wore wool coats and mittens for our walks to school. My father said, "This is not raw. This is invigorating!" Once we saw a few flakes of snow, just before Christmas.

On Christmas Eve, we had all the Cooksons over, and my mother and Mrs. Cookson did a dramatic reading of *A Christmas Carol*, with my mother being the narrator and Scrooge and Mrs. Cookson being all the ghosts plus Tiny Tim. They said they were "reviving a prewar tradition." We could not have currant scones, as they had had before because rationing was still in effect. Even so, the adults said it was better now because Christa and I were here now and not only the boys.

The next day, Stephen and I opened many nice presents. Santa Claus had indeed done his shopping at Harrods, and one of the things I got was the panda bear I had seen in the summer.

With the start of the new school term, I became the first full-fledged reader in my class, and then Christa became one, too. While we were waiting for the rest of the class to catch up, Miss Taylor gave us a book we could read to each other. It was all in rhyme and was about twelve girls who lived in an old house in Paris all covered in vines, and they went everywhere in two straight lines, and the littlest one was Madeline. Madeline was very adventurous, with no one knowing so well how to frighten Miss Clavel.

"I see two sixth formers in the making," Mrs. Cookson said to my mother when Christa and I did a dramatic reading of *Madeline* for them in the Cooksons' sitting room.

My mother said she would put off thinking about the sixth form for a year or so. Nineteen fifty-six was certainly a long ways in the future, but then, she added, "You know, Val, you're definitely right."

Suddenly, it began to be spring. Our crocuses and pansies came up, and then the daffodils, dahlias, tulips, and marigolds. People walking by our house tended to compliment us on our flowers with their grand colors against the side porch, and my mother always said, "Thank you. My daughter and I enjoy gardening together."

School let out as it became high summer. We went on holiday—the first one I had even been on—but we did not go to Devon because my mother said it would be too soon. We went to the Lake District, staying at what my mother called "a charming old country inn." My parents knew the innkeeper, and he allowed cocker spaniels, so Folly came too. In fact, he called her "Princess Folly" and taught her and me to do a jig one evening. For two weeks, Folly did not need to be on a leash, and my parents did not have a social life again. We hiked in the mountains and went boating, and since there were days where it was unusually warm, my parents went into the lake with Stephen and me. In cool, sparkling water surrounded by the green of the valley, they taught us to swim.

Every day that we woke up under the eaves in the inn with Folly on one bed or another was a day that we enjoyed. My father said it was "enchantment," and once again my mother said "enchantment forever."

When we got back home, we found a letter from Jenny, and with the letter was a picture of a tiny wrapped-up baby with closed eyes and a scrunched-up face. This was Jenny's baby, and his name was David Jr. My mother and I hurried out to Harrods and bought him a little blue outfit, a spoon, and a rattle. Right after that, my mother got a letter from her friend in West Orange, New Jersey, in the States, and she had had a baby girl named Barbara. "That's glorious," my mother said. "Who would have thought it?"

Now that we looked for them, we saw babies here, there, and everywhere. There were babies pushed in prams on the sidewalk, babies on blankets in Hyde Park, and babies held on laps in the little park. Fat babies, thin babies, crying babies, laughing babies, sleeping babies! Babies in blue, babies wearing pink! When school started again —my teacher now was Miss Hill, and we had a new subject, which was French—there were even babies waiting in the schoolyard as we came out in the afternoon. Teddy had a baby brother, which meant he didn't have a nanny anymore. As Teddy's mother explained to my mother when we were admiring the baby, since she had compounded the original mistake by having another one, she decided she might as well be the one taking care of them.

I heard my father asking my mother whether we should have a baby. He said the bumper baby crop of 1946 would certainly continue into 1947. They had always been older parents, and now they would just be a bit older. My mother said no, although she sounded wistful. A little one would add to our joy, but it would be too hard to take care of a baby in Africa.

We were going to Africa. My parents told Stephen and me it would be an adventure. My father had gotten a posting, and it was to Nairobi, Kenya. There was no better posting in East Africa. Nairobi was cosmopolitan. We would be able to learn about a very different culture while keeping a link to our own. Stephen and I already knew that the people in Africa had brown skin—some had spoken to us at "People of the World" day at school—but now we would get to know them and their landscape. My mother told us about savannahs, which were somewhat like moors, and about the game preserves. We discussed the different shrubs and trees. "Jacaranda, eucalyptus, papyrus," I repeated, "and the octopus tree is called a Banyan tree." Just like London, different parts of Nairobi had different names. We would live in the part called Westlands, and just like now, my father would walk us to school in the morning, and my mother would meet us in the afternoon. That would be the thing that would stay the same, in spite of all the other changes.

The Colonial Office gave my mother a booklet called *Westlands Has It All!* There were color photographs of green hills, with roads winding past pastel houses with shutters flung back and huge porches called verandas. The houses had bougainvillea on the walls and banana trees and banyan trees in the gardens. A woman and two children played croquet on a trimmed lawn in one picture. In another picture, a family sipped iced drinks on a rock patio with a view of a savannah in the distance.

"It looks like Hollywood," Alice said when she saw the booklet. That showed Alice really was not very bright. Hollywood was not in Africa. It was where they made American movies like *The Wizard of Oz* that Stephen and I had just seen, although it was a little different from the book.

My mother was kind to Alice, so she said, "It does, rather." She added, "But living in a neighborhood is better than being in a fenced-in compound with people breathing in on themselves."

We were not the only ones with a posting. Christa's father had gotten Saudi Arabia. Christa said that on the day they had found out about it, her mother had made her and her brothers go upstairs so the adults could discuss things in private in the kitchen. Christa, Jon, and Ian had sat on the floor by the heating vent in Ian's room and listened. This was how they got all their information.

Christa's mother had said that the first thing that Christa's dad needed to remember was that his name was Donald, not Lawrence. The second thing was that she had no intention of traipsing around someone else's desert, a martini in her hand.

"What's a martini?" Christa asked me. We were at recess, and I was setting up a game of marbles for us.

I said "I'm not sure, but it might be a marionette. A little one. That's why there's the tini." I knew this because I looked at Stephen's lessons whenever I could, and he was studying root words, prefixes, and suffixes.

Christa said that made sense, because before becoming an artist, her mother had thought about a career in the theater. "Anyway," Christa continued. "There was a third thing." Her mother had said that as for sending the ducklings away, if she was going to do that—and don't think it hadn't crossed her mind—she would have done it long ago. The kittens were going to Regency Day for a reason, and it was right there in the title of the school. It was day. Then her mum had asked, without even talking louder, "Does anyone want to leave London?" and Christa and her brothers had called down the heating vent "no." That settled it. They were staying here.

That afternoon in the little park, I heard other mothers speaking to my mother about Christa's mother. They said, "That Valerie Cookson! Always so scattered, so up in the ether and selfish, too. Her husband fought in the war. Now he gets a plum assignment, and she won't let him take it."

"Oh, I don't know," my mother said. "Valerie's just a bit bohemian. I might have been bohemian myself in a different life, or a swimmer. She has bright, happy children. I know that." She paused and added, "Val's fine."

I didn't understand this conversation. Since my mother was highly intelligent, she sometimes had to explain things in complicated language to other adults. That was just how it was.

We were busy now, deciding what to take to Nairobi, and labeling boxes. We got shots that hurt, both in the arm and in the bottom, and we had to tell Folly that she would be in quarantine for a month before she could join us. We felt badly about this. We would think about her every day. We would arrange for her to have treats. However, this was the rule for British dogs. My father could not agree to Stephen's idea that we smuggle her in, hidden in his duffel bag, or to my suggestion that we dress her up in baby clothes. Now that it was raining babies, I thought that my scheme would certainly work, but still my father shook his head no. My mother said that hopefully the time would go by fast and that Folly would not remember it for very long.

Suddenly, we were not going to Nairobi. Our posting was shifted to a place called Dodoma, Tanganyika. My parents said that Dodoma would not be feasible for our family. There were no schools there. My father tried to get changed back to Nairobi, but he couldn't, or even to Mombasa, which was in Kenya, too. Then he asked for Cairo, where there were also many schools. That was not in East Africa, but he could do it, he could learn it. The Colonial Office's answer was that all the slots there were filled. He asked for Accra, Ghana. He could adapt to West African nuances, but again the answer was no.

My mother was always teaching Stephen and me new words like "cosmopolitan," "culture," and "nuance," although not "bohemian." Now, she taught us "compromise." We would compromise and go to Tanganyika, but to Dar es Salaam instead of Dodoma. There was a small international school there, not as top flight as the British schools in Nairobi, but it would do for a few years. She would supplement at home. Of course, the school's color barrier was distressing. She would have to join with other women to change it. That would be one of her goals.

I meant to ask my mother what color the barrier to the Dar es Salaam school was and what she would prefer. Maybe an emerald shade would be nice. By the time I got around to asking, though, the Colonial Office had told my father was that since he knew about roads and bridges, they needed him in an outpost like Dodoma. The only possible alternative was somewhere in India, since a lot of blokes there were coming home.

My father said the idea of India was ridiculous. He knew nothing about India. Besides, the place was too unstable. It was not just the agitation for independence. He rather admired Gandhi. It was more the conflict between the Hindus and the Moslems. He was not about to bring a family into that.

Evening after evening, though, my parents talked urgently about what my mother called their dilemma. They told Stephen and me not to be anxious, not to be concerned. They just needed to sort everything out. Their voices hummed throughout the house, although the door of whatever room they were talking in was shut.

Finally, my father said to my mother one Sunday in Hyde Park as he and Stephen were unwinding a string on a kite, "Maybe we should just stay in London. Don Cookson is staying here, supervising younger fellows going out to the field. He says 'you know—the wife,' but he sort of brags about the constraints placed on family men. I could do the same thing."

My mother, collecting acorns with me, said that she was not sure she wanted my father to go up and down the halls of the Colonial Office saying "you know—the wife." She then talked softly. They had always talked about going to the field. That was what he had planned to do. He had lost five years in the war. She could not deny him this. I moved closer to my mother, and she smoothed my hair. "We want Daddy to do what he would like to do, don't we?" she asked me. I nodded.

"On top of everything, it would mean living in a compound," my father said.

"I realize that," my mother replied, biting her lip.

The following week, when I was home on a school half holiday, some women came to our house. They were not part of my mother having a social life again. They came to give my mother advice, although a bit of tea would be nice, they said. It was a warm for an October day, and I was on the side porch coloring clothes on paper dolls that my mother and I had just cut out. My mother had left the double doors open because it was so nice out, and snatches of talk from the sitting room drifted to me. The wafting smell of face powder and cigarettes mixed with the scent of the lingering asters and zinnias on the other side of the porch. I decided to do a pink and green plaid dress for the girl paper doll. Folly went in to see who the people were, and then when one lady said, "Sit on my lap, doggie," she came back to the porch to stay with me. She licked my knee, and I patted her head with my free hand.

The women said they all had children who had done it or were doing it. They spoke from experience. One woman with a birdlike voice said, "I myself went away from the start, and I turned out all right, didn't I? I even found the right husband after several tries, although I guess you could say that was part of the fun." They all laughed at that except my mother. Spoons clinked against teacups. I heard Alice going in and out.

My mother said she just hadn't thought about it for the pre-preparatory years.

They said, "They survive, Olivia, they survive."

Really, Olivia, really!

Olivia, they do!

My mother said that one of the subjects of the conversation was out playing with friends, but would they like to meet her daughter? I put down my crayon and straightened my skirt, all set to run in when called. The women said no, though. As they had said, this was not quite a "social visit," and they had other people to see. They had just wanted to reassure her. "Stop worrying, Olivia!" they said.

After they had gone, my mother came back to the side porch and said she was sorry she had been pulled away, but the Colonial Office wives hadn't seemed to have known it was a school half holiday. Almost to herself, she said, "but then again, how would they?" She bit her lip.

"Anyway," she continued, "I'm yours until it's time to collect Stephen from the Cooksons. What shall we do?"

We went into the back garden with Folly and played badminton until the sunny afternoon turned into twilight.

My parents thought of another compromise, and this time the Colonial Office said yes. We would go to Dodoma, Tanganyika, if the Colonial Office would put off our posting for six months. They wanted Stephen and me to be a little older when we went away. Especially me —they would feel better if I was at least seven and a half. This was the compromise.

My mother said we should stop thinking of Africa for a while and just enjoy our present lives. We had all been going around in circles, and we needed to just soak up the here and now for a bit.

Once again, the Cooksons came over to our house on Christmas Eve for a reading of *A Christmas Carol*, and this year my mother and Mrs. Cookson pooled their resources, and we had a plum pudding, and everyone got a taste!

Stephen joined a junior rugby team with Jon and Ian and some other boys from Regency Day. I became a member of the Brownie division of the Girl Guides. Mrs. Cookson, who was getting fat, was one of our leaders. In between helping us make braid necklaces with whistles attached to them, she told us that the manual said we should always think ahead and be prepared. She thumbed a few pages in the manual and gave a few examples. We should never go walking in woods without a canteen of water and a compass in one pocket and flint in the other. "I'm keeping out of the woods, myself," Mrs. Cookson said. "I don't care how many sit-upons I have. That goes for you too, Christa. Amelia, you'll need to live by your wits, and I know that you can. As for the rest of you, do what you want."

For my seventh birthday, I asked for *A Child's History of Great Britain*, multiplication flash cards, a handwriting exercise book, and a version of *Le Petit Prince* with questions at the end. My mother said, "Darling, you continue to amaze me!"

I was only thinking ahead and trying to be prepared. Dodoma, Tanganyika, had no schools. I figured that what this meant was my mother would be teaching us at home just as she had taught Stephen (and me) in Devon. The gifts I asked for were necessary supplies. It was true that *Le Petit Prince* had advanced vocabulary, but my mother and I were always practicing French because she had once spent a year in France with her cousin Céline, so I thought we could do it.

My parents also gave me a surprise present of a doll house. The outside was white clapboard. It had windows that went up and down, a china knob on the door, and tiny gutters on the side connected to a peaked roof.

About the same time, my mother got a surprise present of her own. It was a carved model of a Swiss village with a church, town hall, shops including a bakery with little rolls in the window, and many little houses and chalets. It was so cunning that we all clapped our hands, but my mother seemed most amazed by the card.

"It's from Ruth Gold and Henri," she told my father faintly. "Why did she feel she had to do that?"

"She's grateful," my father replied.

"Oh, but why? It was little enough." She saw that I was about to ask a question, so she showed us a picture of a boy who looked a little older than Stephen that had come with the card. She did not read the card out loud, though.

"Mrs. Gold is a friend of cousin Céline and mine," she explained to Stephen and me. "She and her son Henri moved to Switzerland during the war."

"What did Henri's father do during the war?" Stephen asked.

"Let's stop talking and set this up," my father said. "We'll make the town hall the focal point and go out from there."

In midwinter, just after Folly had won a certificate of special distinction at the Regency Day pet show for being the only dog that could do a version of the box step, we began to pack again for Africa. We had another round of shots. "Mummy, they are dreadful," I said.

Where the needles went in, my skin was red until the marks changed into a growing bruise of yellow with dashes of blue black. It was as if I had a lopsided, upside-down rainbow on my fanny, or so the mirror said. Stephen would not let me see, but he said he had a thundercloud.

My mother said she was sorry that Stephen and I had soreness, but she and my father were having the same shots. Even Folly would have shots. It was another part of the price of our adventure.

One night after the last shot, I had a dream. My parents were out, and witches had gotten into the house. They were sprinkled with face powder and smoked cigarettes. Folly stood squarely on her paws and barked, and I said "no, no, no," but they all swept past us, including one who chirped, "I turned out all right, all right, all right." I offered them all my birthday presents if they would leave, since this was not quite a social visit. They paid me no heed and just threw kid gloves into the air as they talked mumbo jumbo. They set an hourglass in the center of my mother's tea table. Cackling that I would survive, survive,

survive, they knocked the hourglass on its side with a thud. With sand now in both bulbs, time was stopped and divided.

As the witches departed, I tried to right the hourglass, but it was framed with bronze and had heavy spindles. I could not budge it, and Folly could only look aghast. I called for Alice, but it was not her department. Stephen was elsewhere, playing rugby. Then Dorothy with Toto under her arm made an appearance. Toto and Folly waved to each other, and Dorothy in her ruby slippers said to me, "Amelia, you saw the bay windows and the way the light came through. You have flint." I nodded. Of course, I had flint. Well, of course. I had started in Devon.

The dream had had a happy ending, but even so I awoke with a start. I looked at the dark shapes of the packing crates in my room and the shadows cast by my empty shelves. My panda bear was all by himself on the bureau. He would go in my suitcase. I began to cry, and my mother heard me and came in. She said, "We still have some time, dear one." She lay down beside me and held me, although she did not get under the covers.

I was tired and did not want to leave Mummy in the morning. For the first time, my father had to hurry me along, and I clung to him at the schoolyard. "What's wrong, love?" my father asked.

I just shook my head, so he said it was probably just a reaction to the shots and that he was free that evening and would play Parcheesi with me after he helped Stephen with his coin collection. Christa had come up to me, and I told her I didn't want to go to school. She said, "Amelia, you just have to come today. You just have to!" She reached for my hand.

"Go with Christa," my father said.

I said, "All right, Daddy" and walked sadly into school.

The day took a turn for the better, though. I was class messenger for the week, and after lunch, Miss Hill sent me to deliver an envelope to the head of the pre-preparatory division. When I got back, everyone was wearing party hats and waving noisemakers. As she fitted my party hat on my head, Miss Hill told me that the class was giving me a *bon voyage* party. She had to commend Christa especially for keeping the surprise. Miss Taylor, my last year's teacher, was there. She had stepped away from her class for a moment just to see my face. I was always glowing, she said.

We played musical chairs and pin the tail on the donkey. Everyone said they would be my friend forever. "Three cheers for Amelia!" they declared three times. We had biscuits with our afternoon milk. Finally, my teacher presented me with a box of sharpened pencils with my name printed on them. "These are from all of us at Regency Day, with appreciation," Miss Hill said.

"Thank you!" I exclaimed with excitement.

When my mother picked us up, Stephen said his party has been nice, but I used an adjective I had just learned. "Mummy, my party was smashing," I said. She laughed and said she was glad.

After I got home, I added my pencils to the other supplies I had packed for Africa. My mother teaching Stephen and me at home would be as easy as 1-2-3!

Before we knew it, it was our last day in London. Alice was not going with us, luckily, and so we had to mark the occasion. My mother gave her a scarf, an envelope of money, and a good reference for the future.

Stephen and I did a card for her on pink construction paper. On the cover, I had drawn a woman with stringy hair. On one side of her was a girl walking away from her. On the other side, a boy was walking away. The message we wrote on the inside said,

> *To Alice,*
>
> *It is time to say good-bye because we are going to Africa and don't plan on seeing you anymore. Good-bye!!! We will sign our proper names to this.*
>
> *Stephen Ord*
> *Amelia Ord*
> *Who are pleased to act on behalf of Folly Ord.*

We had put in the last part because once when we had visited my father at the Colonial Office, he had been doing letters with his clerk, and that was the type of expression he used.

"Well," Alice said weakly, and then looked like she did not know what to say. My mother looked concerned.

Then I had a brilliant idea. I said, "Alice, it's not bedtime now. May Folly and I dance for you?"

"Yes, Amelia. I would appreciate that," Alice said.

I picked up Folly's paws, and we did an original number that I called the cocker tango. With my help, Folly could even dip. Alice smiled a little, and my mother laughed.

Years later, I would be glad Folly and I had done that one thing for Alice.

The next day was the day we were separated from Folly. When the man came for her, she tried to take shelter against my mother's legs and looked so shocked and scared when the man was allowed to pick her up. She squealed and struggled desperately. My mother said, "Goodbye, old Folly, we'll see you soon," but she could do nothing else because Folly going into quarantine was yet another part of the price of our African adventure.

I did not know why it had taken so long to occur to me, but I suddenly decided our adventure was too expensive. This was worse than paying a hundred pounds! As my father called the cab to take us to Heathrow Airport, I spoke to Stephen in private. He did not call me "dummy" because he had been thinking the same thing. Besides, he wanted to go on playing rugby with Ian and Jon. Now that Alice was gone, we would even come out ahead. "And the baby," I said excitedly. "Mummy can have a baby for us, or perhaps two. I'll let her decide how many. We can stay at Regency Day, too!"

We raced to tell my father that we preferred to stay in London. It had just taken us a while to sort things through. We'd help him to do the things he liked to do right here in London. We offered to go visit the Magna Carta with him that very day. The important thing now was to get Folly back immediately.

My father looked at us and seemed both sad and amused. My mother had our coats over her arm, and she handed them to us silently. "The cab is here," my father said. "We are committed."

So, we had no choice but to set out.

It will be your first time on a plane," my father said, trying to cheer us.

CHAPTER 3

Cultural Phenomena

British East Africa, Spring 1947

WE STOPPED IN CAIRO, where we stayed for two days with people my mother and father knew, and I played with a girl next door named Penelope who was lively. However, we did not have time to see the pyramids or the sphinx. My father promised that we would come back on holiday and visit Luxor. Egypt would definitely be part of our adventure. For now, though, we needed to continue on our way.

My parents' friends took us to the Suez Canal, where we boarded a huge ship to go down the coast of East Africa because we were not going the overland route. The reason we were not going the overland route is that my father had asked my mother to pick between stopping in Nairobi on the way down and going to Dodoma directly, so that we could all see where our new home was together. My mother decided we should go straight to Dodoma, although my father reminded her that this meant they could not come back with us to Nairobi. My mother said it was a "Hobson's choice." I didn't know what that meant.

The first day of the voyage, we just got used to the ship and where everything was. It was so funny to be living on something that was always moving. We could look out the portholes of our cabin and see the water sliding by one way as the ship glided another. Up on the main deck where we practiced getting our sea legs, we could see the water rippling all around us when we finally made it reached the Indian Ocean. The ship had a turquoise, crescent-shaped swimming pool in the center of the deck, and we remarked on how curious it was that we could swim in a pool with sides, while being in the midst of the ocean.

"It's a matter of perspective," my mother said as we jumped into the pool. She explained what perspective was, and so that night, before I went to bed in the rolling ship, I drew a picture of railroad tracks heading into mountains to show I understood the concept.

By the second day, we established a routine. Every day, after breakfast, we got into our bathing costumes and went up to the main deck. We would say hello to the guard who was on the lookout for pirates and wave at four-year-old twin boys named Harry and Gary, who ran around with a nanny while their parents slept in. We'd settle in our deck chairs, and it was here that the school supplies I had brought began to be a great help. We always spent an hour working with the multiplication flash cards and reading from *Le Petit Prince* before writing in our travel journals that we were going to send to the Cooksons so they would learn about what we had seen. Study time ended with riddles to make us think.

My mother's favorite one was "What's black and white and red all over?" The answer was a newspaper! "Red" was really "read." The two words were homonyms. Homonyms could often be a great source of confusion when people were talking, because one person would mean one thing and another person could think he meant something else.

My father had a riddle that taught American geography. He had heard it from his friend, the Yank, in the war. "What did Della wear, boys? What did Della wear?" was the question. "She wore her new jersey," my father told us. New Jersey was, of course, the name of a state, and it turned out that Delaware was, too!

I made up a riddle that was also about geography. "If you can buy an orange in West Orange, where can you buy a tangerine?"

No one knew, so I said, "Tanganyika!"

"Good one, Amelia! Good one," my father said.

Stephen wanted to try. "Why did the moron—" he began.

"I don't like that word," my mother said.

Stephen started again, "Why did Amelia throw a clock off the Tower of London?" He paused. "She wanted to kill time!"

"I do not, I never did," I objected. "Why is Stephen saying that?" Remembering my hourglass dream, I frowned.

"Darling," my mother said, "it's only a joke and in keeping with our theme of double meanings." She bent over and ruffled Stephen's hair as Harry and Gary, who were double boys, careened by us.

After study time, we spent the rest of the day having fun. My parents said that once we got to Dodoma, they would be very busy and there would be adjustments for us, but that this week on the ship was our family holiday this year. These days were ours. We played shuffleboard.

We played ring toss. When there was an occasional rain shower, we played checkers and dominos and spelling games. However, most of the time we were in the pool. We perfected our strokes, and we played a game that was like water tag. We had such a good time doing that, that a group of eleven- and twelve-year-old girls who spent all their time talking about lipstick and nylon stockings finally jumped in and joined us. Harry and Gary bobbing around in blown-up tubes splashed us and giggled, and we let them pretend they were part of the game. Even in the midst of gaiety, though, we would sometimes pause and look into space because nothing was complete without Folly.

Stephen and I had dinner with our parents every evening, except for gala night, which my parents had to attend because it was expected. On that night, we had to eat at supervised children's seating with the girls and the small boys, but before we left my mother put on her gown so I could see it. It was silvery blue chiffon with wispy shoulder straps and a straight yet swirling skirt that came down to her white high heels. She wore her string of pearls and a silver bracelet. There was a scent of jasmine about her.

"Don't I look ridiculous in this getup, considering we're off the coast of Africa?" she asked, as she pulled on white gloves that came up over her elbows.

"No, Mummy," I said, "You're absolutely beautiful."

"Indeed, she is," my father said, as he came into our tiny sitting room in his tuxedo.

I was wearing a flowered dress and my patent-leather shoes, and I was smiling, because although I would have preferred it if Stephen and I were not going off to the supervised children's seating—Harry and Gary would probably blow bubbles in their milk—I was determined to make the best of it.

My father turned to me and said, "Amelia, you are as pretty as a picture."

That gave him an idea. He took out our camera, and my mother sat in the one big chair. I put my panda bear on her lap as a stand-in for Folly, and then Stephen and I perched on either arm of the chair. As my father took the snap, we looked at him happily, because this cruise was part of our African adventure.

On the last day of the voyage, everyone was on deck and trying to see whatever there was to see as the ship pulled closer to shore. For hours, we went past smooth white beaches with volcanic cliffs rising up behind them. We saw dark-skinned men and boys standing in the water, fishing. Then a stone tower came into view. The ship made a turn, and suddenly we were in a bowl-shaped harbor with many other kinds of boats. The ship found its place at the pier and was fastened tight, as people lined up, group by group and family by family. Harry and Gary, in between their parents who had appeared out of nowhere, were just ahead of us. We paused as they walked onto the dock. Then with a brief glance back, because we knew this was the end of our holiday, we followed them down the gangplank. We were now in Dar es Salaam.

We stayed two days at a hotel on the wide paved avenue lined with palm trees that ran the length of the harbor. There was mosquito netting around each bed, which made it seem as if we were to sleep in tents, and the window in our room had no glass but was a screen with a louvered shutter. The first night after I was tucked in, I looked through the slits of the louvers at the swaying palm trees. They were sliding one way as the hotel glided another. I would have called for my mother, but I knew this was just an illusion from being on a ship for a week.

The next morning after a quick breakfast of pawpaws and other exotic fruits that could not have been had in England, my father had to hurry off to Government House for something called training and orientation. My mother, Stephen, and I had study time on the hotel veranda, and then we crossed the avenue to see the open-air market. Mummy told us to keep close to her, and we did.

The market was large, with row upon row of wares laid out on the ground. The smell of the sea mixed with the scents of reeds, food, and perfume, as well as the smell of bodies. Sights and sounds were all in a jumble. It seemed a little like a country fair we had been to when we were on holiday in the Lake District, except almost all the people had brown skin, and there wasn't a merry-go-round or Ferris wheel. There were many children about. They wore brightly colored bracelets on their arms and sometimes on their legs, although they did not always wear shirts. Some of them stared and pointed at Stephen and me. One boy ran right up to Stephen, gazed into his blue eyes, and then ran back to some other boys, who appeared to ask him questions. Stephen asked my mother why they were acting like this, and she said it was just because we had unusual complexions for the area. A woman carrying a basket of vegetables on her head and a baby on her back smiled at us, and since my mother smiled back, I did too. My mother bought some beads for me to string and a conch shell for Stephen. Mummy would not buy food, but we concluded that after a slow start, we were having a grand time.

In the afternoon, though, a car picked us up from the hotel to take us to a stucco house on a hill to see a British lady called Mrs. Peck who wanted to show my mother the ropes. What a dreary event that was!

Mrs. Peck was a fluttery woman who said things that did not make sense. After she had led us into a tremendous sitting room with whirling fans, she told us that she had a boy named Johnnie who was Stephen's age and a girl named Brigit who was my age, and she was sorry that they could not play with us, but they were at school. I asked her when they would be home, since I thought if it was in an hour or so, we might still be there. However, Mrs. Peck said, "sometime in July." Then she said that maybe we would meet them coming or go to Nairobi. I just looked at her.

My mother quickly said, "Thank you for having us all over."

Mrs. Peck replied, "It's a pleasure. I know there are difficulties when you don't have an ayah. Now, I have only one question to ask the children before we start our talk." She turned to us and said, "What have you darlings learned about Tanganyika?"

My mother had said earlier that we had to make a good impression on Mrs. Peck, because her husband was in the vice royal governor's office. We each answered the question carefully, although Stephen kept looking at the two antelope heads over the fireplace and some plumes and spears in the corner.

He said, "The short name for Dar es Salaam is Dar. Many crops are grown in Tanganyika, and—and the people speak forms of Kiswahili!"

"Very good!" Mrs. Peck exclaimed.

I said, "The climate and plant life changes as the elevation goes from very low in the humid coastal areas to very high in the dry mountainous areas. Tanganyika is actually a United Nations protectorate and not a British colony. My father says this is to the good, since we can work for the country and its future independence without other motives. Few Asians and even fewer native Tanganyikans are in the professional class. There is something called race prejudice. I just learned about that yesterday when I asked my mother about the signs that said white only, although the sign over the front door of our hotel says European only. Then—"

Mrs. Peck interrupted by saying, "I see you know everything!" That, of course, was a silly thing to say. We had just gotten to Tanganyika. There were lots we still didn't know.

I suddenly felt lonely and out of place. I missed Folly. I wanted to play with Christa. I got up from my chair and sat in my mother's lap. "I have a panda bear," I said.

"Well, she's an intriguing mixture," Mrs. Peck said.

"I think that is what seven and a half is. Do you find it so with your daughter?" my mother said.

"Yes, every time I see Brigit, she has changed."

That was another puzzling thing for Mrs. Peck to say, but I suddenly imagined a girl who had short straight brown hair at breakfast and long curly blond hair at lunch, who was fat one day and skinny the next, with freckles that rearranged themselves on her face when chimes were rung.

Mrs. Peck then said Stephen and I should go up to the playroom now and play with all of Johnnie's and Brigit's toys. We just needed to take the stairs up to the attic. I looked at my mother, and she motioned us to go. As we left, I heard Mrs. Peck saying to her, "Would you like a cigarette? These are a fine brand."

There weren't many toys in the playroom, but after we drank the lemonade that had been poured for us, Stephen got out a lorry, and we put a doll in it and pushed the lorry around the room. Then we got another doll and gave her a ride. This was of limited interest. Next, we found a rubber ball, and we threw it around until Stephen threw it too high for me to catch and it knocked over a lamp. "Why didn't you jump, dummy?" Stephen asked. The lamp hadn't broken, so we just straightened it up, but we didn't play again, because breaking a lamp would not have helped in making a good impression on Mrs. Peck.

The attic was stuffy, so we opened the shutter to the window more. The roof was right on the other side of the screen, and right near the edge of the roof was a frangipani tree that we thought we could jump to. Stephen and I had never been on a roof before, but we were now in Africa and looking for adventure. Stephen undid the bottom of the screen. Then he stood on a chair and crawled out the window, and I followed him. The roof was both rough and slippery on our knees though,

[39]

and Stephen judged the tree too far away for me to jump to, especially if I was such a ninny and would not stand up. What all this meant was that after crawling two steps forward, we edged back and climbed into the playroom again. Bugs came in with us, unfortunately. We shooed out as many as we could. Next, I had to help Stephen figure out how to reattach the screen. It turned out to be a very long afternoon.

My mother had the worst of it, though. She had to be all by herself with batty Mrs. Peck. When we were at last called back to the sitting room, she was pale and biting her lip. Mrs. Peck was saying to her, "All you need to remember is that conviviality is the key."

My mother said, "Yes, I was warned. I mean I was told. I mean my husband explained it. What I mean is I understand." It wasn't like my mother to be lost in her words.

It was a bumpy car ride, since we had to go over a lot of rutted roads to get back to the wide avenue, so we didn't talk very much. After the car left us off at the hotel, though, I said, "I didn't like being there."

My mother said, "And I don't like it that you didn't thank Mrs. Peck for the lemonade she gave you."

"We forgot," Stephen said.

"Yes, we did forget, absolutely," I agreed, in the hope that if I was convivial, my mother would be herself again.

"You know better than to forget your manners! I said we should make a good impression. I was hoping for some cooperation," my mother said.

I burst into tears. We had cooperated. We hadn't broken a lamp. We had fitted the screen back in.

"Oh stop crying," my mother said. She was quite cross, and she knew it. "I can be out of sorts once and a while. We've been traveling too long."

It was my father who read Stephen and me a chapter from *Oliver Twist* at bedtime while my mother packed for the next day. Then, my father arranged the netting around our beds, and my mother came over, and they both kissed us and said good night to us together.

We were all sharing the same room, so after the light was out, my parents went over to the far corner of the room and talked in whispers, so Stephen and I could go to sleep.

"Craig," my mother said in a low voice, "if this is going to be like the Happy Valley crowd in Kenya, I'm completely out of my league."

My father replied, "Of course, it won't be Happy Valley. The British in Tanganyika are more subdued—government officials who need to work rather than bored plantation owners. Actually, there were only a handful of people at the core of that depraved crowd—Dellamere, Hay, the Sackville woman, a few others."

"Craig, do you know how Ramona Peck tried to reassure me?" my mother continued. "She said I didn't need to stir a dollop of absinthe into the cocktails. Craig, I haven't even heard of absinthe since I was at university, and then only because I knew someone who knew someone who used it. I'm not even sure that Val Cookson knows about it, and she's an artist!"

This made my father laugh for some reason. I could see my parents' shadowy outlines as my father drew my mother close to him. Then he said, "Dearest, we have an advantage. Most people coming to field are in their twenties or early thirties. We're older. Our standards are set. We won't compromise."

"We already have," my mother answered sadly. "We're in a segregated hotel. That makes us part of it, and there are the children! We're barely here, and we've compromised, Craig. We've compromised plenty!"

This was getting a little confusing. When my mother had taught us the word "compromise" in London, it sounded like something we should do. Now, it sounded like something we shouldn't do. Perhaps, compromise was a homonym like read and red.

I tried to keep listening to their conversation, but I fell asleep, and then it was morning. We were excited as we got up with the sun, because by the afternoon we would finally be Dodoma.

The train ride was long, but there was much to look at when we got beyond the last buildings of Dar. We went through miles and miles of undulating yellow and green savannahs dotted with thorn trees and baobab trees. We saw boys herding goats. There were grazing antelopes and running gazelles. Then we saw zebras and three leopards. Stephen spotted an elephant, and suddenly there were more zebras. We went by streams and rivers, and all of it was under blue sky. My father said, "I told you that this is beautiful country," and it was.

My mother said after we had been silent for a while, "One could almost think that hope was born in Africa."

At noon, my mother opened the box lunch the hotel had given us, and we ate, never taking our eyes off the vistas we were passing. I

[41]

exclaimed "Mummy!" when a flock of pink flamingos by the edge of a pond came into view. We both clapped.

Suddenly, the savannahs turned into hills and then mountains. All at once, we went down into a valley, and there were rickety huts and little shops and many people. This was Dodoma, and so we had to get off when the train stopped at a wooden depot. "Keep close to us," my father said to Stephen and me as we walked down the steps to the crowded streets.

We took a car through the narrow, noisy streets, with the British driver honking at people who were walking or driving carts so that they would make way. We turned down a wider road and went past concrete buildings that had the union jack flying and then by a clock tower, although it was shorter than the one we had seen in Dar. The driver went around a roundabout. The road led to a wall. It looked as though the car would drive right into it. My mother, who had been laughing on the train, now seemed nervous. Suddenly, a door in the wall swung open. It closed behind us with a thud. We were in the compound. Hibiscus and African flowers called cannas were everywhere. The car stopped for a moment as my father checked us in at the guard station.

The compound had twenty houses set on curvy roads, which made sudden zigzags so that things would look distinctive. Our house was among the bigger ones. It was whitewashed, with a red-tiled veranda that led into an arched entrance. The rooms on the first floor were very large, especially the dining room. Our bedrooms were on the second floor and on the side of the house away from the dining room, so Stephen and I would not be kept up by parties. The grass around our house was sharp and stubby. It would be no good for rolling around in, but our back garden was of good size. One of the first things we did was to put up our badminton net in a shaded space between two jacaranda trees so we would have a touch of home.

The post was waiting for us, and that was exciting. The top letter was from Switzerland, from Mrs. Gold, but it was just for my mother, so she put it aside. The next letter was from Mrs. Cookson and was for all of us. It seems as if it was still raining babies in London, because now the Cooksons had one! They had named him Lawrence in honor of the fact that they had not gone to Arabia. Mrs. Cookson said that everything was chaos. She didn't know how she had ever ended up a mother of four when she just wanted to paint murals, but she was coping the best she could, and everyone was pretty much delighted, although Ian and Jon would have preferred to have a dog just as we did.

Enclosed in Mrs. Cookson's letter was a message in code that Christa had sent me. My mother said I should read it exactly as written and I would know the meaning. The message said

U R
2 sweet
2̲ be
4 gotten.

I wrote right back to Christa in the same type of code. My message was

U R
2 sweet
2̲ be
4 gotten
4 2x sure!

The Cooksons had sent us a picture of their whole family, with Christa sitting in the center holding baby Lawrence. We put the snap on the mantel in our new sitting room, and that was another reminder of home.

Stephen and I got to wear shorts and camp shirts most of the time now. Edna, who was on our household staff, and a member of the Masai tribe, showed us how to weave reeds into baskets. She and her daughter Aumi, who was a little older than Stephen, taught us our first Kiswahili words. *Kikapu* meant basket, but when there were more than one basket, you said *vikapu*, because as Mummy explained, every language had arbitrary grammar rules.

We would usually have lunch on the veranda, and then my mother, Stephen, and I would go to the pool, which was next to a building called the club. The three of us swam laps and played the water tag game and tried to make our time last as long as we could. When my father came back to our house in the late afternoon, he would talk to Stephen and me for a bit about the villages he had visited or the roads or bridges he wanted to build. He would always ask us if we had had a pleasant day. We would both say yes because usually our day had been fine.

Everything was really very different, though. Stephen and I could not go out of the compound unless one of our parents or Edna was with us. When Folly came, she would never be able to go outside the compound. We could not drink water from the taps in our house. Instead, the staff boiled water and put it in bottles in our refrigerator. We could not pick up scorpions for a better look because although the Tanganyikan scorpion was harmless, other scorpions were poisonous, and we might not know which was which. Hardest of all, Stephen and I could not see very much of our parents in the evenings because they had what they called social obligations now.

What this meant was they had to host many noisy gatherings with a lot of laughing grown-ups. These involved cocktails outside and then dinner in the dining room, which went on for hours. On other nights, they had to go to the club, where activities had been set up just for the adults. It seemed to me that social obligations were even drearier than having a social life again. When the party was at our house, one of my parents would dash upstairs at the end of the cocktail part to tuck Stephen and me into bed, and if it was my father, he would seem distracted, and if it was my mother, she would be anxious. My mother said she was sorry about all these evenings—she was trying to spend as much time with Stephen and me as she possibly could—but this was just the way it had to be. I asked her why, and she said she didn't quite understand the cultural phenomenon herself.

We also had to learn new mores. A few days after we arrived, Stephen and I were running races on the veranda before study time, when Stephen knelt down to retie one of his shoelaces. Aumi, who helped Edna by sweeping the steps, hurried over to him and said, "Stephen, shall I do that?"

Stephen laughed and said, "Yes, if you want to, you may."

My mother, who had been gathering together the books for our lessons, was suddenly right next to Stephen and Aumi. She said, "Thank you, Aumi, thank you, but both of the children have been tying their own shoes for years. I would prefer it if they continued to do so. It wouldn't be a help to them if they went back to Britain for university with only a distant memory of how to do the loops."

Later on, my mother talked to Stephen and me in private. She said that we were to treat every Tanganyikan we met with respect and politeness. We were not to assume that special favors from the staff were our due, nor were we to make abundant requests. Many British children came to Africa and acted like royalty in front of the Africans. That wasn't going to be the two of us. That was for double sure, my mother told us. No matter in what high and mighty ways other British children behaved, Stephen and I were to take another path.

"Do you understand, Stephen?" she asked.

"All right," Stephen said.

"And you, Amelia?"

"Yes, Mummy," I answered.

However, except for very little ones, we saw no other English children in the compound. Like Brigit and Johnnie Peck, the children here were all at school all the time.

Each day now, we expected Folly to be brought to us, but she didn't arrive, and she didn't arrive. We were getting frantic, because nothing would be normal without her. Finally, we had my father call Dar es Salaam, but they just said, "All in good time, all in good time."

One morning an open-back lorry laden with packing cases came up to the front of our house. "We were hoping for our dog," my mother said. "We can do without some of our things if we must." The weatherbeaten white man just winked at her, and then unloaded box after box, including one with my doll house.

Finally, he was down to just a crate with air holes, and we heard scratching and miserable whimpering. It was Folly! We were horrified that she had been transported in this manner.

"You could have unloaded her first," my mother said in a tight voice.

"A surprise for the kiddos," the man said. By kiddos, he meant Stephen and me, and it was a surprise, and not a good one!

My father took the man off to one side and gave him money for some reason, as my mother, Stephen, and I all scrambled to release Folly from imprisonment.

When she was out of the box, she briefly went from to one to another licking our hands, and then she slid past us and sat down on the prickly lawn. She just sat there, blinking, swallowing and curling her lips. She looked around dismally.

"Get Folly some water, darling," my mother said to me. "Tap water will be all right."

I raced to the kitchen. I decided to use bottled water and to put it in a silver bowl. Limes had been cut in sections for a party my parents were having later, so I hooked a section onto the rim of the bowl, in case that would be to Folly's liking.

I hurried back. Folly had come up to the veranda with coaxing from my mother and Stephen. She gulped the water down. She ignored the lime. I took Folly's front paws and said "Folly, will you dance with me? Will you dance with me?" I started the fox-trot, but Folly wouldn't move. She seemed frightened. She gave a low growl. I was careful not to drop her paws but to put them down gently. Then I cried, "Mummy, what's wrong with her? Why won't she dance?"

Stephen asked, "What did they do to her?"

My mother said, "Folly is just a bit disoriented. We need to reassure her quietly and give her time." She sat down on the rattan settee and settled Folly into her lap. Stephen and I crowded in on either side and began to stroke Folly's ears. We patted her ruff. We said we were so sorry about what she had been through. It must have been a terrible experience, but she was home now, and although this might seem a very strange place to call home—indeed we all still thought so—the truth of the matter was that home was wherever we were together. We reminded her that when we were in the Lake District, the innkeeper had called her Princess Folly, and he had only spoken the truth. She was our princess.

"And our sweetheart," Stephen said rather surprisingly.

"And our sweetheart," my mother and I echoed.

Folly finally snuggled back against my mother and looked less frustrated. I noticed though that part of her muzzle had turned from tan to white and over one eye was a tiny half healed cut.

Over the next few days, I tried to get Folly to dance. I did the polka. I did the box step. I did the jig. Folly looked at me like she did not know what I was doing. When I started the cocker tango, she pulled her paws from my hands and backed away. She knew that my feelings were hurt, so she came quickly back and touched me with her nose, but still she would not do the steps. My mother only said, "give her more time."

At last, in desperation, I just began to sway as we had when we were young in Devon and had no cares. A little sparkle came into Folly's eyes. She remembered Devon. With a sudden happy yip, she danced. By the end of the next week, we were able to go through our whole repertoire again. We did a recital on the veranda for my mother and Edna and Aumi. They laughed and gave us thunderous applause.

A little while after that, the "kiddos" got another surprise, and it was also not a good one. My parents said that they had made the arrangements back in London and had not told us because they thought we had had enough to cope with, leaving all of our friends.

Stephen and I were going to go to school in Nairobi. There were schools in Tanganyika, too, in Mbeya and Arusha, but these places were rustic and far away enough that we would still have to be full boarders, so it made much more sense that we go to the best and most comfortable schools in East Africa, and these were in Nairobi. Stephen would be going to a boys' school, and I would going to a girls' schools. We would be there for three months at a time having fun—Stephen could play both rugby and cricket—and then we'd be home for a month having fun. Didn't that sound like fun?

I said no, but Stephen was so busy asking about sports and the playing fields and the boys that I don't think they heard me.

I just thought it was so sad that we would be away from my father for so long, after he had been away all during the war. I went into his study, sat in his big chair with him, and told him so. "I don't want to leave you, Daddy," I said. "I will miss you too much. I miss you already."

"I know, love," he replied, "and I'll certainly miss you too. Going away to school is a big step. I was eleven when I went off, and Mummy was fourteen. Stephen is only a year and a half younger than I was. You are admittedly a little on the sooner side. We thought about keeping you here for a year or two and just sending Stephen for now. That was one of the alternatives, but we decided that would not be fair to you." He explained we could not take a break from the British curriculum, that there were tests we needed to prep for, tests at age eleven and then later, the O-levels and the A-levels. "You need to be with other children engaged in the same endeavor," he said.

"No, I don't, Daddy," I replied. That was true. Christa and I were planning to be pen pals. If need be, we could write about the same endeavor.

My father said that when my mother had gone to Oxford, there had been very few women in university. The country—meaning England and not Tanganyika—was so backward when it came to education for girls, but things were finally changing. In fact, Cambridge had just started to give degrees to women. I had shown promise from the start. I could hear a word like Pennsylvania at age four and use it in an appropriate context at age six. I would have quite a future in the postwar world. I just needed to be ready. My intellect had to be nurtured.

"Give your new school a go, Amelia, give it a whirl. That's all I ask. Can you do that, love?"

I said I would, because it seemed to be important to Daddy. It was all very confusing, though, especially since in the six weeks we had been here, Stephen had done nearly a whole term of his work, and I had learned two terms of mine, as well as learning most of Stephen's.

My mother showed me a picture of my house at the school. She said there would be ten girls living there. That was a new idea to me, so I said, cautiously, "two less than in *Madeline*?"

My mother was delighted. She said, "Yes, but otherwise it will be a bit like *Madeline*!"

We would have to wear uniforms, and that was new, too, since Regency Day had let us wear our clothes we picked out, as long as they were neat and smart. My everyday uniform would be a hunter-green linen pleated skirt, a white blouse with a round collar, and a beige vest that ended in points to be snapped to the skirt.

"It looks drab and dull," I said to my mother when she showed me a picture. The gingham rompers for exercise looked even worse. She said she had to concede that school uniforms did not usually have much flair, but she reminded me that my dress uniform would be a white dress with brass buttons.

Stephen's gray knee pants and white shirts would be ready made, but I had to be measured for my things. Edna offered to do it. She had done it for the little girl who had lived in the house before us, but Mummy said, "Thank you, but I would prefer to do this one thing for my daughter."

My mother seemed sad as I stood before her in my shorts and camp shirt and she put the tape measure around my arms and then my waist and measured me from my waist to my knees and then down my back. "You're growing so much, Amelia," she said, "and Stephen is, too." Then she sighed. She probably didn't like us leaving my father for three months at a time either.

"I prefer not to go, Mummy," I said.

"I know, darling," she answered, "but sometimes we all must do things we prefer not to do."

After lunch on the day before we left for Nairobi, my mother, Stephen, and I were on the veranda going through the checklists the schools had sent us. Our uniforms would be already there, but we were supposed to bring things like two small toys, pictures of each immediate family member, and rain gear. We had just checked off cotton socks when I suggested we make a checklist for Folly. Since we were already in Africa, she would not have to go back to quarantine.

"Whatever do you mean?" my mother asked in a surprised way.

"You know—food bowl, water bowl, her rubber ball, her leash."

"Folly's not going," my mother said, still sounding a bit baffled.

"Will Daddy take care of her?" I asked slowly. This was yet another unexpected turn. My father liked Folly, but we were the ones most involved with her. It would not be good to leave her so soon after she had gotten out of quarantine. The more I thought about it, the more I was sure that going to school in Nairobi was not a good idea.

"Daddy and I both will," my mother answered.

"Mummy," I pointed out, "you'll be with us."

A look of horror flashed across my mother's face for an instant. Then her expression went back to normal as she said, "No, I'll be here with Daddy as we eagerly await your return on holiday."

It took time for British people to get used to equatorial heat. Children adjusted faster than adults. Just last week, my mother had said at breakfast that we'd go to the bazaar that day, and I had had to tell her that this was Wednesday, and the bazaar was on Thursday. "You're right," she had said. "I'm so confused by this heat; I don't even know what day it is." Indeed, she had been so busy getting us ready, she hadn't packed herself yet. Clearly, I would have to take charge until my mother was acclimated.

"But, Mummy," I persisted patiently, "we always sleeps in the same house. You are always with us. You are with us even when Daddy can't be. You were with us in Devon."

My mother bit her lip. "That was a totally different situation, Amelia." She paused and then said quietly, "Mothers don't stay with their children when the children are away at school."

My eyes widened. It was like pouring a glass of water and having the water evaporate as you lifted the glass to your lips or like taking an ordinary step only to have your legs crumple as your muscles dissolved. There were things that you never worried about because it never occurred to you that they might happen.

"Oh, Mummy, no!" I said, and I wailed.

Stephen had just been lightly swinging his foot against the rattan chair he was sitting in, but now he said, "Didn't you know that, you silly, you dummy?"

My mother held up her hand and said, "Stephen, this is no time for unkindness. Not that there ever is such a time."

Stephen looked somewhat startled and then said in a distressed way, "Besides, who would she stay with? We are going to separate schools!"

"I'm younger, she should stay with me," I cried.

"I'm pulling rank," Stephen answered. "She stays with me."

"I'm afraid I can't stay with either of you," my mother said. "My role is to be with your father, helping him." She plunged on. She told us that we were not to think that she and Daddy did not want us at home. They did, they wanted it quite desperately. That was why they had tried so hard for another posting. This was all due to circumstances. She said we had no idea how carefully they had picked our schools. "We agonized over the choice," she said.

My mother spoke more and more rapidly. Not only was the education stellar—the schools we were going to took pride in their home-like atmosphere. We would not find them spartan at all. Children were called by their first names. We would each have just one roommate. Perhaps mine would be a lot like Christa. Many adults would be looking out for us. There was no caning.

"What's caning?" I asked.

"Spanking, paddling," my mother replied, and then, sounding somewhat defeated, she said, "hitting, beating. We made sure they don't do it."

I just looked at her. At Regency Day, there had been no caning and also no mention of it.

Still my mother went on. They had signed us up for a variety of extras they thought we'd like. If when we got there we saw something we would enjoy that we hadn't been signed up for, we had only to let them know, and they would sign us up for that for the next term. The reverse was also true. If there was something we had been signed up for that was really not to our liking, we would not have to do it again.

Stephen said, "Dad said I can join my school's coin collectors' club."

"That's for double sure," my mother agreed.

"Mummy," I said in tears, "is this part of the price of our African adventure?"

"Yes, Amelia, it is. It is the steepest part of the price. For a while, we will all have to show the Dunkirk spirit." She picked up Folly and put her in my lap. Folly looked up at me in a concerned way because she wasn't used to seeing me cry so much. She put her paws on my shoulders. Slowly, she tried to lick the wet streaks off my face.

My parents had canceled all their engagements for the evening, so we had supper with them in the large dining room. In Tanganyika, there wasn't really any twilight period as there had been in England. The sun sank in a moment that was almost as fleeting as the gloaming on the moor. My mother had lit candles, and they flickered eerily against the white walls. I don't remember what we ate or what we talked about.

After supper, we played a game of badminton under lighted lanterns that had been set up for the next party. Then, with Folly, we took a walk around the compound, past the guard station, the club, the pool, and through the winding streets with the houses where people lived with no children except babies.

At a bungalow painted green, a man and a woman were coming down the sidewalk. They were the Hobsons, and they said they were on their way to the club. Mrs. Hobson was tottering along in high heels that were much higher than the high heels my mother had. She swooped down on us and gaily said to Stephen and me, "Well, aren't you lucky tykes? Off to school tomorrow!"

We didn't say anything, so she turned to my mother and laughed, "And it'll be liberation day for you, Olivia!"

My mother gave her a look that cut like glass. "I am only free when I'm with my children." I saw my father put his hand on the middle of my mother's back.

"Well, I didn't mean it like that," Mrs. Hobson said. "I like it when my Jory comes home, but I also like it when he goes back. He gets to be with his mates and play rugby, and we get to run on adult time again."

Mr. Hobson, adjusting the bottle of scotch under his arm, said to Stephen, "I hear you want to play rugby."

"Yes," Stephen answered uncertainly.

"Well, Jory's a great player. He aspires to lead his team to victory throughout East Africa when he's old enough for the school leagues.

He's a fair to middling student, but we remind him that if he wants to do this, he needs to be able to at least pass the exams for senior school."

"Jory takes after me, but well, we must be on our way," Mrs. Hobson said. She went tripping past us, just turning back to say cheerily, "These shoes make a cripple out of me!"

"Insufferable woman," my mother said as we went around the corner.

When we got home, it was a bedtime. We had been reading *Lassie Come Home*. My mother had timed it so that tonight we were at the last chapter. Lassie had finally come home. She was allowed to stay. She was having puppies.

I started crying again as my mother tucked me in. I hung on to her neck and asked, "Why, Mummy, why?" I asked so many times that finally she stopped trying to answer. She just said she would sit in my room until I fell asleep. In Stephen's bedroom next door, my father was sitting with him.

My mother woke me early. For the first time ever, I turned my head away from her and said I would not be getting up. "You must, love, you must," she said. Gently, she parted the mosquito netting and pulled me into a sitting position. She had out my pink and white seersucker dress, which we had gotten in London for travel and which looked like peppermint swirl candy. She suggested I wear my oxfords with the dress, since there might be some walking. Somehow I got dressed, my mother helping me when I went too slowly.

We met Stephen and my father downstairs. Stephen was pale. He had on his khaki dress shorts, a white shirt, and a new bow tie.

"Don't we have fine looking young people?" My father said.

"Indeed," my mother answered. They had never called us young people before.

French toast, peaches, mangos, and many other nice things had been fixed for our breakfast, but the meal was rushed. We shook hands with Edna and Aumi, who wished us safe passage. Then it was time to say good-bye to Folly. Stephen and I got down on the floor, and she licked our hands, going back and forth between us. We said we were going away to school for three months and then would be home for a month. We told her that she was not to think that we did not want to be with her. We did, we wanted it quite desperately. This was all due to circumstances. Folly tried to cuddle and play, as we patted her sadly.

She was a very smart dog, and we had always talked to her accordingly, but we could see she really did not understand any of this.

My mother said, "Amelia, would you like to dance with Folly? You always make us laugh when you dance with Folly."

I said, "No, I only dance with Folly when I'm happy."

My mother bit her lip. My father said it was time to go to the airfield anyway.

When we had come to Dodoma, my father had been given a car. Usually when we went out for a drive, my mother sat next to my father in the front seat, while Stephen and I sat in the back. Now she sat in the back between us and put an arm around each of us.

As we drove out of the compound, my parents went over the steps in our journey. We would be flown by private plane to Kenya, but we would not be flown all the way to Nairobi. Instead we would be dropped at a spot on the Athi River where we would go on a party cruise for boarding-school children. It was very highly recommended for first termers. The cruise would take us to a pier in Nairobi, and then vans would take us to our schools.

"The idea is that this way you are always looking forward to something and never back to home" my mother said. "Right now, you're looking forward to the plane ride and being able to see Mount Kilimanjaro in the distance. Aren't you, Stephen?"

Stephen said, "Yes." He looked at his knees.

"Then on the plane, you'll be looking forward to having a good time on the party cruise, and then on the boat, you'll be looking forward to the pier and then to seeing your schools and meeting your new friends. That's the idea." My mother sounded perplexed as she was saying this, as if she didn't know why these words were coming from her mouth.

My father said he had never heard of anyone else who had had the opportunity to go on two cruises in just a matter of months. My mother said she had never had either.

We went over a hill and could see the airfield just three more hills away. The minutes were running out. I didn't usually try to persuade my mother about things, but I tried to persuade her now.

"Mummy," I said, "Mummy, I am your daughter. What this means is that I need to live with you. I have to live with you."

The horror that I had seen flash across my mother's face the day before flickered in her eyes again. She took a breath. "Darling, of course, you are my daughter, just as Stephen is my son. You both still live with us. You'll just be away part of the time."

My father said from the front seat, "Amelia, this is a milestone, but going away to school is a normal part of our culture. All the children in the compound do it. Stephen is nearly ten. I told you that he's just a year younger than I was when I went to Harrow."

"Stephen may be almost ten," I cried, "but I'm not even eight!" I put my head in my hands, and I howled.

My mother spoke slowly. "Craig, she has a point. When Stephen was her age, he was walking to school every morning holding your hand. I know we discussed it and discussed it. We discussed it to death, but maybe we didn't consider all the nuances. Oh, Craig, I didn't prepare them very well. Amelia didn't even fully understand until yesterday that I wasn't going with her. I don't know what we should do. Amelia doesn't cry without any reason. She's distraught, Craig, and poor Stephen is trembling."

"Olivia," my father said in a warning voice, "Olivia, we'll make the children more anxious by wavering. They won't even be gone an entire three months. It will be just twelve weeks, eighty-four days. If there's a problem—and I'm sure there won't be—they don't need to go back, but they should try it."

Stephen said, "Maybe we can go next term and not this term. I still want to go, but not right now."

"I prefer not to go at all," I sobbed. "It didn't occur to me that this might happen. I used my birthday to get learning supplies so Stephen and I could study at home. I thought ahead."

Horror flashed on my mother's face for a third time. What she said now was "Good God, Craig."

My father said, "It'll be all right. It'll be all right. These are very fine schools. Amelia, you'll come to like it."

"Craig, I've heard of a Christian Missionary Society woman in Dodoma who's teaching a few children around her kitchen table. It's makeshift, but they could go there a few mornings a week, and I could do it the rest of the time for just one term."

"Olivia," my father said again. "Olivia."

We were now at the airfield. I was crying so hard my nose was running. My mother took a handkerchief out of her pocket, put it on my nose, and said, "Blow, darling." She patted Stephen's shoulder and murmured, "Good old Stephen."

A small gray plane was there, and a man in a pilot's cap was standing near it. His skin was red, and he looked young and wrinkled at the same time. My father got out of the car and said to the man, "We're here, now. I'm sorry if we're a minute late. This is tough on all of us."

"I can make up the time," the pilot said.

My father opened the car door on Stephen's side and the door on my side. No one moved. My father said, "Um, you need to get out of the car. Come on, Stephen, dear fellow." Slowly, Stephen got out of the car. Slowly, my mother came out after him. Stephen was shaking. My mother was pale.

My father reached for me. "Love," he said, "Love."

"No, Daddy, no!" I screamed. I slid towards the other side of the seat. I put my arms in front of me so I could push him away if I had to. I cried, "I'll find another way to go to university, but I can't leave Mummy. I'm not going, Daddy!"

Now, the horror I had seen flash across my mother's face three times was on my father's face for an instant. He said to her, "Before Stephen was born, I swore no child of mine would ever look at me in fear." He bent over me and kissed me, as he lifted me out of the car and set me on my feet.

I ran over to my mother and buried my head in her blouse. "Mummy," I pleaded, "Mummy!"

"Amelia is crying," Stephen pointed out to my parents.

My father said to him, "At her age, this seems scary. There will be escorting adults every bit of the way. This system has never failed, thousands of children have used it without a hiccup, but you are Amelia's big brother. Can I count on you to look out for her? Will you be right there with her, son, until you get to your destinations?"

"All right," Stephen said faintly. "Yes, I will."

"Amelia," my mother asked, "will you keep close to Stephen?"

I nodded.

The pilot said, "We have to get off now."

My father said, "Yes, hugs and kisses all around, and then it's time."

I wailed and held on to my mother more tightly.

She said, "Darling, you need to let go of me for a minute so I can say good-bye to Stephen properly."

I didn't want to hurt Stephen, so I let her go to him. My father put his arm around me until my mother came back to me.

She stroked my hair and said, "I'll write you, Amelia, you and Stephen both. I'll write you faithfully." She kissed me several times.

I held on to my mother. I held on to her for dear life.

Then there was about a thirty-second gap in time. One instant I was crying against my mother, and the next instant I was crying in the plane and the pilot was briskly buckling me into my seat. Stephen was on my far side, so he must have gotten in first. I think my father had told him that he could help by getting in first.

"She yells like a hyena," the pilot said to Stephen now.

Stephen said nothing. He was jiggling his foot.

The pilot closed the plane's door with a thud, just like the witches had knocked the hourglass over with a thud. Sitting down in his seat, he said, "I wish I had been sent off for an education. Maybe then I would be doing something other than ferrying tykes to school who don't want to go."

He started the engine. My parents were standing together on the ground, waving good-bye to us. They were a few yards away, and I was looking at them through glass and a blur of tears, so they seemed like they were in a picture, their smiles painted on.

The plane began to taxi. I thought my parents would watch us until we were gone, but suddenly my father spun my mother around, and they started walking very fast back to the car. My mother seemed to stumble over a branch, for she sank to her knees and would have fallen headlong if my father had not caught her. He opened the car door and folded her in. Then he looked at the plane and gave us a final wave as we lifted into the air.

I grabbed for Stephen's arm. To my surprise, he let me take it.

"You tykes are in for a treat," the pilot said. "We're flying through the mountains and over for some of the lakes. This is the best way to see Tanganyika."

"I don't care," I said.

About an hour later, the pilot said, "Hey, tykes, off to the right is Mount Kilimanjaro. Better men than me have tried to climb it and failed."

"I don't care," I said.

"Your sister's a charmer," the pilot told Stephen.

"She's upset," Stephen said in a monotone.

Although Stephen was older, I was a little better with words than he was. "I'm not upset, I'm distraught," I said.

In a while, the pilot spoke again to say we were in Kenya now. I said to Stephen that I wanted to go home, and he said that he knew how to roll his tongue; Jon Cookson had taught him. He gave me a demonstration, and then I tried it, but neither he nor I laughed.

We followed a river for a long time, and then the plane flew lower and lower, and we saw a boat with a large paddle wheel in front and a wide deck with blue and red ribbons wrapped around the railings. The union jack fluttered from a flagpole.

The plane landed on an airstrip a short way from the boat. The pilot opened the door, and we silently got out. He gathered up our belongings, and we followed him down the path to the boat. There are crocodiles in the Athi River," the pilot said, as he deposited us in front of a redheaded woman giving out name tags to children getting on the boat. He turned to Stephen and said, "Mind you that you don't feed your little sister to one." He chuckled.

I just looked at the man while Stephen answered dully, "I would never do that."

The man said to the lady, "Here are the Ord boy and girl. They seem to have gotten up on the wrong side of the bed." He carried our suitcases onto the boat.

The lady said to us, "Well, Stephen and Amelia, please put these on and get on board. By the way, you can call me the cruise lady. It is my job to make sure you have fun." She wore a floppy hat and had a big smile for us. She handed us our name tags. A long time ago in Devon, my mother had said we could do better than name tags.

There were dozens of white children running around the deck, but Stephen and I found a spot by the railing and just watched the cloudy, slow river and trees and swampy roots on either side as the boat began to move.

The cruise lady had begun to organize games, and three times she asked us to play. I said "I prefer to watch the river," and Stephen said, "I prefer to stay with my sister. That is what our parents would expect."

In the background, we heard "Button, button, who has the button?"

At lunchtime, we were called to a food table in the center of the deck. Stephen took a sandwich and gave me half. The lady came up behind us and said, "No, no, you each get a sandwich. Two, if you like!"

We said we preferred to share a sandwich.

She said, "No, you must each have a whole one. We can't have it said that children are not well fed on this trip."

Stephen took another sandwich and gave me half of that one, too. Then the woman said, "You should each take a cupcake. Sugar is still dear in England, but we give you cupcakes in Kenya! We want to make it festive for you. They are devil's food." She was continuing to smile brightly.

Stephen sighed and put two brown cupcakes with white icing on top on a little cardboard tray, and we went back to the railing and watched the river some more. Gray birds twittered in the trees by the bank. Something tawny and leathery slithered through the papyrus into the water. It was probably a crocodile, but we did not discuss it.

I was struggling to eat the second of my sandwich halves and started to cry. It had been several hours since we had been with Mummy. She was probably now eating lunch on the veranda. Folly was undoubtedly at her feet. I chewed, but the bread would not go down. I drank the milk, but still the bread did not go down.

Stephen took his second sandwich half and dropped it down into the water and said, "Here's a treat for the little fishies."

That made me laugh, because I had never heard Stephen talk baby talk.

I dropped my sandwich half in the water and said, "Here's another treat for the fishies."

The plate with the cupcakes was resting on the railing. I used three fingers to flick my cupcake into the river. It floated for a moment before it sank. "Ooh, little fishies," I said. "We are so sad, but you are having a festive party."

Stephen picked his cupcake and threw it. "Bombs away!" he said.

I tossed the cardboard plate into the drink and said, "A life raft for fishies." We giggled as it bobbed downstream.

"Let's get more food," I suggested. However, African people were now putting the sandwiches away, and the cruise lady was coming up to us to insist that we go to the lavatory because all the other children had gone. She said, "Last term, a five-year-old wet his pants. No one got mad because he had traveled five days from Rhodesia with Dutch nuns who could not communicate with him—no one else was available—and he seemed a bit worse for wear. Anyway, now I give reminders." She put out her hand to me.

I just looked at her, but Stephen nudged me, and we followed her.

After a sing-along, which we did not join, the boat docked at a pier at the edge of an asphalt lot where waving British adults were grouped. Beyond the lot was a road amid tin shacks and long, low stucco buildings.

The cruise lady clapped her hands and said, "Listen, boys and girls! Everything good must end, and so it is with this cruise. We are now at the outskirts of Nairobi. Please line up, and you will be assigned to your buses."

We walked off the boat, and when it got to be our turn, we had to let a man look at our name tags.

He said, "Amelia Ord, Westlands–King George School, van 23. Stephen Ord, Westlands–Crown School, van 11."

I burst into tears and said, "That's wrong. It's wrong. I am to stay with my brother."

"Sorry, Princess Elizabeth. Separate schools, separate vans."

I cried more loudly, and a boy behind Stephen shouted, "What's wrong with the little snot head? She was blubbering on the boat, too, and throwing plates off the side."

"Shut up!" Stephen told the boy.

"Don't say that to me, you blighter!" the boy answered. He raised his fist. Stephen made a fist.

"Hey, stop the commotion," the man said. "You Ord pair, you can wait together with Mrs. Danvers until your vans come. This is a concession I am giving you."

A tall grim-faced woman with white hair and steel glasses and wearing a gray cap motioned us over to the side. I hooked two fingers under Stephen's belt.

Stephen's van came first. They wanted him to get in right away.

"No, Stephen," I cried. "You can't go, you can't. Stephen!"

Stephen said to the driver, "I need to wait until my sister's van comes. She's only seven and a half. My parents asked me to look out for her."

"No, chap. We have other boys to pick up. She'll be perfectly fine with Mrs. Danvers."

I was all over Stephen. I was leaning on his shoulder, pulling on his arm, encircling his waist. I couldn't say any words now except "Stephen, Stephen, Stephen, Stephen, Stephen!" He had started to pat my back as he tried to explain things to the man.

Stephen said, "My father asked me to stay with her. I prefer to do what my father says. My father helped win the war."

"Well, your father might not have understood that Mrs. Danvers would be here with her. Come on, chap. You're getting off on the wrong foot."

Mrs. Danvers had gotten between Stephen and me. I was screaming. They had called back the cruise lady, who had moved the remaining children to the other side of the lot and was trying to tell them a story. She had three in her lap. One of them turned to look at me, and the cruise lady pushed her head back. She was talking louder and louder, "And the pied piper raised his flute, and all the children fell into line."

I cried, "Up! Up! Up!" I raised my arms. I wanted Stephen to lift me. He glanced at me in horror.

The man said to Stephen, "I represent your headmaster!"

Stephen was crying now. "I need to stay with her! I'm her brother. This is what my father wants. He was away from us for five years winning the war!"

They would not listen. With threats, the driver made Stephen get into the van, while Mrs. Danvers held me back. Stephen, sniffling, had only time to look at me and say, "Good-bye, Amelia. Be back here in three months. Don't forget!"

"Stephen, Stephen," I sobbed. Then the van pulled away. I tried to run after it. I thought I could jump on the running board, but I could not get away from Mrs. Danvers's grasp. She had looped a sash around me and was holding the ends. I shrieked and I shrieked, straining against the sash as the van went out of sight.

"Stop that," Mrs. Danvers said. "Stop that or I'll shake you!"

I changed back to crying loudly, and she undid the sash.

Mrs. Danvers said sternly. "Your father was in the war. I was a military nurse myself, and I have a question for you. How far do you think England would have gotten if the children of London had behaved like this during the blitz?"

I just cried.

"I asked you a question. How far do you think England would have gotten if the children of London had behaved like this during the blitz? How far?"

"I don't know," I cried. "I don't know. I was in Devon with my mother and brother. Jenny, too!"

Just then, my van pulled up, and a man with wet marks under the arms of his white shirt popped out. "Traffic was bad," he said.

"Fred, she's a crier, this one is," Mrs. Danvers replied.

"We get one or two of them every term, don't we?" Fred said cheerfully. "Well, come on, little miss, it won't be as bad as you think."

"She's also cheeky," Mrs. Danvers warned as I got in.

We drove past the wood shacks and the stucco buildings and then tin-roofed shops and more buildings and more buildings and more and more and into the traffic. Fred talked a little and then said when I didn't answer, "Well, I'm going to let you be, since that's what you seem to want."

I cried for some time, and now again I whimpered, "Mummy, Mummy, Mummy," and once I called for my father. I sang "Baa baa black sheep" to myself twice, even though I had not sung it for years. I said "We love you, Alice," and then I babbled like a witch, "Ibble, bibble, ribble, dibble."

"You're screwy," Fred said, even though he had promised to let me be. I looked at him cross-eyed, the way Stephen looked at me when I said something silly. Then I put my thumb in my mouth and took a nap.

When I awoke, we were winding up to the top of a hill past guava trees and Bougainvillea hedges. There was a sign and a gate, and the gate opened. We went up a lane past a brick schoolhouse and several more large buildings. Then the lane became a circle that had grass in the middle, and at the far side of the circle were several white-frame bungalows with wraparound verandas. Fred stopped at the one that said "Margaret House" in green letters over the door. A woman rushed out and smiled at me when Fred opened the van's door. She was big, and her voice was hearty. She took my suitcases from Fred.

"Amelia," she said. "I'm Mrs. Lamberton. You're the last one to arrive. Now, our little house will be complete. Are you delighted to be here?"

"No, I'm not," I said in a small voice. "I would prefer to be home with my mother."

"Well, I'm your house mother." She pulled my name tag off over my head. "You don't need this anymore. This is your home away from home. First impressions count. What do you think of it all?"

I just looked at her. By this time we were in the house, walking around talking girls in a common area with stacks of board games and heading towards the room I would sleep in.

"You're just tired," she said. "You've had a long day. You must be a little worse for wear."

She showed me what she called "the shower room." There were three spigots on the ceiling and a drain in the center of the floor and two tubs side by side so that all the girls in the house could wash in two shifts. She would supervise so there would be no horseplay.

I said, "We have an ordinary bathroom, and I take a bath on my own. I don't like this."

"Amelia," she said, "things can't be exactly like they are at home. My policy is to be kind but firm." Her expression, however, seemed to say: "I've never had a seven-year-old say that to me."

For some reason, I giggled.

"That's a girl!" Mrs. Lamberton said.

The room she called mine was very tiny. The little window had shutters. On the opposite wall were pictures of Snow White, Rose Red, and the royal family. There were two beds with pink bedspreads, and a very pretty girl with long corkscrew curls was sitting on one. She was holding a large stuffed polar bear and was so still she seemed to be part of the room.

Mrs. Lamberton said, "Amelia Ord, this is Samantha Mary Winters. You are the two new girls in the house this term, so we thought we'd put you together. That's quite a bear, Samantha Mary."

"I wanted a giraffe," Samantha Mary replied. "My father left me with the same thing last time. He made a mistake." She was wearing a white lace dress with bows all over it, and her shiny white slip-on shoes had bows on them as well. Now she moved a little to kick at the straw mat between the beds.

"Well," Mrs. Lamberton said, "it'll be story time in the common room in twenty minutes, so I'll leave you two to get acquainted until then. Amelia, I'll unpack you after the nice supper we are having." She turned and left.

Samantha Mary just stared at me as she poked her finger in the bear's ear. She looked at my oxfords, at my seersucker dress, and at my hair, which, like my mother's, was cut at chin length because we had decided that short hair would be cooler for the tropics. "You might as well be a boy," she finally said.

My father had told Stephen and me on one of our walks to Regency Day that sometimes when people were very sick or in deep despair, they would attempt to rally. It would be then that a terrible situation would get better. The tide would turn. He had seen it for himself many times.

I attempted to rally.

"I have a dog named Folly," I offered to the girl. "I sure wish she was here now."

Her sulky expression turned to rage. She was short and skinny in her lace, but she was like a wasp. "You will not bring a dog in here," she shouted. "You will not. I hate dogs. I think I was bitten by a dog when I was a baby whilst Nanny was talking to her boyfriend. Dogs make me throw up. If you bring a dog here, I'll leave. I'll tell my father. He will come get me right away. He will!" She twisted the bear's nose.

It seemed important to get this horrid child to stay. "I do not think Folly will come," I said. "She's a car ride, a plane flight, a boat trip, and another car ride away. I don't think even Lassie could get here, not even Lassie." I shook my head sadly and then started to talk faster. "If Lassie could not get here, how could Folly? Folly is only a little dog. We never let her out of the compound. Folly is—"

"You're folly!" Samantha Mary yelled.

I sat down hard on the other bed and burst into tears. "Folly's not coming," I cried. "She's not coming!" I wrapped my arms around myself and noticed I had added rocking to my repertoire. Even if this ghastly, nonsensical day came to an end, I would still have eighty-three more days before I could get back into my life.

Samantha Mary shouted, "You're common. I hate you, you seersucker bloodsucker!"

That startled me so that I stopped crying for an instant. Stephen, with both Jon and Ian to help him, would not have been able to invent a name like that.

Samantha Mary succeeded in pulling one of the poor bear's eyes off and threw it across the room. "I'm not staying here with you. I'm sending my father a telegram."

"I would send my father a telegram, too," I cried, "but I don't know how. All I have is writing paper," and I cried harder.

Mrs. Lamberton ran in. "Now, girls," she said, "no crying or fighting the first night."

I sniffed, trying to stop the tears.

"Girls," Mrs. Lamberton said, "perhaps you'll feel better if I tell you the extras you've been signed up for."

I had a subscription to the Nairobi Children's Theatre (transportation included), nature walks, double swim time, horseback riding, and something called rhythms. Samantha Mary had curtseying and posture control, place settings, the art of accepting formal invitations, and needlepoint. "I'll be presented to the queen," Samantha Mary giggled, "while she'll be paddling around in a scummy pond." She turned around and wiggled her fanny.

"That's a tad rude, Samantha Mary," Mrs. Lamberton said, "but the opening-night rituals are about to begin, and soon you'll both be as right as rain."

After story time, supper, the giving of the school handshake, the recitation of the principles of the founders, and house prayers, the day at long last was dying. Mrs. Lamberton rang a bell, which meant the girls of Margaret House at Westlands–King George School were sent to bed.

I was scrunching up my eyes, worrying about how long it would take me to get to sleep and wondering what it was like for Stephen when Samantha Mary whispered to me, "Stay wide awake, whore bore, or I'll cut off the rest of your hair, every single bit."

I didn't say anything. I did not know what a whore bore was. It was probably some type of boar. I didn't care. There were no scissors in the room, so she couldn't carry out her threat. I trembled, though, and stayed wide awake, even after Samantha Mary in her silk nightgown had drifted into sleep, her bear upside down next to her. Mrs. Lamberton had said that every night, forty-five minutes after "lights out," she would come by with a flashlight and shine it in each room to make sure everyone was as snug as a rug. When she did it this first night, I was still awake and shaking so much I could feel the sheets moving with me. Maybe, despite the shots, I had malaria. Maybe I would die. Mrs. Lamberton shone the flashlight on my bed and on the other bed. Then she went on to the next room.

The hours passed. My cotton pajamas were sticking to me because it was hot, but still I shivered. The clock on the shelf ticked. It was so late that my mother was probably asleep in Dodoma. It was two o'clock. It was two-thirty. It was only when the dark turned gray that I dozed.

I dreamed of Devon, where the morning sun came through the bay windows of the sitting room and made patterns on the rug.

"Jenny," my mother said, "the war is over. We must get on with our lives."

Jenny replied. "I'll plan a life of games."

"Wonderful, Jenny!" my mother said. "Then, of course, we'll stay."

So we did, and my father came to be with us, and no one ever went to London, which meant Folly never had to go to quarantine because we never heard of Africa.

I woke up. It was the next day. I still had my hair, but my head hurt. I was thirsty, and my eyes felt grainy. Something like a pebble hit me. Samantha Mary, standing on her bed, had ripped the other eye off the bear and threw it at me.

"Why did you do that?" I asked.

"I don't know" she said. "I can teach it to behave however I want. It's mine." She pulled off a handful of the bear's fur and lobbed that over, too. I was glad that last night, while Mrs. Lamberton was putting my name on my toothpaste and hanging my calendar over my shelf, I had zipped my panda bear into a secret compartment of my suitcase for protection's sake.

Now Mrs. Lamberton was walking up and down the hall, ringing her bell and saying, "Arise, girls. Into your uniforms and greet the day. Last one into the dining area may get cold porridge!"

"No cold porridge for me! Only cold porridge for crying soupy poopy!" Samantha Mary declared, jumping down from her bed.

I bit my lip and slowly got up.

I was thin, but I was not the stick Samantha Mary was, and I was strong. I could get her on the floor. I could straddle her and slap her face until blood spurted from her nose. I could yank her hair straight. I could make her scream.

I took a step forward. Then I took a step back. The reason was that my mother was my mother, and I was her daughter. What this meant was that when I finally saw my mother after eighty-three more days, she must recognize me. Mummy could not look upon some mean, glassy-eyed tyke and ask, "Have you seen Amelia? She is one that I am desperate to see." She had to know right away it was me.

"Leave me alone," I said in a fierce way. I gathered up my school clothes and decided it would be best to dress in the closet.

Throughout my time in boarding school, I would feel stranded in immense gloomy woods. I would always feel parched, but before I had even put on my dreary uniform for the first time, I had a compass. That was how I would survive, survive, survive.

Samantha Mary left after three days because she was not making a good adjustment. She would not sit in her seat in the classroom, and she called teachers unusual names like "booby hippo" and "slick lick" when they told her to do her lessons. She threw a whole bottle of ink at one of the day students. She tore up a picture of her roommate's "poodle," and poor Mrs. Lamberton had had to deal with the upset that that act had caused. I heard the last part when I trudged past the junior headmistress's office on my way to "rhythms" in the gymnasium. Folly, of course, was not a poodle.

We were in the common room during our half hour free playtime before supper when her father came walking in. I was copying over spelling words in my exercise book, next to some girls playing jacks. Samantha Mary was on the other side of the room, biting a paw of her bear. The bear was now a little worse for wear.

Her father was very tall, and his black shoes were polished to a high gloss. His steps were long. When Samantha Mary saw him, she took the bear's paw out of her mouth, and her face lighted up for the first time that I had seen. "Oh, Daddy," she said, "I knew that all I had to do was wish it and you would come!" One of her hands held the bear, but she reached out her other hand towards him.

He looked at her with a clenched jaw. "You're such a bore," he said. He jerked her arm, trying to hurry her out of the room. She yelped and dropped the bear.

Mrs. Lamberton snatched up the bear and went after them. "Now, Mr. Winters, this school isn't right for everyone." Pointing at me for some reason, Mrs. Lamberton said, "Just because it's right for a girl like her doesn't mean it's the place for Samantha Mary." She held out the bear.

Samantha Mary tried to grab for it, but he blocked her hand. "You will learn to take care of the things I pay for," he said.

"I was only trying to teach it, Daddy," Samantha Mary cried.

Mrs. Lamberton said, "Girls, let's say good-bye to Samantha Mary," but they were out in the hall. Samantha Mary was whining, "I want to go to Auntie Mim Mim's. Please, Daddy, she will curl my hair."

"Good evening," he said curtly to Mrs. Lamberton. The door slammed behind them.

Some girls started to laugh because Samantha Mary was cuckoo. Someone said, "She called her bear Pee Pee Bradley," and there was more laughing. Mrs. Lamberton stopped it and said we should try to forget all this. Our little house was back to normal now.

Mrs. Lamberton looked at me, copying over my spelling words. She said, "Amelia, you are proving yourself to be a scholar, but this is free playtime, not lesson prep time. Close the book. We strive for balance."

I closed the book. She did not understand. I liked to study. What's more, I needed to study so I could tell my parents I had given this place a go and a whirl and could stay home after this term finally was over.

My new roommate was named Margaret, like the house. Both she and Mrs. Lamberton thought that was amusing. She was chunky, with red corkscrew curls, and liked horseback riding. She liked it even better that riding was available only to the boarders and not to the day girls. "Aren't we lucky stiffs?" she said.

The school allotted us ten pence a week from the spending money that our parents had sent for us. (In London, my allowance had been two shillings, and Stephen had gotten three because he was older.) Margaret used her ten pence to buy crackers that came three to a package. Once she gave me a cracker. I was using all my money to buy supplies because I would need them when I stopped being in this school, so in return I cut an eraser in half and gave one half to Margaret. "Well, thank you," she said. After that, though, she shared her crackers with a girl named Buffy who bought raisins.

At recess during school hours, I played with the day girls because their ways were more familiar to me, and my particular friend was Cassie Townes. She did remind me a bit of Christa because she was quick and pert and an excellent reader. She was also a champion jump roper. What really made us close was that she had a cocker spaniel, although hers was cream color, while Folly was tan. His name was Jambo.

"That means hello in Kiswahili," I exclaimed.

"Yup," Cassie said. "You just need to say hello, hello, Jambo, Jambo, and he bounds over to you and turns inside out."

That made me smile.

Even so, I was sad in this place, and all the time, but the worse was at three in the afternoon when Miss Henning, my classroom teacher, would clap her hands and say, "Day students, you are dismissed. Boarding students, assemble at the side of the room to be organized for your activities." I would look out and see the mothers standing by the gate. One mother who looked a little like my mother would always reach out her arms to the two girls racing towards her. Cassie's mother picked her and her sister up in a car. Cassie would turn and wave, and then they'd be off.

Miss Henning always said, "Amelia, you have riding today," or "Amelia, you're scheduled again for rhythms. Isn't that nice?"

I was required to say, "Yes, Miss Henning, thank you," so I did. The horses were unpredictable, though, tied up but always backing here or backing there when you were told to get on them. As for rhythms, it was just hopping and skipping to music when requested to do so.

The only extra I liked was swimming. The water was silky, and when I did laps I pretended I was doing them with Mummy. Then the pool was shut down for repairs for several days, and the school made up for it by scheduling more riding for me.

There was also Saturday. The day students did not come because there wasn't regular school, and the weekday boarders left Friday night. Only the full boarders were left. In the morning we had to run around in our rompers playing games with balls. I was assigned to dodgeball, which meant I had to dodge a ball when it was aimed at me. In the afternoon, we had extra sessions of our extras. A movie was shown in the evening. The first Saturday, it was *The Ugly Duckling*. I was already familiar with the dreary tale but now had to see it in cartoon form. The ducks called the baby duck names and pecked at him, until he turned into a beautiful swan, at which point the ducks all decided to be his friend. I heard Margaret behind me take a breath and then let it out.

When the movie was finally over, the junior headmistress asked, "Who would like to see *The Ugly Duckling* again this term?"

Almost every hand but mine shot up.

"All right, all right," the junior headmistress said, laughing. "We have *Wee Willie Winkie* scheduled for next week, but the week after that we will show *The Ugly Duckling* again by popular demand."

I did not want to see it again but knew attendance would be compulsory. Once I thought of Christa, playing whatever she liked in the little park after school and helping her mother with tiny Lawrence. She could not have imagined the fate that had befallen me.

When there were seventy-eight days to go, I got a letter from my mother. At the top was a number 1, because this was her first letter to me. She wrote that she knew that from four to five on Sundays was letter writing time at both Stephen's and my schools, so she would do her best to write her letters to us then, too. This was something we could all do together.

She wrote that she and my father had been so glad to get a cable from Mrs. Lamberton saying that I had arrived without incident and that within five minutes of getting to school, I had been laughing. I paused when I read that, because I didn't know why Mrs. Lamberton would tell such a lie. Then I remembered that her expression when she was showing me the shower room had made me giggle for some reason. I went back to the letter. My mother said she was also pleased that they had gotten the same type of cable from Stephen's school, too. She told me that she was trying to give Folly extra attention because we were gone. Once when she was completely and absolutely sure that no one was looking, she had even tried to dance with Folly, but of course Folly would dance with no one but me. The letter went on for a about a page more, and then my mother ended it by saying, "Your father joins me in sending you our greatest love."

I read my mother's letter several times the day I got it and then a number of times the next day, and each long day after that I reread it. Finally I put it in my suitcase with my panda bear because it was the next week (with seventy-one days to go), and I had gotten a new letter from my mother. This one had a number 2 at the top. Again, I read the letter repeatedly until I got another letter—number 3—when there were sixty-four days to go.

My mother wrote me every week faithfully. On some letters, there was a faint scent of jasmine. She told me about Folly, and about the flowers in the garden. She wrote me about the letters she and my father received from Stephen, and she always listed the new Kiswahili words she had learned that week from Edna, so I could learn them, too, since my school didn't teach Kiswahili. Distance could not prevent us from learning together, just we always had. Didn't I agree? She also wrote that she missed Stephen and me. Even when she and Daddy gave parties, they were a little sad because they knew that we were not in our rooms looking down at the colored lanterns and the swirling scene. She always ended each letter by saying, "Your father joins me in sending you our greatest love."

I marked hours at Westlands–King George School by looking at every clock I saw. I marked days by making an X on my calendar each evening, and I marked weeks by my mother's letters. When I got twelve letters, it would be twelve weeks—all the time would be marked, and I could go home and never return.

I had to write all my letters back to my mother in the Westlands–King George School way. Mrs. Lamberton required me to show her the letter I wrote the first Sunday so she could be sure I understood what this way was. First, I had to inquire about my parents' health and assure them that mine was fine. Then I had to write about something I had done in school and something I was looking forward to. Lastly, I was meant to make closing remarks.

I wrote

Dear Mummy,
> *How are you, Daddy and Folly?*
> *I have no diseases.*
> *I had to read some Enid Blyton stories for reading. I agree with you that she is not the best writer. I also got the highest mark in my class on a geography test because I knew where Denmark is.*
> *I am looking forward to going home.*
> *I miss you, Daddy and Folly very much. I would prefer it if Stephen and I were home. I really do, Mummy.*
> *Love,*
> *Amelia*

I had thought Mrs. Lamberton would think it was a good letter. We only had to say one thing that we had done in school, and I had written about two and given a literary opinion besides.

Mrs. Lamberton said that she was not going to ask me to rewrite the letter entirely. She knew that youngsters differed in what they thought was important. I just had to change what I was looking forward to. It had to be something I was looking forward in school.

I thought and then wrote, "I am looking forward to the end of the term."

Mrs. Lamberton didn't like that either, so I tried again. I wrote, "I am looking forward to giving the school handshake tonight."

Mrs. Lamberton thought that was fine. She didn't realize that I was sending my mother a message in code. The school handshake was a special handshake done with three fingers together and the little finger out to the side. Two strangers could meet anywhere in the world, and if both shook hands that way, each would know that the other had been to Westlands–King George School in Nairobi. Every evening, every girl in Margaret House gave the school handshake to every other girl in the house, and then we lined up in front of Mrs. Lamberton so that every girl could give the school handshake to her. It was the last thing we were made to do before we were sent to bed. What this meant was I was telling my mother that I was looking forward to the end of the day, because then I would be one day closer to going home.

I didn't like wishing each day away, but I was in a predicament where I needed to kill time.

I did not write to Stephen at his school, nor did Stephen write to me. Once I saw him at the Children's Theatre of Nairobi, though. I was there with five other girls from Westland–King George and Miss Dahl, the weekend duty matron for primary pupils. It was during intermission, and we were in the drinking fountain line. Suddenly, I glimpsed him talking with some boys on the other side of the lobby. I had swerved away from the line and had just taken two running steps in his direction when Miss Dahl grabbed the back of my skirt.

"Where are you going, itsy bitsy?" she inquired.

I didn't like being addressed as "itsy bitsy," but there was no recourse when the name calling was done by a grown-up.

"I see my brother! I do! I need to talk to him," I said. I was frantically waving to Stephen, but he simply wasn't looking at me.

"I understand," Miss Dahl said, "but you may not leave the group. Many children here are related to another child or two or three in the audience, but if everyone went off searching for brothers, sisters, cousins, and infant uncles, it would be chaos." She was now gripping my shoulder.

"Stephen," I called. "Stephen!" I hadn't seen Stephen in twenty-three days, and now he was right here in the same building.

Miss Dahl said, "It's like you're goats, and my job to keep you herded." That was an analogy, and she seemed to think it was clever. I had heard someone say she was a virgin. I knew virgins had something to do with Christmas, but she didn't seem very Christmassy to me.

The lobby was noisy. Kids were in lines or clusters everywhere, all shouting and laughing. Stephen could not hear me. Now he was turning and following other boys back into the auditorium.

Light flashed twice. That meant intermission was almost over. The drinking fountain line had been slowly moving, and the girl ahead of me had just taken a drink.

Miss Dahl said, "Come, dragon fly, would you like to hold my hand? We will lead our line back in."

I said nothing, but she took my hand anyway. I bit my lip.

The play was about Aladdin, and it was a good play. The genie wore white and gold robes, and Aladdin wore purple pantaloons and a red sash and had a bass voice like my father did. I could not concentrate on the second act, though. I kept looking around in the dim light trying to see where Stephen was. I could not locate him.

After the show, I finally spotted him again. It was just for a second as the bus taking him back to his school—wherever that was—slowed to let the Westlands–King George van go by. He saw me and waved slightly, and then the instant was over.

At the end of four weeks, each classroom had an achievement ceremony. Miss Henning called my name out first and gave me a certificate on parchment that said I was the best in the class. I thanked her, and I meant it. Not only did it show I was working hard, but now I had another way to mark time. When I received three certificates, it would be three months, and I could go home.

I had to go to the junior headmistress's office, though, so I could get her "personal congratulations." Her name was Miss Smallwood, and she was six feet tall with a voice that seemed to come from above. I shifted from one leg to another as I stood before her.

She shook my hand and said she was particularly pleased I was a full boarder.

I just looked at her. Why was she glad about my misfortune?

She went on to say that the school's main interest was the boarders. The boarders get the best of everything. All right, the day students could sing in the chorus, but when had I ever seen them down at the stables or the Sunday sundae social? Yet it seemed that the day students, especially in the primary classes, got most of the academic awards. She didn't know why that was, but she was glad that at least in Miss Henning's class, a boarder had suddenly emerged as top student.

"Cassie does nearly as well as me," I said.

"What is your secret, Amelia?" she asked, appearing not to hear me. I just looked at her.

"How do you do so well?" she asked. "Answer me, Amelia."

I had already learned most of the work at home. Even so, I went over each lesson twice during lesson prep hour. In free playtime, I only pretended to play jacks or cat's cradle with myself. I was really doing sums in my head or thinking up examples of adverbs and adjectives. I needed to be able to tell my father I had given this place a whirl, I had given it a go. I could not explain all this to the junior headmistress, though.

"I don't know," I said. "I need to get ready for university." I bit my lip.

"Well, I think it's a banner day," she replied. "Don't you think so?"

"Yes," I decided to say.

The first month was finally gone. I looked at all the Xs on my calendar before I turned the page.

The second month was dreadful. It was worse than dreary. There was just one long day after another.

It had been so long since I had seen my mother and so long before I would see her. I was desperate to have a conversation with her. Each week, she wrote me a two-page letter, and each week I wrote back in the Westlands–King George way, always telling her two things—or sometimes three things—I had done in school, to make the letter interesting, and always saying I was looking forward to doing the school handshake, which was, of course, my message in code. I still could not believe this existence was real. I always thought I would wake up and crawl in my mother's lap and say, "Oh, Mummy, I had a terrible dream. It was worse than the one about the hourglass," and she would answer, "Well, it's over now, and here is our old Folly looking for some patting."

Finally, I had eight letters from my mother and had gotten two certificates for best in class. It was now the third month. Again I looked at the Xs on my calendar before I turned the page. I had killed fifty-six days, and there were still twenty-eight days to go. Now I was frantic.

Ever since Devon, when my mother read to Stephen and me, she had used special voices when the characters were speaking. One day, I could not remember exactly how she sounded when she did this. I could not remember if when she parted her hair on the side, it was the right side or the left. In the picture I had of all of us, it was parted in the middle. What if she had gotten wrinkly? What if my father had a half healed cut over his eye, or Stephen had lost an arm? Perhaps Folly was dead. I had to get home. This was getting ridiculous.

There were twenty days to go, and after a century, there were eleven and then four. I got the twelfth letter from my mother; she said that she and Daddy couldn't wait to see me, and every morning she told Folly, "Soon, Folly, soon!"

On the last day, I got my third parchment for being best student in class that month and a circle pin for being best student for the whole term. I got an award for best swimmer in the class, and my roommate Margaret got an award for being best primary school rider. Mrs. Lamberton wanted to put both plaques on display in the common room.

"Yes, yes, yes!" Margaret said. "Oh, Mrs. Lamberton, thank you! I am such a lucky stiff."

She began running around the common room singing, "I'm Margaret, and at school I live at Margaret House."

I said, "I prefer to give mine to my mother."

"Well, Amelia, let's compromise," Mrs. Lamberton said after a pause. "You can take it home to show Mummy, and then you can bring it back next term so it can be in its rightful place. This is an honor for Margaret House as well as for you."

I just looked at her. My mother had been the one who had helped me perfect my strokes, and anyway, why was she calling my mother mummy? She was certainly not her mother. I moved the plaque from one hand to the other and then held it against my chest.

During what would have been lesson prep time, everyone was packing, including one girl who was going to Westland–King George holiday camp for a month because her parents were going on holiday themselves. I actually didn't have much to pack. The first week I had been in this place, I had gradually put nearly everything I had brought back into my suitcase with my panda bear, so I would be ready to leave at a moment's notice. I also packed my erasers and other supplies as soon as I bought them. Now, I just needed to add the plaque, my bathing suit, some underwear, and the family pictures that I had slept with. The uniforms, of course, could be left hanging in the closet. Another girl could wear them. The calendar would stay, too.

When Mrs. Lamberton came in to help Margaret pack her miniature horse collection, I was sitting on the chair twiddling my thumbs and singing "Row, row, row your boat" to myself.

That night, we did the silly school handshake, and then I put an X through the last day of the third month. I just had to get through the night.

I was still awake when Mrs. Lamberton shone her flashlight in. Then I knew I had to will myself to sleep, so I did so by thinking about the moor in Devon.

I remembered that the moor was really a great garden of silvery green grass with rises and swells, stretching on and on under the sky. Laced into the grass was heather in all shades of purple, from light lavender to nearly a dark blue. Mingling with the heather were bright wildflowers, as well as . . .

It was morning. I leaped up, went into the closet, and sprang into my pink-and-white seersucker dress, which looked like peppermint candy. It was the first time in eighty-four days that I had worn my real clothes.

When I skipped into the common area, Mrs. Lamberton gave me some bread and jam that had been wrapped up for me. Fred was already there, and he was driving me to the Westlands airfield even before breakfast!

Mrs. Lamberton said, "I don't say good-bye. It's just *au revoir* for now."

"Good-bye," I answered. I really wasn't planning on seeing her again.

Tykes were tumbling into the common room, but I didn't look back.

I got in the car with Fred, who laughed and said, "See there, little miss, school wasn't as bad as you thought, although I suppose there's no place like home, as the Americans say. Yes?"

"Yes!" I agreed, as I suddenly remembered that Dorothy had said that when she clicked her ruby slippers, so I said yes again.

The airfield was much closer to the school than the docks had been, so we were there in good time. We stopped at hanger six, and there was Stephen. I hopped out.

"Hello, Stephen," I said.

"Hello, Amelia," he answered. He took my suitcase from Fred. He swung it lightly. His hands seemed bigger. His fluffy hair was slicked down a bit.

The pilot—a different one than before—beckoned us, and we raced to the plane.

I must admit that even though I was so glad to see Stephen, I played a slight trick on him. I let him be first on the steps into the plane, because I was thinking ahead. Last in would be first out!

After we had taken off, Stephen told me that he and his roommate Ned were on the beginning rugby team. They were both flankers. His house had gone on an end-of-term excursion to Thika.

I said that Mummy had sent me Kiswahili words with each letter, and I had memorized them all.

Actually, we didn't talk very much. We were finally going home. I shared my bread and jam with Stephen. Stephen had cheese and mango slices, and he shared them with me. We both offered food to the pilot, who politely declined, while producing a thermos of water for us. It was really quite companionable on this plane ride.

As we descended to the airfield in Dodoma, we saw my father waving enthusiastically. My mother was right next to him, her face alight with joy. She had relaxed her rule against Folly being out of the compound. Folly was in her arms.

The plane taxied and then stopped. The pilot opened the door, and Stephen and I bounded out, shouting with excitement.

When my mother put Folly on the ground, Folly bounced unceasingly between us, jumping on us, licking us, yipping and squeaking. She even snuggled against my father at one point and then leaped back to Stephen and me. We all agreed that if Folly was any more ecstatic, she would turn inside out.

We went home, and Edna and Aumi were there on the front steps to welcome us. I wondered if Aumi knew how lucky she was. She had never had to leave Edna. She was African. I could not stop smiling.

We had lunch on the veranda. Then my father went back to work, and within the hour, my mother, Stephen, and I were in the pool playing water tag.

By supper time, I was all unpacked, and my panda bear, who had been in my suitcase for three months, was at last out in the light. I gave him many cuddles to make up for his ordeal before putting him in his rightful place on my bureau.

That night, when my mother tucked me in, she said she was going to tell me a secret. The secret was that Stephen had done exceeding well at his school, but I had done even better at mine. They had received glowing, extraordinary reports about me. She told me she felt I should know this—in case I ever got discouraged—but it wasn't something we needed to have great discussions about. Her view was that people should do what they were capable of and not boast about it.

I said, "I gave it a go and a whirl, and that is all." By "that is all," I meant, of course, that that was all I would have of that place. I was finished going there.

My mother seemed to agree, because she covered my face with kisses, starting at the center of my forehead and moving clockwise until she got to back my forehead.

I had popped back into my life.

Stephen and I were the first children back in the compound because we had flown, but after a while, others, who had taken trains or buses, arrived. We saw them in the pool, pushing each other in and splashing or else running around the streets. They talked about strange things such as sitting on a tortoise at Arusha School when they were not supposed to or about a matron who whacked with a slipper. For some reason, my mother wanted us to play with them.

"I prefer to be with you, Mummy," I said, encircling her waist when we were sitting by the pool. "I prefer to be with you."

"All right, for now," she said.

Occasionally Stephen played with the boys, but he told me in private that some of them were blackguards who collected frogs in a pail and then pounded them with croquet balls.

Christa and I were supposed to be pen pals, but I hadn't written her in a long while because I didn't want to tell her about the lengthy predicament I had been in. I was home now, though, so I could write now.

My letter said,

Dear Christa,

How are you? I am fine.

I had trouble for a while. It is over now. I don't expect to have this trouble again.

We like Tanganyika when we are ever able to see it and we like Tanganyikans, especially Edna and Aumi. Aumi goes walking with us but can't swim in the pool due to race prejudice. British people here have customs and do not act like people you have met. We don't like them.

How is Lawrence? We would probably have a baby too if we hadn't gone to Africa. Who will your new teacher be at Regency Day and did Teddy have a magician again at his birthday party?

I forgot to mention that it would have been better for Folly if we had stayed in England.

Write soon.

Your Friend,

Amelia Ord

There came an exciting day when Edna and Aumi showed my parents and Stephen and me their village of origin on the high plains west of Dodoma. My father borrowed a jeep instead of using the car so we could get there over the dirt roads. We went up rocky hills and into green valleys and then back up hills until we came to a tableland of waving grass that seemed to stretch until the earth met the blue sky. This view was breathtaking, although for a time there seemed to be nothing but the endless grass and occasional lines of thorn trees.

Edna had told us that the village was cattle rich, and I was the first to spot the cows—the Kiswahili word was *ng'ombe*—off in the distance. We approached closer and saw that the cattle were in several herds, which were watched over by men and older boys. They waved to Edna and Aumi, and we all waved back, but we could not stop. They were working, and our destination was the village, which was still some miles beyond.

The people lived in huts with rounded roofs, made of hay which looked like thatch, which was what was used in some cottages in Devon, although our own house had been wood (with bay windows). We visited the elder's hut, and he told us a wonderful story about the creation of the world, with Aumi interpreting Kiswahili words that we hadn't yet learned. Then we went to the planting fields and saw women getting things ready for harvest. A few of these women had babies on their backs so they would not get lonely. The children stared at Stephen and me just like some had done in Dar, but Edna and Aumi said a few words, and they taught us a game with pebbles.

"This is a little like marbles," Stephen said, and I was pleased with him for making the connection.

When it was almost time to leave, there was a quick, hard downpour, causing us to take refuge in Edna's aunt's hut and turning the road to mud and making it temporarily impassable.

"This is an example of why more of these roads need to be paved, loves," my father said when we finally got under way.

It was all right, though. We got home too late for my parents to go to cocktails at the club, so they had supper with Stephen and me that night.

The next day, a lady who passed us when we were out with Folly said she was surprised that my mother had not been worried that the natives might do something untoward.

My mother said, "Why, no, these were Edna's friends and kinsmen. They were very nice to us."

"Were some of the women topless?" the lady inquired in a persistent way.

My mother's tone was suddenly sharp. "You mean like Carol Hoyt at the club when—" Then she looked at me and stopped. "Well, we must be getting on," she said after a pause.

When we got around the bend, Mummy said, "Some people here have silly notions."

I nodded. I couldn't have agreed more.

At night, we were reading a brand-new book that an American woman my mother had met in Dodoma had recommended to her. It was called *On the Banks of Plum Creek* and was about a family living in a funny house called a dugout many years ago in a place called Minnesota. Once a cow stepped right through the roof of the house and Ma was a little dismayed, but then she laughed. Eventually, they built a better house, but then they had to hope the wheat crop was good so they could pay for it, and that was what created the difficulty.

We all liked the book, even Stephen, although there were no boys in the family, and my mother said she would make sure we read enough each night so that we would finish it by the end of the month. I didn't know why she said that. There was no longer any need to count days. We had all the time in the world.

It was double sure that I wasn't going back to Westlands–King George. My father had asked me to give the place a whirl and a go, and I had done that, as promised. My mother had said that if there was something we had been signed up for that was really not to our liking, we would not have to do it again. I had been signed up for that place, and it had really not been to my liking, so I would not have to do it again. My father had then summed it up neatly when he asserted that if there was a problem, I wouldn't have to go back. There was a problem. I had found it dreadful. I assumed Stephen would not go back to Nairobi, either, but I thought it was best that he be the one to say that.

I designed a new dance for Folly. It was slow and dreamy. I called it the spaniel swing. We were getting back into a routine. Things were returning to normal, with the only fly in the ointment being my parents' social obligations.

Suddenly, one morning when we were in the garden, my mother said she couldn't believe our holiday was nearly over. It was time for us to start packing again. She looked a little sad.

"Oh, I'm not going back," I reassured her. "Remember, Mummy, we discussed it the first night." I put my arms on my waist. Folly came over to me, and I said, "Don't worry, Folly."

Stephen looked away and kicked at a tuft of grass.

"Well, why wouldn't you go back?" my mother said slowly. "Every report we got was wonderful."

"I hate it, Mummy."

"What do you hate about it?"

"Everything," I answered.

"Do you feel like that, Stephen?" my mother asked.

"I don't know," Stephen said. "The sports are all right."

"I said I hate it, Mummy," I interjected. I stamped my foot for emphasis. That startled Folly.

"Tell me why, and maybe we can do something about it."

"They made me see *The Ugly Duckling* twice. I hate *The Ugly Duckling*. I hate it, Mummy, I hate it."

"Well, you can't give up on a school just because they show a few bad movies. Don't you like Mrs. Lamberton? She writes glowing things about you."

"She's mean. She shines her flashlight into each room every night."

"That's just procedure." She looked anxious. "They need to make sure everyone is where they are supposed to be."

"It doesn't happen at home." I had started to cry. "She also won't let me wear my bathing suit in the shower. I tried, but when she saw it under my towel, she made me take it off. I was going to drip soap suds down the front, but she said that was not the way to wash. I hate her, Mummy, I hate her."

"Did anyone ever, huh, bother you in the shower?" my mother suddenly asked.

"Once a girl named Buffy splashed water in my face, and Mrs. Lamberton told her if she kept that up, she would have to shower by herself, so for some reason she stopped."

I thought and added, "I also hate taking rhythms. They make you hop and skip to music. They tell you when to do it, Mummy."

"I thought you would like it. I did, but that one thing we can change. Would you like to have singing lessons? We made a switch for Stephen. He'll be doing chess instead of going to the Children's Theatre."

"No," I cried. I added, "I also hate the uniforms."

Stephen said, "I'm only halfway done on my fort."

I had not paid much attention to the fort Stephen had been building in the garden while my mother and I practiced Kiswahili with Aunti, but now I said, "Yes, Stephen must finish it. Daddy always says that it is essential to finish what you start."

I was still crying, and Stephen had started to walk around in circles. Folly, for her part, was looking baffled.

"Well, I don't know what to do," my mother said.

I told her, "We can learn everything at home. I've gotten many more supplies for study time. I bought them every week. I made sure I got enough for Stephen, and, oh, Mummy, I borrowed next year's math book and brought it home. I'll mail it back when we're done." I wasn't sure if borrowing something without asking was the same as stealing, but I decided that this was a philosophical question we could discuss at a later date.

My mother said she would talk to our father about our feelings. She reached for our hands. "In the meantime, let's go swimming," she suggested.

In the pool, we swam laps and very fast. My mother and Stephen slightly led, but I held my own, and we all began to laugh and get out of breath. Finally we took a break, and my mother told us something she had never told us before but was telling us now because we were old enough to understand.

As an older girl in school, my mother had been a champion speed swimmer, and everyone thought she should try out for 1928 Olympics. During the holiday between the fifth and sixth forms, her father hired a personal coach for her, and the coach agreed that she was of Olympic timber. However, he said that there was only so much time in the day; she could not possibly prepare for both the Olympics and university. She had been crestfallen, but she and her father had had a serious discussion, and she—they—finally chose university.

"Wait until I tell all the boys I know that my mother could have swum on the British team in the Olympics!" Stephen exclaimed.

My mother told him that there was no need to tell anyone. It had been far from certain, and anyway, as she might have said before, her view was that people should do what they were capable of and not brag about it. She looked around to make sure that no one was listening to our conversation. However, it was still midmorning, so there were only some little tykes with ayahs watching them in the shallow part, and we were sitting overlooking the deep end.

"Did your father and the coach know that you have more time if you get up early?" I asked. We never called my parents' parents our grandparents, because they had all died long ago.

"That didn't occur to anyone," my mother said distantly. "It was all so new then—girls going to university, girls going to the Olympics. It was hard to imagine combining both."

My mother continued. "The point is that I don't regret choosing university. The Olympics would have provided excitement for a season and then receded over the years into memory. University gave me keys to rooms of thought. I'll benefit from it for life." She said that she hoped that whatever sacrifices we made for university, we would feel it was worth it as well.

"I prefer to prepare for university at home," I said. "I can do it."

My mother did talk to my father, but he said we were just having last-minute jitters again. It was just a matter of getting back into the swing of things. We'd certainly enjoy seeing our friends again.

Stephen nodded, but I burst into tears.

He reminded me that my letters had recounted my many activities. I even liked the ritual. I was always writing about the school handshake.

He certainly did not want his children miserable—he would do anything to prevent it, but these were excellent schools.

My mother said, "Her school did make an unfortunate choice in the child they first had her share a room with."

"Yes," my father replied, "and the school apprised us of this, whereas another school might not have. They addressed the situation promptly. Actually, I know something about Sam Winters, and I'm not surprised that a child of his would turn out that way."

He said that I should not let one isolated rough patch color my view. I needed to give the school another try and one more go.

I remembered once in London, Teddy's mother had told him that he couldn't play in the little park because he had a dentist appointment, and he had cried, flapped his arms, and bobbed up and down. Christa and I had just looked at him. Now, I was doing the same thing. "I'm not going back to that place," I yelled. "I'm not going back to that place. I gave it a whirl, and I'm not going back." I waved my arms and kicked at the rug. Folly just looked at me. Stephen did, too. My mother continued to bite her lip.

"You don't persuade anyone of anything by having a tantrum. You're old enough to know that," my father said.

The next day, we played badminton in the morning, did Kiswahili, had lunch on the veranda, and went swimming. Then my mother tried to pack for me because the following day was the day Stephen and I were supposed to get on the plane again. She kept putting my panda in my suitcase, and I kept taking him out.

She finally said, "I thought you would want to have him with you."

"No," I said. "It's no place for him. He would have to stay in the suitcase the whole eighty-four days, Mummy, the whole eighty-four days. That's what happened last time."

"You never took him out?"

I shook my head.

"Well, all right," she said slowly. "If you really don't want to take him, you can leave him here, and he will be ready and waiting for you when you come back."

"I prefer to stay here with him," I said.

That night we finished *On the Banks of Plum Creek*. Pa had been lost in a blizzard, and it was Christmas Eve when he finally walked through the door. He had survived by eating all the Christmas candy while he was sheltered in the creek bank. This meant that there would be no candy for Christmas, but it didn't matter. Pa played the fiddle, and Laura's eyes sparkled. They hoped they would have a bumper wheat crop the next year because then the girls could have candy every day.

In the morning, Stephen and I sadly knelt down to say good-bye to Folly again, and this time she knew we were leaving. She had seen the suitcases being put in the car. She leaned against us. She licked my hand slowly. When my father said we had to get up, she went out to the veranda and tried to block the steps. She was a little dog but determined and steadfast.

My mother said Folly could ride with us to the airfield, so we all got into the car. I cried on the way, and Stephen tapped his foot and played with his fingers.

"You'll settle in more quickly this time," my father said. "You know what to expect."

That made me wail. I knew what to expect.

Folly suddenly whimpered.

"Oh, God," my mother said.

Once again, the minutes were running out.

We got to the airfield. My mother said Folly had to stay in the car. I wanted to stay in the car, too, but eventually I got out with reluctance.

There were hugs and cuddles and kisses. Then the pilot—he was the one who had flown us to Kenya before—stepped towards me.

"No!" Mummy said sharply.

My father took me by the hand and led me up the steps of the plane, with Stephen following. He buckled me in and watched as Stephen slowly buckled himself in. He reminded us that our next holiday would be six weeks and not just a month. We'd do something special. Then he got off the plane. The pilot thudded the door closed.

"Just us chickens," the pilot said. He turned the motor on.

My father and mother were on the ground trying to wave. Folly was in the car, her front paws on the rim of the half open window. She was yipping for us to come back. They all got smaller as the plane lifted into the air.

I cried and cried.

CHAPTER 4

Topsy-Turvy

British East Africa, 1947–1955

WHEN FRED LET me off at Margaret House, Mrs. Lamberton was on the porch, surrounded by Margaret and other girls who were all trying to tell her what they had done on their holidays. She waved to me and called, "Amelia, welcome back!"

I was back to what was called square one, with eighty-four more days to go. The next day, there would be eighty-three.

My calendar was still on the wall in the room assigned to me. The uniforms were still in the closet. It was all the same, the same, the same for me to survive, survive, survive. That was what it meant to be back at square one.

I did have a new roommate, though. Margaret was sharing a room with Buffy, the girl who had given her raisins in return for some of her crackers. The reason was that Margaret's mother had said that Margaret had benefited from sharing a room for a term with a very studious child, but it seemed that all the studying had made me a bit of a sad sack. Margaret was a merry little thing, and over the long run, it would be better if she was with a girl who had the same enthusiasms.

I don't remember my new roommate's name, and I don't remember anything much about her except that once she asked why I got dressed in the closet every morning, and I said, "I just do."

Mrs. Lamberton tried to unpack me, but by the second day (with eighty-two days to go) I had put almost everything back in my suitcase except my pictures of Mummy, Daddy, and Folly, and, all right, Stephen, too. For some reason, Mrs. Lamberton didn't notice that I had no things about. She just used me as an example of a girl who was not only very smart but very neat. What she didn't know was that if my parents changed their mind about my being in this place for the whole term, I would be able to leave on a moment's notice.

In class, Miss Henning was now giving out cards for being student of the week, so that the best students could get rewards even before the monthly achievement ceremony. What this meant was that dreary week after dreary week, I received a card on Friday saying I was first student for that week. (It was yet another way to mark time.) On Sunday, I enclosed the card in the letter I wrote to my mother as proof of the extra special whirl I was giving the place.

I was also careful to tell her four things I had done that week instead of just two or three. I told her about the French verbs I had memorized, the report I gave about the products of Brazil, the songs we were made to sing in chorus, and the fact that in riding I was now required to lead the horse back to the stable after I got off and that several times the horse had tried to butt me with his head.

I also made my message in code easier to decipher. I said I was DEFINITELY looking forward to giving the school handshake each night. I underlined the word "definitely" three times. I was confident that she could see my meaning. For good measure, though, I always added that I was using my calendar to keep track of the future. What could be clearer?

Mummy wrote that she and my father were thrilled about how I was continuing to take Westlands–King George by storm. My success was certainly not unexpected, but even so, it made the hardship of my being away easier to bear. She wrote that the flowers were in constant bloom in the compound, as they surely were in Nairobi. Back in London, they were bound to be long faded, except the hardy asters. When I was home on my next holiday, she and I would do some planting. Did I think we should mix roses with tropical buds? She told me that Folly was a little less perky than she had been, but that was probably due to missing Stephen and me. Lastly, my mother gave me the Kiswahili words to learn for the week, and as before she always ended with "your father joins me in sending you our greatest love."

My mother continued to number her letters, picking up from my first time in this place. I received letter 13, letter 14, letter 15, each week a higher number. This added another variable to the ways I could measure and kill time. When I got twelve letters from her, the last one being letter 24, I could go home. This time I would stay home, and Folly would perk right up. I had my strategies perfected.

In her sixth letter of the term, which was numbered 18, Mummy wrote that she had a new idea. Edna and Aumi had taught her to listen more closely to the rustling of the trees. When there was a bit of breeze, there was only a soft murmur of the leaves. If there was more of a blow, the rustling was distinct. In high wind, there was constant, tuneful rustling all around. Mummy said she was always thinking about Stephen and me, but she would think of us especially when she heard the leaves rustling. She would imagine it was us. Perhaps I would like to think of her and Daddy when I heard the leaves rustling where I was. If so, that would be yet another thing we would be doing together while we were apart.

I was always thinking about my mother, but now I thought about her especially when the leaves were rustling. One Saturday, I edged away from a dodgeball game, knelt down by an azalea bush, and shook it so I could hear the sound.

At the end of the second month, what Mrs. Lamberton called a "sensation" hit Margaret House. The school store was selling enamel trinkets at threepence each. This meant a girl could buy three trinkets a week and still have a pence left over for a gumdrop. The store carried more of some types of trinkets than others, though, with cats and cows being the most plentiful and moons being hard to come by. Girls needed to trade to get the rarer pieces they wanted. The store had set it up that way.

Soon, Margaret House was trading with Elizabeth House and Victoria House. The day students saw items being passed around at recess and asked what was happening. Buffy told them, "You are not to know. This is only for the boarders."

Margaret added, "We are the ones who are lucky stiffs."

Miss Henning complained to the junior headmistress. She said it was harder for her to teach the class if they were such divisions between the boarders and the day students. Miss Smallwood said she would not change the rule that just boarders could make purchases at the school store, but she would limit trinket trading. Trinket trading could only be done in the evening during free play time, on Saturday afternoons, and at the Sunday sundae social. Any girl found trading during the school day would have to forfeit half her trinkets.

Mrs. Lamberton called me into her sitting room—I had never been there before—and said she had noticed that I wasn't participating in trading trinkets. "Why aren't you joining in the fun, Amelia?" she asked.

"I don't know," I said.

"That's not much of an answer," she said. "I think you are a bit too serious. I give you your ten pence a week, and you use it to buy exercise books, rulers, and ink. Once you even bought a compass to measure circumference, even though you won't need that until you are in Miss Pennoyer's class."

I shifted my weight from one foot to another. The fact of the matter was that I would not be in Miss Pennoyer's class, although I had heard from Cassie's sister that she was the nicest teacher there. I needed to lay in more and more supplies so I would have enough to last me for studying at home until university, and I needed to get things for Stephen, too. I had no money to spare for frivolities.

I could not explain this to Mrs. Lamberton, so I said, "At home, my mother and I string beads with our friend, Aumi. We make bracelets and necklaces. There's nothing we can do with trinkets."

"You're not with your mother right now," she replied.

"Yes," I said. "I know."

I thought and then added, "My friend Cassie can't do the trading because she's a day student, so I don't want to do it, either."

Mrs. Lamberton's expression changed. "I can understand loyalty, Amelia," she said.

The last month went by at a snail's pace; it went by at a crawl. I began to worry that I would be stuck in this place with whispering, pointing girls and name-calling adults forever.

At long last, there was only one more day. The art teacher gave me a portfolio to carry home all my drawings in, and that turned out to be a lucky break. The art room was in the upper school, and as I was going to chorus practice for the prize assembly, I saw my opportunity. A door to a classroom was opened, and on the teacher's mahogany desk were three stacks of books, each called *First Year Latin: An Introduction to Julius Caesar*. One stack was higher than the other two stacks, so I quickly slipped a book from that stack into my portfolio. This time, I was thinking farther ahead than usual. I would start studying Latin when I was twelve.

That night was the prize assembly. I won a circle pin again for being best student in my class for the term and also won book awards for being best reader in the junior school and first in French, along with another swimming plaque. This time, Mrs. Lamberton insisted that I give her the swimming plaque so she could put it in a place of honor right next to Margaret's second horseback-riding plaque. She said, "Amelia, remember what I told you before. You win scholastic honors for yourself but sports trophies for your house."

I just looked at her. Margaret House was not my house.

"It is mine," I said finally. "I prefer to show it to my mother."

She replied, "Well, Amelia, I let you take the last one home to show your mother, and you promised to bring it back, but you didn't."

I had promised no such thing.

"I forgot," I said. I was fibbing now. Mummy had put it on her bureau, and that was where I wanted it to be.

"Amelia, I'm waiting." She put out her hand. Then she said, "Amelia, you are as smart as the dickens, but occasionally you are Mary, Mary quite contrary."

I gave her the plaque. I would come back and fetch it when I was older.

The next day, Stephen and I were flown home. When Folly saw us, she didn't bounce between us as she had before, she just leaned against us and softly licked our hands with her velvety tongue. She had missed us severely.

My mother reminded us it was almost Christmas. "We'll have a glorious time," she exclaimed.

It seems so funny that we were getting ready for Christmas at the same time that mimosas were blooming and we were swimming every day. There were, of course, no real fir trees, and we didn't like the ersatz dwarf pines that the club was distributing. We got a potted palm and decorated it with the ornaments and bubble lights that we had carefully packed and brought with us from England. Our tree was splendid.

Christmas cards began to come in, and two of them were addressed to me. One was from Christa, but the other was from Teddy, of all people! Of course, I sent them both cards right back.

The best family card we received was from Jenny. She wrote that Davy junior had a sister now, and her name was Rose Olivia. My mother smiled a little, but then she laughed when I said, "Why, that's a smashing name!"

That evening my father came home and told my mother there would be a function at the club on Christmas Eve from seven on.

The first thing my mother said was "Oh, hell."

Then she bit her lip and said, "Craig, I am not leaving the children on Christmas Eve, or on Christmas, for that matter. Anyway, we gave Edna the night off so she and Aumi can go to Mass."

So it was decided. My mother would say she had a migraine headache and stay home with us while my father would go over to the club, pretend to have a good time for a while, and then make his getaway. We didn't know then that this would be a holiday tradition. My parents would proceed in this fashion every Christmas we had in Tanganyika.

While my father was gone, we completed the decoration of the house. We arranged our cards on the mantel and put our manger scene on the tea table. Then we set up my mother's Swiss village under our Christmas potted palm tree.

"Doesn't that look incongruous?" my mother asked.

Stephen didn't know what incongruous meant, but I did, so I said, "topsy-turvy."

"Like everything the British do in Africa," my mother said. Then she added, "Let's forget I said that. The Swiss village does look nice, doesn't it? I do hope the Golds are having a good season."

"Is this their town?" I asked.

"No, probably not, but we can pretend it is," Mummy replied.

Picking up a white house with a steep peaked roof, she said in a delighted voice, "I call this Henri's house!"

When we heard my father's steps on the veranda, we started singing "The Twelve Days of Christmas," just as we had rehearsed. My mother brought out raspberry tarts. Our celebration had begun. Folly bounced between the four of us, getting pats from everyone.

In the morning, Stephen and I opened our gifts from our parents. I got a new bathing suit and two crossword puzzle books. He got a wallet and a pith helmet. We both got peppermint sticks, but just as I had suspected, Santa Claus, if he existed, hadn't made it to Dodoma.

My mother said, "Let's play badminton before Christmas breakfast."

We went out to the back garden, and there were two bicycles, one for a boy and one for a girl! "I knew the old fellow left the presents somewhere!" my father said.

Stephen's bike was maroon and black. Mine was light blue and had a bell that rang when I pushed the lever. There were also white streamers coming from the handgrips.

Our parents cautioned us that we could only ride on the roads where the compound's houses were. We could not bike up to the pool, and most certainly we could never go out of the compound. If we ever did, even just once, the bicycles would be taken away. My father asked us if we understood, and we said yes. Even so, I was excited. I well remembered the bicycle my mother had had in Devon. Now I had one!

Somewhere, somehow, Stephen had learned to ride a bike, but my father needed to teach me. We practiced after breakfast for some hours, and then I suddenly figured out that to balance I needed to shift my weight a little but not too much. I was off, down the street, my father running at my side and saying, "You've got it, Amelia, you've got it! Merry Christmas!" Folly followed us, happily yipping.

I was nearly eight and really quite accomplished, if I do say so myself. I was an excellent swimmer, and now I could ride a bike. I was able to read just about anything in English. I knew French and Kiswahili, and I was going to study at home until university. The secret of doing that had finally been revealed to me!

The Saturday after 1948 started, Stephen and I went to a party for international children on the other side of Dodoma in a building called a gymnasium. There we happened to meet three American children named Betsy and Bobby Schler and Melvin Whittier. Betsy and Bobby had white skin, but Melvin was a brown-skinned American, and—guess what—they were all from Pennsylvania!

"I've been hearing about Pennsylvania ever since I was four," I exclaimed.

Betsy wore intriguing blue-and-white shoes called saddle shoes. They talked with the funny American accent, and it took me a while to figure out that their game Chutes and Ladders was really our game Snakes and Ladders.

They said, "Oh swell, popsicles!" when my mother and the other ladies helping with the party distributed ice lollies. Melvin wanted to thank Jesus before we ate the popsicles / ice lollies because the reason his family was in Tanganyika was to spread the gospel.

Betsy said, "Well, I'm Jewish, so I'll thank the ladies." She flounced her skirts.

It seems that even Americans who were friends were opinionated with each other.

What was really important, though, was that these children were not going away to school; they were doing Calvert. This meant they received their lessons through the post from the Calvert School in America. Indeed, the boys' school boxes for the next term had already come, and Betsy, who was in what was called fourth grade, expected hers any day now.

"What's in a Calvert's school box?" I asked breathlessly. Stephen had gone off to play ring toss with some Dutch children, but I was sticking to the Americans like glue.

They told me it had everything needed for home study at your grade level—textbooks, workbooks, notebooks, reading lists, lesson plans and instruction guide for parents, and project manual. Betsy said she was going to do a unit on a poet named Edgar Allan Poe. "Quote the raven, nevermore," she said, twirling around.

I suddenly realized my mistake. I had been so busy amassing school supplies and acquiring schoolbooks by whatever means possible (including thievery), that I had overlooked the need for formal lesson plans by subject for each term! How could I have been so stupid? I wanted to smack my head.

In gratitude, I taught the Americans my winning strategy for noughts and crosses, which they called tic-tac-toe. "Not even my brother knows this," I confided. "You go first and get three corners. Let the other person get the middle. Just worry about getting three corners, and you'll be set."

Bobby said, "This is the first time I've ever learned anything useful from a girl."

Melvin said he was pleased to make my acquaintance and that he would try the tic-tac-toe trick on his dad that very night.

I was wearing my pink-and-white seersucker dress, and Betsy said she liked it and wondered if her grandmother could order her one just like it from Macy's.

I asked what Macy's was, and when they told me, I said, "Oh, it's the same as Harrods!"

I had the same thought that I had had at Edna's and Aumi's village. It was amazing how people from different countries could have so much in common!

When my mother asked us how we had liked the gathering, I said, "Mummy, it was not just smashing, it was superb!"

The following day, Stephen and I were playing with Folly in front of our house when a boy from the compound who was walking by said to me, "Well, Miss Stuck Up, did you show the American monkey your knickers?"

Stephen had just raised his fist when my mother came down from the veranda. "You are very rude," she told the boy. "You don't call people monkeys."

"Well," the boy said, "he wasn't supposed to be there. The party was for those of European descent. He just tagged along with the Jews."

"I will have a word with your mother!" she replied.

"My mother says the same thing," the boy said and walked off.

I wanted to tell my mother not to be so upset. He was just a boarding school kid and acted accordingly.

A few days after that Mummy told us ruefully that the committee running the international children's party had changed it to the white international children's party. She said the Schlers were planning to boycott subsequent parties. Explaining to us what the word meant, she asked, "Do the Ords boycott as well?"

We said we would.

Be that as it may, when my mother began talking about how the holidays had flown, I said that there was no need for me to go back to Nairobi, I could do Calvert. That was the solution to all our problems.

My mother sighed. She bit her lip. "I wish we could," she finally said.

She told me she had heard of the Calvert home study division and knew it was a great boon for overseas American children. She was sure it provided them with the education they needed to get into Harvard, Yale, the University of Virginia, or wherever else they might want to go in the States. It wasn't preparation for Oxford or Cambridge, though. It was not for us.

The morning Stephen and I were to leave, I hid in the space between the china cabinet and the edge of the dining room wall. Folly saw me and wanted to cuddle.

"Go away, Folly, go away, now," I whispered. "You'll give me away." I pushed her back, not very hard, but I pushed her.

"There you are, Amelia," my father said, coming into the room. "Stephen is all ready. We must go, love. We're running late."

Folly came in the car with us—she insisted—but I don't know if I gave her a pat when I had to get out. Stephen did, but I don't know if I did.

Stephen said, "Bye, Mum. I'll try to write longer letters. Dad, I'll tell you if I'm elected treasurer of my coin collectors club."

For the third time, I was put on the plane crying.

At Westlands–King George, it was still the same. I even had a new roommate again, which was getting to be part of the sameness. I don't recall her name, either. Truth to tell, I've never been able to remember the names of any of my many school roommates there, except for Margaret and the unfortunate Samantha Mary Winters. All I did was survive, survive, survive, survive.

With sixty-seven days to go, it was my eighth birthday, and I was in this place. That evening, Mrs. Lamberton gave each girl in Margaret House a piece of strawberry cake, after requiring everyone else to sing "Happy Birthday" to me.

My parents sent me a jeweled wristwatch and a gold locket and chain. The locket had a tiny picture of my mother's mother wearing a hat with feathers. In the birthday card, signed with love by both my mother and father, they said that these presents were "grown-up gifts for a grown-up schoolgirl."

I wasn't really a grown-up schoolgirl, but I must admit that the pretty watch came in handy for a person in my circumstances. I could look down at any moment, outside or in, and see how much of the day was still to come before I could slash a red X through the day on the calendar and pronounce the day over and done with.

Two weeks after my birthday, tragedy struck! To be precise, tragedy had struck in Tanganyika three days before, but this was when I found out about it.

During free playtime, Mrs. Lamberton called me into her sitting room and requested that I sit down. She said that my mother had sent her an airmail letter and asked her to personally tell me something.

"I'm all packed," I said eagerly. I knew it! My mother had arranged for me to come home.

Mrs. Lamberton ignored what I said, for some reason. "It's about your dog. A poodle? No, a cocker spaniel."

"Yes, Folly's a cocker spaniel. She doesn't even remotely resemble a poodle." I spoke with some exasperation because this was the second time this mistake had been made.

Mrs. Lamberton's jaw tightened. She said, "I am going to let that remark pass." She hesitated. The pause lasted several seconds. "I guess the best way to put this—is . . . is . . . Folly has gotten her reward."

"I'm all packed," I repeated, with rising excitement. My mother, more than anyone, knew what a good dog Folly was. Mummy had decided to reward her by having Stephen and I come home. I wanted to clap my hands.

"Amelia, she died. She died."

"What do you mean?" I asked.

"I know it's a shock, but dogs don't live forever. In her case, it was a bite from a poisonous insect."

She held my mother's letter up.

My eyes widened. Whenever I thought the most terrible thing had already happened, something even more terrible happened. It never used to be this way.

Folly was dead. Folly was gone. Never again would she lean against me or jump up on Stephen or bounce around my mother's feet. Never again would she yip with joy as we got ready to go for a walk. Never again would she dance "Quote the Raven, nevermore!"

I had pushed Folly away on the last morning I saw her. I didn't know if I had patted her when, crying and distracted, I got out of the car. If I did, it wasn't much of a pat. I was eight years old, and I knew these were acts and omissions I would regret my whole life.

"I'm all packed," I said dully.

"Why do you keep saying that?"

In London, before Stephen and I had seen much of the world, we had thought Alice was not very bright. However, Alice was a brilliant lady compared to Mrs. Lamberton. I needed to exercise patience.

"There's been a death in the family. I must go home. I know my mother is devastated. Remember last term, some girl went home when her grandmother died in Moshi?"

"That was Eileen. But you can't go home for a pet."

I just looked at her. Hamsters and parakeets were pets, not Folly.

"I daresay you have some good memories of her," Mrs. Lamberton continued.

"I don't know," I answered. I looked at the ceiling. Folly used to be alive. Her body was warm. Her tan fur was silky. Her eyes were alight. Now she was a memory.

I felt as if I would break into a million pieces.

When I got my next letter from my mother—it was the seventh letter of the term and letter 31—she told me the details. It might have been a scorpion. Mummy didn't know for sure. She had washed out the bite and given Folly medicine. Folly wouldn't eat her supper but had seemed to enjoy the ice my mother offered. They had one of their parties that night, but she had checked on Folly several times, Daddy had checked on her once, and Aumi had kept constant watch over her, until she and Edna went home. After the party, Folly had seemed both weak and restless and very hot, so Mummy had carried her out to the veranda and rocked her in the settee. There had been a nice breeze and a bit of rustle in the trees, which meant we were all close in spirit. Folly went to sleep, but then, an hour later, she had opened her eyes, and my mother had whispered to her, "Stephen, Amelia." Folly sighed in recognition. She licked my mother's hand. Then she closed her eyes and didn't open them again.

My mother said that Folly had always been so ready to frolic that we had forgotten that she was getting to be an old dog. She had been twelve, two years older than Stephen. She could not withstand the poison from the bite.

My mother had enclosed a lock of Folly's fur. I kissed it and kissed it before I put it back in the letter and then hugged the letter and the envelope just as I usually did.

I wasn't sure where dogs went when they died, but probably they went back in time. If so, Folly was in Devon on one of our afternoons. She was running on the sunlit grassy moor, racing through the purple heather, feeling our presence with her. She would not know that we were stuck back here, struggling on this gloomy earth.

I told Cassie what had happened, and she pronounced the news catastrophic, which it was. A few days later, just before the start of class, she said to me shyly, "Folly would want you to meet Jambo."

I knew instantly that that was so, but I said, "How can I? Primary school girls can't get passes."

Cassie said, "My mother is bringing Jambo this afternoon when she picks Ella and me up, and Miss Henning is letting you come down to the gate for five minutes."

I looked at Miss Henning, and she nodded, smiling faintly.

So at three, I ran down to the gate with Cassie, and her mother was there with Jambo, who squeaked with excitement upon seeing Cassie. I knelt on the ground, and Jambo saw me, gave me her paw, and then licked my face.

"What do you think of him?" Cassie's mother asked.

I only said, "Jambo, Jambo" as I stroked his silky ears. He leaned against me, and for a few minutes I was comforted.

When I heard Miss Henning calling for me, I straightened up and was back in the here-and-now.

When Stephen and I finally went home, my parents showed us the place in the back garden where they had buried a copper urn with Folly's ashes. It was under the banyan tree and near to where we played badminton. They had waited for us to put up a marker. The four of us decided on the epitaph together, and then my father carved it into birch wood that we had brought from London. It read,

Folly Cocker Spaniel Ord
1936–1948
Always Noble
We loved her
She loved us.

Stephen wanted to add "Brave in war," but there was not enough room.

Edna and Aumi were kind. They took us back to their village and showed us two tame cheetahs. Aumi gave me a bead bracelet she had made and said, "Amelia, Amelia, be cheerful. Folly is part of nature."

My mother and I designed a water ballet. Every day, we choreographed a different section. We read *Treasure Island*. I gave my panda bear due attention. We all were trying to go on, but one morning when my parents, Stephen, and I were playing badminton, Stephen hit a shuttlecock out of bounds. It sailed over Folly's marker, past the tree, and into the cannas. We all paused for Folly to retrieve it. Then my father said, "I guess I'll go get it."

Later, I said to my mother, "Daddy misses Folly, too."

"Well, of course he does, darling," she said.

I assumed that I would not be going back to Westlands–King George. We needed to stay together both to mourn Folly properly and to prevent further harm from happening. Indeed, I walked around with a three-foot reed, always vigilant for scorpions that might be in my mother's path, constantly ready to beat them off. However, after a month, the suitcases came out again.

Everything was the same at the school except that Cassie wasn't in class. Her family had been posted to Hong Kong. "Rum deal," Miss Henning said when she told me. She patted my shoulder and gave me a snap of Cassie and Jambo that Cassie wanted me to have.

I would continue to be with the day students at recess, but I would never find a friend like Cassie.

Some children grow to like boarding school. They enjoy the whirl of activities, the camaraderie with their roommates, housemates, and teammates, and all the rituals. They even like being watched over by adults with whom they did not have permanent emotional ties. My early roommate Margaret liked horseback riding, liked Mrs. Lamberton, and loved being a boarder at Westlands–King George School.

It was different for me. I never got used to boarding school. I couldn't ever stand the relentless schedules, the forced games, the compulsory attendance at school-chosen movies, the always being in a group from wash time through free playtime, the uniforms, the school handshake, or the round of ceremonies. I understood my relation to the teachers. They taught. I learned the work—to the extent I didn't know it already. What I could not fathom was my connection to all the other adults who knocked about the place, leaving the day students alone but superintending the boarders in all details, making the boarding machine run.

It was in my fifth or sixth term that I learned the word "bifurcated." I had an unevenly bifurcated existence. The hourglass was horizontal, sand divided and in both orbs. In all instances, I was my parents' cherished daughter. I was double sure of that, but it was only one month in four that I could live that life. For three months out of four, I would be away at school, and time would thicken and tighten. It would coil and knot, a palpable thing for me to get through.

When I was in Miss Pennoyer's class, she asked that if one was in the midst of swimming the English Channel, how would one know how far there still was to go. I was a speed swimmer, not a distance swimmer, but I thought I knew the answer.

"You should have an idea of how long you will have to be in the channel in total. Then keep track of the passing time. Imagine the minutes dwindling in your mind. Tell the elapsing hours by the changes in the sky."

"Would this technique also work if you were arduously climbing Mount Kilimanjaro?" Miss Pennoyer probed.

"Yes, by extrapolation," I said.

"Girls," Miss Pennoyer exclaimed, "this is why Amelia Ord always gets the card for student of the week!"

Student of the week or no, every term I swam the English Channel. Every term, I climbed Mount Kilimanjaro. And although Mount Everest had yet to be scaled, every term I crawled up that peak, too.

Then after each long eighty-four days, Stephen and I were finally home again, wearing our own clothes, sleeping in our own rooms, swimming with Mummy, playing Parcheesi with my father, having family games of badminton, and always speaking of Folly.

Sometimes when I was walking with my mother or we were doing French on the veranda, I would just gaze at her, and she would notice and say questioningly, "Yes, darling, yes?"

I would answer, "I just like seeing you, Mummy." Indeed, I did, and I had to memorize her face and memorize it again and again. When I was little in Devon and we had looked at the way the sun came through the bay windows and made patterns on the rug, she had told me that there were things we needed to fix in our minds so we would have them always.

At home, hours and days glided by naturally, glimmering in their own fashion. Time did not need to be measured, quartered, and killed. When I was home, time just needed to last, and for a while it did, until the last week.

There was a cycle within a cycle. Every year in the middle of our six-week summer holiday (which would have been winter back in England), we took a ten-day trip. We went to the Masai Mara reserve and saw rhinos and hippos and even lions at dawn. We went to the Serengeti Plain, to Ngorongoro Crater, to Lake Victoria and Lake Tanganyika, to the coast and to Zanzibar and to the great Zimbabwe Ruins in Rhodesia. The best trip we ever took, though, was down the Nile to Luxor, when I was nine.

The pyramids made any model we had seen in the British Museum pale by comparison. But then there was the sphinx! Oh, my!

"It's mesmerizing," my mother said.

"It's magnificent," replied my father.

"It's majestic," I said.

"Like a magistrate," Stephen put in, and we all looked at him.

"Well, somewhat ministerial," my mother quickly said.

"Not managerial," my father joked.

"It's magnanimous," I suggested.

"Anonymous," Stephen came up with.

"Inscrutable!"

"Irrefutable!"

"Indisputable!"

Suddenly, we were all laughing and trying to top each other in adjectives, even when the result was ridiculous.

"Magical!"

"Mystical!"

"Logistical!"

We paused for air.

My mother smiled and remarked, "We do have our bits of joy, yes?"

I exclaimed, "Surprisingly, the sphinx seems mysteriously superlatively serendipitous!"

My father boomed, "Good one, Amelia, good one!"

A family who seemed to be American with their flat accents and kids in striped T-shirts chewing gum gave us amused glances. The four of us were acting so naturally and spontaneously that it probably would have never occurred to them that our moments together were rationed, our shared experiences few enough that each was etched and remembered. Our joy, as my mother said, came in bits.

I never ceased my campaign to stop going away to school.

When I came home for the holiday just following my tenth birthday, there was a new boy in the compound. Actually, he wasn't a new boy at all. His family had been in the compound before us, and he must have raced with the pack of kids who ran around the compound during the holidays. I just noticed him now because he was changed. We saw him at the pool in the afternoon doing water exercises with his mother. Once some children laughed, but Stephen, who was getting quite big, raised his fist, and they didn't do that again. Then, the boy's mother asked would I like to come over to their house and play a new game called Scrabble. I usually didn't socialize with anyone in the compound, but I made an exception here, considering the circumstances.

She only had to invite me once. After that, he and I made our own arrangements. I'd ride my bike over to his house a few mornings a week, or his mother would drive him over to ours.

The boy's name was Jordan Hobson, but he said everyone called him Jory. He was eleven and had curly brown hair. When he smiled, his brown eyes sparkled, but his right leg was quite a bit thinner than his left one. He limped, edging along close to a wall, or he took little, stop-and-start steps with a cane.

During our fourth game, he told me how it happened. It had been strange. He had gotten up one morning at school, feeling heavy and achy, and suddenly had sunk to the floor. It was as if his muscles were dissolving. The prefect had thought he was faking and had yelled, "Stand up, you sod!" but even after the prefect had kicked him in the ribs twice, he could not move, so the prefect had called the headmaster, who said it was too serious for the infirmary.

He had come down with polio and had had to spend many weeks in hospital in Nairobi.

"Oh, dear," I said.

Jory admitted that at first it had been quite dismaying, but then his parents had come up to see him. They had given him a model airplane to work on, because he was such a lucky boy, his hands were still good, and they said they would come back once a month to check on him, and people from Government House would come to check on him, too.

He had said, "All right," looking at a crack on the ceiling.

They had left, but then his mother had come back in an hour and said, "Dad really does have to go back to Dodoma for a while, but I don't. I can stay here."

He asked, "For how long, Mum?"

She had answered, "Let's just say that as long as you are in hospital in Nairobi, I'm in Nairobi."

"All right," he had said.

"All right, then," she had replied, "it's settled."

Visiting hours were from three to four so as not to interfere with hospital routine, but his mother had told the nurses that she had come from very far away and that they were related to Danish royalty, which wasn't in fact true—they just had a Norwegian third cousin who sold fish bait. Anyway, they had made an exception for her and let her be there six hours a day.

"I'm glad," I said as I rearranged my letters.

Jory told me that his mother had never been much of a reader, but even so, when she wasn't with him, she had gone to the library and had done what she called research. She was always coming to hospital and saying, "Jory, I found out this," or "Jory, let me tell you what I just learned."

Jory began to feel better after several weeks, but his doctor wanted him to stay in hospital for a year. They would move around his muscles and put him in casts to stretch him out. "Oh, dear," I said again. Jory had just spelled "throat," and it was my move, but I paused. His father had come back to Nairobi, and they had told the doctor that they were taking a different path. It was going to be the Warm Springs approach for Jory.

"That's why you do the water exercises!" I said excitedly. I didn't know how I knew this.

"Exactly!" Jory said. The best part was he had left hospital just before it was his turn to be the subject in a Sister Kenny demonstration.

"What's a Sister Kenny demonstration?" I asked. I couldn't be expected to know everything.

Jory said it was really disgusting, with thirty or forty ladies watching, and he didn't think I should inquire further. He was just happy that he had escaped it.

I nodded. Building off the *o* in "throat," I spelled "orient."

Jory continued talking as he looked at his squares. He explained that polio required adjustment, but it wasn't all rotten. He had never done anything much with his father before, but now they played gin rummy at least twice a week, and they listened to rugby games on the radio together and discussed statistics. His father was always saying, "We won't be defeated, Jory!" and indeed, their team was having a very good season.

He asked me if I knew he had been a champion rugby player.

"Yes," I said, having heard it somewhere.

As for his mother, her memory had greatly improved. When he was little, his ayah would bring him to her after breakfast, and he would say something like, "Mummy, my favorite color is green." Then when his ayah brought him to her at tea, he would ask, "Mummy, what's my favorite color?" and she'd guess "Red? Purple?" and he'd say, "Mummy, I just told you this morning," to which she had no reply but "Oh, Jory, there's only so much poppycock I can fill my head with." However, now she remembered all the model airplanes he had built and always knew the next in line so she could get the kits for him in the proper order. What's more, she had learned to drive so they could get about even when someone on his father's staff was not available.

Jory used the *n* in "orient" to spell "nest." It was my turn again, and I wanted to make the winning move. The next thing he told me, though, really caught my attention. His school had made the suggestion that he not come back because sports were so important there. If they were in England, he might have been enrolled in a school for the physically handicapped "Physically handicapped is the correct term for crippled," he told me.

"My mother and I only say physically handicapped," I assured him. Actually, my mother and I hadn't used any term but polio. Jory went on. There were fortunately no suitable schools of this type in East Africa, so his parents had hired a tutor for him who would start at the end of the holiday. He would have to study very, very hard so he could be prime minister of Britain "Prime minister?" I said.

"Oh, yes," Jory said, suddenly quite grave. "It is the obligation of all boys with polio to grow up to lead their countries. I'm British, so I can't be United States president like Roosevelt. I must be prime minister. Don't you see?"

"Yes, I suppose," I said.

His parents were afraid he might be lonely, but he didn't think it would be too bad. My mother and some of the other women who weren't drunk all the time always talked to him when he was at the pool, and he was going to go over to the American neighborhood in Dodoma twice a week to do science, because one of the fathers there had rigged up a chemistry lab for his sons in their garage. Jory's view was that you had to take the good with the bad, and all's well that ends well. Didn't I agree?

I answered yes, for double sure.

I had an *e, o, x, t, n*. With the *s* on the board, I spelled "sexton." As usual, I won the game.

I went home for lunch, and after my mother, Stephen, and I had eaten, I got up, grabbed for the railing around the veranda, and started stumbling and staggering. I didn't know if girls with polio had to lead their countries, too, but I figured as long as Jory was prime minister, I wouldn't have to be. I'd skip the hospital part, too. I was just about to sink to the floor when Stephen said, "Mum, look at Amelia."

My mother turned to me and spoke sharply: "Well, you can stop that right now, and don't you dare do it again, Amelia! It's not like you to be so unkind. I thought Jory was your friend. If this is the sort of behavior you learn in boarding school, we will have to reconsider this whole proposition."

I straightened right up. My eyes opened wide. I was not like all those snickering girls at Westlands–King George who entertained themselves by mocking everyone else, nor was I like the blackguard children who came back to the compound on holidays. I might lie, steal, or kill time, but I had my principles. On that first horrible morning in Nairobi when Samantha Mary Winters was banging around her bear, I had found my compass, and now, almost three years later, I was still following it. My mother was my mother. I was her daughter. This meant I didn't hurt people. I didn't call people names. I taunted no one.

How could my mother even think I was making fun of Jory? I just wanted to stay home the way he could do now. I was so upset by what my mother said that it sailed right over my head that she had just offered me my ticket out.

As usual, I went back to boarding school at the end of the holiday. The pattern would never end, no matter how many times I swam the channel or climbed Everest. There were always another eighty-four days to get through.

I had always felt uneasy about willing hours, days, and weeks away. I called it killing time. Now, though, that I wrote my age in two digits and we had entered the 1950s, I had some sense that life was fleeting. People just got older. I begin to feel so guilty about obliterating three months out of every four. It was wasteful.

There was something else I felt guilty about. I was learning more and more about the war, the hunger and destruction, continents in flames, and the massacre of the Jews. My mother had finally told us that Mrs. Gold and Henri had fled France for their lives. She would not say what had happened to Henri's father. I had been in Devon during all this. Wartime had been the best time of my life. I wished we were back there. That was my awful secret.

One afternoon in 1951 when there were sixty-one days to go in the term, my extra was horseback riding. Margaret House and the other residence houses were on the far side of the grassy circle that connected to the lane leading out of the school, and the stables were beyond the residence houses by quite a ways, down a hill and in a field. This had begun to make me anxious. It would take a while for word to percolate down to the stables, if by a stroke a good fortune Joseph Kenyatta suddenly came to shut down the place, and maybe by the time I got back to the school proper there would be no one around to drive me to the airfield. To make matters worse, it wasn't guaranteed we would ride in the field. Sometimes the instructor would say, "I have a nice surprise for you all. We are going on a trail ride," and Margaret would get all excited, exclaiming we were all lucky stiffs. This was what happened on this particular day.

We rode into a little forest, went this way and that for a while, then went into an open meadow where we had to go back and forth, making the horse canter and trot. Finally we went back to the stables, but things weren't over yet, although we had exceeded the hour by ten minutes. The instructor said we were now old enough to learn how to check horses' hooves for stones.

"I prefer not to see whether my horse can balance on three legs," I said when the instructor said we would have pick each hoof up, one at a time.

"Of course he can," the instructor said. "Don't be timid. Reassure him."

I lifted up each hoof very quickly, reassuring the horse that I didn't like doing this. There were no stones, but I had to wait my turn to have the instructor verify this.

Finally I was walking back up the hill, thinking how pointless the whole rigmarole had been. I reached the road around the circle. There was enough wind that the azaleas were slightly rustling. I was just about to turn left to Margaret House, where next on the schedule would be free time, when I saw them! I saw only their backs because they were heading towards the gate, but it was them. My mother was wearing her blue linen dress.

I lost a decisive second standing stock still not believing my eyes. Then I was off across the circular green at a run. They were leaving. I had to catch them. They were about thirty feet from the gate. Between them and me was not only the green but also most of the lane. I had to get to them before they got to the gate.

"Mummy!" I screamed as I ran across the diameter of the circle. "Mummy!"

It was noisy on the green. There were several games of dodgeball going on with the smaller girls, and all the players were shouting. Girls from the upper school sat in groups, talking and laughing loudly. Day students who had stayed late for some reason were calling good-bye to each other. My mother could not hear me.

"Mummy," I yelled. "Mummy!"

Despite being so far away, I could see my mother's shoulder blades quivering. My father's hand was on her back. He was trying to steady her. She was upset. They had come for me and had not found me. I had been ready but not waiting.

I had on my stupid riding boots. I could have done better in my oxfords. Even so, I was moving. I was sprinting, I was racing, my legs were going like pistons. I had gotten to the acacia tree, and then I was past it. My riding hat slid over my eyes. I reached up and threw it off.

"Mummy," I shouted as loud as I could. "Mummy, wait!"

A girl in my path giggled, "Look at Amelia crying for her mummy."

I pushed her out of the way. She staggered and fell back.

"What's wrong, Amelia?" a day student who I was somewhat friendly with asked me. I pushed her out of my way, too. I think she stayed on her feet.

I had nearly crossed the green, but I was not covering the distance fast enough. My parents were about ten feet from the gate. Now I knew how Jory must feel in situations where it was important to go like the wind and he simply couldn't do it.

I was at the edge of the green. With a leap, I was on the pavement, pounding down the lane. A teacher came out of nowhere and said, "Amelia, just calm down." I ran around her.

I suddenly thought that if my mother could not hear me, maybe my father could. "Dad," I shouted. "Dad, Daddy!" Then I realized that if he was able to hear me, he would hear me no matter whose name I called, so I went back to calling my mother. Girls were streaming out of the sports building. A fencing class or some such had just let out. Everyone was just so loud. "Shut up," I cried.

I was past the upper school. I was gaining, but my parents were very near the gate. Once my mother seemed to try to look back, but my father put his hand on her shoulder, and she turned forward.

"Stop them," I screamed to the gatekeeper.

I needed to be an Olympic runner. I needed to be Harold Abrahams. Why was I wearing my riding boots? I needed to increase my stride. Increase stride, increase stride, increase rate.

I had just reached the lower school when my parents reached the gate.

"No," I shouted. "No, Mummy, no!"

They were going out. I could see a waiting car.

"Don't let them leave!"

The gatekeeper turned and saw me, running like anything. He smiled and waved cheerfully. I heard the car's doors shut and the motor being turned on. "Vroom, vroom," Stephen had liked to say when he had played cars with Jon and Ian Cookson in London.

I got to the gate just as the car, picking up speed, headed down the hill and out of sight.

Bloody hell! All I had needed was just two more seconds, the two seconds I had lost by not believing my eyes. Out of breath and heart pounding, I fell to my knees.

"Too hot to run about like that," the amiable gatekeeper observed. "This is East Africa."

"Yes," I answered, and let him help me stand.

The teacher who had told me to calm down came walking up to me. She handed me my riding hat as if it was supremely important that I have it.

"Well, that was certainly an unladylike display," she said.

I just looked at her.

"Margaret House is your assigned house?"

That was a good way of putting it, so I said, "Yes, Margaret House is my assigned house." I was breathing heavily.

"On your way," she said, motioning in that direction.

I hated this whole damn bloody place.

Mrs. Lamberton was waiting at the door when I got there. She said that everyone was terribly sorry about the mixup, just terribly sorry, but at least she had gotten to meet my parents, and that was wonderful, yes?

I just looked at her. Topsy-turvy, everything was.

She told me what had happened. My father had had a sudden opportunity to fly up to a conference in Nairobi, and just like that my mother had decided to go with him. They had not sent word to me for fear it would not work out. The conference was set to be over by one-thirty, and their flight back with the other officials from Dodoma was at five, time enough for short visits with both my brother and me. After calling the offices of both schools to see what our schedules were, they had decided to see my brother first, watch a bit of his cricket practice, and then come and see me. Unfortunately, the office looked at my Wednesday schedule and not my Thursday schedule and told them my extra was chorus, and I could be excused from that as soon as they got to the school. They could surprise me at the music room, actually. When they got here, though, they found out that my extra was in fact riding, and what's more, it was the day of the semi-quarterly trail ride.

I should have known these rubbishy trail rides were planned ahead. I should have seen a pattern, not that it would have helped in this instance.

Mrs. Lamberton continued, "I just wish the call had come to me. I have all my girls' schedules memorized."

I just looked at her.

"Anyway," Mrs. Lamberton said, "given how little time your parents had, it simply didn't make sense to locate you. All we could do was give them a nice tour of the school and hope that you would get back and be able to greet them before they absolutely had to leave. They were so disappointed they couldn't see you. They did say they had a nice visit with your brother, though. His name is Stephen!"

"Yes, I know," I said.

Mrs. Lamberton told me again everyone was very sorry about this. Then she added that I had broken a number of rules and would have to see the junior headmistress as soon as I changed back into my uniform.

"Well, all right." I turned and headed to my assigned room.

My roommate wasn't in the room. What was her name this term? Muffy? Duffy? Kuffy? Tuffy? Scruffy? I got it! It was Buffy! No one ever wanted to room with the smarty sad sack. What that meant was that everyone in the house had to take a turn with me. Next term the cycle would be up, and old Margaret would have to do a repeat.

Anyway, since my roommate wasn't there, I didn't have to dress in the closet. I pulled off my boots and hurled each against the wall. One landed on its sole, and the other fell sideways. Bloody hell! Just bloody hell! I ripped my riding pants off and flung them on my boots. My shirt came next, and I threw it in a whole other direction. Oh, dearie, weary, dreary me, I would have to straighten things up tonight or, despite my always being virtually all packed, my roommate and I would fail the bloody room inspection tomorrow.

I yanked my uniform off the hanger and crushed a pleat in my skirt. Goodness gracious, there was no end to the mistakes I was making. God damn! Bloody hell!

I suddenly thought about the day Colonial Office wives had come to see my mother at our house in London, while I unsuspectingly colored on the porch. I understood now that they had been there to talk my mother into getting my father to accept the posting to Tanganyika, which meant talking my mother into sending Stephen and me to boarding school. "They survive, Olivia," they had said. "They survive."

They hadn't even known me, had spurned the offer to meet me. Yet they thought all that I merited was survival. Survive, survive, survive.

Folly had wanted no part of them. When one lady had chirped, "Sit on my lap, little doggie," she had run back to the porch to stay with me. She had known they were bringing trouble.

They were as good as witches. They were witches, the colonial office wives were. Talking their mumbo jumbo, they had confused my mother, and they had knocked the hourglass on its side, causing our time to live together to dwindle.

There was a detail from that day I had overlooked. My mother and I had played badminton the rest of the afternoon, and then we had gone to collect Stephen at the Cooksons. Mrs. Cookson, wearing her painting smock, had said to my mother, "I see you had a visitation."

"Yes," my mother said faintly.

"Well, when a gaggle of biddies and aging glamour girls invited themselves here, I just said 'shoo fly, don't bother me. Unless your talents lie in refereeing cherub boxing matches, we've no basis for a chat.'"

My mother had laughed—and I had too, since we had sung "Shoo Fly" in Brownies—but my mother had become serious again and said, "Oh, Val, I'm so torn."

Mrs. Cookson had touched Mummy's shoulder and said, "Take good care, Olivia, take good care."

The Cooksons, staying in London, had had Lawrence and then two more baby boys, and Christa had gotten a Siamese kitten named Thimble—we learned this in Christmas cards. However, the Colonial Office witch wives had cast their spell on us, and so we had gone on our African adventure, which was no adventure but a disaster, a full-scale, all-out disaster.

The colonial witch wives had done us in, and in Folly's case, that meant literally.

Bloody hell!

I snapped the vest to my skirt, and there I was, dressed in my bloody uniform.

As I went out into the hall, Buffy passed me, saying in a singsong way, "Amelia's in trouble! Amelia's in trouble!" Buffy came from Kenya's Wanjohi Valley, which was otherwise known as Happy Valley, and her claim to fame was that her parents had sometimes been invited to Lady Idina Sackville's parties.

I ignored her. She was a colonial witch wife in training.

When I got to Miss Smallwood's office, she said it was unusual to see me under these circumstances. Usually I was there to receive congratulations for my academic prowess. I had never been there for misbehavior before. She listed my transgressions. I had allowed my excitement to get the better of me. I had recklessly thrown my riding hat. I had pushed two classmates, and one—a fellow boarder—had lost her balance. I had ignored a teacher.

"Yes," I said.

"What is the main thing we teach here?" she asked me.

"I don't know."

"Well, you do know. It is to respect the rights and feelings of others."

I just looked at her.

She told me actions had consequences. She tapped her fingers together. "What should be done with you?" she asked.

After nearly four years, this finally was my chance. I spoke carefully and deliberately. I said, "It is my considered opinion after giving the matter much thought that I be sent home. I have not made a good adjustment." I paused and added, "It would be preferable for me socially if I was with my mother."

Her lips quivered in merriment. "No, Amelia, that's too harsh. We don't want the top girl in the lower school to leave. Let the punishment fit the crime!"

She tapped her fingers together. "Let's see," she said. "I think you should miss horseback riding next week. You can use the time to write letters of apology to Eileen and the day student. Her name escapes me at the moment."

"Sharon Clark," I said. My so-called fellow boarders may have been a blur, but obviously I knew the names of all the day students in my class. They had regular lives, and I still spent time with them at recess.

"Well, anyway," Miss Smallwood replied, "you may not go riding next week."

I sighed and said, "I'll stop riding altogether."

Miss Smallwood laughed out loud. "Amelia, I'm glad you realize your mistake, but why are you trying to make the punishment more severe?"

"I prefer not to take riding," I explained.

She didn't think that was so comical. Her tone changed. "Well, Amelia, that's too bad. You're signed up for riding. After next week, you'll resume it. Amelia, there's one more bit."

I looked at her as she paused dramatically. She finally said, "Tomorrow night, when Mrs. Lamberton lays a piece of red velvet cake on the plate of every other girl in Margaret House, she will not lay a piece on your plate."

Once I had heard some Americans say "Okie dokie." That was what I wanted to say, "Okie dokie." Instead I said "All right."

"Amelia, it's your birthday cake."

I suddenly remembered that tomorrow was my birthday. I would be eleven years old. For the first time, I noticed three wrapped presents on her desk. My parents had hoped to wish me happy birthday in person. They had wanted to see me open my presents.

Miss Smallwood said she would write my parents and tell them how the school had dealt with my behavior. She was sure that they would approve.

My parents in fact did not approve. In my mother's next letter to me, she enclosed a note from my father (in an unsealed envelope) that I was to give to the junior headmistress. In it he said that children were not to be blamed for the mistakes made by adults, and that if he and his wife were people ruled by their emotions, they would take me out of the school right now. It was only because I was doing so well that they were allowing me to stay. They had given the school money to buy me a cake, but only other girls had been allowed to enjoy it. There was a word for this.

On the night that I did not get a piece of red velvet cake, Mrs. Lamberton had still made the girls of Margaret House sing "Happy Birthday" to me. She made them sing it to me all over again ten days later when we had strawberry cake with coconut frosting.

My mother also granted my request that I drop riding. I merely told her that I had no affinity with horses. In fact, the only horse I had ever liked was Stephen's and my old secondhand repainted rocking horse in Devon.

Only my father ever visited the school again. It was actually the next term, with twenty-five days to go and right after I had passed the exam qualifying me for university preparation. I had gotten the second-highest mark among all those taking the exam in Kenya that year and the third-highest mark in all of East Africa. Anyway, I was called to the phone in the office, and it was my father saying he was in Nairobi because he had some business with Stephen that did not concern me, but that after that was done, he'd like to visit with me here, and then we'd go back and collect Stephen and go out to dinner to celebrate my doing well on my exam. He said that he had gotten me a pass so I could stay out until 9 p.m.

This place was run like a jail, and I had never had a pass before, so I was excited for this and other reasons.

At the arranged time, I was waiting in rain gear by the gate for my father. It wasn't raining, but the raincoat hid the fact I was wearing my own dress, even though Mrs. Lamberton had directed me to stay in my uniform. I guess she wanted me to go out to dinner and advertise Westlands–King George at the same time, which I had no intention of doing.

It was confusing at first to see my father by himself, but there were hugs and kisses, and he gave me a book of Tennyson poems from my mother. He asked me to show him my favorite places at school. I had no favorite places, but I showed him the swimming pool and also the azalea bush that I still shook to hear the leaves rustle.

Hand in hand, we walked out of the gate and to the car my father had rented. I took off my raincoat and felt fine and free in my lavender poplin dress. I twirled around, and my father said I was pretty as a picture. He didn't inquire about the rain gear.

We drove down the hill, made two right turns and a left turn and were at Westlands–Crown School. I didn't mention it to my father, but

I was absolutely stunned. I had never had any idea where Stephen's school was in Westlands but had always assumed it was far away. Indeed, he might as well as have been in Uganda. All this time, he had been within a half mile. Even at seven and a half, I could have walked it.

With Stephen in the car—Stephen was wearing his uniform—my father said, "I'm taking you two to the Norfolk Hotel. Your mother and I are not part of the set that would frequent it, but it's a historic place, and I want you to see it."

We went past City Centre, the council buildings, the museums, and suddenly we were in a tropical jungle, quite different from the dry grassland in most of the open areas around Nairobi.

"How did this happen?" I asked my father as I looked at the mass of vines and the riot of color.

"We're on the grounds of the Norfolk. They work hard to make it seem this way."

As my father said this, I noticed a few sprinklers going back and forth. Perhaps it was like this in Hollywood.

The hotel was a large white stucco building, and we went into it and directly out of it. We were having supper on the Lord Delamere Terrace.

China, crystal, zillions of forks, a battalion of waiters calling me "miss" and Stephen "sir" in the midst of a cultivated jungle in Nairobi, Kenya, with my father but not my mother—I didn't know what to think of it.

"I wish Mummy was here," I said.

"Yes, but this was a quite unexpected trip for me," my father said.

Stephen, who had seemed subdued all this time, turned pale. He liked the lamb, though, and he began to relax as my father got him talking about rugby and coin collecting. He and my father were now focusing on getting coins from Persia and the other eastern countries.

We had mint parfaits for dessert, and again my father told me how pleased he and my mother were in my having aced the exam, and even Stephen said, "Your name was in the paper. I was asked if you were my sister. Good show, Amelia!"

My father added, "You're both on the right track. You're both going to go far!" Stephen looked at him and nodded.

The evening had been grand, if topsy-turvy, but my heart sank when we got back into the car. With every mile closer to Westlands–King

George, I felt drearier and drearier. We dropped Stephen off first. It was 8:45. I had to make my stand.

We sat in the car outside the gate to the school, and I began to talk. My results on the important exam had shown that I had really given this place a whirl. Yet, although it would be hard, I would stay here for the next twenty-four days and formally complete lower school. However, I would do upper-school study at home. I was double sure I could do it, studying with Jory and with a little help from Mummy. With work, I would ace the O-levels and the A-levels and then go to St. Hilda's at Oxford. That was my plan.

My father was delighted I had set my sights on St. Hilda's but I was now entering the most intensive part of my pre-university education, and I would be shortchanged if I tried to do it at home.

He said, "What Jory is doing is admirable, but it's far from ideal and forced on him by circumstances."

It was now 8:57. The minutes were running out. Slowly, I got out of the car. I put on my raincoat. The guard opened the gate, and my father walked me to Margaret House. Mrs. Lamberton opened the door. She told me to say good-bye to my father and come inside, and I had no choice but to do so.

My parents did try, though, to maximize what little time we had together. Stephen and I left for Nairobi at the last possible moment and came home at the first possible instant. We were always flown, arriving home sometimes a whole day before the children who went to Arusha or the other closer places but who traveled by bus or train. We never went to camp, as Buffy often did, and my mother refused to go away when we were home.

When I was twelve, the vice royal governor down in Dar invited all the adults in the compound on a five-day safari in Tsavo in the middle of the Easter holiday. My father was going, but my mother wasn't, and that got some of the other women riled. They thought it reflected on the compound.

"Well, how can I go?" my mother said. "When my children are home, they expect to see me, and I want to see them."

The women said she could see us for a week and a half before the safari and for almost two weeks after. "Just five days, Olivia, just five days!" I heard them saying to her at the pool. They said that many of them were leaving children, too. One lady said she would "donate" her ayah to us if that would help.

When my mother wouldn't budge, they started in with me. They told me I was selfish for not encouraging my mother to go. I was a big girl now and didn't need her every second. Brigit Peck in Dar could cope with being home without Mummy. I just shrugged and jumped in the pool.

My father got wind of this and wasn't pleased. How dare anyone question his wife's decisions! How dare anyone make his daughter feel guilty for wanting to see her mother!

My father seldom swore. He always said that in the military during the war, he and everyone else from General Montgomery on down had used words that were not fit for ordinary society twenty times in every sentence. Some of the combinations were really quite amazing. Men had different reasons for doing this, my father said, but for him, it was almost as if he was speaking a dialect appropriate to circumstances, so as to curtain the strange soldier existence off from his normal life. When he had crossed the threshold of our house in London to resume being a husband and father, the dialect had been extinguished. The profane words had reverted to nonsense, he told us.

However, he was swearing now—although probably not the RAF version. What was wrong with the goddamn bastards down in Dar? Didn't those bloody jackasses at Government House ever think? The children were away most of the time, so what do these fools do? They scheduled a damn safari in the middle of school holidays. Well, you know what? He was going to send his regrets, as well. It would be no fun without his wife, and, all right, bloody hell, he'd admit it. He wanted to be with his son and daughter, too.

Mr. and Mrs. Hobson were planning to go, since Jory was home all the time. My mother and I were all set to help him with his water exercises. Then Mrs. Hobson decided not to go. She said that my mother was the only woman in the compound with her head screwed on straight, so what was the point of going without her? Besides, Jory was always more animated when I was around, and she didn't want to miss a minute of seeing him so lively. Mr. Hobson could represent their family on safari.

At the last minute, the powers that be in the compound slapped together a mini-safari for the compound kids at a camp just outside

Dodoma. Stephen and I had no desire to go, but lest we did, the invitation stated in bold letters that this excursion was only for children from four to fifteen whose parents were going to Tsavo.

Just for laughs, Jory decided to ask if he could go. Unfortunately, the two ladies he asked had not agreed on their story. One said that even if you had just one parent staying home, you couldn't go. The other said that the camp couldn't cater to a child who was crippled.

"That's physically handicapped," I giggled, when Jory told us the story. I continued, "The parents turn themselves inside out for a chance to be with the vice royal governor of Tanganyika, but once Tanganyika is independent, having been vice royal governor won't amount to a hill of beans. Yet they don't want their children to be with the future prime minister of Great Britain. It's topsy-turvy."

My mother kissed me twice and then said, "Anyway, Jory, we want you with us. We're going to have more fun."

We did have fun. All the residents of the compound were gone except for us, Jory, and his mother and an elderly couple, the Glovers, who almost never went anywhere. We swam and played all day and into the evening. Jory and Mrs. Hobson either came over to our house for supper, or we went over to theirs. The Glovers were always invited, but they declined. Two nights, we had charades. One night, my father taught us to play poker.

The second day, my mother teamed up with Jory to design a brilliant paper chase for Stephen and me, that took us behind hedges and to all corners of the compound. We were neck and neck until the last clue, which was hidden in the cannas by the post office. The clue read, "Cooling to all who partake, only the divine can walk." Hands on my hips, I watched Stephen race off to the grove of frangipani trees. Then I made a beeline to the pool, where my mother and Jory were waiting with bells and whistles.

Stephen heard our voices and came wandering in about five minutes later. "What type of clue is that?" he asked.

"I came up with the idea," Jory shouted.

"It's slightly blasphemous," my mother admitted.

We didn't stop at blasphemy. We broke all the rules during those five days. There was a dining room in the club where no one under sixteen could enter. We converted that into our game room and used the largest table for ping-pong. There was another room reserved for men who wanted to drink and smoke without women. My mother, Mrs. Hobson, and I marched right in.

"I would so prefer a gin and tonic," I said, spinning around on a leather swivel chair.

"Coming right up," Mrs. Hobson said, pretending to open the liquor cabinet and mix a drink.

"Make mine bourbon straight up," my mother said. "I woke up this morning, saw the hibiscus, and it struck me that London was looking quite odd. My husband had to tell me where we were."

"You mean I'm not in Hempstead?" Mrs. Hobson cried in mock horror. "Well, then, I don't have time to fix you gals drinks. I'm getting sloshed myself."

I laughed delightedly. My mother and Mrs. Hobson were mocking the other adults in the compound and letting me see it.

The last day, my mother did something exceedingly daring. We had a picnic for the children of the staff on the lawn of the club. We ate and played tag and marbles. The air rang with shouts in Kiswahili, and some of us—all right, all of us—ended up in the club's fountain. This included Stephen, who said he could better help Jory get in if he was already in himself.

We had not thought about the older couple. Their house was a ways from the club. It was late in the afternoon, the kids had gone. Aumi had offered to stay to help put everything back together, but my mother had told her this one was on us. We were carefully tidying things up, setting everything to rights. The boys and my clothes were only slightly dripping. Suddenly, the Glovers were standing there. Roly-poly Mr. Glover just glared at us. Mrs. Glover did the speaking. Her dress was boat necked, and one petticoat strap showed.

"Really, Olivia, really! You are the limit! Black children at our club. I never!" Mrs. Glover exclaimed.

"Well, wait," Mrs. Hobson said. "I was part of this, too."

Stephen was starting to get a husky voice. He cleared his throat and said, "My father was left in administrative charge of the compound while everyone else was gone. He gave permission."

My mother said, "Myra, we did no harm."

"No harm?" Mrs. Glover almost screamed. "No harm? I would rather be dead, have my husband dead, my children dead, and their children dead than to share a country club with blacks."

"Then you don't place much value on life," my mother said.

"Yes," Jory said. "It would be better if you said you'd rather you all had polio."

That made me laugh. After a moment, Mrs. Hobson laughed, so Stephen and my mother laughed.

This confused Mrs. Glover. She looked at Jory, and while she did so, Mr. Glover winked at my mother.

"I'm sorry about your son," she said to Mrs. Hobson.

Mrs. Hobson shrugged.

After a moment, Mrs. Glover started spluttering again, "You know what I wish for you, Olivia. I wish you have black grandchildren!"

"You never know," I said, taking two steps forward.

"Grr! Humph! Against nature!" Mrs. Glover said. She took her husband by the arm, spun him around, and they were gone.

"Well," my mother said, after a pause.

"Well," Mrs. Hobson said.

We all looked at each other. Ever since Jory had gotten polio, we and the Hobsons had been friends. Now, it was more than that. In this stifling compound where people breathed in on each other, the Ords and the Hobsons were allies.

For some reason, the Glovers never told anyone about our picnic—Jory thought it was because Mr. Glover was sweet on my mother. Yet I noticed the other women in the compound were waspish around her. Once when we were at the pool and my mother and I were having a race and intentionally splashing each other, one entertaining wit called out, "Olivia, are you a mummy, or are you a mommy?"

My mother had put time with us ahead of socializing with the vice royal governor. She had stood her ground.

There was now increasing national fervor in East Africa. This was especially so in Kenya, where the British had been ridiculously slow in permitting Kenyans seats in the legislature. The Mau Mau from the Kikuyu tribe were associated with the movement, and they were feared. They killed other Kikuyus who did not take the oath of loyalty, as well as some white settlers. They tortured and hanged cattle.

By late 1952, Nairobi was under a continuing state of emergency. Even so, after a longer than usual Christmas holiday (which was very enjoyable), school resumed operation. Now, though, the gate was always locked, and the guards were armed. The few day students who were black all had to swear that they would not take an oath to the Mau Mau. Trail rides were canceled for the boarders, to the dismay of Margaret and Buffy. Some of the younger girls slept upside down in their boarding school beds, in the hope that if the Mau Mau came through, they would only cut off their feet and not their heads.

When we came home, my parents finally let Stephen and me know that they were concerned about the way the British were responding to the Mau Mau's murderous acts. They said they were speaking to us about this totally candidly, because we were older now. In sober tones, they told us they had written to both Parliament and the Red Cross about the harsh screening of Kikuyu and other tribes to root out violent elements. Too many innocent people were getting caught up in the net. Too many families—thousands of them—were being detained and relocated. It was if the British had learned little from the Second World War.

My father gave us a directive he had never given us before. Nothing said about politics in the house was ever to go outside the house. We were not to talk carelessly in the compound. We were not to talk carelessly at school. My mother asked us if we understood. I for one did. There were threats everywhere and from all sources.

My father was now exceedingly glad that he had not been assigned to Kenya.

Unfortunately, Stephen and I still had to go to school in Kenya.

The family as a whole was entering its roughest patch. One term I noticed that my mother's eighth, ninth, tenth, eleventh, and twelfth letters all seemed somehow strange. She still wrote two pages each time and still ended each letter conveying her and my father's greatest love. She responded completely to the things I had written and told me what they had heard from Stephen. Twice, she mentioned Jory. Yet otherwise she seemed to be casting about for things to write. By her last letter of the term, it finally occurred to me that she had written nothing about Aumi this whole time.

When Stephen and I got home at long last, Aumi and Edna were not waiting on the veranda to welcome us. It was then that my mother said poor Aumi had died, and Edna had felt she couldn't stay, so they had helped her get a job in Moshi.

We looked at my mother questioningly, and my mother looked at my father in almost a frightened way. My father told Stephen and me to come into his study.

My father said that Aumi had been in a tribal ceremony and gotten a cut that had become infected.

"What type of ceremony?" I asked.

"Religious coming-of-age ceremony for girls," my father said, sounding uncomfortable.

"I thought they were Catholic."

"Yes, but they still followed some tribal rituals."

"Why did Edna let her be in this particular ceremony?" I persisted.

"Custom," my father said briefly.

"Did they mark her face?" Stephen wanted to know.

"No," my father said. "It was a delicate thing, and I prefer not to elaborate any further."

He told us that Aumi had been listless and exhausted when she came to work with Edna. My mother had taken her temperature, and it had been 101. When Edna hesitantly told her about the cut, my mother said Aumi needed penicillin and quickly. The native clinic in Dodoma had just gotten a supply for the first time—my mother knew that; she and Mrs. Hobson had been part of the committee that had demanded it—but my mother thought it would take them too long to get there. Edna reminded her that the compound infirmary only saw compound residents and not staff or anyone else black. My mother had said, "They will treat Aumi. I'll make them do it."

The trouble was she couldn't. They insisted that if they treated one Tanganyikan, they'd be inundated with them—old people, unfed babies, what have you. Then what would British patients do? My mother had remonstrated that it was an emergency, and indeed Aumi couldn't sit upright anymore without Edna holding on to her. The doctor disagreed that it was an emergency and said she would do fine at a native clinic. He said that penicillin was a miracle drug, and one of the reasons they had been happy to help the native clinic get a supply of it was so the natives could feel they were getting the same care as the whites.

They went on in this vein for twenty minutes, my mother pleading and imploring. She even said that the infirmary could use her name for the medical records instead of Aumi's. This was a very brave thing to do, given the nature of the cut, but to no avail. My father said he had been in the field that day and unreachable. Perhaps if he had been there, he could have gotten Government House to intercede, but probably not.

By that time, Aumi had begun to mix up English and Kiswahili words and mumble about rivers. The doctor thought she was just being a native and wouldn't believe my mother's explanation that she was delirious. Finally, my mother rang Mrs. Hobson, and she came with her car and drove them to the native clinic.

It had taken another twenty minutes to get to the native clinic, and then there was a wait. Aumi's fever was 103 when she was finally seen. She got the penicillin, but it was too late. Her fever rose to 105. She was septic. She died the next day.

They would never know whether Aumi could have been saved if she had been treated at the compound infirmary or if they had gone directly to the native clinic. It was quite possible that Aumi had already been beyond hope when she and Edna got to our house that morning. The point was they just didn't know if the delay had caused her death. They just didn't know.

My father said we were never to speak of this to our mother. "Do you understand, Stephen?"

He said yes.

"Do you understand, Amelia?"

I also said yes.

My father said that my mother was absolutely beside herself.

Edna and Aumi had always been nice to us, trying to make us feel welcome in a foreign land, where the ways of the British were so strange and disagreeable. When Stephen and I were younger, Edna had told us wonderful stories in the kitchen while my parents did their social obligations. They had taken our family to their village several times and had helped us learn Kiswahili. Aumi had strung beads with me and had taught my mother and me to weave baskets. She had stayed with Folly after the scorpion bite. Then she had tried to comfort me by giving me a bracelet and telling me that Folly was part of nature.

I asked my father how old Aumi had been. It turned out she had been sixteen, just a year older than Stephen.

I had learned the term "race prejudice" on our first full day in Tanganyika, but it had always been an abstract concept to me, an attempt to explain something that made no sense, such as Aumi could go walking with us but could not go swimming with us because of race prejudice. Now I know what race prejudice really meant. It meant that people died.

Someone on the staff took Edna's place. Her name was Marian. She was the one who revealed to me where Aumi had been cut, but I never got to know her too well. At night when I was home and my parents were at the club or dutifully giving a noisy party, I ate supper quickly and then went to my room, never lingering in the kitchen as I had with Edna and Aumi.

My mother had some gray hair now and a few wrinkles around her eyes. She smiled at us, but if I looked at her before she looked at me, I saw that her mouth was set in a thin line. My father seemed somewhat wary. He no longer spoke of doing great things. Stephen talked only of sports, and although my mother and I still read out loud together, he didn't join us.

I was thirteen, I was fourteen. I was almost fifteen. I called my mother Mum now, but I was still away three months out of every four. There was a drought in Tanganyika and Kenya. Things were dusty. My only friend was Jory. It seemed as if we would be in this existence forever. Time passed, but we were waiting, waiting, waiting.

On the last night of the spring term in 1955, Mrs. Lamberton as usual had me hand over the plaque for best swimmer that I had won that term since I had supposedly won it for Margaret House. However, a half hour after she had shown her flashlight into each room, I crept into the dark common room with a satchel and put all the swimming plaques I had won for my mother over the years into it. Then I pushed Margaret's riding trophies and Buffy's golf ribbons closer together in the display cabinet so that Mrs. Lamberton wouldn't tend to notice my items were missing until I was gone.

Early the next morning as I was leaving, Mrs. Lamberton said to me, "Well, Amelia, your absence will be longer this time, but I still won't say good-bye, I'll just say *au revoir*." She put out her hand. I think she wanted to send me off with the school handshake.

"Hands full," I said cheerfully, and indeed they were, because I had both my suitcase and the satchel. I walked out the door and to Fred's waiting car.

A glorious thing had happened. Our long-hoped-for home year had finally been approved. In August, the four of us would be flying to Heathrow. Stephen, who was going into the upper sixth form, would be at Eton. It was his choice. He wanted to go to my father's school. As for me? I would be back at Regency Day!

CHAPTER 5

The Home Year

London, 1955–1956

WHEN WE HAD LEFT in 1947, Heathrow Airport had been a small, simple place just opened for civilian use. Now eight years later, it was a bustling labyrinth of corridors. We wound our way into the Europa Building, the immense new terminal. We had never been anywhere so glossy and modern. "It's almost like a pavilion at a world's fair," my mother said.

We kept looking this way and that as we walked, but we did not linger. We wanted to see England. Outside, it was chilly, raw and drizzling. "Typical London weather," we laughed, although we barely remembered it and were shivering a bit.

My father had rented a car—it was silver with blue leather seats; I don't remember the brand. We all piled in. My father followed the signs, and suddenly we were on the new motorway. "You can really drive fast now, Dad," Stephen said. "Vroom! Vroom!"

I said, "Dad, you're Toad of Toad Hall."

My mother suddenly exclaimed, "Goodness gracious, I see an oak tree!"

"Way out yonder, there's a maple," I shouted.

"Statuesque elm on your right," my father put in.

"All right," Stephen said. "I see a birch tree.

"Beech tree, Stephen," the rest of us chorused. "Beech tree!"

"I'm going to drink a gallon of tap water tonight," I declared.

Perhaps we were just exhausted from the long flight and the time difference, but we were all giddy and giggling about everything.

We were not in fact going into the city. There had been some mix-up with the renters of our house. They thought we were coming a week later than we really were, so we said, no fuss, we'd go on holiday straightaway! We were going to the country inn in the Lake District where we had been so long ago.

There, nothing had changed, except the inn had been repainted, and the dining room had more extensive offerings, rationing having eased some. As before, we were under the eaves, but the biggest thing was that it was the same innkeeper, and he remembered not only us but Folly! "Right nice, she was," he said. "A princess of a dog! The little one was always dancing with her."

What he didn't know was that we had Folly with us, right now. We would not leave her all alone in the compound while the rest of us went home. Before we left Tanganyika, we had dug up the box with her ashes and pulled out her marker. We would bury the box in our back garden in London, and we would plant a lilac bush alongside her marker.

The sun came out for our holiday, dappling the green valleys with light and shade. Every day was glorious. We took more adventurous hikes in the mountains than we had before. We picnicked and canoed, and on warmish afternoons we swam in the bracing water. Each evening from a hilltop we watched the leisurely sunset, so different from the equator, where the sun blazed all day and then sank like lead. Three times, we caught the moments of the pink, purple gloaming. My father said it was enchantment.

The week was our buffer between Africa and London, and even as my mother and I read *A Tale of Two Cities* to each other, we tried to make our time last as long as we could.

The innkeeper had a reddish cocker spaniel named Pippa, and the night before we were to leave he took us into his private quarters and showed us her four two-month-old puppies. They had downy, curly baby fur, soft ears, and happy eyes. The one female was so excited to see new humans that she squeaked with joy.

Even Stephen, big boy that he was, got down on the floor and laughed as the puppies bounded between us. The female got up on two legs and put her paws on my shoulders and licked my neck. Then she jumped into Mum's lap and wanted to snuggle. She was the one for us—unless, of course, we got two. They were all adorable.

"She's the pick of the litter," the innkeeper said. "I'd be pleased if she went with you."

"Well—" my mother replied, sounding as if she was tempted.

"Oh, Mum," I said. "She's super."

Stephen added, "I'm for it. Amelia will really like her."

"So will Stephen," I shouted.

"I'm game, Olivia," my father said. "It's up to you."

Under ordinary circumstances that would have sealed it, but suddenly we looked at each other, our delight turning to dismay, verging on horror. It would be wicked for us to get a puppy. In a year, Stephen would be at university but my parents and I would have to go back to Africa. Quarantine had been ghastly for Folly. Never in all our lives would we do that to another dog.

"I'm sorry," my mother told the innkeeper. "Our situation isn't conducive to having a dog." She looked down, and I sadly gave the puppy one last pat.

So our past, which would also be our future, was casting a shadow on us even as our home year started.

The next day, we drove home to London, where we would have to try to act like normal people. For a while, the city seemed as new and different to me as it had when we had come from Devon. Fortunately, Christa was ready and waiting to be my best friend again. Now a tall and willowy girl, wearing her auburn hair in a pageboy, she kept saying, "It's just fabulous to have you back, Amelia, just fabulous."

When we had left, the Cooksons had been a rollicking family of five. Now they were a boisterous band of eight, with Mrs. Cookson still doing murals and making do as best she could. She said, "I didn't have six children. No, indeed, I merely had two groups of three."

"The girl's the unpaid help," Christa added, but she was laughing as a small boy tried to climb on her back.

Ian, a younger version of his good-natured father, was about to go to the University of London. Jon, in his last year at Regency Day, was artistic like his mother, except he did watercolors. As for the new children—at least they were new to us—they were the cat's whiskers.

Lawrence was a naturalist. He had lizards and fish. Dennis was a cowboy, always trying to lasso someone. Kenny played a drum constantly. Mrs. Cookson called them Boom, Boom, and the Final Boom. Collectively, they were known as the Booms.

The baby boomers were actually everywhere. Those who had been infants when we left London were now racing through primary school, and more were coming up behind them. Laughing and shouting, they crowded the little park. They roller-skated in Hyde Park, and they were brassy. They yelled, "Mum, I want this. Dad, get me that," and their parents seemed willing to oblige. The children talked glibly about the atom bomb and how it would destroy everyone and everything. Yet they seemed to feel they owned the universe. They didn't know how hard life could be.

Then there was television. Huge numbers of families had brought sets so they could watch the coronation, and since then television had become so much part of the national culture, with the BBC broadcasting a full schedule every night, that it was affectionately called "telly." The Cooksons considered themselves holdouts because they didn't have one yet. My parents, Stephen, and I had a quick discussion. We decided we would be holdouts, too.

Traffic had increased. It was constant. So many people in the expanding suburbs had private cars, and it seemed all they did was drive around London, especially around our house. The first night, I couldn't sleep and ended up out on the balcony at midnight, watching the city. My mother heard me and came out, too. That made me laugh. I reminded her that when we had done this ten years ago, she had said we weren't doing this again, for double sure. Now we were doing it again.

"Well," she said, "it's just another thing I was wrong about."

The renters had left our house in pristine condition and had complied with my parents' request to use some of the rent money to update what were now being called "appliances" in the kitchen. We even had a machine that would wash and dry the dishes after they were rinsed.

My mother said she would have no social obligations this year, and she and my father would even go lightly on their social life—they had enough of that in Africa—so what did I think of a year on our own, without anyone but an occasional cleaner working for us?

I was thrilled at the idea and thrilled that she had asked my opinion.

"That will be great, Mum," I said. "I'll help you cook supper every night."

"Only when you don't have activities," she replied. "I don't want to you to miss out on anything."

I eagerly said, "We have a deal." I knew that I would almost always be home in time for supper preparations.

It was strange when my father took the train to Eton with Stephen and came home without him, but the next day my mother and I went shopping at Harrods for my school clothes. I would not be wearing uniforms at Regency Day! We could readily see that postwar austerity had lifted a little, and that hemlines were longer and everything more colorful, but after being away for so long, we were unsure about what I should get, so Christa came along as fashion consultant.

After two hours, I had quite an array of things. In addition to several pastel dresses to wear before the weather turned cool, I bought three pleated skirts in different plaids, as well as a gray skirt that hung straight, and also one in beige. The ability to mix and match was the key, so I got an assortment of blouses in both white and solid colors, as well as three cardigans: cream, navy, and maroon.

Then came the *pièce de résistance*. Christa said that it had just become the style for girls to wear wool Bermuda shorts and knee socks when they wanted to look smart but casual on weekends.

"Won't we look like eight-year-old boys?" I objected, remembering that Christa used to wear her brothers' knee pants.

Christa laughed. "No, they are cut differently."

The Bermudas I got were periwinkle blue flannel, and I liked them quite a lot.

The first day of school I followed small children through the door I used to go into, and Christa had to come running after me, saying, "Amelia, we go through the upper-school door now, but it's all right, we'll use the connecting hall today."

My mistake had one benefit. We ran into Miss Hill, who was so pleased to see me, she gave me a hug.

"I still have the pencils you gave me, Miss Hill," I told her.

"It almost broke my heart when you left, but now you are back. Come down and visit Miss Taylor and me when you have a chance," she said.

"For double sure," I replied.

We crossed the threshold into the upper school, and Christa led me into a classroom. Right there was a boy with big brown eyes who said to me in a husky voice, "Remember me, your old partner in crime?"

I didn't remember us committing many crimes together, but still I squealed, "Teddy!"

He had such broad shoulders now.

Suddenly, girls and boys who looked vaguely familiar were all around me, welcoming me back and introducing me to kids who had joined the class while I was gone. A pretty-looking woman of about thirty with long raven hair pulled back and wearing a swirling circle skirt and a silk blouse strode briskly through the throng and put out her hand, saying, "Hello, Amelia. I'm Miss Linfield, history teacher and class adviser. Your reputation precedes you!"

Then she turned to the class as a whole, clapped her hands, and said, "All right, people, find your desks. The school year at Regency Day has officially begun, which means our study of the Elizabethan era has begun."

She waited a moment while everyone found seats. Then Miss Linfield continued, "I pose for you these questions. How does religion change when wedded to the state? How does the state change when wedded to religion? Marriage made in heaven, or union forged in hell, or doesn't it matter?" She lifted her hands in a wondering way.

She went on, "We don't have the framework to address these questions yet, but please remember as we memorize dates and learn about events—and yes, we'll be doing a lot of that—that these concerns will be our ultimate inquiry. Now, as we all know, Queen Elizabeth was the daughter of Henry the eighth and his second wife, Anne Boleyn, who was beheaded. Quite an unfortunate thing to happen to one's mother, yes?"

I knew instantly history would be my favorite subject. Miss Linfield seemed altogether smashing.

It only took me a few days to settle back into Regency Day. I enjoyed wearing a different outfit every day. I liked having boys in class. It was interesting to talk to them and hear their opinions, and it was funny to see them try to behave. I even loved having a locker, a place to hang my coat and stow my lunch and to hold the books I was not using for the next few hours. Lockers were unique to day schools because only students who came and went from home each day needed lockers.

I was too old to need to be walked to school, but since my father was going that way to the Colonial Office every morning, I walked with him. He said that he was glad that we could have this extra time to talk, and indeed we discussed many things. Mostly international politics it was—the iron curtain, the bamboo curtain, the growing might of the States, the changing Commonwealth. The steady stream of traffic still made me a bit anxious, so sometimes I would hold my father's hand as we crossed the street. At the entrance to the schoolyard, my father would say "Have a good day, love," and I'd reply, "So long, Dad."

As he went on his way, I would spot Christa, disentangling herself from the Booms, and we would go through the upper-school door together.

My mother had found an indoor pool in Chelsea where we could go swimming, so two afternoons a week she met me after school, and we got the bus to Chelsea at the next block. The rest of the time I walked home with Christa or by myself, if I had stopped to chat with Miss Hill or Miss Taylor. Almost always in the evening, I'd be in our kitchen, helping my mother make supper, cutting up vegetables, washing potatoes as she did the real cooking. Sometimes we would talk, but we also got into the habit of using the time to recite poetry. As a girl, my mother had memorized the whole of "The Love Song of J. Alfred Prufrock" and still knew it, and I could come in on "in the room the women come and go, talking of Michelangelo."

The sentiments were out of date, but we both loved "The Charge of the Light Brigade." We'd alternate stanzas, saying them louder and louder and faster and faster, reaching a crescendo with the last stanza, which we said in unison. The noble six hundred would not be forgotten, if we had anything to do with it.

I had just read an e. e. cummings poem in school, and although I didn't quite understand it, I was intrigued by the first lines, "anyone lived in a pretty how town (with up so floating many bells down)." It sounded like Devon.

When Christa stayed for supper, we did the witches' chants from *Macbeth*. Of course, the witches were benign witches—not like some witches I could name. They brought only bad weather, and so we were in our element (no pun intended), asking each other, "When shall we three meet again, in thunder, lightning, or in rain?"

Once my father came through the front door, saying, "What through the radiance which was once so bright," and by the time he got to the kitchen, my mother and I were joining him with "Though nothing can bring back the hour of splendor in the grass, of glory in the flower." Who would have guessed Dad could recite a Wordsworth poem?

We were eclectic, but we did have our standards. When Jon Cookson came over to leave off something for Stephen, he requested "Gunga Din."

"Sorry, no 'Gunga Din,'" my mother said. "We don't recite 'Gunga Din,' since it's racist, but would you like 'How do I love thee,' Jon?"

"Well, no," Jon said, vaguely horrified.

We were in the midst of great times.

I remember the evening when I reflected how different everything was now than it had been when I had numbly existed at Westlands–King George. It was not a school evening but a Saturday.

My parents and I had had chicken divan for supper, which was one of my favorite meals. If I suggested a dish to my mother, we might not have it the very next day, but she would see that we had it soon. At boarding school, you ate whatever was put before you, and you were expected to get all excited when they treated you to junket.

After supper, I changed into my Bermuda shorts, a cream blouse, and my maroon sweater and was ready and waiting when Christa got to our house. She was wearing a skirt and tights. This was all right. We didn't need to be in lockstep.

"Have a good time, girls," my mother called from the sitting room. "I think you picked an interesting movie."

I hope that we had. Christa and I had spent fifteen minutes on the phone that morning trying to make our choice. I knew Christa really wanted to see *The African Queen*, but she felt that I wouldn't, which was true. We went back and forth between two Hitchcock movies, *Strangers on a Train* and the old *The Lady Vanishes*. We had decided on the latter, when it suddenly came to me that we should see the American film *On the Waterfront*, since it had a new actor named Marlon Brando, who Christa found entrancing.

The movie was about corruption among dockworkers in an area of New York City called the Bowery, intertwined with the story of a failed prizefighter named Terry. It was absorbing and provocative. Christa and I hadn't known much about the Bowery before. We had thought that Manhattan was mainly Fifth Avenue, Central Park, and the Harlem Renaissance. However, as I told Christa on the walk home, New York undoubtedly had many areas, just as London did. London wasn't all Pall Mall, was it?

I said that Brando would probably become a star. Christa told me he already was one.

"Terry is a funny name for a boxer," Christa said.

"That's the States for you," I replied.

When we reached Christa's house, Mr. Cookson came right out and said that he and Christa would accompany me home and then walk back.

I said, "Oh, Mr. Cookson, the streetlights are on. I can do the two blocks on my own."

He replied, "No, this will be fine. My daughter and I don't get much time just the two of us with that lot of boys we have, eh, Christy?" Only Mr. Cookson called Christa "Christy."

They went with me to my front door, where I said good night. My parents were still reading downstairs and eager to hear about the movie.

I said, "The saddest line was when Terry says he could have been a contender, he could have been somebody."

"Yes, it's hard when a person doesn't realize his aspirations," my mother agreed.

"I think that he wasn't just talking about being a prizefighter. He meant a contender for life, for happiness, for everything!" I exclaimed. I started twirling around the sitting room. If Folly had been there, I would have danced with her. I guess my thoughts were changing from Terry in the movie to what it would be like to be a contender.

I stood still again and said, "Well, I'll be going up to bed now."

"Sleep well, love," my father said.

"Good night, darling," my mother said, kissing me.

I went to my room and lightly shut the door. My panda was sitting on the bureau, and my dollhouse, which I hardly ever played with in Tanganyika, was back in the corner. All right, except for some Penguin classics and the slide rule on my desk, the room reflected the interests of a seven-year-old. As someone once said, I was an intriguing combination. This room was mine, indeed it was. What that meant was I didn't have to undress in the closet!

After I put my nightgown on, I went into the bathroom. On sudden impulse, I ran a bubble bath. I soaked for eight or nine minutes.

Back in my room, I turned off the light, bounced onto my bed, and then slipped under the covers. I heard my parents coming up the stairs, softly talking to each other.

And what would a Saturday night have been like back in boarding school? After glop for supper, we would have marched in our uniforms over to the assembly hall, where we would have had to watch whatever innocuous pap the school had chosen for us. The lower school would have seen *Captain January*, *Snow White and the Seven Dwarves*, or the perennial favorite, *The Ugly Duckling* (although I didn't view that as so innocuous). The upper school would have been entertained with something like *The Corn Is Green*, *National Velvet*, or *The Bells of St. Mary's*. Actually, the last would have been preceded by a few words of warning that we shouldn't be so taken with the film that we would convert to Catholicism.

After the film, we would march back to our residence houses, where next on the schedule would be the nightly giving of the school handshake. Then we would be packed off to bed, and just before lights out, I would take my red pen and slash an X through another day on the calendar. There would be still one event to come. Forty-five minutes later, Mrs. Lamberton would walk the hall with her flashlight, sticking it into each room, shining it on each bed.

That was then. This was now, and I was home in London, and no one would shine a flashlight in my room this night. There was a background hum from the traffic outside. I was getting drowsy. Folly had been such a good dog. Tomorrow, my father and I were going to see the Magna Carta. I drifted into sleep at end of a perfect evening.

School continued to go very well. When I had come back to Regency Day, I found that Ted Sanders—his transformation from frenetic Teddy was really quite amazing—was first in the class, with Christa second. Within a week, I was first and Ted second. That meant Christa was third. I told her that would not do and taught her some tricks that enabled her to wrest the second-place spot from Ted. We didn't want him to feel left out, though, so the three of us formed a Monday lunch study group where we went over the lessons for that week. Ted said he was working harder being third than he ever had being first. He was in fact my rival in conjugating Latin verbs. *Amo, amas, amat!*

Miss Linfield said we were the strength of the class. I was not just best student—I was heading up the trio who were the strength of the class!

Actually, all boats were rising. The others in the class saw how hard we were studying and studied harder themselves. They heard us leading off discussions and became eager to participate. Teachers were assigning us extra reading, and they were doing extra reading, too. We were racing through the syllabus of each course. Topics were being presented in more depth, almost as if we were already at university.

Mr. Young, senior school headmaster, was so pleased. He said that if we kept this up, next year we would be the best sixth form Regency Day had ever had.

There was something I needed to be concerned about, but I pushed it aside. I had once heard the phrase "until the South Sea bubble bursts." I thought it had to do with a failed investment scheme, but it seemed to describe the state I was in. I would enjoy the time—the days, minutes, and hours—until the South Sea bubble burst.

Before we knew it, it was Christmastime. Stephen was back home where he belonged, and on Christmas Eve we revived our tradition of going over to the Cooksons.

"Well, here we all are, again," said Mrs. Cookson, as we settled down to hear her and my mother do a dramatic reading of *A Christmas Carol*, my mother being the narrator and Scrooge and Mrs. Cookson playing all the ghosts and Tiny Tim.

"Yes, here we all are, again," said Dennis, who did not understand why everyone but the other Booms instantly broke into laughter.

We had a real Christmas tree for the first time in eight years. It was a tall, full spruce, and my mother's Swiss village looked grand under it. With careful watering, we made it last through the first full week of 1956.

Our intent was always to see Jenny during our home year. Since she had four children under nine, she could not easily come to London. We would make the four-hour trip to Langley Mill in Notts. My mother and I learned from the encyclopedia that in the last century, Langley Mill had been an industrial village "par excellence" and still had the traditional high street. It was not a place we would have tended to go, but we were excited about the excursion. The problem was scheduling. Obviously, we wanted Stephen to come, so it had to be during an Eton holiday at a time otherwise possible for both our family and Jenny's family. We finally were able to set a date, but then Jenny's kids all came down with mumps, so we had to postpone the visit. We tried to arrange another time, but it never seemed to work out.

However, Mum and I unexpectedly saw someone else. It was our custom to go out to lunch whenever I had a half holiday. In boarding school, half holidays had been a dreary proposition. The day students had gone home, and the boarders were just saddled with more extras. Now, though, a half holiday was indeed a half holiday, and we made the most of it.

On this particular day, we went to a new café on the other side of Hyde Park. We had been attracted by the blue-and-white-checked tablecloths. The waitress coming promptly towards us after we were seated seemed slightly familiar. Yet she had a spring in her step and an attractive perm, which wasn't what I had remembered.

"Alice!" my mother exclaimed.

"Mrs. Ord!" Alice said delightedly.

She looked at me. "Can this young lady possibly be Amelia?"

I smiled and said yes.

My mother said, "Stephen is doing a year at Eton. He's nearly six feet, if you can imagine. Oh, Alice, it's so nice to see you. You are looking well."

"I am well," Alice replied. "I've found someone. We were married last spring."

"Oh, Alice, that's glorious," my mother said.

By mental telepathy, my mother and I came to an agreement. We had been each planning to order just a light entrée, but here miraculously was Alice! We would order an appetizer, entrée, and dessert, so we could have bits of conversation as she served each course and be able to give her a large tip as well.

She said she remembered Stephen and me as a busy and industrious pair and that Folly had been a remarkable dog. I was so surprised that she had thought about us at all. We told her a little about the places we had seen in Africa, although we left out boarding school and other things. She said her husband was a wonderful man. He had had his losses, too, so they had set up a memory corner in their flat. It was too late for more children, but at least they had each other. Alice said, as she served our meringues, "Oh, Mrs. Ord, you were the kindest employer I ever had. I'm so sorry I didn't do a better job for you. I was both numb and raw and could hardly face each day then."

"Alice, you did a fine job for us," my mother said.

"Yes," I put in. "Alice, compared to some of the people I've met since, you were tops!" I meant that sincerely, although I didn't exactly know what we were talking about. "Remember that day I tried to stand up on a swing just because Ted—he was Teddy back then—was doing it. You stopped me from falling right quick."

Alice nodded.

My mother gave her as large a tip as would be seemly. Then she pulled out a five-pound note and said, "Alice, a wedding present!"

I had a guinea in my pocket and reached for it, saying, "On behalf of Folly, Stephen, and me."

Alice said she couldn't possibly, but after some back and forth, we prevailed.

As my mother and I were walking to Hyde Park, I said, "Why did Alice refer to it being too late for more children? I never heard of any kid." As I said that, I realized that if she had had a child, that probably meant she had had a prior husband. I turned towards my mother expectantly.

My mother replied, "Yes, his name was Danny. He died in the blitz. He was four. He was very attached to Alice, and he screamed when she tried to put him on a train to go up north to live with strangers, so she kept him with her until she could garner enough resources that they could leave London together. She had almost had it arranged when there came a night that the bombs started dropping so quickly that she judged it unsafe to get to St. Paul's. They were under their table when he darted out to get the cat, and that was when it happened."

I looked down. I remembered my mother telling Stephen and me that there were things we didn't know about Alice. We had made a joke about it. We had even made a joke about the war.

I looked back up because Mum's voice had started to take a distant cast. "It's the most unspeakable thing to be in circumstances where any decision you make about your child will be at a price. She acted out of maternal feeling in keeping Danny with her, but then she felt it had been weakness on her part that had caused his death."

"Her husband?" I whispered.

"He died at Anzio."

Before I could reply, my mother said, "Well," and seemed to collect herself.

She said it should give us a glow, seeing Alice happy and living a life now.

I nodded. Against all odds, Alice had become a contender!

I was beginning to have the thought that I could be a contender myself. My birthday was coming up, the first one I could celebrate at home since I was seven. Stephen would have the weekend off from Eton, and we were all going to see *The Mousetrap*, a play that had been running in London for a while. As an additional present, my parents were getting me a new type of phonograph called a hi-fi. I thought this was more than enough, but my mother said I was going to be sixteen, so let's do it up round. Would I like to have a party?

I didn't know, so I talked it over with Christa, who suggested that I take advantage of my hi-fi and have what Americans called a sock hop.

I invited all my classmates, and each came with records. We served fish and chips and salad, and a frosted angel food cake that Christa and her mother had made for me. Then the music began, with Stephen and Jon Cookson acting as record changers. Everyone danced with everyone, but I must admit I liked dancing with Ted Sanders the best.

The high point of the evening came when Miss Linfield, who had been tipped off by Christa, made a sudden appearance with a gentleman friend and stayed for twenty minutes. They took to the floor, and it looked like they had choreographed each other. Boy, could they move! It was simply extraordinary, considering she was a teacher. We clapped and cheered until, waving good-bye, they swept out the door.

Our dancing went on until, unfortunately, in no time at all, the clock struck ten.

My parents seemed to enjoy my party as much as anyone. Mr. and Mrs. Cookson had come over to keep my parents company, and I heard my mother saying to them, "Isn't this grand? This is the type of experience we missed with the children when we were in Africa."

Two weeks later, Jill Holmes, another girl in my class, had a party—not a birthday party, just a party for the fun of it—and I went to that with Ted. You might say I had a social life again.

I also had a job, albeit a small one. Kenny Cookson, the Final Boom, had a hearing problem. He was doing well in the starting class at Regency Day, especially after I suggested to Miss Taylor that she always face him when speaking to the class in general. No one bothered him about his hearing aid, since Christa had let it be known in the little park that he used it to receive messages from outer space. However, Kenny's hearing slightly affected his speech, so Mrs. Cookson had arranged speech therapy for him on Monday and Thursday afternoons. She had specifically requested those times because she helped Jon give art lessons on Wednesday afternoon. Unfortunately, no sooner had Kenny started than the therapist came up with a pressing reason to change the Thursday session to Wednesday.

The solution was for me to walk with Kenny to his speech therapy on Wednesdays while Christa raced home to be with the other two Booms. I would have done it for free, but Mrs. Cookson was adamant about paying me. I guess it was a good thing she did, because Kenny sometimes seemed so dispirited after the sessions that I was glad to have money to buy him things—yo-yos, rubber balls, and once, a kaleidoscope—to try to cheer him up.

I probably liked the kaleidoscope as much as he did. "Oh, look, Kenny," I said as I demonstrated it to him. "Look at the swirling shapes! Look! Look!" Then I remembered to hand it to him.

"Kenny, do you see dark blue dancing with silver and turquoise?"

He smiled and nodded.

I felt compelled to add, and in a very distinct voice, "Turquoise is a shade of blue."

"I know," the Final Boom said. "My mother and Jon do all the colors."

"Sorry, Kenny," I said. "You live every day with artists, so that was a pretty dumb thing for me to say."

He said, "The speech lady said it looks dumb to move your hands when you talk." Kenny had a habit of gesturing when he was excited and really wanted to get something out. I thought it was quite sensible on his part.

"Well, that remark itself is pretty dumb, yes? Maybe she just doesn't know any better. Maybe she went to boarding school or something."

The Final Boom looked a bit baffled at my last comment but laughed anyway.

I sat in the waiting room when Kenny had his lessons, but I could hear everything, and now I began to pay attention. Mrs. Leach, the speech therapist, never gave him compliments, never made anything amusing, and seemed inordinately irritated when he hadn't done his phrase inflection exercises or he blew out a candle instead of making it flicker as he did consonant sounds. "Don't you think this is important? Don't you think this is important?" she would angrily ask Kenny, who was all of six.

One day I heard her asking him what he wanted to do when he grew up.

"Play in a band," Kenny said.

"Well, I never heard of anyone hard of hearing playing in a band. That's unrealistic. Maybe you can do manual labor. You'll need vocational training."

"Oh," Kenny said.

Walking home, Kenny kept his head down, and when I asked him if he would like to climb the jungle gym in the little park, he said no. I used two weeks of salary to get him toy cymbals and said to him, "you can too play in a band. You already do the drums, and now you have cymbals. You are a percussionist, a percussionist!"

"Yes, Christa taught me that word. I'm a percussionist." Kenny gave me a radiant smile.

That night at home, I told my mother that I thought Mrs. Leach was making Kenny less confident rather than more confident. Should I tell Mrs. Cookson?

My mother thought for a moment and said I should tactfully mention my concerns to Mrs. Cookson once, but only once. If she wasn't inclined to do anything, I was not to bring it up again. "This isn't easy for her," my mother said.

The next day, I was able to catch Mrs. Cookson in the little park. She had come with the Booms, but they were playing with other boys, and all were racing around in the winter sun and talking loudly.

I told Mrs. Cookson in a quiet voice what I had heard and observed. She thanked me and said she had noticed things as well.

"I thought I might be being too sensitive because Kenny is my son —my baby—and well, I think he's the cat's whiskers."

"He's great," I concurred.

"She did come highly recommended from the Speech and Hearing Association, and what do I know about it? I guess that is why I've kept sending him, despite what she said to me."

"What did she say?" This was a little forward of me, given that Mrs. Cookson was an adult.

"She asked how Kenny was getting along with his peers, and I said just fine. I was thrilled, in fact, that he was holding his own in a regular class. Then I made the mistake of adding that I just wished I could find one other lad his age with a hearing problem so he would know he was not alone in coping with this. Silly me, I guess I was hoping she could make an introduction. Do you know what the old biddy said?"

I looked at her expectantly.

"She said, 'It's the devil's work there are so few of them, but thank God there aren't more of them.' I was shocked speechless, Amelia!"

I clasped my hands in front of me and spoke slowly. "I've been around, unfortunately I have. I've seen Mrs. Leach's type over and over. In all honesty, Mrs. Cookson, they are best to be avoided."

"Quite right, Amelia!" Mrs. Cookson said. "We're making a change pronto!"

Kenny never went back to Mrs. Leach. Mrs. Cookson found a speech therapist who had quite a different approach and who thought Kenny was, well, the cat's whiskers. This lady said that with all the support he was getting from family and friends, he only needed to come once a week and agreed to a time that was best for Mrs. Cookson to bring him.

I had done myself out of a job, but that was all right. What with school and other things, I was plenty busy. My parents had subscriptions to the London symphony and the theater, and half the time my father went with my mother, and the other half the time I went with her. My mother treated me to my first opera, *La Bohème.*

By this time it was March, and the Belgravia flower show was coming up. We had heard that a fellow had won over and over with his big bud blooms. My mother and I decided to take him on with a 3-D display: dahlias, daffodils, and daisies. The basic idea had come quickly to us, but we debated over filler. My mother thought baby's breath would be best, but I was insistent on cute little forget-me-nots. Unfortunately, Mum deferred to me, and we realized too late that forget-me-nots gave the arrangement a hint of clutter.

We didn't win the blue ribbon. We didn't win a ribbon at all. Among 425 entrants, the best we could do was second honorable mention.

The head judge, though, seemed to think that we had done extraordinarily well for newcomers. He said based on what we had learned this time around, there would be no stopping us next year.

My mother thanked him for his words but then told him we would not be in London next year. She bit her lip. Once again, the minutes were running out.

The next day was a half holiday. We had just come home from having lunch in Mayfair, and my mother had gone upstairs to change her shoes so we could play badminton when I heard the knocker at our front door. I opened the door a bit, and there were a group of ladies of varying ages, all with ruby-red lips and so much face powder caked on their faces that it looked like they were wearing masks. Some had old-fashioned little black hats with netting, while one wore a floppy straw thing. Two wore mink.

"Is, uh, Mrs. Ord home?" asked the leader, who smelled like cigarettes. She chirped like a bird, so I knew who they were.

The Colonial Office witch wives!

The last time they had come, I had been not yet seven, blissful in my innocence. Crayoning on the porch, I had heard them but not seen them. Now I was looking at them straight on and was armed with knowledge.

"She's otherwise occupied," I said, making sure I sounded very composed. "Good day!" In my head, I murmured, "Shoo fly, don't bother me."

I was about to shut the door when suddenly my mother was right there. "Do come in," she said to the witch wives.

"No, Mum, they were just leaving. They came to the wrong house." I cried.

She and I had a scuffle by the door, she trying to open it and me trying to close it.

My mother was amazingly strong—but then again, she had once considered being an Olympic swimmer—and she won out and opened the door to the bemused witches.

"I apologize for my daughter," she told them. "You know how adolescents are."

"My daughter was at her school during that time. I couldn't have coped," the one in the straw hat said.

I grabbed my coat —navy blue wool, it was—and ran out.

As I did, my mother called after me, "You're in trouble, Amelia! That's for double sure."

I was in trouble, double sure!

My first thought was to go to the little park and sit on a swing. As I was making the turn in, though, I saw Christa there with the Booms. In my state, I couldn't talk to her or to the little boys. They took living at home every day for granted. They were all babes, even Christa. Fortunately they didn't see me, so I continued walking until I was on Pall Mall.

A few minutes later, I found myself in the direction of Buckingham Palace. Queen Elizabeth II had just received accolades for deciding to send eight-year-old Prince Charles to some boarding place. I would have to write to her and suggest that she rethink her decision, but I didn't have to time to attend to it now. I made a veer and went towards Hyde Park. I was at the Speakers' Corner when it occurred to me that it hadn't been the brightest thing to have left my mother by herself with the witch wives, so I headed towards home at quite a brisk pace.

In my aimless walk, I was able to do some thinking. The conclusion I reached was I strongly preferred to stay in London, but that if I had to—if I had to—I could go back to Tanganyika and the compound. I could do things with my mother and with Jory. What I absolutely could not do was to go back to Westlands–King George. I could not go back to boarding school, not after I had lived in ordinary time for a year, not after I had known what normal was. It was not a question of just not wanting to go back to Westlands–King George. I simply could not do it. I would have to convince my parents that I could do the two years of the sixth form by studying at home. It all came down to that.

The witch wives had gone by the time I reached our house. I told my mother I was going up to my room. She shrugged and said "As you wish."

It was only as it became dusk that I remembered my mother and I had been planning to play badminton. It was too late now.

That night, my parents talked to me. They wanted to know why I had been so impolite to my mother's unexpected guests.

I said, "They weren't guests. It was not a social visit. They barged in here just as they did when I was little, hurling hourglasses and casting spells."

"What are you talking about?" my mother asked. "They were Colonial Office wives."

"Quite right," I answered. "Witch wives! Folly had their number. Well, I can tell you one thing. I'm not going back to Westlands–King George!"

"Oh, is that what this is about?" My parents relaxed visibly. "You don't need to go back to Westlands–King George."

Hey, this was going to be easier than I thought.

My mother explained. "Tanganyika will be independent in a few years. Dad really does have to go back and fulfill his commitment until then, but you can stay in school in England."

"I guess we all know that even though Westlands–King George is the best girls school in East Africa, there are better schools in England," my father put in.

"Like Regency Day," I exclaimed confidently.

This was an alternative that hadn't occurred to me. My mother and I could stay in London, and I could keep going to Regency Day, and my father could go back to Africa if he really had to. We would certainly miss him. It would be far from ideal. However, my mother would write to him, and I would write to him, too. He would write back, sending love. It would be a little bit like old times in Devon, except that on holidays we would go there, or he could come here. We'd be near Stephen, and maybe we could get a dog now!

"We were actually thinking of one of the great British schools," my mother said.

"Yes," my father added. "Stephen has been able to go to Eton, and we want you to have a similar opportunity."

"Uh, Eton is not like Regency Day. It doesn't take girls," I pointed out, triumphantly. I was glad to kill this one quickly.

"Yes, to Eton's shame, it doesn't have a girls' division, but there are a handful of girls schools now which offer nearly the same quality of education," my father said. "You see, Amelia, there isn't any discrimination in this family. What the son gets, the daughter gets—at least as close to it as we can give you, considering how backwards this country is in some respects."

I frowned. In my view, the main way the country was backwards was with its infatuation with boarding schools. Queen on down!

"We were thinking about Longwood in Kent," my mother said. "Their students always do well at the A-levels."

"Well, I can't go to Longwood," I cried. "The junior headmistress at Westlands–King George is named Smallwood. The symmetry would be disgusting!"

The implications of what they were proposing swept over me. "You two are going back to Tanganyika, and you expect me to go to go to boarding school in Kent! In Kent, and you seven thousand miles away!"

"At your age, it's very usual," my father said. "I thought you'd be pleased, actually."

"Brigit Peck is going to school in Britain now," my mother said, somewhat hesitantly.

"Well, I don't care. I don't even know her," I answered.

My mother said that I was not to think that they did not want me with them. They did, quite desperately. It was that they had to think of my future. This was such a wonderful opportunity for me. She spoke evenly.

My parents told me that they would come back for Christmas, each of the two years, and my mother at least would stay the whole month. Stephen and I would come to Africa in the summer, and they would arrange something fun for me to do over Easter term. Of course, since I was under eighteen, I would need a guardian in Britain. This was just a formality. My great uncle Anthony would be the one named, but Stephen had agreed to do any needed legwork.

"Stephen will be my guardian? Jesus!" I exclaimed. I had never used that word as an expression before.

My mother opened her mouth and then shut it.

"I have a better idea," I said. "I will design a curriculum for the sixth form that will let me prepare for university at home."

"I don't see how you can realistically do that," my father said.

"I will do it. You will see," I said.

"All right. We will look at what you come up with. You can try, love," my mother said. In other words, she had agreed.

"Fair enough," Dad concurred.

I wrote a letter to Jory that night and asked him what he thought of our combining educational forces. I sent it air mail the next day, and he responded quickly (also by airmail), saying that it would be great. The plan was that we'd study together each day from nine to one and do prep separately for several hours each night. We'd use his tutors for history, English, and physics. I was sure that my mother would do French with us and supplement in literature. Since Jory was a year ahead of me, he could help me in trigonometry, and I could do the same for him in Latin, because I was advanced there.

Now I was very busy, because in addition to my current schoolwork, I was putting together the course of study that I would follow in Africa. I bought five three-ring notebooks and put four tabs in each, for syllabus, reading lists, assignments, and notes. Miss Linfield was willing to help me pull everything together, even getting information for me from other teachers as need be, and I met with her numerous times after school. She was wonderful. Our sessions were fantastic, an unexpected boon.

She was quite interested in what I was trying to do, because she had been around in the educational world. After university, she had taught for a while in a *lycée* in Paris and then had spent a year in New York City teaching at a school called the Brearley School (which, from what

[144]

I could tell, seemed a ways from the Bowery). Coming back to Britain, Miss Linfield had gotten offers from all the major schools, including Longwood, but had chosen to teach at Regency Day, even though all her family thought she was batty.

"Why?" I asked. I meant why anyone would think of Miss Linfield as batty.

"Well," she said, her gray eyes suddenly serious, "I love teaching students doing university preparation. The interaction in the classroom is usually great. Quite frankly, though, I would not like to be scrambling around at all hours of the day, trying to make school a home and being some type of ersatz aunt to a hundred. There are things about youngsters I don't want to worry about. Oh dear, maybe I said too much."

"Not at all," I answered. "I'm going to be a history teacher, and I'll teach in a day school too, double sure." Up to that point, being a history teacher had not occurred to me, but perhaps that was what I would do. I did love history.

It took me three weeks to complete the five notebooks with Miss Linfield's guidance, but it didn't end there. Rather intriguingly, Mrs. Cookson got involved. She had given me a beautiful book about European art, which depicted many of the paintings of the masters. I was overwhelmed, but she said it was my bonus for doing my job with Kenny so well. Then one day Christa came to school and quietly gave me a six-page outline her mother had written out so Jory and I could study European art as an elective. What a treat!

The *pièce de résistance* was that we would also take an American correspondence course. As I wrote to Jory, there was no reason why we shouldn't give our education a trans-cultural flair. I found out that Calvert only did lesson plans up to what Americans called the eighth grade, but they referred me to another place who did the same thing on the secondary level. Promptly, I requested the catalogue, and promptly it arrived. (I was getting a lot of international post at this point.) Using my saved-up allowance, I purchased a course for us on "Reconstruction and the Gilded Age."

Jory was probably wondering what he had gotten himself into. Seven subjects! He said in one letter that he would be working harder with me than he ever had when it was just he and his tutors. I laughed, because Ted Sanders had said about the same thing in a different context. I tried to reassure Jory. Carpe diem. It was only six subjects and an elective!

[145]

It was the first week in April that I showed everything to my parents. They spent an evening going through the material. My mother even made suggestions on how I could improve the French syllabus and said she wanted to be a part of the European art class, double sure!

Both my parents said what I had done was singularly impressive.

"We're all set, then!" I told them. "I'll do home study in Tanganyika."

"I believe in getting all the facts," my father replied. "Let's not make a final decision until you have your appointment at Longwood on Saturday."

"What appointment?" I asked.

My parents had for some reason arranged for me to meet the headmistress of Longwood, Miss Candida Fox. I said that was totally unnecessary, since I had designed my curriculum. My mind was made up. They thought it would be a nice day trip. Kent was beautiful. We'd rent a car, and after my appointment, we'd do some touring. It would do no harm for me just to see Longwood, would it? They were expecting us. We couldn't just cancel.

"Sure we can," I said.

"We can get Miss Fox's advice on whether doing the sixth form at home is feasible," my mother said.

"Already got Miss Linfield's advice," I answered.

This went on for a while, and then I relented. I liked day trips, and if Longwood had to be a part of it, I'd try to stomach it. What did it matter? No one could make me do anything I didn't want to do. (Although I wanted to be a historian, I tended to ignore prior history.)

Saturday, we got up early. I put on my Bermuda shorts and a jersey, because I thought that would be good for touring, but unfortunately my mother insisted I change to my coral dress with lace around the collar, which I usually wore on special occasions. We had words about it, so to speak, and she won out. Then, after rushing through breakfast, we got a train, which took us beyond the outskirts of London where we picked up a car. I didn't usually notice cars, but this was a Daimler. We were trading with the enemy now.

The countryside in Kent was what they call rolling. We went down one rolling green hill where spotted cows munched, and there was a black sign that said in gilt block letter of varying sizes

Longwood School for Girls
Established 1925
Where Excellence Has Its Home

That struck me as funny, so I laughed.

We drove around a circular drive lined with elms to a large Georgian brick building with three stone columns in front and a white cupola on top. We could see girls in hunter-green outfits running around on clipped playing fields off to the side. Just a usual Saturday at a boarding school. Nairobi, Kenya, or Kent, England, it made no difference. My parents had to tell me twice to get out of the car.

"Put your best foot forward, Amelia," my mother said. Perhaps that was supposed to be a pun, so I laughed again.

An elderly doorkeeper ushered us into an echoing foyer, gave my father a booklet on the distinguished alumnae of Longwood, and, as Dad insisted that my mother was up to handling the interview, pointed him to an anteroom where he could wait. Then he led my mother and me down a marble corridor and through three archways to the office of Miss Candida Fox, senior headmistress.

Her office was triangular, with two windows that were too high to see out of. There was a Persian rug of red and purple on the floor, centered under a sepia picture of Westminster Abbey and two mahogany bookcases to go with her mahogany desk and chair. There were also three fold-up metal chairs for visitors. Miss Candida Fox herself was of medium height, with grayish hair done up in what seemed to be a cross between a bun and a French twist. She was wearing a black academic robe over a chartreuse skirt and sweater, and her pumps were two-toned. In other words, she matched her office.

She greeted my mother with great enthusiasm and then turned to me.

"Oh, Amelia, if I may call you Amelia, I've read your transcripts, and I can say without reservation that you are the type of student who would enhance the reputation of our school. I'm so glad that you are interested in coming here." She smiled brightly.

"Actually, I have no interest in coming here," I said, as I wondered why she had been sent my school records.

"Amelia tends to be a little blunt," my mother quickly said. "I think what she means is that she would like to know more about Longwood."

"Excellent," Miss Fox replied. "Longwood was founded by my older sister and me because we wanted a place where girls could get a first-class education from the word go, study astronomy and all sorts of things, and be able to matriculate at the best universities, where the sky would be the limit!"

"Yes," Miss Fox said, warming to her subject. "It was a daring idea for that time, and maybe a bit daring even today." She giggled a little.

"I remember," my mother said, "when it was considered a big thing for me to go to university. I want opportunities to come easier for my daughter."

Miss Fox continued, "We also wanted a happy school, a warm school where each girl, whether she be six or sixteen, has her place. Judging from the number of alumnae who constantly write and visit, I'd say we succeeded. Any questions so far?"

"No, why?" I said. I had a hangnail. I yanked it off.

"You can ask anything you like," she encouraged.

"All right, this is solely academic, since coming here under any guise is not in the cards for me, but I only interact with day students, regardless of my own circumstances, so how many day students do you have?"

"None. All students are full boarders. We want a total school experience for the total school population."

"Total as in totalitarian?"

Miss Fox's tone suddenly became frosty. "No, total as in complete. We want to shape a girl not just in her schoolwork but in every aspect of her life and development.

"That's totalitarianism writ small," I pointed out brightly.

Miss Fox was angry now. "We are not like the Soviet Union or Red China. No indeed."

"Amelia, you're being impolite," my mother exclaimed.

I shrugged.

"No, she's just putting me through my paces," Miss Fox said, regaining her equilibrium. "I'm used to that from the bright ones. Let's return to the concept of a happy school, shall we? Sixth formers, like Amelia would be, get the privilege of being senior sisters. What that means is that each sixth former is paired with a little primary school girl so that the tot can be introduced in a friendly way to the mysteries and joys of boarding school. You can do things like read Enid Blyton stories together, or—"

"I'm not reading simpleminded Enid Blyton stories to anyone. She's a formula writer," I said. "Mum, can we go?"

"Amelia," my mother said in a warning voice.

I decided to make an effort to be conciliatory. "I would not be an effective senior sister anyway, because I would not know much about this—place myself."

"Amelia likes to focus on her studies," my mother said.

"All right," Miss Fox replied. "I'll let being a senior sister be voluntary in her case, but by not being a senior sister, she won't be part of the senior sister salon. You see, once a month, I invite all the senior sisters to my private quarters, and we discuss art and literature, and I serve *coq au vin* or some other dish I've cooked myself, and we have quite a pleasant time."

"That's sound very nice," my mother said. "I wish they had done things like that at my school."

I just shrugged. I wondered why hangnails could vary in texture. Some of them were just limp skin, but others, like the one I had just pulled off, felt almost shell-like. Then, there were borderline calluses.

"Well, Miss Fox, you've told us many good things," my mother said.

"Hardly," I tried to say.

"Shush!" Miss Fox and my mother said together.

"We want a decision Amelia makes to come to Longwood to be one she is ultimately happy with," my mother continued.

"My decision is that I'm not coming to Longwood."

"Amelia, I'm trying to explain your idea," my mother said sharply.

"Stop interrupting your mother. This is about your education and welfare," Miss Candida Fox put in.

I just looked at her. This was getting ridiculous.

My mother took a deep breath and continued. "Amelia has proposed an alternative to her coming to Longwood when her father and I go back to Tanganyika in the fall. She would like to return with us and do independent study for the sixth term. With the help of one of her present teachers—a very thoughtful and kind young woman—she has put together quite an extensive curriculum. Even when you consider that this is Amelia, it's rather amazing what she has done. We've brought examples."

She handed her a couple of my course notebooks and then went on. "In your opinion, do you think she can do this without putting herself at a disadvantage? My husband and I feel that we should get advice on this."

Miss Fox leafed through my Latin notebook. "This seems well done. I give her a lot of credit. I want her here even more. She's obviously no ordinary child."

"No, she's not an ordinary child, but we try to downplay it both for her sake and her brother's," my mother answered.

I should have sensed that trouble was coming now that the topic was veering off to the happenstance of my being a genius. I should have gotten my mother out of there. Instead I just sat there, checking my fingers for additional hangnails.

Miss Fox was now flipping through my American correspondence course. "How will studying a minor era in the history of the States prepare her for Oxford or Cambridge? She can't just study what suits her fancy. Here, our sixth form courses have been carefully designed to give students the core knowledge they need, as well as challenge them."

"May I interject?" I asked. "I plan to adhere to the full British curriculum. This is added enrichment. Also, Reconstruction and the Gilded Age are very important in understanding the domestic issues America faces even now in the middle of the twentieth century. These were times of great paradox—oppression, racism, equality, philanthropy, and greed all jumbled up together. The era mirrors the paradox of the country itself." I knew all this because I had already read the introduction.

It was if I had not spoken. "How will she explain to universities that she didn't go to school for the sixth form?"

"Due to circumstances," I said cheerfully.

"How will they know she even did the work?"

My mother said, "For some subjects, she'd be sharing a tutor with a boy studying at home—he had polio. For others, she plans to report back regularly to her present teachers, and of course I'll be there and able to affirm she did all of it."

"Righto, Mum!" I shouted.

"Mrs. Ord, I truly don't know how much weight a university would give to a recommendation from a student's mother. By the way, how would she go about taking the A-levels? A-levels are given at schools, are they not?" Miss Fox smiled triumphantly.

That was the missing piece that Miss Linfield had offered to research for me. "We'll figure something out," I said casually.

My mother looked uncertain.

Miss Fox clasped her hands together and said, "Mrs. Ord, you said yourself that she must be given every opportunity. We are a first-class girls' school. Then, there is the social aspect. Our contacts go wide and deep. If she was my daughter, I would send her here."

"Well," my mother said, "I feel that Amelia should play a role in the decision."

Miss Fox, among other things, wasn't a very good listener. Speaking firmly, she said, "I'm saying that if she was my daughter, I would send her here."

If I was her daughter, it would be a moot point. I would have stuck my head in an oven long ago.

My mother thanked her for her time, and she thanked us for coming. "Cheerio, Amelia," she said gaily.

"Good-bye" I said. I would not need to see her again.

As we were leaving, my mother said, "This is of lesser importance, but do you have a pool?"

"Not yet," Miss Fox answered, "but we do have the finest stable of horses of any school in Kent!"

"You're not getting me on a horse," I informed her.

She laughed as if she held all the cards.

We rejoined my father in the anteroom, and he enthused over all the distinguished alumnae—doctors, anthropologists, and such—that he had been reading about. Then, as we were finally walking to the car, he asked, "How did you like the headmistress?"

"She's crazy. She even trumps the Smallwood and Lamberton duo at Westlands–King George," I said.

My mother said, "Let's mull things over for a few days. Now, shall we plot out what to see in Kent?"

I decided the least said, the better. I had a lot to do at school. Our class play was going to be *A Doll's House*. Christa was playing Nora, Ted was Torvald, and I was Nora's friend Christine. For some reason, I was also heading the props committee. Actually it was a committee of one, which meant I had to go around scrounging stuff from my mother and Mrs. Cookson. In addition, prep had started for the end-of-year exams. I was hardly giving Longwood any thought. That idea had died on the vine. Some days later, when a letter addressed to "Miss A. Ord" came from Longwood, I just threw it out.

No one was more surprised than me when two weeks after our peculiar jaunt to Kent, my mother announced that she had made an appointment for me to get measured for my Longwood uniform.

"What?" I shouted. "I'm not going there! I thought that was settled."

"Amelia, this is one of the best girls' schools in the country. The faculty is top notch, the headmistress is very distinguished, and—"

"She and I do not get along," I said in a calmer voice.

"Amelia, this is not about personalities. It is about what she and the school can do for you and your future. Dad and I have discussed this at great length. We have agonized over it."

"I am not going to another boarding school! What's the matter with you?"

My father had heard us and came into the sitting room. "Amelia, I wish you would not talk to your mother so heatedly. You're doing it more and more."

"All right," I said, knowing my father liked moderation. "I prefer not to go to Longwood. I would rather stay at Regency Day, but since you have to go back to Tanganyika for a reason that escapes me, I'll go with you and study with Jory. We have it all set." That was true. Jory had just sent me some revisions for my trigonometry notebook, and I had made them.

"We feel you'd be shortchanged if you didn't go to Longwood. Why are you so averse to going there?" my father asked.

"I don't know. I just don't want to," I said.

"No one planning to go to university just studies at home these days," my father said.

"Jory does!" I replied confidently.

"People do admire his determination. He's a positive influence in the compound. I've told his mother that many a time," my mother commented. "He's one of the few people I'm looking forward to seeing when we go back."

Then she sucked in her breath. "Amelia, I see now we sent you to Westlands–King George before you were ready. Stephen might have been old enough to slide into a new routine, but you were not. I am very, very sorry, Amelia. We relied too much on the advice we got and on the fact that everyone in the compound sent their children away to school. I apologize."

My father told me that he was sorry too, but be that as it may, I was more than the right age to be away at school now. Almost everyone in the sixth form was in residence at school. Wasn't Stephen at Eton even as we spoke? This was the British system. Day schools offering a sixth form like Regency Day here in London were the exceptions rather than the rule.

"Conventionality is not morality," I snapped.

"Who wrote that?" My father asked. "Rousseau? Mills? Engels?" Sometimes my father sounded just like Stephen, or maybe it was visa versa.

"Charlotte Brontë!" Mum and I said in unison.

Pressing my advantage, I turned to my mother. "If we were Chinese, would you have bound my feet?"

"I would like to think no," she said hesitantly.

I was going to ask her whether, if we were Tanganyikan, would she have had me go through what Aumi went through. I glanced at my father, though, and remembered he had told Stephen and me never to speak of what happened to Aumi to my mother. I was silent. There were some arguments that could not be marshaled.

My father said, "We're trying to expand your horizons, not narrow them. Miss Fox thinks you'd be compromising your chances for the best place at university if we let you study at home in Africa."

"Well, Miss Linfield thinks I can do it."

"Miss Linfield's very nice," my mother said, "but she's young, doesn't have the perspective of Miss Fox."

"You just don't think I am up to doing the sixth form on my own!" I almost howled.

"Darling, you are obviously up to it, clearly you are. You'd do the sixth form and then some. That's not the point," my mother said.

By this time, no one seemed to know what the point was. Maybe it was that I was so smart it would not be smart to let me do my own education.

My father said, "You say you want to go to Oxford, to St. Hilda's, but—"

"Yes," I said, "and Jory wants to go to one of the Cambridge colleges. We will both do it."

"Why does Jory keep coming into this? Jory would not be able to handle a boarding school where everyone is racing about. Your circumstances fortunately are different!"

[153]

My mother suddenly thought she had figured it out. "I know you and Jory have suddenly been sending many letters back and forth. If your love is true, it will last, it will. You can see each other in the summers, and when you are both at university, you can see each other all the time!"

I look at her in total and utter amazement. There was no romance between Jory and me. Jory had repeatedly told me that his ideal girl was sophisticated and leggy, a young Katherine Hepburn with auburn hair, who would be a good helpmate in a political career. Except for being slim, I didn't resemble Hepburn, and I certainly didn't want to be a prime minister's wife. Those poor women probably had even more social obligations than Mum had in the compound! It was Ted Sanders, with the husky voice and broad shoulders, who was so distantly related to the old goofy Teddy, who gave me the heebie-jeebies.

"This doesn't have anything to do with Jory," I exclaimed, strangely echoing Dad. "I just don't want to live at a school."

"Amelia, we don't see any alternative," my father wearily said. "You may be too young to see this, but we would be failing our responsibility as parents if we let you pass up Longwood to study on your own in Dodoma, Tanganyika."

I looked at him and then at my mother. I decided in an instant that the devil I knew was better than the devil I didn't. "All right," I shouted. "I give up. I'll go back to Westlands–King George. Is that a good compromise? Everyone's happy now?" I hit the arm of the sofa so hard, it left a mark on my palm.

My parents glanced sheepishly at each other. Finally, my mother said, "Darling, you said quite emphatically that you didn't want to return there. I just sent a letter to Nairobi, telling them to release your place. Longwood has so much more to offer you as a sixth former. We're betting you'll like it."

"Oh, Mum, no!" I said, and then, just as I had at age seven, I wailed.

"What you don't realize, Amelia, is that this is hard for your mother and me, too," my father said. "When we agreed to go to Tanganyika, we didn't fully understand the implications for our family. We should have, but we didn't."

"And you don't really want to go back there," I said.

"No, we don't really want to go back there, but I have to see it through." My father was winning his argument with me but sounded defeated.

My mother was pale and almost twitching. She said we should try to enjoy what remained of our home year. Stephen would be home for the Easter holidays in a week. Wouldn't that be grand? We'd see *A Midsummer Night's Dream*, go on an excursion to Hampton Court.

I tried to enjoy the dwindling time, but there was a difference. I had to tell Miss Linfield that I would not be using the notebooks she had helped me to prepare, and she said it was a rum deal, but she was sure I would light up the sky at Longwood. After that, we didn't speak of it. She was actually very busy helping Christa, Ted, and the others in the class pick their sixth-form courses. Christa was voted president of the history club, and Ted was assuming the reins of the Latin Club. Everyone else's lives were going to go on.

We put on *A Doll's House* to great applause, and Christa, as Nora, slammed the door that reverberated throughout Europe. I wished I could have done something similar.

Ted asked me out to a snack bar. I think it was supposed to be a date, because it was a Friday night; and since I was sixteen, my parents let me go. We talked about school and music called rock-and-roll and ate ice cream. He seemed to look at my front a lot as I scooped my mint ripple. My breasts were small but round and perky, creating a hint of cleavage. I had to admit they were my best feature. I decided that if he asked me out again, I'd wear a little tighter sweater.

He did, and I did, and we went to a movie, *North by Northwest*, after which he said, "Should I kiss you?"

We were a block from my house and had been lightly holding hands. I leaned towards him—his shoulders were even broader than they were at the start of the year—and his lips met mine. We kissed several times, but then I murmured sadly, "I can't, Ted. I'm being sent away again, and I just don't know what's up or what's down."

He accepted what I said, which made me want him more.

A few weeks later, he asked Christa out, and she said that under the circumstances, she really couldn't. Next, he asked Jill Holmes, and she said yes. I suspect he kissed her quite a bit. Maybe they went farther.

I got the highest mark that any Regency Day student had even gotten on some national exam—I forget which—earning me a royal merit certification. Miss Linfield smiled at the end-of-year ceremony, and Mr. Young shook my hand over and over. "You're the strength of the class and the pride of the school, even though we had little to do with it. We all wish you well in your future endeavors."

"Thank you," I said faintly.

Then it was the summer holidays, which meant the minutes and hours were really running out. Stephen, graduated from Eton, was home, running in and out of the house with friends and boisterously packing for Cambridge. He thought the world was his oyster.

Only a few months ago, I had had the hope of being someone, of being a contender. Now I had no idea how I would turn out.

CHAPTER 6

Top Student

Kent, England, 1956–1958

THE SUNDAY IN September my parents dropped me off at Long-wood was one of the saddest days in my life. It was quite soon after we had had three fleeting weeks in the Lake District, but still they made a little trip out of it. The day before we had gone up to Cambridge with Stephen and helped him set up his digs, which he would be sharing with Jon Cookson and a fellow he knew from Eton. Then we went out to one last supper as a family and stayed overnight in a university guest house.

"Get in touch with me if you need me, sis," Stephen said as we were about to start out towards Kent in the morning.

"All right, Stephen," I said tonelessly. I had a miserable, gone feeling in my stomach.

At 3 p.m. I was standing by the side of the circular drive of Long-wood School. I had already been checked into Victoria Hall, the three-story stone building where all the sixth formers were stuck, and had met the matron, who was called Matron. Now my parents were trying to say good-bye to me.

"You will be so far away, "I said, my eyes filling with tears.

Both my parents sought to reassure me that the distance was only geographical, although once my mother tripped over her words and said geological.

They reiterated that they were coming back to London the day before my Christmas holidays. That was just three months, just like when I was at Westlands–King George.

Déjà vu! It made me cry more, oblivious to the milling girls giving me strange looks.

I clung to my mother, who was trembling slightly, but finally we had to disentangle. They would have to hustle to Heathrow as it was.

"Best of luck, darling," Dad said. "It will be all right. You'll see!"

They got into the rental car, turned back and waved, and then as the car began to move I saw my mother put her head in her hands. I watched the car go down the drive and out of sight.

I trudged back to the room that had been assigned to me and found my roommate there. She looked like a version of the girl named Buffy back at Westlands–King George, except that she wore makeup and was curvier. She was putting things into the bureau.

Straightening up and putting her hands on her hips, she said, "Well, Ord, what's your story?"

I said, "I've been in boarding school most of the time since I was seven. That's my story."

She said, "That's not a story. I've always been here. If I had had to stay with my parents and gone to a town school—ugh, ick, and vomit —it would not have worked."

Then she said, "I've got the top three drawers of the bureau. I've got rank. You can use the bottom drawer."

I answered, "I don't need it. I never really unpack. I keep almost everything in my suitcase."

"Oh, all right," she said. "Suit yourself. So what's your sport?'

There was no point saying swimming, since the place didn't have a pool, so I said, "I play badminton with my mother, and—and I used to play Scrabble with my friend Jory."

I was tired and wasn't thinking, so I added, "He had polio."

"Sounds like the games were exciting," she said, smirking.

I just shrugged.

She curled a strand of her strawberry blond hair around a finger and asked, "Why did you get out of being a senior sister?"

"Don't want to lie to the little ones," I replied, as I hung up my calendar on my side of the room.

"Oh, all right," she said, and made a funny face.

I asked, "Do they poke a flashlight in forty-five minutes after lights out here?"

"What?" she said. "Yeah, they do, but that's not a problem. If you have a place to go or want some exercise, so to speak, just line up three pillows under your covers, and Matron will never be the wiser. As she is starting down the side hall, make a run for the back stairs or, if you're daring, go down the trellis. Did you bring extra pillows?"

"No," I said.

"Anyway, I'm Roxanne, but you can call me Rox." She cast a merry look at the pictures of my parents, Stephen, and Folly I was putting on a shelf.

"Well, I've got no more time to waste on introductions," she continued. "I want to talk with my friends." She sashayed out of the room.

It seemed almost instantly that a clutch of girls or maybe a coven had collected just outside in the hall. My roommate appeared to be a leader. She just had to murmur something, and they all laughed.

I had the rest of the afternoon to get through, and then there was dinner in the cavernous dinner hall. After the meal of stew or something was over, everyone was steered into the cavernous auditorium for a weird ceremony called First Rites and Assembly. The lights were switched off, and the teachers in black robes and carrying candles marched in single file behind Miss Fox up to the stage. At a certain moment in center stage, she boomed out, "Veritas!"

The teachers replied, "Veritas!"

Next, everyone in the audience shouted, "Veritas!" and the lights went back on. I don't know if this was meant to be symbolism or what. I was shivering a little, because I knew this was about the time my mother was getting on the plane to Dar with my father, and I was stuck here.

There was tuneless singing all around me, a song that had a one line chorus, "lovely, lovely Longwood."

I looked up at the stylized naked cupids carved into the molding.

Miss Fox spoke for about a half hour. The gist of it was that learning was thrilling, and being seduced by knowledge was better than being seduced by men. There were a few titters. My mind wandered to Ted. He and Jill Holmes had lasted as an item only until the summer, but I assumed that he would find someone else.

"Praise God from all blessings flow!" Miss Fox shouted.

Finally it was over, and we were sent back to residence halls.

"Ta, ta," my roommate said, when we were in our room. "Sometimes I take the trellis route." With that, she climbed out the window.

I took out my red pen and slashed an X through the date on the calendar. There were eighty-three more days to go.

I was just about to lie down when I heard a plaintive voice cry out with a twinge of cockney, "Crickets! First night away from home and I can't get down in bed!"

It was Charlotte Barnard, the other new girl in the sixth form and the one scholarship student.

I ran down the hall and said through her closed door. "It's just a boarding school trick. They short sheeted your bed. Just untuck everything and make the bed up again."

"All right, I'll try," she said. "Thank you."

I didn't offer to come in to help her. I felt too dreary.

It was hard to get to sleep. When the flashlight shone on my bed and the three pillows in the other bed, I was still wide awake. My parents' plane was crossing Europe. It was over the Mediterranean, maybe over Malta, and I was here, and even Stephen was all the way in Cambridge. I was just drifting off when my roommate clambered in the window, followed by three other giggling girls. I hoped this wasn't going to be a regular 2 a.m. occurrence.

The next morning, it was no small feat, putting on the Longwood uniform in the cramped closet. The cream scooped-neck blouse fastened up the back. The long, heavy hunter-green skirt had a series of side buckles, and the matching jacket had ten fabric-covered buttons that needed to be secured with loops. In addition, sixth formers got to wear (had to wear) nylon stockings with a school-issued garter belt.

I thought of Christa getting up in her own, if tiny, room, quickly donning a plaid kilt and a mock turtleneck, pulling on knee socks, and then running down the stairs for the first day at Regency Day, calling, "Hey, Mum, are the Booms organized? We need to get a move on."

I couldn't find my hairbrush. I opened the door so I could see while I rummaged around in my suitcase. It had just fallen to the bottom under a lot of things, but next to it was a small paper bag. I undid the tie that held it closed and saw that it was full of dark weedy stuff. It had a faint dusky smell, which I had smelled once walking by the house next to the Hobsons. Jory had told me what it was. He said that there was a certain set in the compound that used cannabis quite regularly.

"This yours?" I asked, holding the bag out to my roommate.

"We were in a scurry hurry last night and didn't know where to put it," she said, grabbing it. Then she added with a hint of menace in her voice, "It would not be in your interest to tell."

"I'm certainly not going to tell," I replied. That was true; it was not my job to help enforce the rules.

Her face relaxed a bit.

"I just don't want to find it mixed in with my things again," I said. I paused, as I realized that I could put one over on the headmistress.

"There's a compartment here." I pulled back some elasticized fabric on the left inside of the suitcase. "You can put the stuff there. The deal is that you are not to tell me when you put it in or when you take it out, and I won't look. You also need to be sure that there's nothing in there by the holidays or when I'm otherwise leaving. Those are the only times I'll check."

"Righto, good girl!" Rox agreed, faintly smiling. While we had been ironing this out, the bag had disappeared.

My existence at Longwood was now in full swing.

I was older now, but in many ways it was just like being in West-lands–King George, only more so and in a cold clime. I went to classes and then to my extras—ceramics, chapel chorus, and ice skating in this reiteration. Every minute was regimented, and time was coiled in on itself again, halt, heavy, and spastic, a palpable, enervating thing I had to push through. I had eighty-two days to go, then eighty-one, then eighty.

With eleven weeks to go, I got the first letter of the term from my mother. The last letter she had sent to Westlands–King George in the spring of 1955 had been numbered 306. The first letter she sent to me at Longwood in the fall of 1956 was numbered 307. She said nothing had changed in the compound in the year we had been gone. There was still the endless social whirl and an air of unreality. Jory was several inches taller and looked well. He still did water exercises, although the Hobsons were now resigned to the assumption that he would always need a cane. My mother said she missed Stephen and me. It was hard being in Tanganyika with us in England. She couldn't wait to get our letters. As always, my mother ended the letter by saying, "Your father joins me in sending you our greatest love."

I wrote back and said that Longwood's library was adequate—if not creatively stocked—and that the chemistry lab had slides, microscopes, and chemicals. The good class was Greek, where only one other girl had signed up, and so we had a tutorial. Mrs. Lefko promised us we would be reading *The Iliad* in short order. Otherwise, the teaching was uninspired and consisted of mainly of lecture, with the emphasis being on the regurgitation of assumed facts. For example, my first assigned history paper was on how the assassination of Archduke Ferdinand had plunged the world into war when a better question was, of course, why the assassination of Archduke Ferdinand had plunged the world into war. Nevertheless, I had just gotten my first merit card for being first in the class, which was no great feat in this place. I wrapped up the letter saying I missed her and my father and I guessed even Stephen, although he was at least in the country, and in case anyone was wondering, I would have strongly preferred not to have been at Longwood. I signed the letter "love, Amelia."

I did not mention to my mother in this letter or in subsequent ones that under the gloss of the minute-by-minute scheduling and total regimentation, it was a free-for-all in this place, the Wild West, if you will. The fact that half the girls in the sixth form dormitory went out on the town after compulsory lights out was only the beginning. Taught to speak like cultured ladies, Longwood girls cursed like combat soldiers. Some of the word combinations were really quite inventive. Smoking was forbidden, so kids smoked cigarettes (along with weed) in the tunnels that connected the academic buildings. Ditto for drinking. Daughters of members of Parliament chafed at how the school doled out their spending money. They stole from the school store—and from village shops. A third cousin of the Rhys-Joneses got pregnant by some boy or other because she thought it would be amusing to do so, given that she was a third cousin of the Rhys-Joneses and it was just some boy or other. (This got her out of Longwood, so I didn't know the end of this story.).

There was a certain general nastiness here that hadn't existed to quite the same degree at Westlands–King George. Perhaps it was because here there were three large dormitory halls, one for each division of the school, while at Westlands–King George, each girl was assigned to a small residence house where she stayed all the way through. Mrs. Lamberton at Margaret House did her job entirely without feeling, in my view, but she did do what she considered to be her job, one aspect of which was to see that no girl was constantly harassed or picked on. Even at age seven and eight, I had had the vague notion that she was protecting me. At Longwood, Matron ineffectually shined a flashlight into each room each night, but otherwise she just wandered around vaguely. She seemed to have no desire to be in the right place at the right time.

Actually, I was somewhat insulated, because my being an academic whiz-bang inspired a modicum of awe. The fact that I provided a place to stash didn't hurt, either. Apart from calling me "note kisser" because I kissed my mother's letters, my roommate and her friends left me alone. The same was not true for pale Charlotte Bernard.

Her complexion was blotchy, and it was felt that she did not wear the dreary school uniform with flair. From the drabber side of Marylebone Street in London and with a bit of cockney in her voice, she occasionally said "me" when she meant "my," which our classmates found wildly amusing.

Equally hilarious to them was the fact that her mother worked in the hardware section of Harrods and moonlighted as a dog groomer. No one seemed to hear when Charlotte said she had only a flicker of an actual memory of her father, who had died on D-Day.

Having been welcomed the first night with a short-sheeted bed, she found the hem of her nightgown sewn together the second night. It went on from there.

Although she had probably never been on a farm, some clever girls had taken to calling her Charlady Barnyard. It would be an exaggeration to say everyone joined in, but Roxanne's group—I called them the gaggle—made animal noises whenever she passed by. "Gobble, gobble. Oink, Oink. Cheep, Cheep, Cheep. Baa-a!" Then someone would say, "Hey Charlady, sweep my barn!"

One afternoon—there were fifty-six long days to go—everyone was in the meeting room of the dormitory for delivery of the post. I had finished reading my letter from Jory when I saw Charlotte look up sadly from the letter she had received.

"Me—my mum and I were never apart for a night before this fall," she said. "She misses me ferociously."

"Ferocious like a bull?" One girl said. "Moo! Moo!"

"That's a cow," Roxanne pointed out.

"Her mother looks like a cow. I saw her picture," a third girl said.

Charlotte fled the room in tears.

"Drop dead, you creeps," I said. I was still trying to follow my moral compass, but the circumstances at Longwood were such that I had somewhat relaxed my rule against name calling.

"Bugger you," the girl who had started it said.

"Oh, forget it," Rox said to her.

Matron wafted in. "Enjoying the post, girls?"

"Yes, Matron!" There was a chorus.

A few evenings after that—we were finally into the second month —only Charlotte and I were eating supper in the sixth-form section of the dining hall because it was the night of the senior sister salon. Unlike me, Charlotte had wanted to be a senior sister, but my idea that you shouldn't be a senior sister unless you really knew about this place had really caught on with Miss Fox. She had disqualified Charlotte.

I was sitting on the right side of a long table at one end, and she was sitting on the left side of the table on the other end. I was trying to compose an essay for literature class, comparing *Of Human Bondage* to *Goodbye, Mr. Chips*, although the fact that boarding school figured into both books made me want to throw up, so I guess this wasn't the right activity for dinner. Charlotte was just mechanically shoveling cod and boiled potatoes into her mouth.

"Why are you here?" I asked her suddenly.

She gave a little start and looked at me with perplexed, baleful eyes.

"No, I mean, you can do lots better, so why are you here with this crowd?" I got up and moved my plate so I was sitting closer to her.

She spoke deliberately. "It is because the vicar says I'm smart and I will have a wide-open future if I prepare in the right way for university. My mother believes it, too."

This sounded eerily familiar if you deleted the vicar part.

"Listen, Charlotte," I said. "There are boarding schools everywhere the British are—or think they are—but these schools don't quite have a monopoly. There are a handful of day schools, especially in London, that offer the full pre-university curriculum."

I had her attention.

"Yes, I'm only here due to circumstances," I continued, lowering my voice a little. "If my parents hadn't gone back to Africa, I'd still be at my real school, Regency Day. I had friends there and everything." I couldn't help boasting.

"They offer calculus?"

"Double sure, in the upper sixth form," I answered.

"Whereabouts in London is it?"

"The part of Belgravia closest to Hyde Park."

A smile came across her face, making her almost pretty. "Why, that's near Harrods! I could take the tube in with my mother and then walk a few blocks."

"Definitely," I said.

"There's the money part," Charlotte said doubtfully.

"We'll figure it out as we go along," I assured her.

Thus began the project to spring Charlotte.

It helped that her mother was agreeable to Charlotte making the change, and it helped ever more that the vicar who Charlotte and her mother considered to be the authority on everything had heard of Regency Day.

There was lots to do, and it all had to be done on the sly. One night, I told Matron I had to call my brother to talk about our sick aunt. (We didn't have an aunt; both our parents were only children.) When she left me alone in her sitting room, I didn't ring Stephen, I rang Christa and asked her to get a Regency Day application and send it to me pronto.

Two days later, I had it in hand, and in the flurry of everyone getting mail, I handed it to Charlotte.

As part of the application, she had to write an essay, and she wrote a bang-up one. The title was "This is really true," and it was about how when she was in primary school, her mother would write her a note every morning in which she told Charlotte one thing about her father. If her mother began by writing "this is really true," that meant she was telling Charlotte something factual, such as her father had been six feet two. If, on the other hand, she wrote "this could be true," she was telling Charlotte something that might have happened but for her father's death in the war, something like her father would have saved all his change for weeks so he could take Charlotte to the circus.

In the afternoon, when Charlotte let herself into their flat after using the hall phone to tell the vicar's wife she was home, she would find the note on the kitchen table. She would read it straightaway and write a reply note, which she always started with the phrase "this could be true" before she described something that might have happened that day if her father was still alive. For example, he would have played eight games of crazy eights with her when he learned how well she had done on her spelling test that day.

With the letter finished, Charlotte would change out of her school clothes so she could wear them the next day and be presentable. Then she would wash the vegetables for supper, set the table, play with her doll, listen to the wireless, and above all, remember never, ever to open the door to strangers. Finally, finally, the clock would say five-thirty, and she would hear her mother's footsteps on the stair, and Charlotte would be ready to greet her with the letter the second she walked into the flat. Her mother would read it straightaway and then say something like, "That's my bright girl for doing so well in spelling. After we eat and do the washing up, we'll have ourselves ONE game of crazy eights, we will."

It was in this manner that Charlotte got extra practice in reading and writing and didn't feel so latch-key. She never knew what she had and what she didn't have, except that whatever it was, it was more than many others had, and that was really true.

I read the essay at Thursday afternoon tea when Charlotte and I were sitting in a corner behind a potted plant, pretending to enjoy the plain little biscuits. The piece was so good it gave me shivers. I made some suggestions about syntax, and that was it.

She had her grades from her old city school and a recommendation from the vicar, which she put in the application package. However, she also needed a recommendation from Longwood, and obviously she could not ask for one. I thought for a while, and then told her that I had credibility with both Mr. Young and with Miss Linfield, who, as luck would have it, was head of the admissions committee. I would write the recommendation.

This was daring—letting the gaggle store cannabis in my suitcase did not have a patch on this. I wrote the letter in proctored study hall, my stationery placed inside my Latin notebook, my chemistry text-book propped up in front of the notebook. I wrote that Charlotte might lack polish, but she was a conscientious student who was more than holding her own in her classes at Longwood. I thought she would blossom in Regency Day's more progressive social atmosphere.

I loaned Charlotte extra stamps, and just when the postman was leaving the school after collecting the outgoing post from the designated tray in the dormitory's foyer, she ran after him and slipped him the package as he headed out the gate.

The following Tuesday—it was the ninth week, and I was not expecting anything in the post because my mother's letters usually came on Wednesdays—I received a small cream-colored envelope. I opened it and took out a scalloped-edged note card on which was written in delicate script:

Dear Amelia,
   I think this is possible. Be of good cheer.
   Fondly,
   Claire Linfield

I read the note over and over. She had written "fondly." She had signed her full name. It was a small gift in the gloom, this letter from Miss Linfield.

In a few days, Charlotte had her formal acceptance into Regency Day, starting with the next term. The problem for me to solve now was fees. It was never publicized. It was just a private matter between the school and the student's family, but the school reduced the tuition in many cases. What this meant, though, was there were no full scholarships. They were offering Charlotte the highest reduction, seventy-five percent.

Charlotte said that she felt that if she and her mother tightened their belts, they could come up with some of the additional money. The vicar said the church would also contribute a share, since from day one, she had been the hope of the parish. I came up with five pounds from the funds I secretly kept for a quick getaway, but twenty-five pounds more was needed to get her through a year and a half at Regency Day.

From the Rhys-Jones business, I had heard in swirling conversation that there was an organization that helped rich girls in trouble. Briefly, I thought about going to them, saying I was in trouble, which was more than true. I was in Longwood, wasn't I? Then I would get the money and give it to Charlotte. I began to worry, though, that they would insist on giving me some icky medical exam. Well no, I couldn't do that.

Perhaps I could raid the cannabis stash and sell a bit of that, but there were problems with that approach, too.

In desperation, I wrote to my mother. I told her about Charlotte and how her widowed mother missed her, about the class prejudice she was subject to at Longwood, and how Regency Day would be much better for her. I asked my mother if she and my father would contribute the needed twenty-five pounds.

My mother wrote back by return mail or at least what passed for return mail between Kent and Tanganyika. She did this even though she had just posted my usual letter for the week. Letters number 316 and

317 arrived just a day apart, a boon of sorts. Her answer was yes. They were delighted to do this. In fact, they had wired Regency Day thirty-five pounds, so Charlotte's mother could buy Charlotte a few outfits with some of the money she had planned to use for tuition.

That gave me pause. Next term, I'd still be wearing the heavy, stiff Longwood uniform every day, while Charlotte, like Christa, would be able to mix and match according to her own inclination.

I went back to my mother's letter. She was pleased that I had taken an interest in another's well being. She said I was a good girl. She and my father were counting the days before they flew back to London for Christmas with Stephen and me. Weren't we fortunate to have renters who went away for the holidays? We would have a grand time! She ended the letter as she always did: "Your father joins me in sending you our greatest love."

I read the letter several times, kissed it, and put it in my pocket with the letter I had received from Mum the prior day. The two envelopes rustled together like leaves. I wondered if my mother still listened for the rustle.

I got up and beckoned Charlotte into the cloakroom off the foyer. There among the swinging hangers and the green umbrellas with Longwood insignia and the regulation mackintoshes, I said, "You're set! You have a benefactor."

"Who?" she asked breathlessly.

"Wishes to remain anonymous," I replied.

"Well, when I have a career, I will find out, and I will pay the money back. In the meantime, please extend me—my—gratitude." She smiled, and just as before, she looked almost pretty.

We left the cloakroom, and I went one way and she went the other, so as not to arouse suspicion.

That night after I had slashed another red X on my calendar, I licked my finger and drew the figure one in the air. I had helped save one. One, I had helped save!

At long last, one of my schemes to bust out of boarding school had worked, not for me but for someone else.

I don't know how Miss Fox reacted when she heard Charlotte was giving up her scholarship and leaving Longwood at the end of the term. Charlotte didn't say, and I didn't ask.

I did see the gaggle set upon her when they heard the news. "Gobble, gobble, Charlady" they said. "Are we not good enough for you? Going home to roll in the hay with a chimney sweep?"

Charlotte, in a somewhat doubtful voice, said what I had suggested she say. "Dobble, dobble! Go sell witch jelly!"

"You're strange!" they said as they backed away.

"Why are they so mean?" Charlotte asked me.

"A lot of them were imprisoned in attic nurseries as babies and then sent here as soon as they could hold a pencil. They just didn't have the advantages you had in childhood, and that's really true," I explained.

"Oh!" she exclaimed, her whole face lighting up.

The days were finally at long last waning; bold Xs covered almost three months of my calendar. Just as I had at Westlands–King George, I killed the time methodically. I won this award, that award, and the other award, and then the twelve weeks were over and I went back to London, where my parents, who had just flown back from Tanganyika, were waiting for Stephen and me.

Stephen talked quite a bit about Cambridge and being what he was happy to have my father call a Cambridge man. My parents hardly spoke about the compound, and I said nothing about Longwood except that it should be blown up. We set up our Swiss village under a six-foot Christmas tree, and once again the smell of pine filled the sitting room and we saw the Cooksons and my mother and Mrs. Cookson read *A Christmas Carol* as they always did when we had Christmas in London.

I tried to pretend this was still our home year, and I was almost successful, until two days before New Year's, when Christa and I went on a double date with Ted Sanders, meaning Christa and I were Ted's double date. We went to the American film *Bell, Book and Candle*, which was good enough if you overlooked the fact the screenwriter had probably never met a witch. After the movie, we went to an ice cream place, and the two of them started talking about a Latin banquet they were having at school in January. They'd both be at the head table, Ted as Julius Caesar and Christa as Caesar's wife, who must be above suspicion. Hence she would not be able to sit in his lap, much less feed him grapes. They were laughing until Christa looked at me and quickly changed the conversation back to Jimmy Stewart.

I smiled wanly. There was no reason for them to be in stasis just because I was.

The next afternoon, my mother and I went as guests to the indoor pool we had belonged to before. Suddenly it seemed everything was running short, and even though I did laps as fast as I could and even beat my mother, I could see minutes and hours dissolving. I kept looking at Mum's face when we got out of the water, and as she had when I was younger, she said, "Yes, darling, yes?"

A week and a half later, I went forlornly back to Longwood as my parents flew back to Africa. Surprisingly, old Rox had chosen to continue as my roommate. I guessed that a convenient hiding place for cannabis was too good to give up.

The main difference for this term was that I would not be going home for the next holiday—wherever home was. Tanganyika was just too far for Stephen and me to go there, or for my parents to make a second trip to London. What this meant was there were 196 days to go, twenty-eight weeks to expire, more than a half a year to endure, counting the holiday that would be no holiday. All my rituals, all my calibrations based on eighty-four days were thrown topsy-turvy. How was I to massacre that much time?

I finally I decided that, whatever the reality, I would continue my prior practice of killing time in day-by-day bites and twelve-week chunks. Maybe something would happen. I just hoped my mother didn't die in the interim.

The morning after the new term started, with some infinity of days to go, Miss Fox required me to see her so she could tell me I won first prize in a national independent school French essay contest.

"Everyone at Longwood is so proud of you," she enthused.

I just shrugged, knowing the gaggle could not have cared less.

"Why did you pick that Sartre play, *No Exit?*" she inquired.

I said glumly, "The instructions were to write about what you know, but do it in French."

"That really doesn't answer my question," she said.

I shrugged.

"Well, study hard," she said brightly. "It's a new term, and I'll get you on a horse yet."

That wasn't worthy of a response, so I turned and left.

At least Charlotte was out of this place. She was apparently settling into Regency Day well. According to a letter I got from Christa, they didn't see much of her after school because she lived in another part of

London and had to help her mother with things, but everyone really liked "Lottie." She could do a Charlie Chaplin imitation that had people rolling in the aisle. She won all the class debates. Given fifteen minutes to formulate her position, she could argue like she was a barrister or something. Christa was somehow hanging on to first in the class, which she had assumed after I left, Ted was second, but Lottie was quickly beating out Sebastian Gray for third. They all missed me, Christa kindly added.

I was happy for Charlotte—Lottie to her friends. Truly, I was. I had had a hand in it, but that didn't help my predicament. I was so oppressed by time, so pressed in by time. Matron shined her flashlight into each room every night. You've heard it all before.

I turned seventeen that term but felt I had slid back from sixteen. Matron put a pound cake in front of me at Thursday afternoon tea and had me blow out the one candle she had lit. There was a smattering of applause, led by Rox. My parents sent me a card, a new watch, and *Too Late the Phalarope* by Alan Paton. Delivered from a florist shop was an Africa violet with a note that said, "Have a nice day, Sis! Love, Stephen." Stephen had never done such a thing, and I didn't know whether he meant it as a joke or what, but I gave him the benefit of the doubt and wrote him thank-you note.

Somehow, I got through that term. Somehow, I got through a month in Bath with my great uncle Anthony whom I barely knew and Stephen zipping in and out, when he wasn't occupied with friends. Somehow, I got through the next term (in my usual stunned blaze of academic glory). Three times, I climbed Mount Everest.

With the dead weeks littered about, it was finally summer, and Stephen and I flew to Tanganyika. My parents met us in Dar with cheers, and I cheered, too, because I had made it through. Stephen just looked around and said, "Well," and then "Hello, Mum. Hello, Dad." My father patted him on the back, calling him "our Cambridge man," and he was pulled in.

Just as we had when we had first come to Africa ten years ago and thought we were going on some kind of adventure, we took the train up to Dodoma, the four of us. Once more, we saw the plains and the baobab trees and the goat herders. We saw flamingos, zebras, and gazelles. I was aware, though, as I hadn't been back then, that we had to sit in the "European only" section of the train, and it was the only section with upholstered seats. Holding on to my mother's hand, I started speaking Kiswahili, and my mother followed suit, and then my father and finally Stephen, whose Kiswahili was the most limited. Despite the strange glances of the whites around us, we spoke Kiswahili the whole trip.

In the bubble of the compound, nothing had changed. Even the cannas were laid up in the same fashion. The prevailing notion still was that existence was an art best practiced with drinks at the club. I saw my mother's face take on a weary and constrained look every time she and my father had to go out for the evening or people had to be invited in.

It was good, though, to see Jory after almost two years. He was taller and more solid looking, except for his thin leg, and he was, as always, merry and optimistic. The great excitement was that he had been accepted at King's College in Cambridge for the fall.

I regretted that Jory and I had not been able to study together as planned, so he, my mother, and I formed a study group for the summer. Every morning on either our or the Hobsons' veranda, we pursued the American correspondence course on Reconstruction and the Gilded Age that I had gotten when I had the delusion that I could avoid Longwood. For an hour or two, we would be in the years following a foreign country's civil war, the nation still bleeding, Lincoln gone, reconciliation abandoned, racism unabated and on a parallel track, the rise of the industrial age and industrial wealth, Fifth Avenue figuratively paved with gold.

Often, Jory's mother would join us to be what she called an auditor. As she enigmatically explained it, "This old dog wants to learn new tricks!" She astounded us one day when we were talking about the financial scandals of the 1870s and she timidly speculated that maybe part of the problem was that business enterprises became bigger and more complex without a corresponding change in bookkeeping.

"I think you are right, Grace," my mother said. "Double-entry accounting wasn't in use yet."

"That's what I think I mean, yes!" Mrs. Hobson said, looking pleased.

We spent every afternoon at the pool. Jory and I talked politics in the water and laughed and played water tag. I swam laps with my mother, back and forth and up and down. We were trying to make our time last as long as we could.

The days fell into a pattern, Stephen going to a job of some type that he had in my father's office and I staying close to my mother and doing things with her or Jory and then reading in the evening as my parents went to or hosted endless parties. As always happened, though, the minutes and the hours began to sift and dissolve. Soon, it was the next to last day.

I told my parents that I really preferred not to go back to Longwood. The first paper I had written for the correspondence course had already been graded in Philadelphia, Pennsylvania, and returned. I had gotten an American A+. The director of the program had written me a personal note, saying that my referring to the disbanding of the abolition society in 1866 as "tragically premature" was very insightful. He hoped I would be able to stop by the next time I was in the States. (I had wanted to try out a new identity, so I had sort of implied that I was from the East Coast, and had been extra careful to spell colour "color").

Anyway, I said to my parents that if I could do well enough in a course designed in another culture about an era that I was not familiar with, I could certain handle the British curriculum with a little help from Mum for just one year. I could just update my notebooks. I'd write to Miss Linfield, with whom I was now on a first-name basis, and she would make suggestions.

My parents would not hear of anything but my going back to Longwood.

"We'll be in London for the Christmas holidays, just like last year," my mother said brightly.

I would have fallen apart at the airfield, except that all three Hobsons were going on the flight with Stephen and me. Jory would be in residence at King's College, and his parents had decided to return to Hempstead. Mrs. Hobson said they wanted to see him now and again and during the holidays. After all these years, they had grown accustomed to his face.

On the short flight from Dodoma to Nairobi, Jory and his parents were fairly quiet, looking out the window and occasionally making "we were here and now we won't be" remarks. For the last half hour, they were absolutely silent. I was silent too, of course, although Stephen had moments of chatter with the pilot.

It was different, though, on the tedious trip from Nairobi to Heathrow. Jory, Stephen, and I sat three abreast, with Mr. and Mrs. Hobson across the aisle. Jory was right between Stephen and me in age, but he had always been more my friend than Stephen's. Stephen had protected Jory from the blackguard kids in the compound when needed, but that had been about it. Stephen was not an outstanding Scrabble player. He played sports, and Jory couldn't. Suddenly, now, as the plane plowed through the clouds, though, Stephen and Jory became as thick as thieves, discussing Cambridge dons, Cambridge clubs, Cambridge pubs, and Cambridge political activity. Somewhere over Italy, the conversation veered into the nature of the Cambridge women's colleges and then into the nature of the women at the Cambridge women's colleges.

Stephen was saying, "One Friday night, I met this girl from Lucy Cavendish. She looked like she had been poured into her dress and—" He stopped and glanced my way.

I said. "Don't look at me. I'm going to St. Hilda's at Oxford."

BOAC had just passed out tiny trays of lamb cubes over rice with bits of carrots and pineapple as an excuse for dinner, and I was trying to get that down when a question belatedly formed in my mind.

"Jory," I asked. "Jory, what did you do in place of the A-levels? Did Cambridge have you write special compositions for different subjects, or what?"

"I took A-levels!" Jory replied in a somewhat indignant tone.

"Yeah, Amelia, he took A-levels," Stephen said.

From across the aisle, Mrs. Hobson said, "Amelia, he took four A-levels."

Clearly they had misinterpreted why I thought he hadn't.

When I had gone for the interview at Longwood, Miss Fox had given the death blow to my studying at home by saying, "By the way, how would she go about taking the A-levels? A-levels are given at schools, are they not?" She had smiled triumphantly.

I said to Jory now, "I thought A-levels were just given at schools." It was as I spoke that the genius me realized that she had not said *just* at schools; she had not said *only* at schools; she had not said *exclusively* at schools. I wanted to smack my head.

Jory said, "They give A-levels once a year at City Centre in Nairobi for students not associated with British schools. First time in seven years I was there for anything besides an orthopedic appointment."

His father said, "After Jory took his exams, we stayed a few extra days, saw the sights, took in a show. We enjoyed it."

I said, "So how many kids were there? You and three others?"

"Amelia, why are you turning nasty?" Stephen asked.

I don't know why I kept being misinterpreted.

"About three hundred," Jory said.

"Oh, three hundred, imagine that," I commented. "Quite a crowd."

"Yes, about a third were English, the rest were Americans, Europeans, and Indians who wanted to study at our universities. Also, some Kenyans, although they had to take them in a separate room. That's still a British rule."

"Let's hear it for the bloody British," I said rather loudly. The stewardess taking our trays away looked at me.

"Amelia," Stephen said, "Dad thinks the system will change. He believes that with independence—"

"Oh shut up, Stephen," I said.

That caused Mrs. Hobson to say "Amelia!" This was getting to be some trip.

I turned back to Jory and said, "Did my mother know you were taking the A-levels?"

"Why, yes," he said. "She helped me get ready for the French A-level." The plane was now flying above France.

"Your mother was incredibly generous with her time," Mrs. Hobson put in.

"Oh, she was," I said. "I'm personally often in circumstances where I kill time."

The stewardess was coming back down the aisle, giving out clammy washcloths.

"Well, sis," Stephen said, "What extras are you signing up for?"

"What do you think? Basket weaving, as befitting a freak," I replied. Then I felt cold and guilty that I had said that. When we had first come to Tanganyika, Edna and poor Aumi had taught us to weave baskets with reeds. They had sat with us companionably for hours. *Kikapu* —basket—had been one of the first Kiswahili words we had learned.

"Oh, I don't know, Stephen," I said dully. "What difference does it make?"

The plane was over the channel now. The stewardess announced we were making our descent. Mr. Hobson told her, "My son will need his cane."

Stephen said to me, "Sis, the number where you can reach me at is still the same."

I was in the upper sixth form at Longwood now, doing my last prep for university, with my days as usual passing in a dreary, interminable blur. As planned, I took five A-levels. My fingers felt as if they were welded to my fountain pen, but I passed each with distinction. I now had entrée into every women's college at Oxford, at Cambridge, and at every university in Great Britain that gave degrees to women. I even got into Radcliffe in the States.

My mother was now writing twice a week—I guess she had learned that she could do so when she wrote me twice that one week the previous year—and she said I had free choice to go where I wanted to go. My father wrote me a letter echoing my mother's sentiments and asking me if I thought now that everything had been worth it.

I even heard from Stephen. He sent me a postcard of Big Ben, on the back of which he had scribbled, "Congratulations, Sis! You're really smart! Love, Stephen." Of course, with Stephen, you never knew if he was serious.

I chose St. Hilda's College, since I had always planned to go there. It was my mother's college, and although on the small side, it was reputed to be the most intellectual of all the Oxford women's colleges. I appreciated the opportunity to become part of such a good college, I really did. I felt removed from the jubilation, though. The simple fact was I could have been accepted at St. Hilda's if I had been at Regency Day. I could have been accepted if I had studied on my own in Tanganyika. Even if I had adhered to the American curriculum, I could have been accepted. It had all been such a charade.

Three weeks into Lenten term, I became eighteen. This surprised even me. So much of my life had slipped away. My childhood was for all intents and purposes over. Yet I felt twelve, perhaps eleven, infinitely regressed from the age I had been during our home year.

My birthday fell on a Saturday, always the worst day for me in boarding school and filled with compulsory sports. I was forced to play hockey, since I would not do riding. The puck was always being aimed right at me. I was always getting hit by a stick. To compound matters, my birthday was the night of the upper sixth-form promenade ball. Since four o'clock, the gaggle had been eagerly getting ready for the arrival of their dates from the various boys' schools in Kent. Afternoon showers, as long as they were only five minutes in duration, were even being allowed. Up and down the hall, there was the swish, swish of evening gowns being stepped into.

I didn't know and didn't want to know anyone from a boys' school in Kent, so for me it would be stew in the dining room and then the movie *How Green Was My Valley* with the rest of the Longwood senior school. Actually, perhaps I'd really celebrate being eighteen the right way and watch *Snow White and the Seven Dwarfs* with the waifs in the primary school.

I had read and reread the birthday card that I had received from my parents in which they had sent me their greatest love as Roxanne, who somehow had permanently stayed my roommate, looked at herself in the mirror this way and that. She was fiddling with her neckline, rearranging the rolled-up socks she had shoved down her crimson brocade dress, when Matron came in.

"Don't you look a vision of loveliness!" she said to Rox.

"Thank you, Matron!" Rox said, beaming. She was a little asymmetrical, one sock being less tightly balled up than the other.

Matron turned to me, "Miss Ord, you have some young visitors. I said they could wait in the courtyard, and I am giving you a pass for the evening, since it's your birthday. However, I'm not doing it again. If you want a pass, you'll have to give eight days' notice, just like everyone else.

"Oh, all right," I said, taking the pass.

"Now, how often does she have an opportunity for pass?" Rox asked.

Matron shrugged.

She left, and quick as a flash I leapt out of the Longwood uniform and into my own skirt and sweater and slip-on flats.

Young visitors! I couldn't imagine who they might be. However, as I was running down the hall patting down my hair, I heard one of the gaggle announce, "Ord's boyfriend Limpy Gimpy is here accompanied by a dreamboat and his girlfriend who looks like some actress."

Being a genius, I figured out my boyfriend Limpy Gimpy was Jory, and I did hope that he hadn't heard what had been said. Perhaps the other two were Ted Sanders and Christa, who had decided to dress like a movie star. Jory was from one side of my real life, though, and

Ted and Christa were from the other. I could not figure out how they would have gotten together.

I was right about Jory, at least. The dreamboat turned out to be Stephen, and standing between them but closer to Jory was a tall, slim girl with long auburn hair. She looked like Kate Hepburn in *The Philadelphia Story*.

"Happy Birthday!" they cried. They waved noisemakers.

"Jory! Stephen!" I exclaimed. "You, too!" I added turning to the girl. They all laughed. The girl was Katherine—Kate—Burnham, and taking English literature at Cambridge and starring in campus plays. "Awfully glad to meet you," she said, stepping forward in tippy high heels and shaking my hand enthusiastically. "I've heard awfully lots about you, and I'm awfully glad you pushed Jory towards university, because otherwise he and I never would have met."

Jory grinned sheepishly, giving me final proof that she was his girl-friend, not Stephen's.

"Well—" I said, since I had done nothing to push Jory towards university.

"How did you all get here?" I asked.

Stephen had rented a car, and it turned out Jory and Kate had been free for the evening, so they had come too.

Apparently, somehow, somewhere, Stephen had learned to drive.

"What shall we do, sis?" Stephen asked. "You have a pass until ten."

It didn't escape my notice that I was the only one who needed a pass.

We discussed crashing the promenade ball and doing the hokey pokey, but we decided Longwood wasn't ready for that.

Stephen said that when driving through the village, they had noticed a pub that featured a band, and he suggested we go there. We all piled into Stephen's rented car and took off. He drove somewhat on the fast side but stopped at red lights, so I guess he knew what he was doing.

The pub in a Tudor-style building was dimly lit and crowded, not what I was used to, but the candles flickering in green bowls on each table lent some cheer. "Welcome!" the proprietor said to each of us as he seated us near the postage-stamp dance floor. He handed out the menus with a flourish, looking appreciatively at Kate.

It was fun doing something normal people did and being with my brother, Jory, and Kate Hepburn. Stephen said that Mum and Dad had sent him money for our dinner. I guess that explained why I had gotten a card but no present from them. Anyway, he ordered the lamb chop blue plate special for each of us and asked if I wanted a drink to celebrate being eighteen.

I declined, because what I had seen of alcohol in the compound and also at Longwood had given me a low opinion of the stuff, but I urged them to have some.

Stephen had just a half glass of ale because he was responsible for the rental car. Jory had a glass and a half, and Kate Hepburn had three drinks—ale and then two scotches.

I entertained them with an account of my latest acts of subversion at Longwood. I said that when I had first been unfortunate enough to meet the headmistress, she had said I couldn't study anything I pleased. Well, boy, was she wrong. I had learned last year that you could do just about anything in proctored study hall, as long as you arranged books and papers artfully, so when I won a free American correspondence course for getting the highest mark of any American in East Africa in "Reconstruction and the Gilded Age" last summer—"

Kate looked perplexed.

"I was trying on the guise of an American," I interrupted my narrative to explain. "I chose 'The Outsider in American Fiction,' and I use the Cooksons as my mailing address, with Christa being the go-between for assignments," I continued. "But I do home study right in the citadel of the enemy! I do everything in study hall. What this means is, even though the proctor might think I'm doing chemistry equations, I'm really reading "Bartleby, the Scrivener"!

"What's that about?" Stephen asked.

"It's about a hardworking fellow who preferred not to do things and consequently didn't do them, which I guess gives him a leg up on me."

"Well, when do you prep for chemistry?" Kate asked.

"At lunch or at these teas we're forced to go to, or sometimes when I'm able to be on the bench in field hockey, although then I'm more likely to do Latin," I said.

"Amelia take risks!" Jory said, and they all laughed.

I briefly consider telling them that the school's cannabis was in my suitcase, but I wasn't quite sure how Stephen would react.

"I played an American in a play once," Kate said meditatively. "My name was Tammy, and I had to wear shrunken trousers called pedal pushers and say 'Hi, there' and 'Hey, there' and 'Gee, this is keen.' The director wrote it, but I came up with the title, 'Backyard Bar-B-Q.' That was when I was younger. I lean towards classical roles now."

Jory looked at her with adoring eyes.

"Speaking of scriveners," Stephen said, "Jory just became corresponding secretary of the Liberal Party Club at Cambridge."

"Yes, between my political science courses and that, I'm always busy," Jory said.

I bet he was, when you threw in Kate Hepburn.

"How's your mother?" I asked Jory.

"Fine. She and my father came up when Kate was in *She Stoops to Conquer*. She's suddenly thinking of working in social services, if she can manage the courses."

We all had lemon sponge cake for dessert, and as we were finishing, I saw Stephen look at his watch.

"Oh no, Stephen, don't make me go back," I cried. With them, I at least could live vicariously, which was better than what I usually did.

"Well, perhaps a dance first," Kate said. She grabbed Jory's hand.

The band was playing swing, and with Kate's arm on Jory's back and his arm on her back, he could glide with her, no need for a cane. They seemed practiced, her head on his shoulder, his thighs close to her hips. Stephen saw me looking at them, and so there was no help for it. He and I got up and did a chaste brother-and-sister waltz.

It had somehow been revealed that it was my birthday. When we sat down, everyone in the pub sang "Happy Birthday" to me, and the manager brought me an extra piece of cake and said it was on the house. He gave Kate an extra piece, too, for good measure.

Then Stephen said it was time to go. My pass was only until ten.

I ripped up the pass. "I can stay out as long as I want, now," I announced.

"Absolutely," Kate said.

"I'm not going back," I told them.

"Just a term and a half more," Jory said encouragingly. "University is much better."

"Amelia," Stephen said in a level voice, "it'll be a long drive back to Cambridge after we drop you off."

"All right, Stephen," I said sadly.

He paid the bill, and Jory left the tip and money for Kate's extra drinks. They had suddenly become grownups.

"Come back anytime, if you're passing through," the manager said.

"Actually, I might be playing summer theater in the area, so who knows?" Kate Hepburn answered.

When we got into the car, which wasn't that big, Kate accidentally jabbed my ankle with the edge of one high heel.

"Oops! Awfully sorry. These stilettos are deadly weapons, but I must be fashionable," she said.

"It's all right," I reassured her.

"You're always fashionable, bunny," Jory said, reassuring her, too.

Kate giggled. She was good-natured, but I didn't know if she would wear very well. She reminded me of someone else in addition to Kate Hepburn. I couldn't think of who. It didn't really matter. The minutes were running out.

Then I had an idea. "I say, my good brother Stephen, why don't we show Jory and Kate the land of our early life?"

"What?"

"Devon, Stephen, Devon! All we have to do is head straight west."

"Amelia, that must be 160 or 170 miles! You know we can't do that," Stephen said. He made the turn into Longwood School and started up the drive. It was 9:55.

"Oh, come on, Stephen, be a sport!" I pleaded.

"Sis," he said, sounding wary.

At 9:56, we were in the courtyard of Victoria Hall. Matron was looking out the window. It suddenly occurred to me that the promenade ball would not be over until 11:30. Yet she had made me be back by 10.

Everyone got out of the car, Jory using the car door for support as he stood. They wished me happy birthday again. I said good-bye to Jory and to Kate Hepburn, who wished me luck in my secret studying.

Turning to Stephen, I said, "Thank you, Stephen. This evening was super. I'll see you at Uncle Anthony's in sixty-two days."

"Um, I'm not sure that you will. I'm probably going mountain climbing in Scotland with some friends. Dad sent me some advice on itinerary."

I looked at him incredulously. I would have to get through the whole entire month at our great uncle's on my own.

"All right, Stephen," I said shakily.

"I'll see you in June, sis," he said, briefly touching my shoulder.

It was 9:59. I walked up the steps of the dorm and then looked

[181]

back. They were waving. I could barely give an answering wave before Matron was telling me to come in. The place was quiet enough that I could hear the murmur of their voices, Kate's laugh, then doors closing and the car engine starting. I could have watched them going down the drive, but I couldn't bear to.

Matron said, "I didn't say you could be out of uniform for the evening."

"It's my birthday," I answered, starting to walk by her.

"Well, you should think before taking liberties. Sometimes you act as if you aren't even part of this school."

I took that as a compliment and thanked her.

She looked a bit baffled and then said, "Well, here's a telegram from Tanganyika. It came when you were out. I read it to make sure it wasn't an emergency."

I gave no verbal response but just grabbed it from her hand. I had never received a telegram before.

I read it in my room. It said:

HAPPY 18TH BIRTHDAY TO MY SMART AND WONDERFUL DAUGHTER AMELIA. FOR A COMBINED BIRTHDAY/GRADUATION PRESENT, YOU WILL SPEND THE EASTER HOLIDAYS IN MALTA WITH MUM. DETAILS TO FOLLOW. WITH GREAT LOVE AND ADMIRATION, DAD.

I reread the telegram six times. I would not have to go to my uncle's for the holidays. I would be on the entrancing island of Malta with my mother. As I slashed another day off the calendar, I felt a soupçon of joy.

The next day, in enforced letter-writing time, I wrote to my mother, thanking her and my father for their two presents. I said I had not expected anything else after the surprise dinner with Stephen to which he had brought Jory and his girlfriend. Then I had gotten Dad's telegram telling me about the real surprise.

In my mother's reply letter, letter, number 373, she said that Malta was somewhat equidistant between Tanganyika and England, and so when she heard about a cottage to let, she had consulted my father, who had said "just the thing for you two," so she had grabbed it. She was glad that Stephen had made the trek down from Cambridge to see me on my birthday. Stephen always rose to the occasion, didn't he? However, she was a bit confused as to why I thought this had somehow come from her and Dad. This had been on Stephen's own time and shilling.

That was interesting about Stephen coming on his own initiative. This made me remember that somehow I had forgotten to write him a thank-you letter, so I belatedly dashed him off a note.

It took forever to get to Malta, both in terms of crawling through the rest of term and the long flight down alone, but then I was there, my mother smiling in a light linen dress, waiting for me at the tiny airport.

Our three-room house was made of pink stone with cream-color shutters that we always threw open in early morning so that the light could leap into our front room, dappling the wood grain of the floor. Our view was of the aqua sea glistening and sparkling as the sun ascended in the changing sky. We could always hear the water lapping in the crescent cove, and our garden had roses and also an orange tree. There we spent four weeks, my mother and I did. It was a time outside time, a reprieve and a reprise.

There was nothing we had to do, so we had a routine but no schedule. Mondays and Thursdays were usually for sightseeing. We saw the palaces and museums in Valletta, and the Byzantine architecture. We explored the coast and took boats to Comina. On the other days, we walked to the local village in the morning, strolled through the ancient streets, and bought provisions for our meals: bread, cheese, fruit, vegetables, seafood, or meat. We were learning to cook with tomatoes and olive oil. We discovered tuna. Afternoons we spent at the cove, hiking on the cliff paths, sunning on rocks, finding shells, and floating for hours in the gentle frothy waves.

One evening, my mother and I were sitting in the garden after our Mediterranean supper. It was dark, but millions of stars were out, and moonlight shimmered on the ocean. The salt breezes mingled with the scent of flowers, and the shrubs softly rustled. My mother had on sandals, but I was in my bare feet.

We had been silent for a while, listening to the crickets, when I spoke. "I wish we could stay here forever. I never want to go back to England or anywhere."

"It has been lovely, hasn't it?" my mother said. "You'd get bored if you were here indefinitely, though. You'd want to get on with your life."

"This would be my life," I answered." All we need is a dog."

Once again, the minutes were sifting out. I was loath to return to Longwood for the last term but knew better than to bring it up. It would just break the spell.

Anyway, Mum had her own plans. She was not going back to Tanganyika in the interval before my graduation. She was first flying to France to see cousin Céline and then to Switzerland to see Mrs. Gold, who had remarried, and Henri.

"I haven't seen Céline and Ruth since 1931 during that year after university, and of course I haven't met Henri. We just have pictures of him."

The Golds and my mother had been in touch regularly, but I never quite understood the relationship. My mother either glowed when she mentioned them, or was quite hesitant to discuss them. In any event, after one last silver, pink, to blue sunrise in Malta, I was going on one plane to England, and she was going on another to the Continent.

My final term was like any other of my boarding school terms. I felt no nostalgia or sense of impending freedom. I was just impatient and miserable. My uniform felt rough against my skin.

I climbed Mount Everest. I swam the English Channel.

My mother, as she had during all my terms, wrote me faithfully. Finally, her last letter, postmarked from Basel, Switzerland, and numbered 403—she had written me a total of 403 letters since I was seven and a half—arrived. I had marked time by each.

I began the countdown.

My parents, with Stephen in tow, arrived the day before graduation for baccalaureate dinner. I suggested that we skip the festivities and awards and just head for London. I was certainly all packed and set to go. They would not hear of it.

I could not even spend the night with them at the inn they were staying at. All my requests for a pass had been refused. Matron said I had to enjoy one more night in the dorm with my classmates before we scattered to the winds the next day. I would regret it always if I didn't do it. I just had to trust her.

As a consequence, I was forced to watch my family leave at nine-thirty. Miss Fox came over to the dorm, congratulated us for getting to this point, and gave us each a bar of Yardley soap, as a personal gift.

"Just can't wait until tomorrow!" she said, beaming.

I couldn't either.

She left, and Matron sent us to bed. "Lights out as usual in twenty minutes, girls! All rules still in effect!"

Of course, most of the gaggle lit out after lights out, to spend one final night on the town.

As they swung from window to tree or climbed down trellises, I slashed the last day off the calendar. I took the calendar off the wall, tore it in half, and put it in the wastebasket. I had killed all the time dead and would get a diploma tomorrow to show for it.

Humming a bit, I turned down the covers and tried to slide into bed. I couldn't do it. Either my legs were meeting resistance, or they were not working. Was I finally getting polio when it was too late to do me any good? Did the Salk vaccine not work? Being a genius, it only took me a few seconds to figure out that the oldest boarding school trick in the book had been played on me. My bed was short sheeted!

I lay down on top of the bed, pulled just the bedspread over me, thought of Devon, and drifted off shortly after Matron stuck her flashlight into the room.

Then it was the last morning.

Rox and I were both brushing our hair, and I felt that, given the day, I should make a try at conviviality. I said, "Rox, thanks for making sure the weed was always out of my suitcase before the holidays."

"What?" she asked. "Oh, we only used your suitcase one more time, and that was just for a few minutes when Matron was prowling and it was an emergency. Actually, we didn't think it was fair, since you avoided the stuff yourself."

"Then why did you stay my roommate all of these two years?"

"Well, why not?" she answered. "I guess your gloomy nonconformity intrigued me. You gave me a break from my entourage."

She paused and added, "You grew on me."

"Thank you, Rox," I said faintly.

"Well, we are not likely to see each other after today, since roommates here or not, we definitely do travel in different circles—but fare thee well," Rox said. Then surprisingly, she kissed my cheek.

I was the star of the graduation ceremony. After Miss Fox and the Longwood faculty in their black robes marched into the assembly hall, I, as top student, led the Longwood class of 1958 onto the stage. I wore the prescribed school graduation attire, a high-neck white satin dress with a silk yolk collar and low scooped back. It had been designed by the headmistress with her usual fashion flair, and I just hoped it wouldn't fall off my shoulders. I kept doing spastic things with my arms to help it stay up. As everyone turned to sit in their proper places, one of my fellow graduates had a tennis ball pop out of her front, but fortunately she grabbed it before it bounced on the floor. An Anglican rector led the multitude in prayer, and then I was on.

I hadn't wanted to do it, but Miss Fox had said I couldn't shirk my duty. I was valedictorian by any measure, so I had to give a speech, yes, indeed. Thus, I had thrown together some rubbish about fortitude and endurance and how, like soldiers in a war, Longwood students were changed by the experience, or at least I was. I had written the thing so that you had to really listen to figure out that I was slamming the place six ways to Sunday. It had passed the censors.

After my brief conversation with Rox, though, I had thrown it out. I wanted to say something that it was worth her time to listen to. I had had just a half hour to jot down some notes. Now I moved to the podium and launched in. I said that my friend Jory, who had preceded me to university, did not let himself be defined by circumstances. He was thrown something out of the blue. He does more than cope. He seizes the day. He sets his own sights. "Circumstances are not everything," I told the class. "Whether you liked the way you were here or whether you didn't, you are going on to new things. The paths you can take in your lives are infinite. Be true to yourself and be critical in the best sense. Each day gives you—us—more chances."

I said that *A Christmas Carol* was a holiday book, but the story's themes of new life, renewals, and changing the future were surely well in keeping with commencements. I continued, "Consider the paradox of Scrooge. The name is synonymous with being a miserly misanthrope, a stranger to empathy, set in one's miserable ways. Yet when shown what was, what is, and what terribly might be, although not inevitably will be, he awakens figuratively and literally. His inner spark, tiny but always there regardless of circumstances, has met the tinder, and he chooses to transform himself. He does it for the person he now wishes to be. He does it for the world. We can do the same."

After some elaboration, I ended with the charge to the class. "I exhort you all to be like Scrooge. Be like Scrooge when he became his best, on Christmas day, after the visits from the three ghosts. Go out and change the future! Fare thee well."

There was moderate applause and then greater applause.

Finally, the diplomas came. When Sir Colin Witherall, head trustee of Longwood, gave me mine, he said, "Splendid finish."

For me, the salient word was "finish," so I replied, "Why, thank you."

After the ceremony or show or whatever you want to call it was over, I raced to find my parents and Stephen in the milling crowd outside the assembly hall.

"Here it is, Dad," I said, tossing my father my diploma.

"Congratulations," he said. "You worked hard, wasn't always easy."

"Congratulations," my mother said.

Stephen said, "Yay, sis!"

I said, "Well, I'll change out of this shroud one two three, and we can get on the road." My suitcase was already in the rental car. All that was left was a satchel and the polka-dot dress I was wearing back to London.

Mum unfortunately reminded me there was yet a luncheon in the dorm's common room.

I was chomping at the bit, but I had to let it play out.

We walked to Victoria Hall. They headed to the common room, and I went back to the room where I had spent 504 nights. I quickly changed and then walked out without a backwards glance.

In the common room, I gulped down two cucumber sandwiches and tried to hurry my family along. It seemed to me that they were chewing too slowly.

"Don't you want to let us meet your friends?" my mother asked.

I introduced them to Rox, since I guess she had been a closet friend, so to speak.

It was quarter past one when we were finally on the way out. We were going by the main building and its columns, and who should appear but the headmistress!

My parents greeted her nicely.

I decided to short circuit this. "Good-bye, we're leaving, but there are oodles of people still at lunch."

She said to Stephen—it seemed like, "May I steal Amelia away for just a minute? I'd like to personally wish her well in my office."

"No need and no time," I said. "We have to get to London!"

"We have time," my mother contradicted me. "The Cooksons aren't expecting us until six."

[187]

"Yes, we'll put your satchel in the car, wheel around, and just meet you here," my father said.

"Sure," Stephen added obligingly.

Apparently, even though I had graduated from this place, Miss Fox was still allowed authority over me.

"Yes?" I said to her, as I stood in her office.

"Your speech was jim dandy," she said.

I shrugged. I may have somewhat risen to the occasion, but I hadn't done it for her.

She smiled. "You may not remember this, but you were ambivalent about coming here."

"No, I wasn't," I said.

"Well, that was how you acted!"

"Sorry, I didn't make my position clear," I said.

"Glad we cleared that up!"

I just looked at her.

Adopting a confidential tone, she continued, "We have many good students here, but when I saw your previous school records, I knew you were tippy-top tier! You were definitely one to snare."

She had snared me, all right.

"Great," I said. "Listen, I have to get going. My friend Christa is graduating from Regency Day tomorrow, and—"

"What's she doing next year?"

"Going to St. Hilda's." I paused. "Charlotte Barnard is, too."

"How do you know that?"

"Grapevine," I said. Apparently, she had never connected the dots.

"Well, let's get back to you. Did you notice that in the graduation program we had an exceptionally long list of colleges and universities our students were accepted into? Well, many of these were places only you had gotten into."

"Yup, I know. Good-bye. My parents and brother are waiting."

"Then, there's the national recognition, your royal merit commendation, your inclusion in one hundred best sixth formers in Great Britain, all the essay contests you won, and, of course, all the class prizes you were awarded at baccalaureate."

"Well, the hour is running late."

"I just wish we had gotten you sooner. You have been our top student for the two years you've been here. More than that, you have enhanced the reputation of the school. We will write up your achievements in our promotional material."

Then it clicked. The advice she had given my mother against allowing me to do the sixth form on my own had been biased. To use a phrase I had picked up from my first American correspondence course, she had had a conflict of interest. It was so obvious I wanted to smack my head.

She had told my mother that I must be given every opportunity. She had said that if I was her daughter, she would send me to Longwood. Then there had been the clincher—A-levels are given at schools, are they not?

Perhaps she had thought Longwood would be good for me. Perhaps she had. This did not change the fact. She had snared me for the benefit of this bloody place.

Miss Fox was now putting out her hand. "Well, I just wanted to give you my personal congratulations. I hope you'll be an active alumna. We do need a pool. Maybe you can spearhead the fund-raising for that.

"Come back and visit often," she said.

I shook my head. I was going to curse her. I had nothing to lose. The shock effect would be good, but then I decided to merely say, "The only remotely brilliant thing I did here was to be willing to hold the stash."

Miss Fox looked perplexed, but she hesitantly put out her hand for me to shake. I did not take it.

I turned and strode out. My boarding school days were over, and I had survived, survived, survived. I just wondered how long it would take for me to curtain that existence off.

The joint graduation party the Cooksons gave for Christa and me was smashing. It was just four Ords and eight Cooksons around the Cooksons' extended dining room table under a mural that Mrs. Cookson had done of little Ords and little Cooksons playing in the Little Park. There was even a little dog in it who looked a lot like Folly. My mother and Mrs. Cookson had teamed up on a roast beef, Yorkshire pudding, asparagus with hollandaise sauce, and a peach trifle for desert. We talked and laughed about the days when Christa, Jon, Ian, Stephen, and I had just started at Regency Day.

Mr. Cookson said, "Everyone talks about how postwar was so grim, with everything conceivable thing rationed and people unsure how to start their lives again. But they were splendid days for us, when we were all together."

"Indeed," my mother said. "Val, remember how we each saved our sugar coupons for weeks to make a minuscule plum pudding so each of the children could have a taste?"

"Well, where was I?" Dennis, the second Boom, asked.

"Before your time, love, "Mrs. Cookson said. "But you're here now, and Larry and Kenny, so this is a splendid time, too."

"It's Boom time," Stephen suggested in an unexpected burst of creativity. Everyone but the Booms laughed, and then they laughed too.

With so many mentions of Christmas on this day, Mrs. Cookson and my mother had no choice but to agree to do a dramatic reading of *A Christmas Carol* after dinner. As the twelve of us sat in the Cooksons' sitting room listening to my mother being the narrator and Scrooge and Mrs. Cookson playing all the ghosts and Tiny Tim, with both of them speaking distinctly for the benefit of the Final Boom, I felt content and wished that these moments could last forever.

Finally, we said good night. Christa, as Regency Day valedictorian, still had to put the finishing touches on her speech. As for us, we had to get organized. We were leaving for Tanganyika in the morning.

CHAPTER 7

Needing to Wake Up

Dodoma, Tanganyika; Oxford and London, 1958–1964

IT WAS THE usual strain being in the compound, and even more so now that the Hobsons had left. I sent Jory a postcard that said, "Having a crummy time. Be glad you aren't here!"

Stephen had a job again in my father's office, and I helped my mother organize supplies for village schools. She was surprised when I brought out a whole box of erasers, pencils, several pens, a compass to measure circumference, and a great deal of slightly yellowing paper to contribute to the cause. I also donated a primary school math book and *First Year Latin: An Introduction to Julius Caesar*, although I felt it best not to tell my mother that these were hot items.

In the afternoons, my mother and I had our swims, which was the part I enjoyed. We did laps and water ballet and tried to make our time together last as long as we could.

My parents still had their social obligations and functions in the evening. I was now old enough to go to these things, but I rarely did, even though Stephen, who, being a dreamboat, seemed quite a hit with the girls, often went. I preferred to read in my room or look out the window. My mother explained to people I was "studious." (Once I heard someone saying, "At least the boy turned out halfway normal.")

This was to be our last summer in Tanganyika. The country was set to become independent as the 1960s started, with, hopefully, Julius Nyerere, who like me was reputed to be studious, taking the helm. England was recalling its officials in waves, and my parents would be in the group leaving in the spring of 1959, with my father getting his old desk job back. I was glad, since that meant I could come home for even the shortest holidays, and certainly I had no regrets over our family leaving the compound.

Yet I was also furious at the irony. My parents were coming to London just as I was university age and would not have lived full time at home anyway.

My mother asked me if there had been anything I liked about Africa. I answered slowly.

"I liked seeing the plains, I liked the flamingos and the giraffes. I liked our trips. It was good to learn Kiswahili. I'm glad I know Jory. I liked it when Edna and Aumi took us to their village."

I paused, and we were silent thinking about Aumi. We would find ways to remember her always.

I continued, "There was lots I liked about East Africa, but not how we had to live here, so topsy-turvy."

My mother nodded. "I agree," she slowly said. "We thought Dad could just concentrate on building the infrastructure. We didn't know how much we would be pulled into the racism and colonial culture. It was naïve."

As the days ran short, Stephen and my father did something they had always talked about doing. They climbed Mount Kilimanjaro together. They seemed wholly impressed with themselves, oblivious to the fact that, at least figuratively, I had climbed Mount Everest alone repeatedly for years.

We took a final holiday at Lake Victoria, and then my parents delivered Stephen and me to the airport at Nairobi. I was sad and jittery when I boarded the plane as Mum and Dad waved cheerfully. This was just the same old pattern of separation. I would have to survive, survive, survive.

After we landed at Heathrow, Stephen and I made our way to the train station, where he bought a ticket to Cambridge—he was in his third year now—and I dispiritedly got a ticket to Oxford. Suddenly, Stephen went back to the ticket counter and exchanged his ticket for a double ticket, first to Oxford, then to Cambridge. He said, "This way, I can help with your luggage."

"All right, Stephen," I said. Over the course of all these years, Stephen had fallen into the habit of coming through for me.

For some people, university is largely a socially experience. It wasn't like that for me. At St. Hilda's College in Oxford, I spent all my time studying. University was what my childhood had been oriented around, so I thought I should make the most of it (academically).

Jory was right. University was better than boarding school. There was true scholarship here, and I appreciated it. Also, there wasn't relentless scheduling. So long as I went to lectures and kept my appointments with the dons, I could set up my own routine, which was to be mainly at a carrel in the Bodleian Library.

Longwood had somewhat imprinted me educationally, much as I tried to resist it. The way they had taught history there had been abysmal, with nothing but memorizing, and so I had drifted away from history as a discipline. My classes in Greek had been well taught, though, and I had always been fascinated by words. One thing led to another, and so my area of concentration at university was in linguistics, with a specialty in Greek. I threw myself into analyzing language.

Of course, I wasn't literally at my books one hundred percent of the time. Christa and Lottie were there, and they were willing to include me in what they were doing, as much as I wanted. Christa even ran interference for me, telling people who called me "the ice scholar" that I was really a very nice girl. I just hadn't had the childhood that I had expected to have.

Although she didn't have the aspirations or pretensions Jory's girlfriend had, Christa had some interest in theater, and she was able to get me to join the drama society with her. We were two of the benign witches in Macbeth, chanting the same chants that we had chanted with my mother in our kitchen during the home year, and we played minor characters in a few Ibsen plays. Then, in *The Diary of Anne Frank*, Christa was cast as Miep, the linchpin of the Franks' support group, and I was Ellie, her assistant.

The director said we should model our character after someone we knew who embodied key traits that we thought the character had. Christa, for some reason, took my mother as her model, and I tried to play Ellie with the openheartedness I remembered from Jenny, although she was now a dim memory. We must have done something right, because when the college newspaper reviewed the play, they mentioned us. The write-up said, "Lively Christa Cookson and quiet Amelia Ord gave standout performances as Miep and Ellie. They made one believe that caring, moral people can exist and do exist."

What else did I do? Sometimes I visited Jory at King's College, but not too often, since he was busy helping in local political campaigns and getting more and more involved with Kate Hepburn. Occasionally, when I was in the Cambridge environs, I saw Stephen, who, to the wonder of the world, had decided to pursue an advanced degree in chemistry.

I had been told I had a good voice, so I joined an intercollege chorus. That brought me two dates with a bookish tenor.

I swam in the indoor pool but opted not to join the swim team.

After my parents came home from Tanganyika, my mother came up to St. Hilda's on some of the weekends when I didn't go home. I usually saw her twice a month actually, not counting holidays. We walked in the gardens and went boating on the River Cherwell and tried to make our time together last as long as we could.

Mainly though, I just studied. As a consequence, I did extremely well. I got not just firsts but double firsts and a congratulatory first. When I told my mother the honors I would be graduating with, she was pleased. It was our secret, although I suppose she let my father in on it.

My professors did everything they could to get me to stay on at Oxford for graduate study, even virtually promising me a faculty appointment when I was finished, quite a rare thing for a woman in 1962. On one level, the offer was tempting, but I resisted. I thought academia would only accentuate the increasing tendency I saw in myself to be three steps removed from emotional life. I needed to be back in the hustle and bustle of London and not just because my mother was there. I needed to wake up.

I think my parents had assumed I would be a professor, but they accepted my decision with equanimity.

For about a year, I worked with Christa organizing and listing books in a rare book store on Charing Cross Road. (It was not the one at Eighty-Four Charing Cross, although Christa swears she met Frank Doel once at a book conference.) The job was good enough, and I enjoyed being with Christa, but the work really wasn't right for me the way it began to be for Christa, who would have her career in antiquarian books.

Finally, a chance reading of an article about people who had had strokes that left them with full cognition but unable to verbalize started me down a different path. My study of linguistics, combined with a vague desire to help people (I was bored with thinking about myself a hundred percent of the time), led me to go into speech therapy—or, as it later began to be pretentiously called, speech pathology.

I already knew a bit about bad speech therapists from the Final Boom. I thought I could be an acceptable speech therapist.

Jory, who was getting a doctorate in political science and still going out with Kate Hepburn, didn't want me to do it. He said I would have to learn a lot of sucky medical stuff. I admitted that was true but pointed out that at least I wasn't going to be a physiotherapist, which we both agreed would be absolutely disgusting.

One of my Oxford professors, when he heard about my plan, was more straightforward than Jory in expressing his distaste. He wrote to me on official university stationery, saying, "You were the best student I had in five years. We wanted to give you the keys to the kingdom. Now you are entering a pedestrian profession for muddled reasons. I'm astonished."

Oh, well, you can't please everyone. With my parents and, for some reason, Mrs. Cookson cheering me on, I started the certification program at the London Logaoedics Centre in the summer of 1963.

I almost quit the program, though. Halfway though, we had to go on a field trip to one of London's showcase institutions. It was in our "Social Situations and the Handicapped" course, and as the teacher explained, it was to expose us to the range of conditions we might encounter. I didn't want to go. I just thought it was a hazing, an initiation rite. However, I was told that this was just as mandatory as the visit to the cleft palate clinic had been. I said I hadn't much liked that either, all these kids brought in right after the other and forced to open their mouths, for our professional edification.

The institution was built around an inner courtyard, with a garden where families could visit with their confined relative on Sunday afternoons. I guess this was what made the institution "showcase." Unfortunately, we were there on our Thursday, and no one was in the garden, and all the windows were shut tight. The air in the building was more than stuffy; it was heavy with the smell of disinfectant, decay, and sweat. If you reached out your hand, you could have grabbed a fistful.

The assistant director, a large woman named Mrs. Duckworth, greeted us cheerfully. She wanted to tell us a little about the population before we started the tour. She said that there was every age group, with those that were retarded and those that were crippled all mixed in together and jumbled up because if a body couldn't care for itself, it didn't really make a difference, did it? She looked straight at me.

In my head, I disagreed. The latter group at least had a shot at being prime minister. However, as we went to the first ward, I began to see what she meant. The residents all seemed suspended in such interminable nothing. It did not matter what they had begun with.

The floor for the elderly was bad. People with crumpled skin and crumpled muscles stared vacantly into space. Mrs. Duckworth snapped her fingers in front of one, and the man did not move. A few of the more agile walked around in circles fitfully. One old lady was crying for her mother to pick her up from school. "Ma, we were let out hours ago. Why aren't you here?"

I bit my lip

"Oh, Hattie," Mrs. Duckworth laughed. "Your mother died in the nineteenth century."

The floor for the middle-aged was worse. Two of them were trying to play patty-cake, and one was reading a magazine but mostly just sat, staring off vacantly. Amid the tangled limbs, people who had been denied youth were growing gray. I began to get fixated on the pallor, which I realized I had noticed with the old people as well. Everyone was a waxy white, except for one person who appeared to be Pakistani and who was waxy brown.

Much worse was the floor for the young adults. The despair here was palpable. They knew their future had evaporated. Some of these inmates seemed to have had polio, probably as the result of the epidemics of the late 1940s—just like Jory.

Mrs. Duckworth, ever eager to show us students amazing things, went up to a fellow whose arms just dangled and said, "May I?"

She did not wait for him to respond. He was not apt to have a speech impediment, so there would have been no educational value in hearing him say words. She lifted up one of his arms and then let go. It just dropped, slapping against his side.

"That's what the upside-down type of polio does," was Mrs. Duckworth's commentary.

We had been told that we could ask questions at any time, so now I did. "Has Harold Macmillan ever been here?"

"No, I don't think so," Mrs. Duckworth replied, "but Princess Margaret came a few years ago, and we were all spruced up for the visit. Wasn't that a banner day?"

No one in the throng of residents answered, so she asked again, "Wasn't that a banner day?"

A chipper sort of a lad spoke up, "A banner day, yes, quite a banner day, indeed it was a banner day, truly, truly a banner day, yes."

Mrs. Duckworth said, "That's James. We call him the mayor."

We were now going up to the children's floor. I found my teacher. I whispered that I was feeling sick. I played the "it's that time of the month" card, telling her I was leaving now. The teacher wouldn't hear of it. "Just hang on for a bit longer, Miss Ord. You'd be proud of yourself later that you did."

"No," I said.

"Miss Ord, I'll help you. I'll stay right here at your elbow."

I should not have gone up to the children's floor. It was totally dreadful. Some of the older ones wearing green romper type things lolled around on the floor pushing at balls; others, who were strapped into chairs, played with their fingers. The smaller tykes, though, were confined to cribs, even in the dayroom. They wore peasant shifts that barely covered their hips.

"We show them films on Saturday. *The Ugly Duckling* is a special favorite," Mrs. Duckworth said.

Mrs. Duckworth moved us over to a crib where a little boy was wailing. Although his legs were wobbly and rotated in, he had pulled himself into a standing position. There was still a bit of rose in his cheeks. He had clearly known better days.

Mrs. Duckworth was explaining, "Sometimes children who have been the center of attention take a while to adjust. They need time to understand that things can't be exactly like they were at home. Our policy is to be kind but firm."

I cringed. Hadn't Mrs. Lamberton said about the same thing?

My teacher whispered to me, "You're just having a nervous reaction, Miss Ord."

You bet I was.

I stood still for two more seconds. Then, to use a phrase that would come into vogue several decades hence, I was out of there.

This was the fifth floor, but when the elevator didn't come instantly when I slammed my hand on the call button, I bolted towards the stairs. I hadn't moved so fast since I made my desperate run after my mother at Westlands–King George School. I was leaping two and then three steps at a time. I dashed across each landing. I slid down the banister for the last flight. My skirt rode up to my hips. I didn't care. Finally, I was on the ground floor. I sprinted out the building. I ran a hundred feet up the sidewalk and then stopped. I gasped and gasped in the city air. I leaned towards the smell of traffic. I took in the honking noises.

Everything was a jumble in my mind. Everything was topsy-turvy. Jory would not have been sent to such a place. If I had been disabled, my parents wouldn't have sent me to such a place, either. Nowhere I had been had been remotely like it.

The place nonetheless had seemed like boarding school to me, but boarding school without classes, without extras, without awards, without holidays, without presentable uniforms, and without hope of the future, just boarding school forever until death. I also knew now an aspect of boarding school that I had loathed but which I had never able to adequately name or describe to my parents—even as a teenager the concept had eluded me. Boarding school underneath the glitz and the horseback riding had been institutional.

I took the underground to Belgravia but got off two stops before our street because the subway was moving too slow for me. I ran the rest of the way to our house. I burst in just after my mother had put one arm into the sleeve of her coat.

"Darling, what a surprise," she said. (I had moved to a flat; I'll say more about that later.) "But I am just on my way out."

"No, you're not," I said.

She looked at my face and said, "You're absolutely right. I'm not. Let me just make one phone call."

She took her arm out of her coat and put the coat in the closet. She dialed a number on the phone and said, "Hello, Lillian. My daughter has just popped in, and since she doesn't pop in on a weekday afternoon very often, I'd like to spend some time with her. Please give everyone my regrets."

My mother rang off and said to me, "Would you like a bit of sponge cake and some tea, dear?"

"This is not a social visit," I said calmly.

"All right, let's just sit in the sitting room."

"No, we're sitting on the sunporch. I don't like being cooped up."

"All right, love. It's November, but it's warm enough. Sitting on the sunporch would be quite nice. I don't like being cooped up, either."

She opened the glass doors, and we went out to the porch. It was chilly actually, but we settled in chairs anyway. I could see our old badminton net in our back garden. My parents had put it back up when they had returned from Africa for old times' sake. I said, "Do you ever think about Folly? I do."

My mother said, "Why, certainly, I think about Folly. I think about her often. She was such a wonderful dog."

I went on in my incoherent way, "When I was a child, all I ever wanted—all I ever needed—was to live every day with people who loved me. What is wrong with that?"

"Nothing is wrong with that. It's the paramount thing, or at least should be. That is what we overlooked. That is what we brushed aside."

She continued, "You yourself thought of alternatives, and I—I should have followed my instincts. Oh, Amelia, I wish we could undo our decisions. Dad does, as well. We are just so sorry. It was a mistake in judgment, not lack of love. You must know that."

"Of course I do. Even at seven I did," I said, and felt the rage subside.

I told my mother about the trip to the institution. I cried about the little boy who still had a bit of rose in his cheeks.

I said Jory was right. I didn't like the things I was learning. I didn't know why I had ever thought about being a speech therapist. I was leaving the program. I'd go back to the bookstore or else be a char lady. My mother told me not to make any hasty decisions. She pointed out that I certainly wouldn't need to work in an institution. There were a great number of settings where I could work. (Actually, I made a similar argument to my teacher when I had tried to get out of the field trip.) My mother said that at some point, I could even do speech therapy out of my home, if that was what I preferred. It was something I could meld with having a family.

"I'd never be so lucky," I said. I gave a short laugh.

"Think carefully. Don't let this one thing change everything," she said.

I shook my head sadly.

"Anyway," my mother continued, "I'm yours now for as long as you want. What shall we do?"

As we had done on the day sixteen years ago when the Colonial

Office witch wives had come to our house, we went into the back garden and played badminton until the afternoon turned into twilight. I tried to imagine Folly threading in and out around us.

My mother's words were not enough to persuade me to stay in the program. Strangely, it was Jory, who had tried to talk me out of starting the endeavor to begin with, who more or less persuaded me to stay. I was too tired to get in touch with him that night, but the next morning I cut class and called him up long distance. He said I was exactly the kind of oddball that should go into the rehabilitation field. Because of my experiences, I would give credence to "unheeded perspectives."

"You mean that I'm halfway to handicapped myself," I said.

"Exactly!" Jory said enthusiastically.

He said that maybe I would tip the balance in someone's life just enough that the person would be able to stay clear of an institution, and maybe I would never even know.

"Perhaps," I said. It was now a Friday, so I would have all weekend to think about it.

Jory knew I was feeling dismal, so just before we rung off, he tried to make me laugh. He said, "Ask not what people with speech problems can do for you; ask what you can do for people with speech problems!" Jory and I were both so fascinated by America's president, and indeed by the ethos of his whole clan.

Yes, it was Jory who more or less persuaded me to stay in the program, but the salient words here are "more or less." A totally unrelated event helped to tip the balance. Because of the time difference, the event happened for Britain in the evening.

I had eaten supper, and then went out to post a letter to Jory, thanking him for talking to me that morning. As I was walking back, I suddenly noticed a lot of agitation among people on the street. A man shouted out, "The governor was shot, too."

What governor? Which governor?

A woman threw up her hands, and someone said, "It can't be true."

Someone else was holding one of those new little transistor radios to his ear and said, "Yes, it is true. Johnson has been sworn in."

Who's Johnson? Which Johnson?

It took several moments for me to understand. President Kennedy's life had been ended in a place in the states called Dallas, Texas.

In the shock and sadness everyone was plunged into, I decided my personal dismay didn't much matter. I would become a speech therapist and do what I could.

When I went back to class, I learned that I had missed the "Mongoloid" wing and also the top floor for the grossly deformed. (A classmate told me that Mrs. Duckworth had not gone to the top floor with them. She had pleaded a meeting and let a hapless lackey take over.) My teacher said they were willing to arrange a special make-up visit just for me so that my grade in "Social Situations and the Handicapped" would not suffer. I flatly refused. I said that I would never in my life set foot in an institution again.

I made good on this vow. More than forty years later, in a totally different incarnation, though, I would read an article in the *Times* by an activist who compared institutions not to boarding schools but to "gulags," and I would think of the pale people I had seen.

What my refusal to complete the field trip meant, though, was that when I got my certificate, the school would not recommend me for a job I wanted that involved working with people recovering from strokes after they were discharged from hospital. My adviser explained that I had shown myself to have rather a weak stomach and to have "still some growing up to do, to speak frankly." The London Logaoedics Centre prided itself in knowing their students and matching them with the right job. Their reputation was at stake.

I took a position in a clinic for adults who stuttered. The environment was meant to be welcoming, and both I and the person I was seeing sat in leather armchairs. My office was carpeted but didn't have a window. Although there were a few other bells and whistles, and my supervisor favored some technique with marbles that I eschewed, the main idea was to tell the individual to relax, think of what he or she wanted to say, and then say it purposefully. Once in a while, I was helpful. For example, there was one fellow who had trouble only with *b*'s, and I told him that it was my clandestine suggestion that he should stop working on *b*'s and come up with synonyms for *b* words.

"Never say 'baby,' always say 'infant.' And 'big' is nothing more than 'large,'" I said by way of illustration.

"A b-b-boy is just a young male," he replied, to show he was catching on.

We spent several sessions coming up with word lists, and when the man felt he could manage on his own, he shook my hand, saying,

"You're tops, Miss Ord, you're tops. And did I tell you that my wife and I are expecting an infant?"

I laughed. It wasn't he would stop using *b* words. That would not be natural. It was just that he was armed with alternatives, if he needed them. He could relax, so to speak.

Anyway, the job was a living, I guess.

After I had gotten out of Oxford, I had lived at home for a while, but then I started to share a flat in Chelsea with a sensible, straightforward girl named Susan, whom I had met at the bookshop. Susan just happened to be Stephen's steady girlfriend. Actually, I had met her when Stephen had brought her into the bookshop to meet me. In any event, the bonus of the arrangement was that I got to see Stephen a lot. Actually, although he had a mail address elsewhere, Stephen was essentially living with us. Perhaps it would be more accurate to say that I was living with them.

I filled up my nonwork hours somehow. I did some things with Christa and saw my parents, especially my mother, a lot. As we had during our home year, Mum and I went to concerts and plays together, and we usually went out for lunch on Saturdays. On Sundays, my parents had Stephen and me and increasingly Susan over to dinner. (Susan's family lived in London, too, but she didn't seem to see them much, except for holidays.)

I had settled into a routine. I was not miserable or killing time. It was more as if I was biding time, absorbing the world but not quite awake yet. It bothered me. I had never forgotten the ill-fated prizefighter Terry in *On the Waterfront*, the film that had made such an impression on me during the home year. I guess I still had a sliver of hope that I could be someone, that I could be a contender.

CHAPTER 8

Razzle-Dazzle

London, 1964–1966

CHRISTA WAS JOINING an amateur musical theatre troupe called the Globe Light Opera Company, or GLOCO, for short. The troupe was mainly made up of Cambridge and Oxford graduates, although others with the requisite abilities were admitted as well. Its focus was on Gilbert and Sullivan, and two productions were put on a year. People had sometimes told me I had a good singing voice, and I had done a bit of acting with Christa at St. Hilda's, so when Mrs. Cookson suggested I try out, too, I hesitated, but then said I'd give it a whirl.

Christa and I were both in the chorus in *Iolanthe*, but then she had to quit after only one season because the bookshop wanted her to travel to manor houses all over England looking for rare books. I wasn't too happy being without her—the whole idea was that we'd do it together—but the next production was slated to be *The Mikado*, and that had always been one of my favorite shows. I thought I'd do that and then quit. I was cast as Pitti-Sing, one of the three little maids.

The troupe was still in the midst of casting when an American fellow walked in, wanting to be part of it all. He sailed through the auditions, and then we arranged ourselves in three rows in front of him, and he had to talk about why he wanted to join the troupe. I sat in the back row and listened absently.

His name was Michael Klein. He had gone to Yale and was now at the London School of Economics getting a master's in mathematics. He loved math, and since he didn't want to teach, he'd probably be an actuary. He had acted at Yale and also had done summer stock since he was fourteen on Shelter Island off Long Island or Nantucket or wherever his family happened to spend their summer vacation. He wanted to join GLOCO for two reasons. First, he thought anything named GLOCO had to be a hoot. Second, his mother thought that all work and no play might make Jack—or in this case Mike—a dull boy. She had actually come to this concern late in life, he said. When he and his little sister Pam were kids, they had had desks in their rooms from the word go—which they were quite free to use once they had completed their homework at the kitchen table. Even in high school, there had been old Mike sitting there in the kitchen conjugating French verbs night after night for his mother to check. His friend Derek had thought it was a riot, until his mom had instituted the same regime.

I looked up at him. Being an American, he was wearing American-style clothes—a sport shirt under a V-neck sweater, "chinos," and well-stitched leather shoes. He was sort of lithe but bouncy in that way some people from the States had, moving around slightly as he talked. I smiled, thinking that if he joined GLOCO, he would be all work and a play.

He said he was from New Jersey.

"Well, that's near Pennsylvania," I suddenly interjected. Everyone looked at me. It really wasn't my habit to shout things out, and anyway, who was I to instruct an American in United States geography? "It's also near Delaware," I felt compelled to add. "My father once told me a riddle about it."

Michael laughed and said he knew the same riddle, as well as one about Mississippi and Alaska. Then he said Montclair, where they lived, was actually part of the New York City metropolitan area. His father worked in the city, and that was where they had usually gone on their frequent excursions, both his parents having been big on excursions, as well as junkets and outings.

I thought of how after the war, with my father home, we had seen all the sights of London.

I said that I like junkets too, but not junket. Again, everyone looked at me.

He laughed. It was a nice laugh he had.

The director of the troupe stood up and said Michael had put on a good chat. He could have the part he had tried out for. He would be Ko-Ko, Lord High Executioner.

The troupe was actually quite glad to have him. First, the disadvantage of his being from the States and talking like it was offset by the fact he was male in a troupe where women far outnumbered men. Moreover, he could sing. He could act. He could dance. (I didn't really pay much attention to him, but once I had to overcome a terrible temptation to say, "Michael, will you dance with me? Will you dance with me?") My disinterested guess was that he was probably good at sex, too.

He was also willing to help in set construction, even though most of the other leads seemed to think backstage matters were other people's affairs. He said that he had never made anything other than lots of bird-houses with his father—it had been an easy way to earn arrowheads in Cub Scouts, and his mother and Pam had always been obsessed with feeding birds—but he figured construction was construction.

There was one other huge benefit to our having Michael Klein. We were meant to bring snack-type things for rehearsal breaks. Everyone else, if they remembered, brought dried crackers, celery sticks, or the like. Michael brought box after box of American-style "cookies." They were of many types: oatmeal raisin, something called chocolate chip, which were apparently an American classic, peanut butter squares with cashews, macaroons, sugar cookies with cherries, butterscotch, and the *pièce de résistance*, ginger snaps made with a secret ingredient to give them zing.

I didn't have reason to talk very much to Michael. However, one famous evening, we were at the refreshment table at the same time, so I thought I should say something. Nibbling a macaroon, I said, "Michael, how do you come by all these cookies!"

He replied, "My mother is going bananas since I've never been so far away from home, so she keeps exhorting my father to whip up batches of cookies for me. She thinks they'll keep me safe." He laughed, "At least I'm faring better than Derek. When he went to California for six months, he kept getting pairs of socks from his mother. He even got socks from my mother. He hardly knew where to put them. At least we can eat the stuff I get, and it is a reminder of home. I do miss everyone, I admit it." He suddenly looked self-conscious.

"Michael, I won't elaborate, but I'm just like that!" I exclaimed. "I've never met anyone who was."

"Kindred spirits," he replied. "By the way, I'm Mike to most people."

I considered that for about two seconds before I spoke.

"Well," I said, suddenly giving a little coquettish giggle, "my friends and those otherwise in the know call me Amy." There were several things strange about my response. I was not a coquette. None of the lessons Christa and even Lottie had given me about flirting had even taken. I didn't know who I meant by "those otherwise in the know," and, to top it off, nobody had ever called me Amy. The name had popped out of my mouth from absolutely nowhere.

I had to move this to safer ground. "Is your father a baker?" I asked.

"Not commercially, although he always ran the PTA bake sales," Mike said. "Commercially, he's a commercial architect. It's just that my mother is a community volunteer and homemaker par excellence —she was always out there building snowmen with us when the other mothers were inside—but she draws the line at making cookies, so my father bakes the cookies. I guess it's sort of weird."

"Not at all," I assured him. "I don't even know how to bake cookies." Now that was true. The only times in my childhood—in London—when Mum could have taught me how to bake cookies (or as we would say, biscuits), sugar was still being severely rationed. Even during our home year, sugar had been a dear item.

But then I said, I certainly did, did I, "What this means is that when we are married, I'll live in America with you. I'll even live in Montclair, New Jersey, but you'll have to make the cookies. I'm not doing that!"

"Fair enough," Mike said, "but let's live in Manhattan for a few years before settling in Montclair. That's my suggestion. My mother says everyone should grab a chance to live in the city when they are just starting out."

"For double sure," I agreed boisterously. Wasn't it curious how words could frolic out of one's mouth like sprites or even nymphs, free as the breeze?

"Oh, I'm sorry," I said, suddenly aghast. "I can't even blame this on liquor. I don't drink."

"And you only nibbled an oatmeal raisin cookie and not even a ginger snap," Mike noted.

After that I made sure there was at least fifteen feet distance between him and me at rehearsal breaks. Once he cornered me coming in and asked whether I would like to learn set construction, since they were down a person. I said, "No, too busy" and dashed by him.

I even had to get the director to change the blocking on one scene. Originally when Ko-Ko (a.k.a. Mike) sang his song about his little list of people to execute, the three little maids were fanned out diagonally to one side of him. Mike got in the habit of looking straight at me when he sang, "the lady novelist! I have HER on the list." I didn't know why he did this. I hadn't written any novels. I convinced the director that it would be very artistic if the little maids were rearranged in a vertical line with Pitti-Sing (me) farthest in back. What that meant was that Mike couldn't look at me without turning half around, and of course the audience would have found that strange, and he was too much of a professional to do that.

One April Saturday afternoon, I was walking across Hyde Park after having met my mother for lunch and thinking how nice it was that it was finally getting warmish. My mother and I had worn sweaters and dined alfresco.

"Howdy, stranger," Mike said when he saw me. He was sitting on a bench with a stack of letters.

"You have a lot to read," I said, surveying the five opened letters and four unopened letters.

"Courtesy of a freak blizzard. Blanketed the whole Northeast. Snow, sleet, and gloom of night may not stop the mailman, but it does stop planes, which is to say that I got no letters for almost a week, and then today I got three letters from my mom, two letters from my father, two letters from Pam at Wellesley, and one from my friend Derek's mother."

"You must spend all your time answering mail," I said, pleased that I had used the American word for post.

"Mom makes it easy. Montclair built a new library several years ago, and she was vice chair of the fund-raising committee and came up with the idea for flagstones out front as well. So now she thinks she owns the place and is there all the time. They have a mimeograph machine. You know that makes copies, making the ink white and the paper dark. All I have to do is write one letter, and she makes mimeographs for Pam or whoever."

He paused and then said, "However, I've lately taken to writing Pam individually. I've met this girl with hazel eyes and a Cheshire Cat smile, and since Pam's a girl, I'm hoping Pam can advise me on how to get to know her better."

"Well, better to ask her than me," I replied. "I don't specialize in social relationships." He had probably figured that out. I had faint memories of the heebie-jeebies I had gotten years ago with Ted Sanders, but that was about it.

"So how long did the pony express last?" I asked inanely, after I had a sudden image of him riding, riding, the muscles of his male shaped thighs rippling under his chaps. The saddle was, of course, western, not froufrou English.

"Not long," he replied. "More of an experiment, I think. Railroads took over fairly quickly."

"Yes, I've read that in the nineteenth century, America was pretty can do, as you would say. There was a lot of bad stuff mixed in, though."

"Agreed," Mike said.

"Also, ponies can't swim across oceans," I felt the need to say. Good God, what was wrong with me?

Mike laughed and said, "Yup."

"Listen," I said. "I need to be on my way. I have to look up something in a textbook." Now, that was true. I wanted to find out if there was a label for a condition where words popped right out of your mouth on their own accord. I was just glad that I had successfully resisted the temptation to rip off my blouse. My perky breasts were still my best feature.

"Hey, Amy," he said. I looked around to see who Amy was, perhaps the girl he wanted to go out with. Oops, Amy was me.

"I also got three packages—socks and two containers of cookies. I'll bring the cookies to rehearsal and possibly wear the socks."

"You have a fabulous family," I said. I could feel him smiling as I walked briskly off.

I purposely arrived at the next rehearsal at the very last minute, when people were getting in place onstage. At the break, I left after grabbing two ginger snaps, since the rest of the rehearsal involved blocking scenes that I wasn't in.

I guess I hadn't learned my lesson, though, because when Saturday afternoon rolled around the next week, I was once again in Hyde Park, this time taking a stroll. The daffodils and tulips were just about in bloom. The leaves, soft and green, were coming back on the trees, and there was Mike on the same bench.

I had begun to notice that his nose was lightly freckled. I liked the contrast with his very dark brown hair wisping over his ears.

"Hi there, Amy," he said, hailing me. He had several opened letters beside him, but he was holding a book, *Too Late the Phalarope*.

"Reading in the park?" I asked, having nothing better to inquire about.

"Yes, I like to be outside for hours, especially when the weather is this wonderful and color is coming back into the world."

"Likewise," I said, but resisted the temptation of adding, "See, we're a perfect match."

"My parents just sent me this book," he said.

"My parents sent it to me as well, although it was years ago, for a birthday. I've never met anyone but my mother who has read it. It's lyrical, but it's so sad, a man undone by the intersection of his impulses with terrible cultural dictates." I paused and wondered whether I should have said that impulse thing. It was not like I was talking to Christa. Oh, well, who cared?

"And it's ironic. He's a celebrated Afrikaner policeman, sworn to enforce the ghastly apartheid law, but he breaks it, and not for, um, the most enlightened reasons," Mike commented.

"His aunt is set apart by a handicap, I think," I said. "She is aware of the whole thing, knows what is going on, and even why. She thinks she can save him by getting his father to accept him or give him advice or some such thing. Yet she does not speak. She holds her peace, a peace that was no peace at all." The last was a quote from the book.

"Yes, but she was bound by cultural norms, too. Her brother had included her in his household. She didn't feel she could tell him how to interact with his son."

"I suppose," I said. I didn't tell him that I hadn't quite understood the father-son angle.

Mike went on, "My mother has always said that the hardest thing for people to learn is when to stand back from one's culture."

"Yes, I can understand that," I said. "In *Huckleberry Finn*, which you've probably read, Huck has been raised totally outside of society —indeed he has almost raised himself—but he has still absorbed the notion that it would be wrong to help in an escape from slavery." Oh great! I was interpreting a classically American novel for an American.

"Yes," Mike said. "The moral climax of the book is when Huck decides to do the right thing, even at the risk of going to hell."

I had been standing up, but now, for some reason, I sat down on the bench, although on the other side of the stack of the letters.

Then I said slowly, very slowly, "For a lot of the time when I was growing up, my family lived in Africa—not South Africa, where *Too Late the Phalarope* is set, but Tanzania, when it was Tanganyika."

Mathematically speaking, I had probably spent more time in Kenya, but I opted to save that for a later day. I would have told him, though, how long we had been in Africa, but I have never known how to calculate that. Our home year had started eight and one-third years after we had come to the compound, but after that my parents had gone back while Stephen and I had stayed in England, except for summers. Did I count that period? I remembered I had never known exactly where home was at that time.

"We stayed for quite a while," I said, and then realized that was redundant with what I had already said.

"How was that for you?" Mike asked.

I took a deep breath, as I suddenly realized that there were two things I liked about his question. First, people who found out I had lived in East Africa were usually besides themselves with excitement. You did! That's great! It must have been amazing! What an opportunity! Mike had made no assumptions. Instead, he was just asking. Second, he had indicated he knew that my experience was only my experience and no one else's. Not Stephen's, not the Hobsons', and you bet your life not the Tanzanians.

I looked at my fingers. "My parents told my brother Stephen and me it would be an adventure. It wasn't, not once we were there. We would be living with the British in Africa—not with the Africans, we knew that going in. My parents recognized that the British in Africa had some, um, rather unfortunate customs, but they thought my father could just design roads and bridges and we would not be ensnared. It was all so topsy-turvy. My mother had to give alcohol-fueled parties, she had to bend to racism, and—and although we were a close family, we were in a milieu where distance between parents and children was deemed right and proper." I silently gave a little laugh. I guess that was one way of putting it. There had been hundreds of miles of distance between Dodoma and Nairobi. "Once we were there, my parents didn't know how to get out of it."

"Must have taken a toll," Mike said.

"My very early childhood was very nice, though," I told him. "During the war, my mother, my brother, and I lived in a little house with a bay window in the west of Devon with our cocker spaniel and a girl named Jenny. Even though my father was fighting in Europe, and my mother was worried about him, she pulled out all the stops to make us safe and happy. She had gone to university, but once she and Jenny searched all through the village for a secondhand rocking horse to give to Stephen and me for Christmas. They repainted it and put a bow on it." Why on earth was I telling him this?

"One of my early memories was helping my mother make a rag doll for my baby sister. We followed a nineteenth-century pattern," Mike replied.

"Smashing!" I exclaimed in my new robust style.

He laughed. Then he asked, "So after the war, you went to Africa?"

"First we went back to London, although in my case, I had only lived there previously *in utero.*" I simply didn't know what was wrong with me.

I paused and then continued, "Anyway, my father got out of the RAF, and we learned to pay badminton, and we all had a pleasant enough time for about two years. Then we made our mistake and went on our Africa adventure disaster. Actually by the time we embarked, none of us really wanted to go, but there were forces." Yes, I thought to myself, that's one way to describe the Colonial Office witch wives.

"From the age of seven on, I had a rather strange childhood," I said. Eureka! I had just figured out why I became a rather strange person.

Mike spoke now. "My parents are from the New York area. They met when my father was president of the Latin Club at Columbia and my mother was president of the Latin Club at Barnard. Each was the first in their families to go to college. They married several months after graduation, and I arrived a year and a half later. We spent the war in southern Virginia, on a naval base where my father was stationed, designing ships. Pam was born there."

"You were able to be with your father during the war?" I asked.

"For most part, except for three months at the end where my dad was in the Pacific preparing for the invasion that never came. We stayed with my grandparents then."

"Virginia was where my parents first saw overt segregation," he continued. "For example, the drinking fountain in the park had a "whites only" sign. My mother didn't want us to drink out of it, so she always brought a thermos of water. Then she began bringing several thermoses, packing them in Pam's baby stroller, so she could offer water to the black women watching the white kids who drank and splashed their hands in the fountain."

I nodded appreciatively.

"Anyway," Mike said, "after the war, we settled in Montclair. Both my parents have characteristics—but my mother in particular, because she is so helpful and gracious—that make them highly respected and admired in town. Yet we don't exactly fit the mold. My father is Jewish, and at the time we moved in, Montclair had few Jews. My mother was Catholic. There were more Catholics, but almost none married to Jews. Then she left the church because of a dispute she apparently had with a priest over Pam's and my upbringing. I don't think she was formally excommunicated, but almost. Also, she's Irish. We became Presbyterians because she wanted us to have some religious base, but everyone knew that wasn't really what we were. On top of that, our closest friends are black. Let's see what else. We're Democrats, even though everyone for miles around is Republican. My father, like the other fathers, gets on the train to New York every day, briefcase in hand, but he's practiced in the domestic arts. This is just for starters."

"Double smashing!" I said, and I meant it. Then I said abruptly, "Well, I best be running on!"

"Cheerio!" Mike said.

I wanted to respond in kind. I was going to say "so long," but it somehow came out as "See you later, alligator!"

Mike said, "What can I say but in a while, crocodile."

I strode off. My hair was at chin length, as it had been for years, but it bounced. I was aware of that. I wondered if he was aware of that, but what did it matter? Mike Klein was nothing to me, just an entrancing American with an entrancing American family (who I would have died to meet).

It was now the week before the show, and it was called "hell week," because we rehearsed each night. I managed to keep away from the man of the hour. I had other problems. My part was making me sick. I just didn't see how I could do it.

The main song sung by the three little maids was "Three Little Maids from School." That was how Yum-Yum, Peep-Bo, and, unfortunately, I as Pitti-Sing, were introduced. I had originally not thought much about it. When I was first a little maid, I had gone to Regency Day. Now, though, I began to focus on the phrase in the song "Come from a ladies' seminary." We had to sing the stanza in which it appeared twice.

I did my research, just to make sure. In the nineteenth century, certain types of girls' boarding schools were referred to as ladies' seminaries! My character had come from boarding school. Had she been sent there when she was as young as I was when I had gone to Westlands–King George? Her name, Pitti-Sing, was undoubtedly code. You should pity her as she sings.

I considered Yum-Yum, self-absorbed, overconfident, loving Nanki-Poo to a point, but only to a point. She might as well be the girl named Buffy. In fact, she was more Buffy than Buffy. Now that I thought about it, the three little maids were a mean little clique, always together, Peep-Bo and Pitti-Sing constantly simpering and giggling with Yum-Yum. It was right there in the sixth line of the song, "Nobody's safe for we care for none." They were the gaggle! All right, I had conflated Westlands–King George and Longwood, but nonetheless it was inescapable. I was playing a boarding school lass, who was one of the gaggle! How had I ever gotten into this?

I sang more and more dispiritedly with each rehearsal. My line delivery became anemic. Finally, at the second-to-last rehearsal, the director stopped the first act and said, "Amelia Ord, you must display more enthusiasm!"

"I'll try," I murmured.

Mike cornered me at break. "Would you like a molasses and raisin cookie? Fresh from the postal service today!"

"No, thank you," I said primly.

"Amy, did I do something to upset you? If so, I apologize. That wasn't my intent."

"You exaggerate your importance."

"My sister has always said the same thing."

I took a breath. "The main result for me of the African adventure disaster I told you about was that I had to go to boarding school. I don't want to be a character with that in her background. It's like I'm endorsing the experience!"

"Amy, I'm playing a supposed executioner. I would never promote that as a profession, though. For one thing, mom would kill me!"

I smiled faintly and then said, "I know it doesn't make sense."

"Amy, this is all a parody."

"Yes, but in the instance of the three little maids, Gilbert and Sullivan are parodying women's education, not boarding school. There's a big difference! They probably liked the concept."

"Actors and actresses can interpret a part any way they want for the benefit of the play."

"I considered boarding school to be ridiculous. I always made double sure I stayed remote."

"Then convey that!" Mike said.

"All right, I'll try," I replied. I grabbed a cookie, and Mike smiled. I must admit he had a grand smile, truly joyous and lighting up his whole face.

At the dress rehearsal, I moved slightly away from Yum-Yum and Peep-Bo. In the first stanza of our song, I had a quizzical look on my face, which got more quizzical when we got to the line "filled to the brim with girlish glee." It wasn't true for me, folks! Then I gave the other two a sidelong glance just as we sung "for we care for none." I looked wary each time we sang "all unwary," and I discreetly pointed at Buffy Girl Yum-Yum and her sidekick when we got to "come from a ladies' seminary." I'm not really a part of this. It's all due to circumstances! For the *pièce de résistance*, I folded my hands in prayer when the three little maids sang "from three little maids take one away." The line was about Yum-Yum, but it was as if I was saying, oh, please, let it be me!

"Amelia, what are you doing?" the director asked.

"Yeah, Amelia, what are you doing?" the girl who was Yum-Yum demanded.

"I'm the dissident little maid," I demurely said.

"Quite creative," the director said. "It stays in the show!"

"Bonanza!" yelled the Lord High Executioner. I gathered that was an American expression.

On opening night, Mike showed me a telegram his sister had sent him. It said,

"Brother, dear—break a leg. Get the girl. Love and Hugs, Pam"

I couldn't quite see writing "love and hugs" to Stephen, but then again, they were from the States.

The audience loved the show. The reviewers said that stodgy GLOCO had turned "lighthearted, coy and effervescent." My parents, who came to three out of four performances, said they didn't know when they had enjoyed anything more. Even Kate Hepburn was impressed. She and Jory, who had just gotten a faculty appointment, came down from Cambridge for the last night. When we went out afterwards for a drink, or rather to watch her have a drink, she said, "God, Amelia, you may not have the fire I have, but you have a quirky dash. You took your supporting part and fairly ran away with it. Yum-Yum seemed a bit thrown, although she was trying not to be, and that made it funnier. Of course, the American chap who played Ko-Ko was the linchpin. He made it come together, definitely he did."

"Well, thank you," I said with a proprietary air.

Jory gave me a delighted glance.

"Oh, it's not anything, Jory," I said. "He gets his master's at the end of the month. Then he's flying back to the States in time for his sister's Wellesley graduation. After that, he and his sister and some friends are going down south to do civil rights stuff. At the end of the summer, assuming he doesn't get killed, he'll be working in Manhattan. I'll not see him again. He gave me a novel, *To Kill a Mockingbird*, as a goodbye present." (All right, Mike and I had talked a lot at the GLOCO patrons party.)

"I read books," Kate said. "However, when it comes to gifts from men, I prefer tokens of love—flowers, chocolate, jewelry, especially jewelry. Should we tell her, Snuggly?"

Jory nodded. "Yes, let's. Amelia became my first friend after I had polio, and my fortunes changed. She should be the first after family to know!"

"My parents are putting the announcement in the *Times*!" Kate announced. "Rising actress Katherine Burnham to wed Cambridge professor!"

"Congratulations! Fabulous! I'm glad," I said. I lightly patted Jory's arm. I was sincere in what I said, or at least ninety-eight percent sincere. Kate was egocentric, but she was entirely without guile and seemed totally enamored of Jory. It wasn't like they were rushing into anything. They had been going out for almost seven years. It was just that Kate continued to remind me of someone, other than Kate Hepburn. I just couldn't figure out who it was. It slightly disconcerted me.

"Thanks to me, he plays quite a game of Scrabble," I told Kate, tipping my water glass to her glass of scotch. We all laughed. I told them they both deserved the best.

I was restless that summer of 1965. I was four-square for the people I saw at my job, but the work itself could not hold my attention. Nothing could. Christa, ever loyal, arranged a few dates for me. Feeling I should make an effort, I would try to talk to whichever well-behaved fellow it was about the voting rights law that had just been passed in the States. They never seemed all that interested.

Sometimes, walking around Hyde Park or swimming with my mother, I'd think about Mike and his sister Pam and Derek and Derek's cousin down in the American South. They were helping black people, who might have previously been intimidated or worse, to register to vote. I had asked Mike if he was worried that they would be hurt, and he had said no, not really. They were not going to the Deep South, but instead to southern Virginia where they had once lived, and perhaps a tad into North Carolina. They would be staying with friends of his parents rather than with volunteer host families who might have mixed motives. They would call home at regular intervals. Heck, let's put this simply. He wasn't about to let harm come to his sister.

I started subscribing to the *Herald Tribune*.

Life seemed to be swirling about me. Ted Sanders, who was climbing the rungs of the banking world and had married a girl he had met at university, became a father. I told Christa that I couldn't quite fathom Teddy, the playground daredevil, with a tiny daughter cradled in his arms.

"And she—um, Flora Elise—is to have a christening ceremony!" Christa said. Our laughter was tinged with awe.

Christa herself had been promoted to head of acquisitions at the bookshop and took occasional trips to the Continent. Ian was a stockbroker, and Jon was selling his paintings. Even the Booms were growing up. Lawrence would be heading to Oxford in September. His sights were set on being a naturalist. Dennis and Kenny were in the upper school at Regency Day. Dennis wanted to be a philosopher. No one knew where that came from, but he said it so often that we decided he was serious. Kenny, the final Boom, was an increasingly accomplished percussionist and played with a youth symphony. This summer —with some assistance from me, because as a speech therapist I was supposed to know about something or other—he was giving drum lessons to other hearing-impaired kids. The Cooksons were all so proud of Kenny. I was, too, feeling as if I had been present at the creation.

As for the Ords, shortly after Jory and Kate announced their engagement, Stephen and Susan said they were tying the knot, too. This was not unexpected, especially to me who had shared a flat with Susan (and Stephen) for some time. At the same time, it was surprising to think of Stephen age twenty-eight and a married man.

Of course, we all liked Susan. She was always looking at Stephen with adoring eyes and telling me how good to her he was. She encouraged him to keep going on coin-collecting forays with Dad and even seemed interested when he proudly showed her some rare guinea they had picked up. Indeed, she was very accommodating, saying "I'd love to share the flat with Amelia" when the idea had first come up. She did all the grocery shopping. I just had to contribute my share of the money. A quite good cook, she did most of the meal preparation and even left fixings for me when she and Stephen were going out. Her parents had given the flat a portable television, and I personally thought she watched it too much, but that was minor. Most of the time she was so quiet, I hardly knew she was there. Anyway, Susan was marrying Stephen, not me.

Her parents lived in the London area, and she saw them on holidays but not too much otherwise, so we didn't know them very well. My mother and I decided a good way to start the process was to have her mother over to tea at our—or perhaps I should say my parents'—house. (I wasn't quite sure where I lived.)

Mrs. Dale was pleasant looking like Susan but seemed to have a tightness about her that Susan didn't have. She thanked my mother for everything, the chair she sat in, the tea, the sugar, the biscuits, the napkin. She liked the sunporch, she liked the begonias and petunias in our garden. She had nice things to say about the azaleas.

"We've asters in late fall," I put in helpfully.

"Amelia and I have always enjoyed gardening together," my mother said.

"Swimming as well," I added, but then was silent for a while, as I realized we should be talking about Stephen and Susan.

Mrs. Dale liked Stephen very much, very much. "He just seems so steady, everything you would want in a man. Susan is so lucky, I've told her so, haven't I, Suse?"

Susan nodded. "I know I am."

"Well, Stephen is lucky to have Susan. We're extremely pleased," my mother said.

"Thank you, Mrs. Ord," Susan said buoyantly.

"Yes, thank you, Mrs. Ord," Mrs. Dale said in her polite, wary way.

"Please call me Olivia," my mother said.

"Of course, Olivia, and please call me Connie," Mrs. Dale said. She turned to me. "Susan tells me you are a speech therapist."

"I had to do something," I said.

"Susan's an office manager for an accounting firm," my mother said. Everyone seemed to be telling everyone else things they already knew.

Mrs. Dale nodded. "Isn't it nice that young women of today are taking serious jobs? Gives them options, don't you think?"

"Agreed," my mother said.

Then we went back to Stephen. We talked about his job as a chemist for a company that was about to become international. His prospects were bright, exceedingly bright. This brought Mrs. Dale full circle. Stephen was nice, so kind and steady. Mrs. Dale would have no care about Susan. Susan was just so fortunate. Not every man was like Stephen.

Susan said, "I enjoyed the hike I took with Stephen and his father last weekend. They seem to have a grand relationship."

Mrs. Dale put in, "Mr. Ord, um, Craig, sounds wonderful.

I said, "He's Stephen's prototype!"

Susan laughed out loud, and her mother, twisting her napkin, smiled a little. My mother changed the subject to how tourism was flourishing in London.

"Well, that was stilted," I said to my mother as I was helping her put away the tea things after Susan and her mother had left.

"It just takes time to break the ice," my mother replied. "I thought Connie Dale was very agreeable."

"She's as nervous as a cat."

"She has clearly done her best with Susan. Stephen mentioned that Susan's father has some difficulties resulting from the war. It's probably been hard for them."

"Oh," I said, imagining he had a tremor or something. "I've never heard Susan mention it."

"Well, it's nothing we need to have a lot of discussion about." My mother added, "They love Stephen, and we love Susan, and that is all we need as the starting point for cordiality between the two families."

It flashed through my mind that Mike's family—the Kleins—would be the most amazing in-laws that anyone ever saw. I wondered if the girl Mike had been interested in before he left Britain had reciprocated his interest. I wondered if she thought about him.

I said, "Mum, let's play badminton. I don't want to go back to the flat just yet."

"All right, let's," my mother agreed. "And do stay for supper, love. That would please Dad."

It was August by now, and then it was September. I had not intended to go to the fall organizational meeting for GLOCO. I had thought *The Mikado* would be my last show. However, I had nothing planned for that particular night. It wouldn't hurt to see what they would decide to put on next.

We were just taking our seats when Mike, wearing a blue suit and green tie, came flying in. He had two cookie boxes under his arm.

"Mike!" the crowd shouted, "Here you are!"

"Yup, it's me!" he said.

He put the cookies on the table and then slid into the only available seat, which happened to be next to me.

"There's a question I've never asked you," he said.

"What's that?" I asked. I caught myself and didn't add: "We already know where we are going to end up." I could keep myself under control when I had to.

"Amy, do you like the Beatles' music?"

"Well, I've always said, you would have to be off your rocker to love rockers," I said. Three things were wrong about this response. First, I had never voiced this sentiment before. Second, he had not asked if I loved the Beatles, but if I liked their music. Third, I did sort of like their music, especially now that they were well past the "I want to hold your hand" stuff. In other words, Mike and I were back to where we started.

"Yes, somewhat," I amended. "However, I have a question as well. Did you bring ginger snaps?"

"I brought ginger snaps!"

I suddenly wanted to hold his hand, so I did briefly. He had a nice, firm grasp.

Why had he returned to Britain? We didn't have much more time to talk. The meeting was starting, and at the break, a lot of people were fluttering around Mike, so I learned only that he had a job at Lloyd's of London. Exchanging only a few words at the end of the evening, since I had to get home to pick out my clothes for the next day or some such thing, we made tentative plans to meet at our "usual place" in the park on Saturday so we could catch up.

[219]

We had a usual place in the park!

I didn't know how tentative our tentative plans were, but yes, indeed we both showed up at our usual place in the park. He was wearing blue jeans, and the denim looked soft from many washings. When we sat down on a bench, I wanted to pat his knee, but I managed to hold back.

Mike told me he had had a good summer. Voter registration, at least in the places where he and his sister and Derek and Derek's cousin had been, had gone well enough. There seemed to be some recognition on the part of many southern officials that the country had made a moral decision, and they had best go along with it.

"A little like England finally figuring out that the regrettable colonial era is finally over and done. Couldn't jettison it soon enough, if you ask me," I commented in my sophisticated way. "Hey, I thought you were going to work in New York."

Mike's plans had changed for a multiplicity of reasons. Just before he left for the States, he had been offered the opportunity at Lloyd's— he would be replacing a fellow who was going to Paris for a year—and he had been given time to mull it over, talk to his family. It seemed like a great chance, something that would only help him down the road, but it was unexpected, and he wasn't sure. Then, on the plane to Kennedy, he had been excited about seeing his parents and Pam and everyone, but something gnawed at him. He had spent his first few months in London, nose to books, also seeing sights but really interacting only with his professors and with the cluster of Americans at the school. Then, just when he had branched out in his activities and began making British friends—present company included—it was all over.

He felt better when he got home—it was, well, old home week. He was enveloped in warmth and the familiar routines. The smile never left his mother's face. His father was always patting him on the shoulder. At her Wellesley graduation, Pam led him around by the hand, introducing him as her wandering brother. However, he had begun to sense the change in the national atmosphere that had occurred in the nine months he had been away.

Coextensive with all the social progress occurring under the Johnson administration, Vietnam had become VIETNAM, as Derek put it. American's involvement had escalated exponentially since the Gulf of Tonkin resolution. Reading it in the paper was not the same as coming home and seeing how it was playing out.

"It's playing out more in Vietnam, south and north, than in the United States," I said. Boy, wasn't I trite?

"Exactly, exactly!" Mike shouted, as if I was a genius.

As guys were increasingly getting drafted, more and more people were looking into the situation critically. Actually, his mother was part of a League of Women Voters' study group on the country's involvement in Vietnam. That did not make her an expert, she was the first to admit, but she was extremely concerned. Things were less clear-cut than they had been in previous wars. Was the US repelling an invasion, or in the middle of a civil war, the cultural dynamics of which Americans did not fully understand? Had the change from presumably an advisory role to the South Vietnamese government to large-scale US military action been inevitable? There was the domino theory and the desire to spread freedom on one hand, but mounting death and destruction on the other.

"With so much murkiness, it is impossible to balance factors," Mike said.

"Quite right," I said, as if I knew anything.

Mike knew someone who had publicly burned his draft card. He hadn't burned his. That wasn't his style. He had an asymptomatic heart murmur, though he wasn't sure if this would disqualify him from service, and he had not researched being a conscientious objector, since he wasn't a pacifist, not really. There was just this one-year job offer at Lloyd's, which he had half a mind to take anyway, and his parents were not adverse, and Pam had said enigmatically, "forces are colliding!"

"So I telegraphed Lloyd's and accepted the offer. Guess I told you more than you wanted to know," Mike said.

"No, not at all," I said. "I guess I will stay in GLOCO this season, although I wasn't planning to." His country was in chaos, and was this all that I could come up with? Jesus, Mary, and Joseph, as the Catholics said. I wondered if his mother had said that when she was Catholic.

"Your mother sounds great," I added.

"She is great, everyone thinks so."

"I assume I'll meet her before our wedding." Jesus, Mary, and Joseph, squared and cubed and once again—I hadn't even been eating ginger snaps.

"Yes," he said. "I'll throw in my father, sister, and friend Derek too."

"I call with my mother, father, my brother Stephen, and his fiancée Susan, and I elevate the stakes with my friends Christa and Jory."

"I think you mean you raise me with your friends Christa and Jory."

"Yes, I suppose, I do," I said. "I haven't played in about ten years." That was true. It had been about ten years since our home year when I had entertained hopes about Ted Sanders.

"Well, I call with Derek's parents."

"I have a full house, so I call with Kate Hepburn."

"Kate Hepburn?" Mike laughed.

"Oh, her name is really Kate Burnham. She's marrying Jory. I just call her Kate Hepburn because she has long legs and is a rising actress—professional, that is."

"Kate Hepburn is not a rising actress. She's already there—professionally, that is," Mike pointed out.

"You might say she is raised," I said. "Professionally, that is!"

The remark wasn't that witty, but we both started to laugh so much that our shoulders nearly collided, to use his sister's word.

"Oops," I said, suddenly straightening up. "I see one of my speech customers coming our way." Speech customers? I guessed I better explain the use of the term, if not to Mike, at least to myself, since I had never used it before.

"At my shop," I babbled, "we're supposed to call the people who come for services 'patients.' However, I don't want to call them that for two reasons. First, that would imply I am doing something quasi-medical or ersatz medical, to be more precise. Instead, I see myself essentially and at the core as just giving practical tips to make communication easier, not that communication is ever something you can trust, even when oral musculature does not hinder you. I'm surely the proof of that! Second, and this is key—" I paused. Was I writing a paper, or what?

"The word 'patient' objectifies individuals, make them more abstract, and I'm trying to avoid that, so I call the people 'customers' at least to myself, right here, right now," I said. "Guess I told you more than you wanted to know." I suddenly realized he hadn't even asked.

"No, this is interesting. You shouldn't take things at face value."

"Anyway, the coast is clear," I announced. My speech customer, never in earshot, had veered off in another direction, just exchanging a wave with me.

Then I made a disclosure. "I may have hinted at this, but I have arrested development."

"Well, as I told you, I'm a mama's boy," Mike said.

"And a gentleman," I replied.

"My mother would be glad to hear you say that."

We both laughed.

"Oh, I need to thank you for *To Kill a Mockingbird*," I said. "It has a few flaws. Atticus is put on a pedestal for merely behaving decently —not that it was all that easy—but, gosh, I enjoyed the book. I read it twice and gave it to my mother, and she liked it as well. We discussed it while we were planting begonias." Where had my sudden penchant for mentioning inane details come from?

"I'm glad, "Mike answered. "I liked it too. I read it on the plane coming back."

I gave him a sidelong glance.

"Well, both my mother and sister had enjoyed it."

I clapped my hands and laughed. He joined in. Our shoulders kept touching.

So, talking about the weighty and the mundane with occasional bursts of merriment, we passed a hour more. It was a classic mid-September day, blue sky, grass green, leaves still on trees, with the softness of summer in the air. Yet there was something about the play of the sun and the shade that hinted that a more sharply etched season was coming.

I suddenly looked at my watch. "Gosh!" I said. Was "gosh" my new favorite word? I hardly ever used it, and that afternoon I had said it twice. Maybe I thought it was an Americanism.

"I must run," I explained. "Christa is having a party tonight to celebrate our friend Charlotte—Lottie—passing the barrister exams, and I promised to help her get ready for it."

"Sounds like you have a lot of friends."

"Not really," I said in surprise. "Oh, perhaps I do. I don't know." I was nothing, if not a clear thinker!

"Walk with you to the edge of the park?"

"Why, thank you, sir!"

We shared a quick kiss.

Fortunately, Christa was having the party at her family's house, which was not far away and I walked briskly, but even so, I was later than I should have been.

"I was beginning to get worried," Christa said when she opened the door.

"Sorry, it's such a beautiful day, I went to Hyde Park, and I tarried there, but I'm here now. In the flesh, as they say!" Where did that last thing come from?

Mrs. Cookson, in an apron with flour on the flowered pattern, came out into the hall. "Amelia," she said, "you're smiling like the Cheshire Cat!"

"Just excited to see Miss Linfield tonight. Glad Christa got in touch with her. She's the one that pointed Lottie in the right direction."

"Miss Linfield was fabulous, but you got things rolling," Christa wanted me to know.

"Well, anyway," I answered. "Let me put up the streamers. We're celebrating Lottie tonight! Let's hear it for Lottie! Do I smell angel food cake?"

Christa and her mother looked at each other, since I usually didn't talk so exuberantly.

"She is indeed smiling like the Cheshire Cat," Mrs. Cookson murmured.

Hadn't Mike said something about a girl with a Cheshire Cat smile? He had mentioned hazel eyes, too. I had hazel eyes.

I had to hold myself in check.

GLOCO was in a muddle. A second organizational meeting was needed, since at the original meeting, after the election of officers, everyone but Mike and I had voted to take a break from Gilbert and Sullivan. We had gotten smashing reviews with *The Mikado*, but some people had been bent out of shape with the reference to GLOCO being formerly stodgy. A critic's comment about the natural conservatism of university graduates had further caused ire. The consensus opinion—probably relating to a misunderstanding of Gilbert and Sullivan—was that the best way to avoid stodginess and conservatism was not do Gilbert and Sullivan.

Now the group had to decide what to do instead.

The decision was fraught, and suggestions ricocheted. *The Merry Widow*! *My Fair Lady*! *The Magic Flute*! *Mary Poppins*! *The Music Man*! *The Music Man*!

The idea had not come from Mike, but now he spoke. "If we are going to do an American musical, that's the one we should do. A lot of musicals have great songs, but *The Music Man* has something more."

He explained. The story was predictable, yet it wasn't. There was an ambiguity about it. Professor Hill was a flimflam man who was sort of onto something. Marian was not the usual lonely pretty lady. She was the head of her household and pursuing two careers, the intellectual touch-point of her town. "She owns the books," he said.

"Yeah," someone objected, "but amateur British actors are not going to get British audiences believing in the think system."

"That would just make it funnier," Mike said. "I admit, though, that I may be biased. I did *The Music Man* at Yale."

"Actually," I exclaimed, "I practice the think system constantly."

"*Kiss Me, Kate*, perhaps?" someone else suggested.

That curiously garnered a lot of enthusiasm, but the faction stridently supporting *The Merry Widow* was also gaining strength. Forty minutes of back-and-forth ensued, and then a hour. Feathers were getting ruffled, so Mike rose and started handing out chocolate chip cookies.

It was getting late when, by some alchemy, the divide was bridged. We would give Iowa a try. GLOCO's 1965 fall production would be *The Music Man*.

The show was cast a few days later. Several fellows tried out for Harold Hill, but Mike won the part handily, based on his rendition of "Ya Got Trouble." Beth Brantley, our strongest soprano, if a little wooden as an actress, became Marian, the librarian. I was cast as one of the Pick-a-Little ladies ("Pick-a-Little, Talk-a-Little, Cheep! Cheep! Cheep!). I knew I would have to suppress the suspicion that the Pick-a-Little ladies were a sanitized Midwestern version of the Colonial Office witch wives. Hopefully, I could do it.

Just a week into rehearsal, we had trouble right here in River City. It was trouble with a capital *T* which rhymes with *B* which stands for break. Beth Brantley tripped on a cobblestone on her way to play practice and broke her tibia. Mike and I then put our heads together—and I called Jory and got some tips from him—and we developed a plan for staging the show so Beth could still be in it. For example, for the Marian, Madame Librarian, number, Beth would be seated in a swivel chair, earnestly trying to check out books, and Mike would start swiveling her all over the stage, Mike rapidly alternating between being behind her and being in front of her. However, the director—who had been agreeable to letting one of the boys whom the Final Boom gave drum lessons to play Winthrop—was quite skeptical here, and besides, Beth didn't really want to do it.

That left the understudy, Buffy Yum-Yum. (I don't know when I had turned into such a name caller, having so valiantly resisted the temptation as a child.) Now that she was faced, though, with actually taking over the part, she said she wasn't up to it. Sorry, she'd stay the mayor's wife.

What would we do? The company stood in a circle around the director, trying to figure out a solution. The construction crew hammered away in the background.

"Hey, why not Amy?" Mike asked.

"Who?" everyone inquired.

"Um, he might mean me," I said. "But I've only played small parts. I can't do this."

"Amelia, I think you can," the director said. "I wouldn't have said it earlier, but based on how you approached the character of Pitti-Sing, I think that, with work, you can."

"Of course, you can, Amelia!" said Buffy Yum-Yum, who had reneged on being understudy. "You'd only be playing yourself. You read all those books, act like a music teacher."

"It would certainly take extra effort and time," the director told me. Then turning to Mike, he said, "And extra rehearsals for you, too."

"Barkis is willing," Mike said.

I was glad that everyone was so focused on whether we could salvage the play, no one caught the implications of that.

"I don't know," I said.

"Amelia, it's your decision, but you would be fine," the director said.

"I think so, too!" This came from the boy playing Winthrop.

"Well," I said, grabbing seconds to think. It was my decision, indeed. It would take extra effort and time and extra rehearsals with Mike, and then we would need to go out to discuss our characters and how they interacted. Time and more time.

"Well, why not?" I said, taking one step forward.

For some reason, everyone clapped.

There was no time to lose. The next night, Mike and I met at a café for supper to talk about characterization and how best for me to quickly learn my lines. It was a nice night, so afterwards we went on a bit of a walkabout past Regency Day, the little park, my mother's and my favorite flower shop, our dentist's office, and other points of interest in Belgravia. On Saturday, we were in our usual spot in Hyde Park, where we went the script over some more and otherwise chatted away the afternoon and then took the underground to the business district around Trafalgar Square so I could see where Mike spent his work days. We repaired to his tiny flat, where once more we discussed the play before I had to hurry off for an engagement I had previously committed to. Sunday, Mike came to dinner at our house, and my parents, Stephen, and Susan all obligingly acted as if I regularly brought home American fellows who called me Amy. Monday, the director had a special rehearsal for Mike and me, and Tuesday, we had our regular rehearsal where everyone complimented me on how quickly I had stepped into the role of Marian.

I was suddenly having the time of my life. Slam bam alakazam! I can't describe it.

Two months later, just before the American holiday of Thanksgiving, GLOCO put on *The Music Man* to cheers, whistles, applause, and, on the last night, a standing ovation. The review in the *Times* said, "The production is extraordinary. As usual, GLOCO's chorus is strong, and various cast members manage an authentic Midwestern American twang, in this reviewer's opinion. Randy Bothwell, who plays Winthrop and apparently comes by his speech impairment naturally, is a scene stealer. However, it is the leads, Michael Klein and Amelia Ord, who take the play into the stratosphere. Their showcase number, 'Marian, the Librarian,' sizzles. When Marian, trying to check out books and irritated that that the Music Man is twirling her in her swivel chair all around the room, leaps up and pushes HIM into a waltz, the air becomes electrified. Later, by the footbridge, as Marian sings 'Till There Was You,' we are convinced that these two very different people have fallen head over heels for each other. Seventy-six trombones to them!"

Actually, Mike and I thought "Till There Was You" was the sappiest song in the show. We made up a parody that we sang at the cast party, which went, "There was ping pong, in the gym, but I never heard the pinging, no, I never heard it at all, till there was you."

[227]

We had fallen head over heels for each other, though. Seventy-six trombones to us!

While the play was going on, we had essentially kept our connection under wraps. Only my family knew, but then with the play over, everyone seemed to know. Christa was a little nonplussed. "Well, I did pick up on certain things. You could have clued me in, Amelia, really you could have," she said.

"Christa, it was all so new, so different, so too good to be true, that I just couldn't," I said. "I had to get used to it first."

Christa paused, and then smiled her wonderful smile. "I'm happy for you. We all are," she exclaimed.

A friend of mine at work did say, "God, Amelia, you really know how to fry your parents, taking up with an American who's half Jew and half Irish Catholic." Actually, she wasn't a friend, just a colleague, and she didn't know my parents at all.

My parents liked Mike. They liked him very much. He could talk international relations and economics with my father, and, since his college minor had been in French, French literature with my mother. They discussed how she had spent several months right after university with her cousin Céline east of Paris and spent time with their friend Ruth before she went to the French-Swiss border, where she helped set up English literature sections in rural libraries. This was one of the few stories about her past that Mum liked to tell. Although I enjoyed it because it showed my mother being daring, I had heard it many times. To Mike, it was new and fresh, a bit about my family that he was eager to hear.

I knew that we had crossed the Rubicon when, on Sundays after dinner, Mike began to organize what we were now calling the "six of us" into round robin games of badminton.

"This is enchantment," my father said.

"Yes, it's delightful," my mother echoed.

"Sis, you do well," Stephen said.

"Couldn't happen to a better girl or one who has a better brother!" declared Susan.

Although our families were truly very different, Mike and I discovered some intriguing similarities. We had grown up at a time where smoking was nearly universal among adults—our houses had been filled with ashtrays for visitors—and yet none of our parents had smoked. In both families, bedtime reading had been the rule when we were small, and both my mother and his had used special voices for the elephants in the Babar books. It was amazing to think that we might have been reading the books on some of the same nights, although owing to the time difference between England and the East Coast of the States, never at the same moment. In London, while we spent Christmas Eves with the Cooksons, listening to the mothers do a dramatic reading of *A Christmas Carol*, in Montclair the Kleins spent Christmas Eves with Derek's family, the Gibbses, and Mike's mother would do a dramatic reading of "The Gift of the Magi" by O. Henry, an American short story writer.

The Kleins liked swimming. We liked swimming. My family was competitive, academically and otherwise. If there were awards to be had, we would try to win one. The Kleins were somewhat the same way. Pam had been the New Jersey state spelling champion of 1956 and had been a semifinalist at the nationals. The whole family had gone down to Washington, DC, for it, and they still talked about it; Mike had gotten slightly less raves for being a national merit scholar finalist.

"What did her in?" I asked.

"Afebrile," Mike said. "She thought it started with an "e" but my mother told Pam that since she had never expressed an interest in medicine, it was nothing to worry about."

"I just love your mother!" I said, and I did.

I reflected on this in alone moments. Here I was attracted to a man partly because I loved what I heard about his mother. What sort of basis was that for two adults to build a relationship on? Maybe this was lunacy. As for the institution of marriage, I didn't know if I approved of it. My parents seemed a unit, an unshaken "we," but there were things about them together that had always confused me. My mother had always appeared confidently in charge of things in Devon but somewhat hesitant later on. I didn't know how my parents made their decisions. Whose views were the more important? Who deferred to whom, or was it a blending of desires? I had the feeling that my mother always held the veto—she could have nixed Africa easily—but did that imply that my father essentially set the course? Yet that wasn't true all the time. Everything seemed to change, depending on circumstances.

Everything was a muddle to me.

Well, I would let it play out. Que Será, Será. Whatever will be, will be. I was fatalistic in my joy.

In April of 1966, Stephen and Susan got married in a large church wedding, meaning there were about 150 on Susan's side and about 30 on ours, and we were glad to have eight Cooksons plus Mike to bulk up our numbers. Susan was glowing, and Stephen seemed quietly proud and happy, and they said their vows well.

Afterwards, I loved it when we were all on the dance floor. My parents could really cut a number, which was something that I had forgotten or more likely had never noticed. Mike and I could cut a number as well, and I also enjoyed doing a few steps with my father, as in days of yore. The reception went on a bit too long, though, with Susan's father, a hearty glad-hander without a trace of a tremor, plying everyone with so much liquor we might as well have been back at the compound. Mrs. Dale looked increasingly wary, nervously smiling and telling everyone how nice Stephen was and that good men were hard to find. We were glad when Susan and Stephen made their escape to Heathrow.

While Susan and Stephen honeymooned in the Azores, I had the flat to myself, meaning I shared it with Mike. Having lived so cerebrally for so long, I was surprised to find out how possible, how very possible it was for two people to lose themselves and become themselves in each other. I hadn't even had a glimmer that there could be such ecstasy on earth. It was then that I started calling Mike my king of glory.

Mike called it razzle-dazzle.

When Stephen and Susan returned, I moved back to my parents' house, to live every day with them for one last time before Mike and I formally started our life together. Sometimes, though, I would leave in the evening and not come back until morning. This was just the middle sixties, when such things were still frowned on—Stephen had lived a double life for two years—but my mother and father never said a thing.

It was Mike's and my habit in nice weather to read the *Times* and the *Herald Tribune* in Hyde Park on Sunday morning before meeting up with Stephen and Susan to have dinner with my parents. We eschewed benches now and sat tailor fashion on the grass, since I had purchased some paisley bell bottoms, to the excitement—not of Mike—but of Mrs. Cookson, who told Christa that she never thought she "would see Amelia go mod." The times they were a-changing.

Mike and I never actually became formally "engaged." We had in effect been engaged from our first conversation at the refreshment table.

All that remained now was to set a date so that our families could write to each other. I chose not to get an engagement ring, preferring that we use the money for our future. Mike was thrilled. "I had to come to England to find a girl who doesn't like frippery!" he said.

I told Christa, trying to amuse her, that I was a war bride. She laughed only slightly, and I never made the remark again, since more and more people were dying in Vietnam. A funnier joke was that Mike and I were having an arranged marriage. First we had arranged our marriage. Then we had fallen in love.

Mike was adaptable—he had to be, to link up with me—and readily agreed to what I called a family honeymoon. It was my mother who was far more dubious when I told her that Mike and I would have one night of abandon at our old inn with the cocker spaniels in the Lake District, and then I wanted her, my father, Susan, and Stephen to join us there for a week.

"Are you sure?" she asked. "Are you sure? I've not heard of anything like this, Amelia." I hadn't either, but I was sure. It would be both a celebration of my wedding and a kind of Ord last hurrah, because shortly thereafter, scattering would occur. Stephen and Susan were going to Toronto, Canada, where his company was opening a new division, and Stephen would be chief chemist. Mike was twenty-six now, not likely to be drafted, so, on my initiative, we were heading for the States, to the Big Apple.

It wasn't as if Stephen and I disliked Britain, but more that we didn't feel a firm connection to it. We had spent so little of our childhood in England except for Devon, which for our purposes had been a country unto itself where my mother had gently ruled as queen, goddess, and prime minister, assisted by her loyal page, the still remembered Jenny. For my part, America and the way Americans seemed to chart their own course had always fascinated me. Being with Mike gave me courage. I wanted to try the new world.

When my mother accepted the idea of a family honeymoon, finally saying it would be delightful, I asked Mike if his family would be miffed that it would be just Ords, except for him.

"Double sure, not," he said. (He had begun to use some of my family expressions). He explained that Pam, having so recently landed her dream job as an editorial assistant at Condé Nast publications, would have to fly home right after the wedding. Meanwhile, his parents had

reservations for Paris, so as to kill two birds with one stone and celebrate their twenty-seventh anniversary. He told me not to worry. We'd
see his family constantly when we moved.

It was full steam ahead.

The minutes were now starting to run out, each day going by more
quickly than the day before. May had given way to mid and then late
June. I suddenly wanted time to freeze. Nothing could be better than
what I had now. At Mike's urging, my mother and I were taking tennis
lessons together. Everything was great the way it was. I began silently
to panic.

I met Mike's parents and his sister for the first time at the Sheraton
Belgravia two days before the wedding. They were all wearing well-
stitched American leather shoes, just as Mike did. That was the first
observation about the people who were poised through happenstance
to become part of my family. His father was tall and sturdy, his mother
was shorter and lithe, with curly hair, and Pam, well, looked like an
Americanized Christa, except a bit more athletic, and she had bangs
like me. Yet they all somehow resembled Mike. Derek Gibbs, Mike's
best man, was there as well, and also wearing well-made shoes. He
seemed to look a shade like Mike, too, except that he was black.

Mike's father had a strong handshake. "Alan Klein, at your service!"
he said.

"I love the ginger snaps. The raisin molasses are good, too." I said.

"You'll always be supplied with both," he promised.

Pam said, "I'm the strategist. I told Mike to discuss books with
the Oxford scholar, and I said that if she likes to hear about Mom—
and who wouldn't?—tell her about Mom! I may have even suggested
paying off the understudy, but let's make one thing perfectly clear. I
had nothing to do with the original Marian the Librarian breaking her
ankle. Neither did my brother, insofar as I know. We do have our principles! You do need to know what you're getting into, though. He has
been known to return library books late."

"Yes," Derek added, "and the first time he parked a car on Bloom-
field Avenue, he got a parking ticket."

"Well, I didn't know how long a movie *The Ten Commandments*
was," Mike objected.

"I kept nudging you through the burning bush scene to get up and
put more change in the meter," Derek said.

This devolved into telling Mike stories. Once Mike had sent Derek's mother a birthday card and signed it "your son, Derek," and it hadn't even been her birthday. They were all laughing, and I laughed too, to meet them and see how they were with Mike.

In a lull, I said, "Mrs. Klein—"

Mike's mother said, "Amy, we're going to be family. Please call me Janet."

That reassured me right away to know she didn't expect me to call her some appellation of mother.

"Well then, Janet," I said, "I will like it so much if we become the best of friends."

Janet clasped my hand in both of hers. "I'm certain we will be, Amy, the very best of friends."

"You can be friends with me, too!" Pam said.

"And me," Derek echoed.

"Amy's already friends with me," Alan bragged.

"Well, friends," I said. "My mother would love it if you'd all come to supper tonight."

I had worried that my parents might find the Kleins too breezy, but they seemed to hit it off with them. (I had begun to use American expressions.) My parents knew just a handful of people from the States, but incredibly, my mother and Janet had a common acquaintance. West Orange was just over the ridge from Montclair, and Janet knew my mother's friend from St. Hilda's. Her husband had retired from the New York Yankees and was engaged in philanthropy. Janet had worked with them on several Easter Seal fund-raisers.

"Won't Honora be surprised to hear about the connection!" Janet said.

"We've gotten a little out of touch over the years," my mother admitted. "I will write her immediately now. She has a daughter Barbara?"

"Yes, Barb's at Swarthmore, and they have two younger girls as well. When you come over—and I hope you and Craig come over as much as you can—we'll get together with Honora's family."

"Oh, we'll be crossing the Atlantic often," my mother replied with complete confidence. "One thing you need to know about us, we're quite attached to Amelia and her brother. Can't bear to be separated from them for too long."

"Then, we can do many things with Honora," Janet said, smiling.

I felt strangely comforted that my mother would have a social life in America.

Mike and I were married on July 16, 1966. There was not a cloud in the sky that day, which was a good thing, since I had opted for an outdoor ceremony.

"The sky is blue for me," I said to my parents during breakfast that day.

"It is blue for everyone," my mother remarked enigmatically.

We wanted to linger over breakfast, but we couldn't. There wasn't enough time.

Stephen and Susan and then Christa, my maid of honor, came over, and we all briefly chatted. They told Amelia stories. I had known the names of twenty-five flowers at age two, and so on. Then I had to get ready.

My mother had a lemon silk dress that I remembered from Devon and that I had always liked, so she, at my request, had had it altered, and I was wearing that. My mother had lent me a silver flower-shaped pin with a little pearl in the center, which we pinned on the dress just above my right breast bone. At Harrods we had bought a cream-colored belt lightly dotted with blue, which went well with the dress. So I had something old, something new, something borrowed, and something blue (apart from the sky). That was where tradition ended. Christa and Susan, who was my matron of honor, were in white chiffon. The three of us together looked like daffodils. My father, taking a photograph, said we were as pretty as a picture.

In addition to my family, the Kleins, Derek, and Christa, the guests were the rest of the Cooksons, Jory (Kate Hepburn was rehearsing *As You Like It* and couldn't come), Lottie, and, to Mike's surprise—I had been in a conspiracy with Janet—Derek's parents. Lottie's vicar, from the wrong side of Marylebone, was officiating, and after the ceremony we were going to have an American-style barbecue, and our wedding cake was an apple pie. This wasn't the usual Belgravia wedding.

The minutes were running out. After many cuddles, my mother left me and went out with Stephen. Just five minutes later, right at eleven, a quartet we had hired started playing Pachelbel. Susan and Christa went outside. Now it was my father and me. I wasn't sure I wanted to do this, but it seemed to be happening. My father gave me his arm.

My father walked me from our side porch to the center of our garden. He kissed me and whispered in my ear, "This is enchantment." I took his hand briefly, and then he stepped back to join my mother. I was surrounded by roses, by smiles, by everyone I most cared about (even Folly was there in the lilacs), and Mike was at my side. There was nothing to be frightened about.

Mike and I exchanged thin gold rings, the only rings we would ever wear. We said our vows slowly and carefully. From here on out, we would never be apart. What, never? Well, hardly ever!

CHAPTER 9

The American Revolution

New York City and Montclair, New Jersey, 1966–1973

MY PROPER NAME was now Amelia Ord Klein. It had a ring to it—AOK—and I would use it on applications and documents. However, in the new world, friends and those otherwise in the know would call me Amy Klein.

It was in September 1966 that we hit New York. Mike always said I was part of the British invasion. From my perspective, it seemed more like the American revolution, everything shifting for me even as the country at large was going through upheaval.

I almost didn't get there. Leaving England or, more precisely, leaving my parents in England wasn't real for me until Stephen and Susan nonchalantly packed up and left for Toronto in August. Blissfully happy with my husband, I began counting the days until our departure with dread. Glumly, I packed my clothes, books, and photographs. Dutifully, I read *Time* magazine, the *New Yorker*, and *Glamour*, sent to me by Pam to prepare myself for immersion in the States.

Lottie, mistaking my concern, said she would visit my parents often. She had apparently figured out almost from the start that my parents had contributed the extra money she needed to attend Regency Day, and she had insisted on paying it back with her first paychecks as a barrister. My parents had agreed to accept it only if she permitted it to be used to start an aid fund for students at the school. She and my mother would be setting it up this fall, and I would be in America. They would do it by themselves, because I wouldn't be there.

The minutes were running out.

I went to pieces when I said good-bye to my parents at Heathrow. "I've changed my mind," I yelled at Mike. "I can't leave!"

"Oh, Amy, it'll be fine. If you don't like it, we can always move back to London, we can definitely."

"I'll miss my mother!"

My parents reminded me that they would be coming over for Christmas. "That's just over three months away, dear," my mother said brightly.

That made me burst into tears. Was this going to be like boarding school?

"Amelia, you're embarking on an adventure," my father said, trying to helpful.

"Adventures can turn into disasters," I cried.

"It's not that you've never been abroad," my father added.

I cried harder. They would probably tell me next that Stephen would be on the same continent.

"Dear," my mother said, "remember, Stephen and Susan are coming to see you the weekend after next. Won't it be fun showing them Manhattan?"

I shook my head.

Mike was shifting back and forth. They were calling our flight. "Amy," he said. "Amy, my mother will there, and Pam, too. You'll enjoy them. My father has found a Y for you in midtown, a brand-new place. You can swim there all winter. He picked up a membership form." Then Mike looked sheepish, since he had just admitted that he had enlisted his parents' help in setting things up the right way for his emotional wife.

I loved him so awfully much.

"All right, love" I said. "All right. I guess our life awaits! I will go."

I took Mike's hand, and we said our last farewells to my parents. We walked down the jetway, turning around once to see them cheerfully waving, although Mum was wiping her eye a bit. We got on the plane.

New York City seemed to have even more neighborhoods than London, and we hit the jackpot. Our neighborhood was Greenwich Village. Pam's boyfriend Ben Klein (no relation to them) had a cousin who knew someone who had a one-bedroom for rent on University Place, and so we slid right in.

Everything was all hustle and bustle, with people always on the sidewalks and steady traffic going by and intermittent honking every hour of the day or night. The first night in the apartment, I couldn't sleep, and so at midnight, we found ourselves looking out our living room windows at Washington Square and the endless tall buildings beyond it, all the way to the Hudson River.

It was all so new and different, the skyscrapers so imposing, and I missed home terribly, but yet there was much I liked from the start.

The first Saturday we were in the apartment, Mike and I were going to meet Derek and his new wife, Lynne, at the Frick, and we were a little late getting off, so we decided to splurge on a cab. Mike told the driver where we were going, and he replied, "Sure thing. Cute little museum."

In London, the driver would have said, "Very good, sir," to reflect the class difference between him and his passengers.

As he eased onto Fifth, he said, "What in blazes do you think is going on with those Yankees?"

"Can't win the pennant all the time," Mike said.

"They're not even close, probably be tenth in the league," the driver said. "It's the Dodgers who will make it to the Series. Still feel any sentimentality about them?"

"Not really," Mike said. "They used to be my father's and my team, but after they were in Los Angeles for about a year, we made the switch."

"Same for me. You move out of Brooklyn, I don't know you," the driver exclaimed.

"Um, what do you think of the Mets?" I asked.

"Thursday's child, far to go," the driver answered.

We were just three New Yorkers, discussing baseball teams.

Five minutes after this conversation, I met Lynne Gibbs, who was destined to become my best American friend after Pam. Her father was a prominent journalist and her mother a concert violinist, but she was straightforward and down to earth, telling me dryly that the Manhattan experience varied widely, based on the block. We soon discovered an incredible coincidence. Before her family moved to Montclair, she had been one of the first black students to attend the Brearley School, and she had been there the year Miss Linfield taught there. My favorite teacher in London had been her European history teacher in New York! Pandemonium broke out in the main hall of the Frick museum!

What other surprises would be in store for me in the Big Apple?

The city had such a beat, such a sophistication, everyone regardless of their individual reality rushing about pursuing their aspirations, and American shoes were so well made! When I started working, I bought a pair of walking shoes, a pair of loafers, and some blue pumps with Cuban heels.

The food was extraordinary. Rueben sandwiches at delis; take-out pizzas with every type of topping; cheese soufflé, which was Pam's specialty; lasagna; western omelets; chicken fricassee—these were all new to me. For some reason, I was intrigued by herb rice, which came preseasoned and which you boiled in a pouch, and also by 3-in-1 Jell-O. Indeed, I wrote my mother a whole letter on 3-in-1 Jell-O.

Once when I was on my own, I slipped into a toy store and bought an Etch A Sketch. I had never seen anything like it. For months, I etched a sketch in odd moments.

The first time I saw the Klein house on Highland Avenue in Montclair—and this was right after we got off the plane—several things registered on me. Highland Avenue was on a ridge of the Watchung Mountains and nearly the highest street in Montclair, and so the Kleins' backyard had a breathtaking view of the New York City skyline. The backyard also had a built-in swimming pool; Mike said they had put it in, since they had never wanted to join a county club, and even if they had, it would have been a neat trick finding one that would have taken them. The last thing I noticed was that in their welcoming living room, interspersed with pictures of Mike and Pam at various ages, were two wedding pictures of Janet and Alan. In one they were standing before a judge on someone's sunporch. In the other, they were standing before a priest in an ornate church. Janet looked glowing in both and wore the same long white wedding dress, although in the church picture it looked a little tighter.

All right, I was a bit tired from the trip, perhaps a bit overwhelmed, but I asked Pam, "Is it common for American couples to have two wedding ceremonies?"

"No," she laughed. "I've never heard of anyone other than Mom and Dad doing it." She explained that her mother needed two dispensations to marry her father in a church, one for marrying a non-Catholic, and another one for marrying a non-Christian. The priest was slow in filing for the dispensations, and there were some bureaucratic snafus; her mother thought no one was very committed to the effort. Meanwhile, she and Pam's father were desperate to begin married life, so to speak, with the result that they finally had a civil wedding. However, receiving the sacrament of holy matrimony was still important to her mother, so when the dispensations finally came through eight months later, when she was beginning to show with Mike, they married again in a cathedral.

[239]

"I always thought Dad was rather a good sport about it," Pam said.

"Oh, he was," Janet said, overhearing us. "I married outside the church for love, and he married in the church for love."

"I'm in love with love," I said rather inanely.

By the time the holidays arrived and my parents came for their first visit, I felt somewhat settled and was able to show them confidently around the metropolitan area. However, my mother noticed one thing I hadn't. In towns like Montclair, people brought their Christmas trees home strapped to the roofs of their cars. We simply couldn't get over it.

My father said, "Marriage and the States become Amelia."

Mike and I could not just sightsee, eat, and have sex. We did have jobs. Mike worked in the actuarial area of a major property and casualty insurance company. He converted the probability of risk into mathematical equations and seemed to like it. I landed the first job I applied for, providing speech therapy in the outpatient unit of the neurological institute of Columbia Presbyterian Hospital. The Kleins joked that I was giving a nod to the Presbyterian guise of the family. Actually I didn't really think I'd get the job, because my experience was so thin, and I really didn't want it, because it involved being in a medical setting. However, the people interviewing were quite taken with my Oxford record and probably my English accent. When they made me an offer, I felt the easier thing to do was to accept it.

I generally liked the individuals I provided services to. They were the population I had originally wanted to work for, and their concerns were interesting. It was just the environment that got to me.

The therapist was supposed to keep file notes that reflected objectivity. We were to refer consistently to the person involved as the "patient" and to use phrases like "the patient presents with" or "the treatment plan to address the patient's most severe deficit is." I felt like objectivity was being confused with objectification. I more or less adhered to this format for the first several weeks while my boss was checking my notes, but when he stopped, I stopped. Instead, I wrote things like "Hilda Wexler (alias the patient) is an F. Scott Fitzgerald buff. She read the opening paragraph of *The Great Gatsby* with cadence and inflection. She then discussed the book with animation. I suggested to her that when she was enthused about her topic and focused on what she was saying, rather than how she was saying it, she spoke in a less halting way."

Well, it paid. Mike and I had a vague sense that we should add to the quite generous wedding gift from my parents and sock away as much money as possible for wherever the future led. My job helped in that endeavor.

Our routine was to work all week, do city things either by ourselves or with friends on Saturday, and then take to bus to Montclair on Sundays for dinner with the Kleins and a pleasant afternoon where I did things with Pam and Janet and the men made the family's weekly supply of cookies.

Five years went by, and they were happy and productive years, the first half decade of Mike's and my marriage.

Mike had to study for a series of exams to be a full actuary. I used the time to get two master's degrees. The first one was in speech therapy, because that was the way the profession was heading. Fortunately, the program didn't feature field trips to institutions, and I did well enough, writing some gobbledygook about the distinctions between language, communication, voice, and speech for my thesis.

The second one was more interesting. It was in American history, and I focused on the period running up to the Civil War, because I thought it was a time of great moral questioning among the body politic, just as our current time was. My thesis explored why, in an era when women were expected to stay out of civic discussion, they instead were the muscle of the antislavery movement.

I discussed the topic with Mum by letter and with Janet in conversation. We agreed that it was facile to think that women abolitionists identified with the slave status. Regardless of their legal disabilities, most of these women were well educated, seemed to have high self-esteem, and saw marriage as a loving partnership.

My mother and Janet both said that women might be more likely to see the moral dimension of every issue because the day-to-day caring for children involved constant moral decision making. What was best for the child? What values did you want him or her to have? How did you want him or her to view the world and people's place in it? If you have to choose between education or nurture for your child, what do you choose?

It was my mother sitting in England who wrote that certain ramifications of making black people, including children, commodities must have had peculiar horror for any woman who was willing to think about it.

"Yes," I wrote back, "Harriet Beecher Stowe became concerned about the plight of slave women who had their children ripped away from them after her own baby son died. That was when she wrote *Uncle Tom's Cabin*."

On a day when Pam and Lynne were with us, Janet said, "Your mother is right. After the importation of slaves stopped, successive generations of slaves were produced to a great degree by rape. Certainly that must have resonated with any decent woman who knew about it."

Involuntarily, I looked at Lynne.

She said, "My great-grandmother's father was white, and he gave her to his other daughter on the other daughter's eighteenth birthday."

Pam and I sucked in our breath.

I titled my thesis "The Bonds of Sex: Women's Power in the Underground Railroad." My adviser said it was the best thesis that had been submitted to him in five years. I had beaten out all the natural-born Americans in my class! My professor wanted me to expand it into a book, and I said perhaps someday.

Part of the reason I studied for a master's in American history was that I wanted to understand the enterprise I was signing up with. As a child, I had lived for long years in East Africa while receiving daily messages that I was expected to remain English. It was topsy-turvy. Never again would I live in a country indefinitely and not be a part of it. I applied for citizenship as soon as I had been in the United States for the minimum length of time required.

The Kleins laughed. Alan noted that most people prepared for the test to become a citizen by reading a civics handbook, but I had gone to graduate school!

There was one element of dissonance, though. I was opposed to the war in Vietnam, increasingly so as the bombing continued. Mike and I signed petitions. We wrote to members of Congress. We solicited money for newspaper ads. With Janet's antiwar group in Montclair, I assembled informational packets, which we distributed outside supermarkets. I worried whether it was hypocritical or at least contradictory for me to swear allegiance to the country while protesting the government's actions.

Mike said, "Well, I'm doing the same thing, and it has certainly never crossed my mind to give up my citizenship. That would be shirking my duty as an American, so to speak."

I didn't quite understand what he was saying, so I just replied, "That's different. You were born a citizen. I'm seeking it."

I talked to Janet's group about my concern as we were stuffing envelopes with invitations to a forum where John Galbraith would be speaking.

A woman named Meg said, "Amy, as I see it, no country has hopes and ideals greater than that of America. It's in the practice where we fall short. It is an act of loyalty to work to bridge the gap."

"Yes, Amy," Janet said. "The issue is not whether you accept everything the government does. No informed person will. The issue is whether you believe in the hopes and ideals of the United States. To put it more technically, do you accept the Constitution?"

"I do," I said. "It builds on concepts in the Magna Carta, which I saw often as a little girl."

All the women clapped for me.

That bridged several gaps for me.

Everyone, including my parents who had come over for the event, clapped for me again on the day I became an American.

By this time, helped by some tricks I knew from being a speech therapist, I had dropped my British accent. The reason was that when Mike and I had to be at social gatherings, someone would hear me say a few words and get all exited over the fact I was from England. I would be deluged with questions about the place, and that would lead sometimes to Africa and always to boarding school. The worst was when some well-meaning person, who had lived at home through high school, would wax eloquently about what people called the British system. "It must make you all so independent" was a typical comment. It was easier just to avoid getting into it. I didn't adopt a New York accent, though. Instead, I settled into the accent of the Kleins, which was deemed to be no accent or, in other words, a standard American accent.

Stephen came to visit, and he asked me why I talked funny.

Mike and I loved each other. We loved the city, and we loved our life. We could have gone on like this forever.

Along about the sixth year, we began to notice that other people were making changes. Specifically, Pam and Ben, who had married in 1967, were now living in Montclair. They had an adorable baby son named Robbie. Derek and Lynne Gibbs had also moved to Montclair, and Lynne was expecting. Mike and I were not about to just say "us too." Yet we were in our thirties now, and we thought we should take stock.

Mike was easygoing. He said we could either have children ourselves or be the best aunt and uncle the world has seen.

I pointed out that we'd be the latter either way.

I didn't know if I wanted children. Aspects of my mother's maternal experience confused me. She had loved Stephen and me, been devoted to us, had managed Devon for us, and had done other wonderful things for us. She had also allowed us to be separated from her for three months at a shot. I thought a lot about her and Janet's comments about how raising children involved constant moral decision making. How were these decisions made? How much was dictated by chance, circumstance, or culture? What were you supposed to do with children? It all baffled me.

Mike and I began to talk about what we called the Question a lot. We talked about it on the bus going downtown. We talked about it during the intermission of *Hair*. We talked about it at supper.

We were in Central Park one Saturday in late April. Daffodils and tulips mingled with lilacs, and the trees were turning green.

"I just love it when the leaves return," I said, as we sat down on our favorite bench, Fifth Avenue at our backs.

"Leaves don't return," Mike said. "New ones appear, instead." We had this discussion every year.

"That's just a technicality," I said. "But listen, love, if we do this thing, we must be all out, go-for-broke parents. They can't be ornaments or appendages."

"Absolutely!" said Mike, who over the years had learned to interpret my speech. "The specifics will be different, but we will care for our kids the way our parents cared for us."

That was it! The specifics would be different—in my case, oh God, would they be different—but the depth of feeling, the love would be the same. We would care for our children the way our parents cared for us. I felt a rush of joy. Once you got beyond the details of upbringings, our families were greatly alike. That had been our magnet, our point of attraction.

It flashed though my head that even on that ghastly day when Stephen and I were first put on the plane to Nairobi, my conviction in my parents' devotion had been unshakable. Mike and I could give our child the same security.

I bent my head down, letting my hair cover my face. Then I tossed my head back. "I love my husband, indeed I do," I shouted to passers-by. An elderly couple walking a Pekingese smiled at us as I covered Mike's face with kisses.

Still, we were not sure. We decided to do laissez-faire. Que Será, Será. Whatever will be, will be. By midsummer, I was pregnant.

We did not tell people right away. We did not want to raise hopes only to be disappointed. I had a vague sense that my mother may have had a miscarriage before Stephen. We also wanted to enjoy a secret just ourselves for a little while, to be able to look at each other in a crowded room and signal to the other our wonder. Ord genes were mingling with Klein genes and, on the maternal side, Brook with Mullin, back to the first person. This was to be the fruit of our union.

Keeping mum with Mum when we went to England for a visit in late August was one of the hardest things I had ever done, but I did it. That was part of being an adult and preparing for parenthood.

One Sunday afternoon in October, Janet, Pam, and I were sitting in the Kleins' backyard, chatting while the menfolk were baking cookies. Pam had Robbie in her lap. Mike brought out a plate of chocolate chips for us, and I said, "Thanks, love, I do have a craving for these."

Mike laughed and went back to the house. Pam looked at me and said, "You know, Amy, if you drank, I'd give you the drink test."

"What's the drink test?" I asked.

"Offer a woman a drink, and if she says no, she's in the family way," Pam replied.

"All in good time, Pam," Janet said. "All in good time."

"I don't indulge in drink," I said, taking a chocolate chip. "I indulge in cookies! That is why my marriage is such a success."

"Cookie?" Robbie queried.

"Cookie!" Pam said emphatically.

The next night Mike and I made several calls, to my parents in London, to his parents, to Pam and Ben in Montclair, and finally, because we were feeling expansive, to Stephen and Susan in Toronto.

Joy cascaded.

There then followed a flurry of activity. We were looking for a house, one that would be big enough to accommodate what would be our growing household, for as soon as our baby was on the way, we knew there would be siblings, there would be pets. It wasn't a foregone conclusion that we'd live in Montclair. Sandy, our real estate agent, showed us houses in Maplewood, Cedar Grove, and Ridgewood as well. We even wasted an afternoon in Paramus, where there were housing developments nestled between malls and highways. It was Montclair, however, that had so much of what we wanted. It was a well-established town rather than a bedroom community. It had racial and ethnic diversity, which was important to us. The schools were quite good. The iris garden was renowned. We had family there. All right, it was a foregone conclusion, we'd live in Montclair.

We were taken with a modern house with skylights on Macopin Avenue, and Janet and Alan agreed it was a good buy. We were just about to make an offer on it when Sandy said she wanted to show us an older house that had just come on the market on Erwin Park Road. We weren't that interested but felt we should oblige her.

It was a three-story wood house painted slate blue with cream-color trim. Built in the 1920s, it had been totally updated inside. The windows were large, and all the rooms had at least two exposures. There were nice little nooks and crannies, lots of closets, and a sunporch that was somewhat similar to the one we had in London. The other house had caught our eye because it was crisply geometric. This house was equally well built—as Alan would confirm the next day—and it had character.

The planting was a bonus, even though we couldn't see the full effect in November. (At the Macopin house, we would have started from scratch.) There was a copper beech surrounded by pachysandra in the front yard, and a fir tree on either side of the door. We had a maple and an oak and two crabapple trees on the property. There were flower gardens both in the front and the side yards. The *pièce de résistance* was the rosebushes set in five-point pattern in the backyard.

"A quincunx!" I exclaimed.

"Yes, we'll have roses in a quincunx formation," Mike said. "What more can you ask?"

Sandy looked at us rather hesitantly. She never quite knew what to make of us. "Well, roses are rather sexy," she finally said.

Erwin Park Road was also a grand location. Both the train station and a small shopping center were just a short walk away. Erwin Park itself was a grassy square around which the houses at the end of the road were grouped. The real park was Edgemont Park, just across Valley Road, and it would be through this park that we would walk with our child to Edgemont School, which had been Mike's school.

Two days later, we signed the contract. Pam in particular approved of our choice. Nearly a straight line could be drawnfrom our house on Erwin Park Road to Janet and Alan's house two miles away on Highland Avenue. Exactly at midpoint at the rise of the hill was Pam and Ben's house on North Mountain Avenue. "Little sister is now at center!" she announced.

We started to call this swath of Montclair "Kleinland."

Incidentally, the Gibbses were right in back of us, on Midland.

After saving our money as a matter of course for so long, it was a bit disconcerting to be going on a spending spree. We were buying a car too, a four-door blue Chevelle, since I did like the color blue, and it would match the house. We'd use it for excursions on weekends, and during the week I would have it for errands and such.

"Good God, I don't drive," I said to Mike.

It was true. I had never had the need or desire to, having lived in London and then New York, places where everyone used public transit, and cabs could be gotten quickly, if required.

Mike set out to teach me on Sundays when we were in Montclair. We were a good team in most enterprises, especially since I was usually the one in charge. However, here we were a bust.

We'd be in the high school parking lot, and I'd asked, "Well, where's the clutch? I saw it in Pam's car. Stephen talks about the clutch all the time."

Mike would answer, "We're practicing in my parents' car because it has an automatic transmission, just like our car will have. There's no clutch."

"You expect me to use deductive reasoning at a time like this?"

I told him I didn't like the hand-over-hand stuff.

"You need to do it on sharp curves."

"Well, why can't cars have rudders or maybe a horizontal bar that you could push down on one side or the other, depending on how you want to go?"

"Write Detroit!"

We'd come back to the Kleins with me biting my lip and Mike looking frustrated.

Finally, Alan said that he had taught Mike and Pam to drive, and he could teach me. He would do it if Mike would temporarily do all the cookie making.

We accepted the offer with alacrity.

Alan was calm and patient, explaining everything beforehand and saying that practice yields improvement, a maxim that seemed far truer than practice makes perfect. Whenever I did something right, he said "excellent." He said "good job, Amy!" often. He told the family that my sense of spatial relationships surpassed that of most people, and that was why I was becoming adept at parallel parking so quickly. I really should have been an architect.

Thus, at age thirty-two, increasingly pregnant, winter bearing in, and with my kind father-in-law at my side, I learned to drive. I aced the written driving test and did fine on the road test. Lynne and Derek, upon seeing my license, pronounced me "a real American now!"

I would never totally enjoy being behind the wheel. I'd walk or bike whenever practical. Mike and I would have only one car at a time, even as nearly everyone we knew acquired second cars. At least, though, I had the mobility I needed as a Montclair mother.

The momentous year of 1972 had begun.

At the end of February, I gave up my job at Columbia Presbyterian. Some of the speech customers with whom I had worked the longest seemed a bit dismayed to see me go, but I assured them I would keep in touch with them. My colleagues, who had already given me a baby shower, gave me a farewell party and a hundred-dollar gift certificate to Macy's. My boss thanked me for my work, and I thanked him for the opportunity. After leaving the building for the last time, I had a lump in my throat that lasted until the middle of the evening.

It was much harder leaving our apartment. It was a small little place. We had to lean sideways to open a bureau drawer, because there was only enough space for us to stand between the bed and the bureau if the drawer was closed. My desk was jammed catty-cornered in the living room. Mike's desk was the dining table (also in the living room). We used to joke that doing the dishes was a job for one, because two people couldn't fit into our galley kitchen. We had been here six years, and we had been so happy all of that time.

The movers came early on a Friday morning in March. As they methodically took furniture and box after box out, I stood at our large window and looked down at Washington Square. I felt dismal. Why on earth were we moving? A lot people had kids and even dogs in the city. We could put the baby's crib in the alcove outside the bedroom. We'd make Washington Square our little park and go to Central Park weekly. If the baby was a girl, she could go to the Brearley School. I was just about to broach the idea to my husband when he came up to me and kissed me.

"Ready, love?" he asked.

"Guess we have to move on to the next stage," I said, fighting back tears. Then I laughed. We were joining the Montclair Operetta Club.

Mike knew that I would feel better if the house was pulled together fast. Once the movers had unloaded everything and arranged our old furniture around new pieces that had already been delivered, all Kleins and Gibbses worked tirelessly, opening boxes, putting dishes in cabinets, and hanging pictures. Except for our clothes and linen, which I put away myself, all I had to do was sit on the new couch, hands on my expanding stomach, and give directions. By Sunday night, when we took the whole crew out for pizza and salad, we were totally settled in. Mike had even baked a batch of cookies, and the aroma of lemon squares wafted from kitchen to sunporch.

On Monday, Mike took the train into Manhattan with his father, and I spent the day with Pam and Robbie and Lynne and six-month-old Derek junior (called Ricky) so I could experience the rhythms of life with little ones. Pam and Lynne gave me baby things and baby tips and smiled at me indulgently when I said I foresaw no problems in taking my child out to a restaurant, because I would explain the necessity for good behavior beforehand.

"You just need to state your expectations," I said.

"Yes, Amy, right, of course," Pam agreed, trying to keep Robbie from chewing on a block.

"Do tell us if it works," Lynne added.

The next morning, I walked around the yard, planning out the flower gardens, what was already there and what I would need to get. Then Janet came by, and we went to a League of Women's Voters meeting. I already knew a few women there because they were also members of Janet's antiwar group, including Meg Tilson, who had said such a helpful thing when I seeking citizenship. As luck would have it, she lived right on Erwin Park Road with her husband, daughters, and sheltie. Meg was organizing the candidates' forum in the fall, and since she was a gracious and efficient person, I volunteered to help.

No sooner had I gotten back to the house than she called me, inviting Mike and me to supper Thursday night.

"You'll get to meet all of us, since Lauren has college vacation this week," she said.

"Thank you, we'd love to come. I like dogs," I replied, and then hoped she didn't think I was downplaying the merits of meeting Lauren or, worse yet, comparing the girl to a dog. Oh, well, the neighbors might as well know how I was from the start.

Meg appeared not to mind. "Wonderful, we have a lively one! How's six-thirty?"

By the end of the week, I was becoming acclimated to Montclair. One thing was wrong. I wanted my mother. When my parents were with us at Christmas, they had said they would come back just before my due date and stay for a few weeks. Unfortunately, Dad had been ill later in the winter, some mild heart thing, they said, now totally under control. I told Mike it was probably angina. He had missed a bit of work and didn't feel he could take more time off so soon. My mother had given me a choice. She could come alone for several days when the baby was born, or they could both come for a longer period in August. I drearily picked the August option. It only seemed sensible, but I was beside myself. This was just the old-time rationing. I was in so much trepidation about having a baby, and I would have to wait four months to see my mother. Somehow I would have to survive, survive, survive, survive. I put up a calendar in the kitchen, circling both my due date and the date my parents would be in Montclair. Mike told me that it would be all right.

One afternoon, Janet and Pam, with Robbie acting as our consumer panel, were helping me select wallpaper for the nursery. Robbie was entranced over a pattern that involved clowns holding balloons, everything very colorful, and we liked it, too. It would work with either a boy or a girl. I purchased several rolls, and as we were going out of the shop, I burst into tears.

"Hormones," I said, wiping my eyes, embarrassed.

"Hormones!" Janet and Pam both agreed.

"Hormones!" Robbie sang out from his stroller, and we all laughed.

On April 10, I woke up early, with twinges of increasingly severity. Two hours later, we knew it was time to go to the hospital. Labor was the worst pain I had ever experienced. Yet it wasn't as bad as I had expected, and the worst thing I said to Mike, who was at my side throughout, was, "You'd better not ever leave me after this, buddy." Actually, it was somewhat like climbing Mount Everest, which I had done in the past. To the top, to the top, summit, start down!

At 4:45 pm, Olivia Ord Klein was born, seven pounds, eight ounces, and with the cry of health. She looked like a rosebud about to unfold, our Livy did.

Medical clean-up stuff was attended to, and then Mike made the phone calls, London first. For the rest of the evening, it was just the three of us, getting to know each other. Her feet and toes were entrancing. The joints in her tapered fingers were miraculous.

After a long while, I let Mike snuggle Livy, and being very tired, eventually I slept. I dreamt of Devon where the sun shown in the bay window of the sitting room and made patterns on the rug. I was standing with Livy in the light, and my mother and her lady group were around us in a circle, clapping and cheering. I said I wanted to have more.

The next morning Lynne and Derek started off the visiting, and then the Kleins were in and out all day. They thought Livy was wonderful and that I looked beatific holding her. They congratulated Mike, who gave out ballpoint pens in lieu of cigars. Janet ruffled his hair, and Alan, who had taken the day off work, called Mike "my son, the father." Pam told him he had been replaced as the eighth wonder of the world, and he said, "No, that happened twenty-nine years ago, when you arrived." They were all so excited and happy for us.

My parents sent a telegram and flowers, and we had two transatlantic phone calls that day. Yet they were not here, and although it was just bad luck that my father had been sick earlier in the year, it seemed that time in my family was a mercurial resource, out of reach, fleeting, or overwhelming.

The Kleins left before supper, and after I ate the stringy pot roast with peas and cubes of roast potatoes, I started feeling dreary. I knew that at seven-thirty, Livy would have to be back with the other babies, and shortly afterwards they would force Mike out. I wanted my mother.

Just then a nurse came in and said, "Uncle is sorry that his plane was delayed, but he is here now. May I show him in?"

"Yes, all right," I replied, a little surprised that Mike's uncle Phillip, whom I had only met twice, would hop a plane from Chicago.

I had picked up on the grandparent thing but had forgotten that a whole set of new relationships had been formed. It was not Mike's uncle. It was Livy's uncle! Once again, Stephen had come through for me.

"Oh, Stephen!" I cried. "Oh, Stephen!"

Stephen did not want to hold Livy at first, but finally he did when Mike showed him how. Livy was a sleeping new life all wrapped up in white in his arms. "She's beautiful, sis," Stephen said. "Absolutely." Mike took a picture.

Our love for Livy was immediate and extraordinary. Mike and I would just gaze at her for hours as she slept. We could not believe she was here. Yet in the very beginning, I felt overwhelmed and in an exhausted haze. She always needed to have things done for her. When she was awake, she was either eating or crying, or her diapers had to be changed. I didn't know what I was doing. Mike took ten days off, which was quite a long time in the days before paternity leave. The first morning that Mike left Livy and me to go back to work, though, I burst into tears, even though I knew Janet was coming over in less than two hours. It was all I could do not to slap him, as he stood there in a suit and tie, about to go out the door.

Janet was marvelous, spending time with us almost every day, not to tell me what to do but to give support and be companionable. Pam with eighteen-month-old Robbie came too, whenever she could.

I felt more myself outside, and so as April turned into May, we spent long afternoons together in the backyard, Livy sleeping on her pink blanket under the oak tree. Sometimes when a light wind caused the trees to rustle, she would murmur, and I would pretend my mother was there, too.

June came. The flowers were in full color. The rose quincunx bloomed. Livy smiled quite a bit now, especially at me. She turned her head at the sound of a familiar voice. She grabbed at toys Mike held out to her and laughed when we clapped for her. At the end of the month, the afternoon venue changed to Janet's and Alan's house for the summer. That was where the family pool was, and besides, I needed to get used to driving with a baby on board.

I would usually do a few quick laps while either Janet or Pam held Livy. Then I would sit on the shade side of the pool with my legs in the water and Livy on my lap, and sometimes I would dip her in, which she liked. Indeed, she was a water bug from day one. Pam would be in the pool with Robbie, who splashed around in an inner tube, and Janet would be alternately with them and with Livy and me.

I finally confided in Janet that I didn't enjoy nursing. "All I want to be is close to Livy," I said. "I never get tired of holding her, but when she sucks on me, I feel like a milk machine or something. It's hard for me, Janet. I imagine that she's nipping me. Once I called her a piglet." She was also making me switch metaphors.

"Then change her to a bottle, Amy. She's three months."

"That's what my mother writes."

"Then listen to your mother, Amy, if what she says coincides with your inclination, anyway."

"It's just that I read constantly about the benefits of nursing."

"There are pros and cons to everything," said Pam from the pool.

"I nursed Mike for just a few weeks. With Pam, I nursed much longer, but I saw it as a wartime measure," Janet said.

Pam said, "Here's to the babies of 1943!"

"It's all about striking a balance," Janet continued. "In general, the child benefits from whatever makes things more relaxed and comfortable for the mother."

"My motto is express love, not milk!" Pam said.

"Well, we'll take that under advisement, won't we, Livy, Civy, Divy?" I said, sprinkling water on Livy. That made her giggle and wiggle.

Pam stepped out of the pool with Robbie, who wanted to play with his matchbox cars. I watched as droplets of water dripped from the skirt of her bathing suit onto the flagstones. Janet put out her arms, and I handed her Livy.

I felt like a contender, so I said, "Pam, you want to race?"

"You're on!" she cried.

We dashed into the water. Back and forth, we raced. We started some races from the shallow end. Other races, we began by leaping into the deep end. Either way, I won most of them. We started splashing the other. We blocked each. We swam under and around each other. Robbie was yelling, "Yay! Yay!" and Janet was moving Livy's hands so they were clapping. We were all laughing.

Janet must have heard Alan coming up the walk, because she called out, "We're right out here, dear. The kids are having so much fun!"

I was thirty-two, married and with a daughter, and I was just thrilled to hear myself included as one of the kids.

When I climbed out of the pool—ladder, not the steps—so I could get Livy and myself ready to meet Mike at the train, Alan put his hand on my shoulder and said, "Isn't this the life?"

"Indeed," I answered.

I began to hit my stride as a mother.

Although we usually saw one another constantly, one of the paradoxical customs of Kleinland was that each household took separate vacations. This was the exact opposite of my family; we saw each other only on holidays. In mid-August, Janet and Alan left for Ogunquit, Maine, and Pam and her family went to Cape Cod. This meant I had one week of going solo during the day with Livy until my parents came. I had a vague sense that Janet and Mum may have coordinated on this, saying to each other, "Let's build her confidence by giving her some time on her own."

I would have been nervous even a month earlier, but now I felt ready. Meg Tilson said that she was available if I needed any help, and actually I had invited her and her daughters for lunch and then a swim in the Kleins' pool on Tuesday. On Thursday, Lynne and I were venturing with the kids to Verona Lake. I could cope with the other days, for double sure.

It was beautiful out on Monday, not too hot and with a sky that was blue for everyone. Livy and I got to Edgemont Park early. She was becoming increasingly alert to the world, and as I pushed her stroller, I talked about whatever she looked at.

"Yes, the leaves are green now, but, oh Livy, in a month or so, they will begin to turn crimson red, yellow, gold, and brown, and a little while after that, they fall, all to the ground, dear, all to the ground. They come back in the spring, though, as green as before. Indeed they do, never fear. Now your father, being of a literal bent, maintains that it is new foliage, but I say the leaves return. That's my view."

Livy turned to look at the ducks in Edgemont Pond. "Ducks, Livy, ducks! Soon you'll be old enough to feed them bread, and that will mean they will quack and honk whenever they see us, because they will know it is truly party time!"

I was going to imitate honking and quacking, but then I saw Deena Silva—the Silvas had just moved onto our street a few weeks ago—sitting on a bench and looking off into space as she repetitively bounced her baby son Brian in her lap.

"Glorious morning," I said.

"If you say so," she said in a monotone. "I'm exhausted."

I wasn't going to let her rain on Livy's and my parade now, so I started to push on when I suddenly heard my mother's voice in my head saying, "This is no time for unkindness, not that there ever is such a time." It suddenly occurred to me that Stephen had never once called me silly or dummy after Mum said that.

"Livy has just started to sleep through the night," I said lightly. "Boy, was it rough when she wasn't."

Deena immediately said she was sorry. She hadn't known everything would be so hard. Her mother was a more than a hundred miles away in Albany. Her mother-in-law was closer but had other things going on. Her husband was in the city all day, and when he got home, he barely looked at his son. He just wanted to eat and watch TV.

I felt it best to refrain from telling her that Mike referred to early evenings around our house as "Daddy's time with Livy."

Instead, I said, "I'm lucky that the Kleins all live here and I get so much help from them. If we were stuck someplace like Paramus, I don't know what I'd do."

Deena brushed her hair out of her eyes and nodded.

I then said, "Here's a thought. Especially as fall progresses, I expect to be here with Livy most mornings, and my sister-in-law Pam will be here with Robbie, and either Lynne or her mother will be coming with Ricky. Lynne works alternate mornings as a social worker."

"Ever notice that black woman with kids are apt to work?" Deena asked.

"Um, this may not be so with Lynne, but I assume in many cases they need the money." I decided not to say that in a few months I'd be working part time, too, and that Pam was doing some freelance editing.

"Anyway," I continued, "we don't have to do anything formal, but when we are all in the park, we can gravitate together. The little ones can play or at least shake their rattles at one another, and we can talk."

"That might be good sometimes," Deena said, again pushing her long hair out of her eyes. "I hardly know anyone here. I'm sort of at sea."

"Well, I sort of came here with the hometown advantage, so to speak. Montclair is the Kleins' town, so I was already familiar with it. If we were living in Paramus or somewhere, God knows what I would do."

Deena smiled a little. "Right," she said.

Livy was babbling contentedly and looking all around. Brian had been whining at a low level all this while, but now he broke into a howl.

"Guess I should get Mr. Crank home for nap time. He sleeps half the day so he can keep me up half the night." Deena fastened him into his stroller. I noticed it was one of those umbrella-type ones. Livy's was padded, and the back was upright, giving her a lot of support. Of course, Deena was probably nine years younger than me, and it showed.

"So long," she said. "Enjoyed chatting."

"Same here," I replied. "Hey, Deena, if you're in a jam, call me, and if I'm not home, call Meg Tilson. She's a helpful person."

"She's the one with a little Lassie dog."

"Yes, her family has a sheltie. Hang in there!" I added.

That night I told Mike about the informal plan for an informal playgroup. "I will be a mover and shaker in Montclair, just like your mother!" I exclaimed.

"You're a mover and shaker everywhere" was his comment.

My parents were flying in to JFK on Sunday. That morning, Mike baked molasses cookies and ginger snaps, and after lunch we got ready to go to the airport. I put on a new turquoise linen sundress with a scalloped hem and my silver bracelet. Then, when Livy's rest time was over, I changed her into her frilly pink party dress.

"You have four grandparents, Livy," I said, lifting her high. "Four of them!"

I twirled her around the room, and she cooed with glee. "Riches, dearest," I shouted. "Riches!"

Mike was waiting in his chinos and blue oxford shirt when we came downstairs. He took a look at us, raced upstairs, and came back down wearing a tie.

Thus we were quite the well-dressed family as we stood in a throng of people in cutoffs, T-shirts, and flip-flops at the airport.

When my parents cleared customs and we saw them coming through the door, Mike gave Livy to me, and I held her close. She was smiling.

My parents, looking radiant, raced to us.

"Mum and Dad," I said joyously. "May I present Livy." I made a little flourish.

"Oh, what a lovely baby," my mother said, and then kissed us both.

My father just gazed at us in silent wonder. I had seen that look before.

"Oh, Mum," I exclaimed. "You just don't know how much I love her, you just don't know!"

"I think I have some inkling," my mother said, suddenly sounding a bit shy.

"Well, does being a family man agree with you, Mike?" my father asked. For some reason, he and Mike were repeatedly shaking hands.

"Double sure," Mike said.

"Gluba gaga, da, de, dub," Livy declared with verve, and we all laughed.

I was afraid my parents might think that our house was a bit of an overreach—Stephen and Susan had a two-bedroom ranch in suburban Toronto—but they reacted very enthusiastically. I took them from room to room, and they complimented me on how light and airy everything was, our things comfortably spaced and no clutter.

"Oh, my, this is cheerful," my mother said when we came to Livy's room. They admired the clown wallpaper, the white crib with the planet mobile hanging over it, the rocker that matched the crib, and the set of colorful wicker baskets that held Livy's growing collection of toys.

"Janet helped with all of this," I said.

My mother winced a little. I was sorry, but the fact was that Janet had been the one who was here.

My mother quickly recovered her equilibrium and said, "I'm very glad, darling. Just one thing—where's the dog?"

It was a joyful group who sat down at our dinner table that night.

For the first few days, my parents shared hours with Livy and me in Montclair. Then Mike's vacation started, and we all repaired to a cottage on the tip of Long Island for a week. We took excursions to Shelter Island, Sag Harbor, and Montauk. Most of the time, though, we were at a small, quiet beach surrounded by reeds and rushes that went right up into the lapping water and with a view across the cove of the cedars of Orient Point, and beyond that the lighthouse heralding the open sea. Every day, the weather was warm and sunny. We swam, walked, talked, picnicked, and played with Livy. Sometimes we just read on the sand. This was our holiday this year, the first year of Livy.

"This is enchantment," my father said, and we all agreed with him.

My parents wanted Mike and me to have a night out on our own while they looked after Livy. I told them that there was no need. Less than a month ago, Janet and Alan had stayed with Livy for an evening while Mike and I had grabbed supper and then saw the film *The Go-Between*.

I said, "No, let's keep the family together. We just want to be with you."

Finally, after some back and forth, it was decided that my mother and I would go out to a nearby seafood restaurant and Mike and my father would stay with Livy.

I was a bit anxious, but it was my mother who suddenly asked when we were getting into the car, "Can they cope?"

I said, "Mum, listen!"

Through the open window, we heard Mike saying earnestly, "It's my experience that the best way to have a baby settle into sleep is to put your hand very lightly on her side, but it does have to be very lightly."

"Just a whisper of a touch?" my father inquired.

"Correct!" Mike affirmed. "Just a whisper of a touch."

My mother and I looked at each other, trying to muffle laughter. "What would we do without our fellows?" Mum asked.

"I don't know, Mum, I just don't know."

Something between us had shifted. We were still mother and daughter, absolutely, but because of Livy, we were also women who could be together and react to things as women.

Mum was impressed at how expertly I pulled out of the drive and onto the lane that led to the road to East Marion.

She said, "If I could do it over again, I would have learned to drive when Grace Hobson did, so she could take Jory places."

I resisted the urge to say that if she could do it over again, the first order of business would be to scotch our African adventure. Instead, I just said, "Why don't you do it now? If I can learn to drive at thirty-two, you can certainly learn to drive at sixty-four."

"I think the time for that has passed, dear."

"Oh, don't say that. Anything is possible." I paused and added, "Mum, I believe I am someone. I am a contender."

My mother still remembered my long-ago reference to Marlon Brando's famous line. She knew I meant that I was a contender for life, for love, for everything.

"Of course you are!" she said. Her smile was bright.

The next night, the suggestion was that I go out with my father. I don't know why the assumption was that I was utterly desperate to eat in restaurants, especially since Mike and my mother were both marvelous cooks. However, I said I didn't want to miss Livy's bedtime two nights in a row, so ultimately it was Mike and my mother who went out. My mother was a little perplexed as to why she was the one going out twice, but we said it couldn't happen to a nicer person.

So it was my father, Livy, and me. We had broiled scallops, which I was able to do credibly well, and then Livy went to sleep after six riotous games of patty-cake, with Grandpa Craig guiding her tiny perfect hands through the motions, and four lullabies, my father and I singing to her together, and last but not least, kisses from both of us as she nodded off.

"I never got to do much of these things with you," my father remarked quietly.

The war had taken him away two months before I was born.

"We can seize time now, Dad, and pretend it is both now and then."

He nodded, seeming to know what I meant.

His once sandy hair was gray now, his face lined, but he looked fit and well. I had written to him in London, asking if I should make an appointment with a Manhattan cardiologist for when he came, and he had written back, saying no, he was fine. Being with him, I could see that certainly seemed to be the case.

Leaving the door open, he and I went out to sit on the back porch. We took in the salt air and listened to the lapping waves. One by one, the stars came out over the darkening water. The chirp of the crickets mingled with sea sounds. I wished my father had been with us in Devon, but he was here now at this time, at this moment, and Mike and my mother would soon return, and we had Livy.

"Dad," I asked, "have you ever noticed every beach is different? Stephen and I loved the rock pools in Devon and the crashing of the surf, and Mum and I were impressed by the grandeur of the Malta coast the month we were there, and then there was the beguiling Indian Ocean, but now, here, I'm enamored of the reeds and grasses in the sand flirting with the gentle water."

"Yes, every shoreline has its own feel, its own virtues, its own romance almost, just as each family has its own romance."

"Our family has always made the most of being together, every sense heightened during those passing moments, nothing forgotten, nothing unappreciated."

"Yes, I used to love seeing you look at your mother when you were a little girl."

"Oh, Dad, you noticed!"

"Of course, I noticed. You just said every sense was heightened."

We laughed, and then I said, "And we played badminton, too. Stephen and Mum on one side and you and I on the other, just to mix it up."

We were sitting on a wood bench, and his hand gently brushed mine. "Your mother and I have so enjoyed this holiday. Just what we needed."

"Same for us," I said. "I don't want it to end. This is the life."

"Yes, love," he agreed. "We're living the life."

Despite my talk of seizing time, once again, the minutes were running out.

Two days later, I felt quite glum as we dropped my parents off at JFK. They were flying to Toronto for a visit with Stephen and Susan before they headed back to London. I was forever saying good-bye to them.

On the way back to Montclair, as Livy napped, Mike tried to cheer me by reminding me that his parents were back from Maine. When that didn't entirely work, he pointed out that we'd have a very busy fall. I had to admit that was so, but still it was hard to know that every time my parents saw Livy, she would be different.

Yet I had Mike and her, and family in town, so I got back into the swing.

The Montclair Operetta Club was putting on *The Music Man*, and Mike and I were reprising our starring roles. Seven years, and I still remembered every line. That was why it was practical for me to do it. Mike attended all the rehearsals. I attended about two-thirds, and Livy came, too, along with Sharon Tilson to keep her entertained. If my daughter cried and I rushed off the stage in the middle of practice to comfort her, so be it.

The *Montclair Times* gave the play a very good review, lauding the chorus and supporting cast and saying that Mike had given a "commanding performance" and I was "sparkling." They called us "wonderful additions" to the company. There was, though, no mention of the air being electrified, but that was probably due to the director wanting to stage the play very conventionally—he would not allow Marian to be whirled around in a swivel chair—rather than because of any change in Mike and me.

Mike and I certainly were not settling into a companionable arrangement. At night, when it became adult time at our house, the razzle-dazzle was still there. I can be trusted on that one!

I cast my first vote in a presidential election that fall. Unfortunately, the candidate whom the Kleins supported lost rather badly. We braced for four more years of Nixon.

As Livy turned six months, I started a small speech therapy practice, seeing school-age children several afternoons a week, our den becoming my office. I had never liked having a boss or working in a clinical environment, where institutional rules had to be adhered to. Also, I would not separate myself from Livy. The only way I could continue in the profession was to be out on my own. True, some of the kids had difficulties like cleft palates and cerebral palsy, which I had no previous experience with, but since my approach had always been intuitive rather than scientific, I didn't see that as a problem, as long as I made proper disclosure to the parents.

I had to think about how to refer to the kids. I would not call them "patients," and "customers" or "clients" didn't seem quite right either, since they were children. "Students" would not work, because this was not school, and I took pains not to make it seem like it was. I decided just to call them the "speech kids."

Livy was the icebreaker and the comic relief. At the first appointment, I would meet the child and the mother at the door, with Livy dressed in a bright outfit in my arms.

I would say, "Hi, I'm Amy Klein, but more importantly, this is bouncing baby Livy Klein." That always got a smile, even when the child was coming quite reluctantly.

During the sessions, Livy sat on my lap or played with her toys on the floor and would participate as the mood struck her.

Once Sara, a little girl who was especially taken by Livy, and I were doing drills for the letter *L* in preparation for practicing *L* words.

"Lalalala, la!" I said.

"Lalalala, la!" Sara responded.

"Lalalala, la!" Livy added.

"Let's see if she will do it again!" I said. We repeated the drill, and Livy came in right on cue. Sara nearly fell off her chair laughing.

I said, "Give me a *L*! Give me an *I*! Give me a *V* and then a *Y*, and what do you get?"

"Livy!" Sara cried, getting up and doing a jumping jack.

I let the kids call me Amy, because I wanted a certain informality. Besides, "Amy" was easier for someone who lisped or was dysarthic to say. Yet I always changed into a skirt and blouse for the appointments, because I wanted to convey that we were engaged in an important endeavor, even as I tried to make it fun. I never had the kids bring notebooks for me to fill with exercises that they would ignore until the next appointment came around. Instead, I made up tongue twisters that they could practice when they thought about it, or better yet, teach to family and friends.

Sara's main tongue twister was "Lively, lovely Livy likes lowly lazy lizards."

For Ned, who had trouble with *R*'s, I made up, "Rowdy red rats ransack real rag refineries."

Kyle liked to move, so when I had him say phrases to the beat of a metronome, we threw in dance steps. The word "rap" had not yet come into general usage, but I guess that was what it was. Livy, when she got to be a bit older, loved that part. Kyle and I would be chanting and shaking it out, and she would be spinning.

Most of the parents appreciated how I did things and realized that their child was gaining confidence in communicating, which was the goal. However, one parent did say that I was "sort of loosey goosey." Mike and I laughed so hard on that one, since there was nothing in my background to incline me to be "sort of loosey goosey."

My most challenging speech kid was Tricia, a junior high school girl with cerebral palsy. She was very smart, with a lot of potential, but was resentful of the idea that she had areas where improvement might be helpful. On top of that, she liked acting the part of a sullen adolescent. It was nearly impossible to engage her in conversation, and it was not because of her slurred speech.

Her three favorite expressions were "Well, no," "I guess so," and "I don't know."

I often asked her what she enjoyed doing.

She always said, "Hack around."

"What does that mean?"

"I don't know, do whatever."

I often asked the kids to read poems out loud. It was a good way to practice phrasing and inflection. For Tricia, I chose poems by Emily Dickinson. We started with fairly easy, straightforward poems like "I'm Nobody." Then, one afternoon, hoping to pique her interest, I threw in "Wild Nights."

She read it dutifully.

Then I said, "I find it an extraordinarily passionate poem. Don't you?"

"I don't know."

"What's interesting is that she makes clear that this is something she's imagining rather than something that is happening."

"I guess so."

"Dickinson is a Victorian lady who is rather daring in a classy way." I continued, "For example, the phrase 'Might I but moor—tonight—in thee' is pretty suggestive, but I don't find it off-color. What would you say is the difference between eroticism and pornography?' I might have been going too far, but I was desperate to get her attention.

"One's fun and one's disgusting?" Tricia ventured.

"I think that's getting close to it. It's sort of like the difference between tradition and ritual. Tradition has meaning, there's a warmth to tradition. Ritual isn't always bad the way pornography is, but it can be rote, reflexive, and exploitative rather than thoughtful."

"I guess," Tricia said, looking both intrigued and bored.

"Read the poem out loud, one more time."

"Wile nigh," she started.

"Tricia, it's wild nights," I said, emphasizing the *d* in "wild" and the *t* and the *s* in "nights." "Your bugaboo is that you leave off the last sounds in words."

She looked at me and said quite clearly, "What are you? A pronunciation Nazi?"

That lit a fuse. I slammed the book closed.

"Well, wait," I exclaimed. "Just wait, I'd rather have the worst obscenities hurled at me than be called a Nazi. You baby boomers—"

Tricia looked faintly pleased that I had identified her as a baby boomer.

I repeated, "Yes, you baby boomers throw around the word casually and, to continue this afternoon's theme, promiscuously. Someone is rigid or preoccupied with order and you call him a Nazi."

"I-I-I—" Tricia was trying to say something.

"No, you listen to me," I shouted. I was really getting worked up. "In the time and place where I come from, a Nazi was a mass murderer! They killed millions, including the husband of a friend of my mother's. My parents knew people who died trying to stop them. I had a classmate—Charlotte—who had no memory of her father because he was one of the first ones out of the boats on D-Day. My own father easily—easily could have died, and you know what, he would have died willingly, yes willingly, to keep Nazis out of England and away from my mother, brother, and me." Actually, I had never thought of it like that before, but of course it was true. My father had been ready to die for us.

I continued. I would not be stopped. "I only saw him twice in my first five years. Once when I was two, and once when I was four and a half. I don't know what I thought the first time, but the second time I wasn't even sure who he was. My brother had to clue me in."

Livy looked up at me. Her big brown eyes were anxious, and her lip was starting to tremble. She had never seen me this agitated with a speech kid. I picked her up and put her on my lap. "It's all right, love," I said, kissing her soft hair.

I went back to what I was for some reason trying to tell Tricia. "We lived in the country because it wasn't safe to be in our house in London. You heard of the blitz, haven't you? How about the battle of Britain? Dunkirk?"

Tricia nodded meekly.

"My mother only had a young girl to help her, and together they worked all the time to take care of Stephen and me and keep our small household going. They got up early to light the gas fire in the sitting room. We only had cold water, so they boiled water on the stove for our twice-a-week baths. My mother grew vegetables in our back garden in the summer and in the neighbor's greenhouse in the winter to supplement our ration coupons. Our source of transportation was feet, or my mother's bicycle. My mother had to teach my brother at home because the village school was four miles away, too far for him to walk at age six." Well, wasn't this something? I was spontaneously recounting the flip side of Devon. Actually, I didn't know how I knew the village school was four miles away, but it was a poignant little detail.

"We tried to have chickens, but they were done in by foxes." Really? I had no memory of any chickens in Devon, nor of anyone ever mentioning chickens. Maybe I had gotten this confused with Miss Fox trying to do me in at Longwood.

"My mother rolled bandages. She wrote letters for a blind woman, and she was part of a group helping the war effort in other ways, but I'm not sure what all they did, but they tried."

"She had contacts," I confidentially explained to Tricia.

I knew I was being unprofessional and that Tricia was only a young girl, but still I went on. "I'm not a baby boomer. There was a group before you, the war babies. At the time, we didn't even understand what the war was, but it was an undercurrent to everything the whole time we were growing up. It imprinted us."

"That's why you keep calling World War Two the war," Tricia said.

"Correct," I replied. I spontaneously decided that after I wrote my book on women power on the underground railroad, I'd write a second one on the war babies. This conversation wasn't a total loss.

"I'm sorry I called you a Nazi. I didn't mean it," Tricia said.

"I know you didn't, and I'm sorry I flew off the handle. I do that sometimes, don't I, Livy Divy?"

"Actually," I added, "I had a very nice early childhood in Devon. But Tricia, I had obstacles, too. I was sent to boarding school when I didn't want to be." Oh, so I was getting into that now.

"You don't act like someone who went to boarding school," Tricia said.

That was a compliment, so I said, "Thank you. I tried hard not to act that way. I kept myself apart. I was just passing time." Well score one for me. Passing time sounded better than killing time.

"You seem to be a good mother, at least," Tricia commented.

That was even more of a compliment, so I said, "Thank you. I try. I do so try."

Then I said, "Tricia, you are completely right. I shouldn't harp on pronunciation. Your listeners can get used to unusual pronunciation. It's like an accent. It seems to me, though, that you might like to say things faster. Give me a sentence, and I'll tell you how to express the thought in fewer words."

Tricia thought and said, "Sometimes I have no idea why I say the things I do."

I said, "I don't know why I say things I do. Your sentence was twelve words. I got it down to nine."

I looked at my watch. We had blown through the forty-five minutes. I told Tricia to tell her mother that since the session had been about me, the session would be on me. I wouldn't bill for it.

Even so, I knew her mother would call me, and she did an hour later, when I was blowing bubbles for Livy. I was anxious when I heard her voice. What would she be angriest about? My blithe mention of eroticism? My yelling at Tricia, or my making her listen to some weird version of my childhood when I was supposed to be patiently trying to help her speak better? I should probably have my license revoked or at least be barred from working with kids.

After some pleasantries, her mother said, "I heard you laid into old Tricia today. Far out! Of course, I'm paying for the appointment! Keep up the good work."

"I aim to please," I said weakly.

I intended to write to my mother that evening to ask whether we had tried raising chickens. However, after supper Mike was on the floor playing with Livy, who was standing, holding on to the coffee table with one hand—it was March, and she was eleven months now. Mike had her little stuffed dog besides him, and he said, "Livy, come get Rover," and just like that she let go of the coffee table and took three steps to Mike! A few minutes later, she took five steps to me and giggled as she received my hugs. Hence, I did write Mum that night and very excitedly, but it was all about Livy.

I did ask Stephen about the chickens, though, when he ecstatically called many weeks later with the grand news that after eight years of marriage, Susan was in the family way. Livy would have cousins on both sides!

I congratulated him several times, and just when we were finishing the conversation, I said, "Hey, Stephen, do you recall us having chickens in Devon?"

"What? Yes, for about two weeks. I'm surprised you remember them. You were probably hardly three!"

"Well, what happened to them?"

"Why the sudden interest? Jenny and I went out one morning to look for eggs, and when we found the first chicken mangled, she had me go back to the house. Apparently, all four of them had been killed, probably by foxes. Mum felt bad that she hadn't reinforced the coop."

"Well, she had many things to think about at that time," I said.

"She did," Stephen agreed. "And she was a novice at country life. She just knew what she had gleaned from living with French Swiss farmers for a few months after university, and that was a decade before."

"She did remarkably well, but what about me?"

"What about you?"

"How did I react?"

"Sis, it was all so long ago. I don't know. I think Mum told you that the chickens had moved somewhere else, and you accepted that. Why?"

"No reason. Congratulations again, Stephen! If you and Susan get even half of the joy, the steady joy from your baby, that Livy has brought to Mike and me, you will be the happiest couple in Toronto, double sure." I told him.

"Thanks, sis. We are right now the happiest couple in Toronto, double sure."

I smiled as I said good-bye. The Ord family was growing.

Livy was growing, and as she turned one year old, she started saying words. The first four were approximations of "Mommy," "cookie," "Daddy," and "flower." It was spring now, leaves back on the trees, and the perennials I had planted the previous year were blooming, a palette of color around the house.

Pam inquired, "Is it acceptable to say that the English can really garden?"

I said, "Yes, stereotype or no, that's one attribute of the nationality that I'll own up to."

The roses set in a quincunx came out next, and it was summer again. The speech kids dwindled as they became immersed in their summer activities, and those that still came, I switched to early mornings. This allowed Livy and me to once again spend long hours at the Kleins' pool. Livy, true to her genes, was indeed a water bug! Whether with a tube, wearing a bubble or a life preserver, or on a float or in my arms, she wanted to be in the pool all the time. Robbie would come out for a break, but Livy might insist on staying in.

"Can I spell you, Amy?" Janet would ask.

"No, thank you," I would usually say. "I love it."

In late August, Mike and I took Livy to England for the first time. It was the holiday of holidays, fourteen indelible days with my parents.

The first week we were in London, living the life there. Jory came up from Cambridge for a day—Kate was acting in a play—and was totally besotted with Livy.

"I'm Uncle Jory. Correct?" he said.

"Yes, Jory," I affirmed. "You're Uncle Jory!"

Livy was fascinated by his cane, so we tied red and blue ribbons around it, and when Jory left, he kept the ribbons on.

Christa wanted to be "Aunt Christa," even though Jon, Ian, and Lawrence had now made her an aunt several times over.

My heart filled with joy when my mother and I took Livy to the little park and slid her down a slide that I had slid down as a child. Some of the children playing around her were children of children who had played in the little park with me. I recognized Jill Holmes, now Jill Carroll, who had been one of our classmates at Regency Day, feeding birds with two children. Although we had not seen each other in fifteen years and had only been casually friendly in school, we hugged and hugged. Having a baby had opened worlds for me on both sides of the Atlantic.

The best by far was yet to come.

The second week we spent in Cornwall on a beach that was flat and wide because my father said it was always nice to be at the seaside with Livy. Now sixteen months, she was really starting to do things, and Dad seemed to soak her up like sunshine. He said Livy looked just like I had at that age in all those pictures my mother had sent him from Devon.

"At last, I see my little girl." he said.

My heart swelled.

He built sand castles for her. He made seaweed necklaces for her, which caused her to laugh, so he made some more. They collected shells, and he would discuss them with her, saying things like "here's a most interesting one. See, Livy, it has ridges on one side and is smooth on the other." Whenever Mike or I took Livy into the water and pretended she was riding the waves, he accompanied us to make sure we were exercising every precaution with his grandchild.

My mother and I laughed at how we'd have to go through a check-list every morning as we left for our day on the sand.

"Livy's sunhat?" he asked.

"Yes, we have Livy's sunhat," we would say.

"A bit of a book for after lunch before naptime?"

"Yup," Mike answered. "It's theme consistent, Scuppers the Sailor Dog!"

We all thought, to use my father's expression, that this was enchantment. My mother had a perpetual smile on her face. Mike and I had brought a video camera just before we left for vacation, and now we took enough film of all of us, and especially of my father and Livy, to last a lifetime.

The afternoon before we had to go back to reality, Mike and my mother took a walk down the beach, and my father and I sat talking while Livy in her pink bathing suit napped on a towel. My father had adjusted the umbrella several times so she would be completely in the shade. We discussed how we were all looking forward to Stephen's and Susan's baby's arrival in December. Susan had had severe morning sickness early on but was now fine.

"Next summer will be glorious," I said.

"Indeed!" Dad said. We were planning a spectacular family holiday for July of 1974 at Lake Placid in New York. There would be eight of us—my household of three, Stephen and Susan with their little one, and my parents.

"Dad," I suddenly asked. "Do you ever think about retiring?"

"Yes, I do. Possibly next year or the year after. There are other things I want to do, people I want to see more of." He nodded at Livy.

Livy stirred in her sleep and murmured "Grandpa Gray," which was her version of Grandpa Craig.

I chose my words very carefully and spoke slowly. "Dad, when you retire, could you and Mum move to America?"

My father said, "We've been mulling that over. We'll probably never leave London entirely. It is our place. Everything good happened for us there. Even if we sold the house, we'd want a flat."

"Yes, Dad," I said, hardly daring to breathe.

"But we could also have a home base in North America. Certainly, we could, dear! We would like it."

I felt a rush of holy joy. My father and I clasped hands.

Livy woke up. "Swim now?" she said.

"Of course, darling! You beautiful girl," I cried, picking her up and covering her with kisses. Livy was our redemption baby!

The next day at Heathrow, I didn't have the down, dour feeling I usually had when I left my parents. I actually had a spring in my step, which impressed Mike to no end. Mum and Dad accompanied us to the gate (which could be done in those days), and when we entered the jetway, we turned around, and there they were standing very close to each other, my mother cheerily waving and my father blowing kisses. Mike was carrying Livy. She leaned over his arm and without prompting, she said, "Bye, bye Grandpa Gray!" She was a very smart child, if I did say so myself.

I smiled through to takeoff. My father had said that he and my mother would live in the United States. New York or Montclair, I could cope with either. After all these years, finally, finally, we'd all be living the life. We'd have so much time together. Time would stretch to the horizon!

Seven weeks later, it was the quintessential autumn Saturday in Montclair. The sky was blue. The sun was warmish but with a hint of crispness in the air. The leaves had turned red and gold, and many were on the ground.

"Fall is such an American season," I remarked to Mike at breakfast.

"At least in the Northeast," he relied dryly.

"Another spoonful of Wheatena?" I suggested to Livy.

We had the day planned. In the morning we would rake leaves, and Livy could roll in them just as Mike and Pam had when they were kids. Later we would be going to a pumpkin patch in Cedar Grove with Janet and Alan to pick out Livy's Halloween pumpkin.

"No one can pick out a pumpkin like Grandma Janet," Mike told Livy.

"Pumpkin!" Livy exclaimed.

The Gibbses were coming over for supper.

Mike glanced at the *New York Times*. "Nixon's going to force Richardson to fire Cox," he said.

"I think Richardson will refuse," I said. "At least, I hope so."

In the midst of breakfast, in the midst of life, the phone rang.

Mike got it. "Why hello, Olivia," he said. He paused. "She's right here."

My mother's voice was subdued and distant, more distant than the miles between us. "It was very strange, Amelia," she said. "First, your father was here and then he wasn't. He was gone in an instant."

My father had just disappeared? I almost asked her if she had called Scotland Yard. Then I began to grasp what she was saying.

Livy clanked her spoon against her cereal bowl. "All done!" she announced. Mike picked her up. He had one arm around her and one arm around me. Livy patted my hair, a small pause between each pat. They were here with me.

It was after lunch, and my mother had been doing the washing up, while my father lingered at the table, which was unusual for him. They were talking about going walking in Hyde Park later.

My father said, "Do you remember how we use to take Stephen and Amelia to Hyde Park every Sunday during those twenty months we had?"

My mother said to him, "Of course, dear, that was grand."

Then they spoke about how they needed to get the plane tickets for Christmas. My father said, "It will wonderful to see Stephen's baby for the first time and then Livy."

"Indeed!" my mother agreed.

"Olivia, love!" my father said urgently. "Olivia!"

Before she could get to him, his head hit the table. His arm knocked a stray tea cup which fell to the floor and shattered.

She had called the paramedics, but she knew he was dead, very dead.

In the last minute of life, he had spoken all our names.

"First he was here, and then he wasn't," My mother repeated. "The breath of life is everything, isn't it, dear? When that vanishes, a body is just a body."

I wasn't used to my mother talking like this. I wanted to say, "Well, yes, but hey, do you want to speak to Mike again? How about Livy? She knows eighteen more words."

What I said was "Oh, Mum!"

"I'm afraid I'm not telling you this very well, darling. It was all so unexpected. I just never imagined, even though we did all know he had the widow maker."

We did?

Apparently they had found out about it when I was pregnant. They hadn't wanted to worry me. Things were under control, or so they hoped. They had just told Stephen.

I let out a long breath. They had never wanted to worry me; better for me to be hit over the head with no warning. However, being the mature person I now was, I decided that this was not the moment to pick a fight with my mother.

She said after a pause, "I'm so glad your father knew Livy."

"I am too, Mum."

"He was a natural grandfather."

"Yes, Mum."

My mother said Mr. and Mrs. Cookson were at the door, so I let her go to them.

Mike and I immediately made plans to fly back to England.

Alan and Janet came over, and while Alan went out with Mike to get traveler's checks and the other things we would need for the trip, Janet stayed with me.

She offered to take Livy for the week we would be away. She said, "Pam will surely help. We'll make it so fun for Livy, she won't have time to miss you."

That was a very generous offer, so I hoped my face didn't convey my horror. "Oh, no, Janet," I said. "I don't leave Livy. She goes where I go."

"Of course, I wasn't thinking. I'm sorry, dear, and she will be a great comfort to your mother as well. May I cancel your appointments with the speech kids?"

I had forgotten about that. "Thank you, Janet," I said, bringing her the notebook containing my roster. (This was well before the privacy laws.)

We migrated outside. It was such a beautiful day, the sky so blue for everyone that I didn't want Livy to completely miss it. All right, we migrated to Edgemont Park, where Livy walked about in the leaves, liking the crunchy noise they made. She was wearing her first pair of sneakers, having just gotten out of high shoes.

"Is there anything else I can do, Amy?" Janet said.

"Yes, if you have time. Could you get Livy's pumpkin? We won't be able to do it today, and I'm just afraid that by the time we get back, all the good ones will be taken, and then what will we do?" I was just about in tears.

"Certainly, I will," Janet replied. She gave me a little hug.

"Oh, Janet, why did this have to happen just when things were going to be so good?"

"I don't know, dear. It's a mystery."

Livy came up to me and handed me a crimson and gold leaf. It was still supple and must have just fallen.

"Pretty leaf," I told her.

She stooped down and picked out a leaf that had some red in it but was more brown and a bit drier.

I said, "New ones will come in the spring, darling. They always do, but the old ones don't come back. They don't come back."

"Yes, but the new ones always come. That's the promise," Janet said.

Livy wanted to feed the ducks, and I was about to say we had not brought any food for them when Janet, as if by magic, pulled out a bag of bread bits from her pocket.

Livy was a little perplexed being at JFK that night, especially since there hadn't been much preparatory talk about it. She was adaptable, though, among her other virtues. She spent the first twenty minutes of the flight turning a boarding pass this way and that and bending it and unbending it, and then she went right to sleep upon just one singing of "The Muffin Man." After a while, Mike dozed too, but I stayed wide awake, I was so angry.

If anyone had asked me, how long we had been together in London before going on our goddamn African adventure disaster, which had killed Folly, by the way, I would have said nearly two years. However, my father had known the length of time exactly: twenty months. We had been a family of four who lived together every day without fear of separation for a mere twenty months. My father had not been with us in Devon, and then after we arrived in Tanganyika, Stephen and I had gone off to lousy boarding school, away for twelve weeks at a shot, everything topsy-turvy. The home year had been glorious, but it had just been my parents and me for a lot of it, Stephen being at Eton. After that, our childhood had been pretty much over. Some force had knocked an hourglass to its side, causing so much of our time to be lost. Twenty months as a family of four living together every day had been all that we had had.

That wasn't quite true, but after those twenty months we had had to grab time where we could, in bits, in intervals, in segments. Mike had told me that his childhood memories were kaleidoscopic, a colorful swirl of hundreds of mainly pleasant days in slightly different and evolving patterns, bright dashes of occasional surprises in an aqua sea of security. My memories of family life were etched and distinct, grains of slipping sand that I needed to hoard. I remembered each homecoming with Stephen, who always seemed a bit bigger, every welcoming by our parents, all of our trips, the books we read, the tricks we used to pretend that our shared time was greater than it was. I remembered my evening alone with my father during our glorious vacation to the Long Island shore. We had pretended our always having to seize the day to have been some type of crazy advantage. Talk about looking at the bright side!

Now, just when my father had said that he and my mother would move to the United States so we could all finally be close together again, with the hourglass righted and time in abundance, he had fallen down dead. Was this the Colonial Office witch wives' idea of a joke?

My father had always been kind to me, always loving, and in the last few years we had had a mutual admiration society; but the truth was I hadn't known much about him. I didn't know what he had done in the war, other than he had been in the RAF and commanded some sort of missions. I didn't know exactly what he did at the Colonial Office, or whatever it was called now "to reflect changing times," as it was euphemistically put. Oh wait, I got it! It was the Foreign and Commonwealth Office, FCO for short. I didn't know why he had been posted to Dodoma, Tanganyika, or what his role there had been, except that it had had something to do with roads and bridges. I had the feeling his career had stalled somewhere along the line, preventing him from being sent to a larger place, but I didn't know why, except that Mum had once said that the powers that be had found him not flashy enough but too outspoken at the same time. I hadn't known he had the widow maker. I probably didn't even know what else I didn't know about him.

I thought about Stephen. It seemed to me he had had even less time with my father than I had, since he had only been partially home during the home year. He and my father must have passed like ships in the night.

Livy stirred. She was smiling in the Land of Nod, her tiny hands loosely curled into fists below the turned-back cuffs of her turtleneck.

I had so been looking forward to getting to know my father through Livy. Now she would be the one slender link between her generation and my father, and she would not remember him.

What a cheat! What a measly, measly gyp! I wanted to scream and scream and scream.

I slept for only about twenty minutes before the pilot woke us all up to tell us to prepare for the descent. Livy was crying, Mike was trying to reassure her, and I didn't even know if I was on American or British time, or neither.

The headlines of the papers were screaming all around us as we made our way through Heathrow. In the evening, just as we had boarded the plane, there had been quite some goings-on in Washington. Nixon had found someone to fire Cox, the Watergate special prosecutor, but not before Attorney General Richardson and his deputy had departed the Justice Department. Mike hastily bought the last *International Herald Tribune*. It was being called "the Saturday night massacre." Impeachment was now being discussed. I didn't care.

We hadn't tried to coordinate our flights at all, but when we got to the cab stand, we saw Stephen in the queue.

My mother was still remote and distant when we got to the house, preoccupied with how my father had died in an instant. First, he was there. Then he wasn't. I was so glad that either Mrs. Cookson or Christa had been with her constantly until Stephen and I arrived. Livy was too young to ask explicit questions, but during the week we were there, she kept looking in the corners of rooms and under chairs. One night, she said, "To beach, to the beach!"

"It's too cold, Livy Divy, it's too cold," I told her, whereupon she cried inconsolably. I rocked her and rocked her and gave her my old panda to hold, but still she cried and cried.

"I want to find him too, darling," I said.

Curiously, it was Stephen—he had come alone, because Susan was so far along in pregnancy that it was judged unsafe for her to fly— who seemed the most devastated. His eyes were red. He looked off into space. I was able to get Mum to play badminton with me, but he wouldn't join us. He slammed things around. He ignored Mike. Once he lit a cigarette, but I looked at him so reproachfully that he snubbed it out quickly.

I decided to get him to talk to me one morning when Mike had taken Livy for a walk and Mum was getting papers organized for the solicitor.

Stephen said that Dad was practically the finest man he had ever known. Dad was his touchstone. He looked to Dad for guidance on everything. He couldn't even manage his coin collection without Dad. Dad was the reason he had gone one way when so many boys he had been to school with had gone another, although Mum had helped, of course. That time in Nairobi with the Indian man's shop, Dad had been up there so fast that Stephen had barely gotten out of the head-master's office. The fathers of the ruffians who had actually been in-volved hadn't come at all, he said.

By sheer force of will, I turned a sudden urge to laugh into a cough.

At first I had been totally baffled by what Stephen was referring to, but then asked, "Hey, was that the time he took us to the Norfolk?" I remembered that Dad had come up to Nairobi because of some busi-ness with Stephen that he said did not concern me.

"Yes, wasn't that wonderful of him to do that, instead of leaving me to contemplate my sins?"

"Well, I never knew exactly what you did. Could you clue me in sometime?"

It was if I hadn't spoken. Stephen bit his knuckle. Now Susan was fi-nally pregnant, and Stephen had been expecting Dad to teach him how to be a father, because he simply had no idea, and he just didn't know what he was going to do.

Seeking to reassure Stephen on that point, I said it seemed to me that Alan had been a pretty good father, doing things with Mike and Pam every day of their childhood, and Mike had been great with Livy from the word go and now had eighteen months of experience under his belt. When things got back to normal—not that they ever really would—Stephen should come to Montclair for a fatherhood preparation weekend. Susan should come as well. There were lots of things Janet, Pam, and I could tell her—Mum too, if she had moved by then.

Stephen suddenly looked at me so wildly, I stood up and stepped back.

"You wouldn't understand," he hissed venomously. "For you, Dad was always an add-on!"

"Stephen," I cried. "I gave up a chance to go walking with my hus-band and daughter to talk to you." I was in the hall. Mike had said they were going to Pall Mall. Livy, in her stroller, often called a halt to look at cracks and twigs and such. I could catch up with them if I hustled.

"Oh, keep your shirt on," Stephen said. "Livy gets more walks than any kid on the planet."

I thought that was vaguely amusing, given that I was putting on my jacket.

That afternoon when Mum, Stephen and I went to the solicitor's, I nearly fell asleep. He droned on and on. I did vaguely catch that we were moderately well to do, as a result of my parents' parents' investments, which my parents had managed prudently. Ho hum, I guess that explained the house in Belgravia, the plane rides to and from expensive schools, all the trips, my parents coming back from Africa to London for Christmas. Genius here had never made the connection.

Stephen kept saying in a flat voice, "All I care about is that my mother is all right." Actually, he spoke for both of us.

As we were leaving, my mother paused to say good-bye to the solicitor, so I leaned towards Stephen and attempted some off-the-cuff sibling chit chat. "Glad you stayed awake," I said in a whisper.

He nearly shoved me.

"Mum, I'll hail us a cab," Stephen said. I was lucky that he let me crawl into the backseat.

That night, after briefly explaining our financial situation to Mike, which didn't seem to surprise him, I told him that I would never understand Stephen. "Oh, Amy," Mike began, and then we both folded our hands and said in unison, "Everyone grieves in their own way."

I then thought about how Stephen might have taken my innocent remark about how many things Alan had done with Pam and Mike.

"No," I said laughing. "No, your mother would say, 'Perhaps, dear, this is not the best time to be comparing people's fathers.'" I collapsed against him.

Then I felt guilty, not for making fun of Janet, because we really weren't, but for acting like a Klein when there was so much sadness in the house of Ord.

The next morning, I helped my mother design the program for my father's memorial service. I didn't like writing CRAIG TIMOTHY ORD, June 12, 1907—October 20, 1973, on the cover. It made him seem so dead. We chose a picture of Dad in middle age to appear above the dates. It was probably from our fleeting home year. However, my mother said that if it was all right with me, she also wanted to include a photograph on the inside that had been taken when they were young and thought the world was their oyster, and his face had had a joyful radiance that it had not had to quite the same degree after the war.

I said that was fine.

"It was before you," my mother said cautiously.

I said I understood that they had had a life prior to Stephen and me, I understood completely. No two parents could love a child as much as Mike and I loved Livy. Yet we would always cherish the memory of the six years when it was just the two of us. We had needed that time to grow together and create an unshakable home for Livy to come into.

Mum showed me the photograph. My father did have a radiance I had never quite seen. Indeed, he was beaming as he sat on the floor of the sunporch spinning a top, to the delight of his toddler son.

Well, of course, I had seen pictures of baby Stephen with one or both of my parents. Of course, I had known that Stephen had been a little over two when my father went to war. What genius me had never figured out—even though I had been looking right at it even since Devon—was that in those two years, Stephen and my father had forged their bond.

"Daddy," he had exclaimed breathlessly when my father had come home on his brief leave. "Daddy!"

I had been the only one totally frolicking on the moor, as unconcerned as Folly. Jenny had longed for her Davy, and my brother had stood with my mother hoping and waiting for my father's return.

I had to make amends with Stephen.

I got Stephen to come to the little park with Livy and me. Jon Cookson's wife and their kids were there, and she welcomed Livy into their group, so I had a moment with Stephen. I said, "Listen Stephen, I know it's especially devastating for you that Dad died before your baby arrived. The one thing that keeps me from despair—and I have discussed this with Mum—is that Dad did intersect with Livy."

He looked at me sadly.

I continued, "It's a grain of sand, Stephen, but we have it. He did know that your little one, his second grandchild, was nearly here. He was very, very excited. He died awash with joy and expectation. How often does that happen?" My chin trembled.

A little light came into Stephen's eyes.

I felt the need to say one more thing. "Maybe when we were growing up, Stephen, it was harder for me to be away from Mum than from him. Maybe it was, but he was my father too, and I always knew it. My first memory in life was of Dad, the way he told us he loved us in all the letters he wrote to Mum."

"I know, sis," he replied. "I was sorry I snapped at you the minute I did it. It's just such a stressful time."

"For all of us," I agreed, patting his shoulder. "This is all so unexpected."

Livy came up to us. "Swing?" she said.

"Let me," Stephen said, picking her up. "I need to get into training."

"Good uncle, good father," I commented.

Stephen in his good gray suit and slate-blue tie seemed noticeably energized at the memorial service as he walked around, shaking hands and thanking people for coming. He especially liked it that so many folks from his and our father's coin collector club were there. (Yet another thing that I hadn't known was that Dad has been one of the leading hobbyist numismatists in Britain.) Indeed, people had come from far and wide. Mr. and Mrs. Hobson, whom I had not seen for seven years, were there with Jory, although Kate was caught up in rehearsals. Lottie had come and sat at the service with my old friend Ted Sanders, now a slightly portly businessman. Jill Carroll also kindly came.

All the Cooksons were there, and it was quiet Mr. Cookson who gave the eulogy, lauding my father as his north star, who by word and example had guided him in how to be a husband and father again after having been in the horrors of war.

He told of how he and my father would drop their respective children off in the schoolyard and then continue on to work together, calling each other family men. When Mr. Cookson confessed to the fear that battlefield obscenities would pop out of his mouth in front of his six-year-old, my father said, "Would you talk to her in mathematical equations? Soldiering was a temporary parallel existence forced upon us by circumstances and duty to humanity. Our lives as we know it are with our wives and children. It is there we find enchantment."

I nearly cried, especially since I remembered my father and Mr. Cookson meeting every morning at Regency Day and never guessed they were putting their ordinary lives back together. However, I laughed instead when Mr. Cookson said that there indeed must have been some type of enchantment, because three Cookson children turned over time into six Cookson children.

He went on. Craig Ord was not flashy or ostentatious. Despite what he saw in war and elsewhere, he never lost his sense of wonder. Referring to the sadly beautiful Wordsworth poem, Mr. Cookson told us, my father looked for the glory in the flowers.

All in all, the memorial service went well, and, yes, everyone thought Livy in her lacy dress was adorable—and she was very good, quietly playing with pipe cleaners—but there was a letdown afterwards. My father was still dead, and we didn't know what we were supposed to do next. My mother sighed as I set the table for a light supper, and things still weren't entirely right between Stephen and me.

That night, it was totally at my initiative—perhaps the comment about the six Cookson kids had got me in the mood—and Mike and I tried to be quiet, we really did, so much so we got the giggles. The next morning, as Stephen came into the kitchen for breakfast, he frowned at me. "Life must go on, Stephen," I said lightly.

"Of course, it must, dear," my mother said, not knowing what we were talking about.

In the couple of days remaining in the week, I tried every manner of persuasion to get my mother to embrace the idea of moving to America. I said Mike and I would be pleased if she lived with us, but if she preferred, she could have her own place, either in Montclair or in the city. I said there was an Oxford University Club in the metropolitan area. I hadn't joined because I was sure a lot of the members had been to boarding school, and that was not my milieu. However, if she was there, I'd definitely sign up, and we could go together. I reminded her that her old classmate Honora was right in West Orange.

My mother said it would be strange not to see the Cooksons.

I said we could invite them over for a visit. In my mind, the *pièce de résistance* was proximity to Janet. "She's fantastic, Mum," I said. "You won't believe all of her interests. She'll be your custom-made best friend."

"We're mutual grandmothers to Livy," my mother commented.

"Well, there you go!"

"Janet is grand. We do have many common interests, and she has become one of my best friends, but really, Amelia, that's not the point. London is my home."

I took a deep breath. I told her that Dad and I had discussed their moving across the Atlantic when he retired. Owing to unfortunate circumstances, the timetable had sped up, and it would just be her, but she could still carry on with their plans.

"Yes," she said. "We talked about it quite a bit. In fact, we got some brochures for townhouses in Toronto several weeks ago."

"He was alive then," she added somewhat vaguely.

I had read that grief made people confused. This was especially true when people were older. The day before the service, Mum had said to me, "Come, we need to get pastries for the reception, and I had had to say, "Mike is getting the pastries. He has an eye for pastry. We are to get the flowers," to which Mum had replied, "You're right. I don't know if I'm coming or going."

Now I said patiently, "Mike, Livy, and I live in Montclair, Mum. It is Stephen and Susan who live in Toronto."

"It's close enough to Montclair that we could have come down for many long weekends," she said after a pause. "It's just that Toronto made sense for many reasons. Canada is a commonwealth country. The cultural adjustment would have been easier. Toronto certainly is a nice, manageable place, and, besides, you know how unbearably close Stephen and your father were."

"Well, I do now," I said, slightly rocking back on my heels.

"Stephen and Susan are there without other family. You have the Kleins."

I was nonplussed. I had not thought that I was exchanging one family for another.

My mother went on. With my father being gone, she wasn't moving at all, though. Instead, she would come over for visits three or four times a year, staying several weeks with Stephen and Susan and several weeks with us.

"But I want to go on living here, darling," she said. "London is where I had the happiest times with my love."

It sounded strangely like something Dad had once said.

I knew I had to accept my mother's decision.

I set up a game plan with Mrs. Cookson for making sure my mother got out and had plenty to do, but still it was so hard for me to leave her at the end of the week. I even had a lump in my throat when Stephen went off to a separate gate at Heathrow. However, I was tired, tired of my father being dead, tired of my mother's daze, tired of trying to make things happy and normal for Livy in the midst of all this sadness, tired of being guilty about moments I had with Mike, even tired of trying to explain to people in the little park that we couldn't solve Watergate by calling for a new election. I just wanted to go home.

In Montclair, it was quite close to Halloween. Janet had gotten a beautiful round pumpkin for Livy, and we decided to paint a clown face on it instead of doing a jack-o'-lantern. Livy was thrilled, calling it "pumpkin clown" and hugging and kissing it at every opportunity. I bought some Indian corn for the door and made an arrangement for the porch with bumpy textured green-and-yellow gourds that fascinated Livy. Much to my neighbor Deena's surprise, we held off on trick-or-treating for another year, but Livy enjoyed seeing the costumed children who came to our house, recognizing two of the speech kids and shouting, "Hersheys for you!"

A month earlier, the Tilsons' sheltie had had puppies, and several times in November Livy and I went over to see them. We would sit on the floor, and they would climb in and out of our laps. "Puppies!" Livy squealed, as four living puffballs wriggled, snuggled, and leapt around us. "Puppies!"

Mike and I, excited because this would be the first decision the three of us would make together, talked seriously to Livy. We told her that a puppy, like a baby, needed lots of love. Would Livy help provide it?

"Yes," she answered solemnly, but her eyes sparkled.

Our puppy was tricolor, a little larger than average, which we thought would augur well for her personality, and was animated and affectionate. Livy wanted to call her Puppy Clown, and certainly she was a clown, carrying Mike's socks all over the house, but we thought the name might not stand the test of time. I opted for Molly. I told people we were trying to celebrate Livy's mixed heritage, Molly being an Irish name, and the Shetland Islands being English. The real reason, of course, was that Molly rhymed with Folly. Livy kept her promise and always was gentle in her hugs and patting, and Molly was gentle back, treating Mike and me as her chew toys but only giving Livy lots of licks. Many times I would come upon the two of them on the floor curled up together.

Just as we were settling Molly in and Livy was beginning to talk in six-word sentences, I had confirmation of something I had suspected. Another American baby was on the way.

With each happy new thing, there was an element of bittersweet. It was yet something else that my father hadn't lived to see.

CHAPTER 10

Come to the Kleins!

Montclair, New Jersey, 1974–2003

WE WERE IN THE midst of a baby boom for the Ords and Kleins. Susan and Stephen had a son in mid-December, which, to no one's surprise, they named Craig. Pam had a daughter, Rebecca, in February, and I was due in August.

My mother was in Toronto when Susan and Stephen's baby was born and stayed with them through Christmas. When she came to us at New Year's, she still seemed sad but interested in everything again and much more herself. She told us that Craigy was just a beautiful baby —she had many pictures to prove it—and that though Susan seemed a bit anxious, Stephen had taken to fatherhood like a duck to water.

"I almost wish he could be the one staying home with him," Mum admitted.

She thought Molly was a great addition on our walks and said she was thinking about getting a dog as well when she went back to London. A little company in the house might be nice.

"Do, Mum, do," I encouraged her.

Upon her return home, my mother followed through and got a Yorkie. Displaying a touch of the Kleins, she named her New Yorkie, although she usually called her York.

By the end of spring, I was quite big, and Livy, two years old and talking fluently, told more than one speech kid that I was becoming a clown. I spent most of July floating around the Kleins' pool with Livy, and I still sometimes beat Pam in lap races. I only had to make a salad for supper and perhaps slice potatoes, because Mike usually grilled something, and we'd eat on the patio, admiring our quincunx of roses. Deena, who had produced her second quite close to her first and always seemed harried, felt sorry for me being so pregnant in summer. However, I was living the life of Riley.

Our second daughter, Janet Mullin Klein, conceived in London the night after my father's memorial service, was born the day Nixon resigned. Celebrations all around! My mother was able to be in Montclair for the birth, and so while I, with Mike at my side, was occupied with bringing Jan into the world, my mother and my mother-in-law planned a day of games for Livy. The three of them were at the Central Park Zoo at the moment Jan emerged, which was probably excellent preparation for Jan. Life in our heretofore quiet and controllable household would never be the same. While Livy was merry and docile, Jan from the first was perpetual motion, perpetual noise, and with an edge. As Mike said, Jan was all Ord and all Klein, taken to the max.

By the time she was eighteen months, I would lay her down in her crib for an afternoon nap, and no sooner had I gone downstairs for one-on-one time with Livy than Jan would shout out, "Finished, Mommy, finished!"

Livy would say, "Oh, brother!" even though Jan was her sister.

The day after she was two, I foolishly asked Jan if she would like her nap, and she replied, "No thank you, Mommy." That was the end of the pretense of nap time.

Her favorite literary character was Noisy Nora, and she would dash around the circle of rooms on our first floor, yelling, "And I am back again, said Nora with a monumental crash!"

One rainy day, Livy and Derek junior were peacefully playing Chutes and Ladders on the living room floor while Jan as Nora was dashing about, Molly at her heels. They ran from the kitchen through dining room into the living room and straight through the game, scattering the pieces hither and yon. We all thought that was quite amusing, and fortunately, being a genius, I had memorized where the pieces were on the board, so I was able to get Livy and Ricky set back up quickly.

"You and Molly need to take a detour from now on," I told Jan.

They went running off, making the loop, and this time Jan stopped abruptly just shy of the board, while Molly went scurrying through, sending the pieces everywhere.

"Hey!" Livy cried.

"Molly doesn't always listen to Mommy," Jan explained, giggling to Ricky.

Rick was six at the time, and when Lynne came to pick him up, he informed her gravely that Jan was the most disruptive girl he had ever met.

My mother, who from her frequent visits to us had increasingly absorbed Americanisms, thought Jan was a hoot. We all did.

Jan was our child who was planned. No laissez-faire with her. Mike's and my original idea had been to have our kids four years apart, until circumstances had compelled us to decide differently. On that night in London, Mike had reminded me that we had packed in haste, not bringing certain things.

"So be it?" I had asked.

"So be it!" he had affirmed.

"Here's hoping!" I had exclaimed, intertwining myself with Mike.

By the time Jan was one, I had phased out my speech therapy practice. I had thoroughly enjoyed it when I just had Livy, but now I wanted to be free to plan the girls' and my day without constraint.

Deena, who had just had her third child and was now in business school, told me I had it all backwards. "Really, Amy, you do. You worked when it was rare for mothers to do it. I used to watch those kids going into and out of your house and wondered if you guys were having trouble paying the mortgage or what."

"We're doing fine with the mortgage," I said.

"That's good, but anyway, now that women have finally figured out that they can be more than household drudges, you become content to stay home and bake cookies."

I decided not to point out that it had been work keeping me home afternoons, and now I could be out and about with the girls for hours. "I don't bake cookies," I told Deena instead, just as I would tell Hillary Clinton years hence. "My husband bakes the cookies."

When I repeated the conversation to Pam and Lynne, they laughed. "Good old Amy, always swimming upstream!" they said.

Unlike Deena, they knew it was all part of a master plan, the germ of which had been my getting an advanced degree in speech therapy years before Mike and I had considered having children, after Janet had asked me, "Should you be getting your master's, dear? Is that the way the profession is heading?"

Perhaps it had started even before Mike, when Mum, in trying to persuade me to stay in the certification program, had said that I could do speech therapy out of my home. It was something I could meld with having a family.

The strategy had been to get credentialed for the future and then, with my first child, devise a model for pursuing a practice while mothering. With my second, I'd have the luxury of not working but would know that if I ever needed to or wanted to, I could jump-start my career at a moment's notice. I aimed to have it all, consecutively. So far, things had proceeded without a hitch.

Mike and I enjoyed our household enormously. Livy now attended a cooperative nursery school several mornings a week with Ricky and her cousin Robbie, with Lynne, Pam, and me alternating as volunteers, which made it cozy. The kids sang a song there that had the line, "If you're happy and you know it, clap your hands." We never sang it at home because I didn't especially like the tune. However, I was happy and I knew it. Often, I remembered to clap my hands.

Although my father's early death left an unfillable void, he had seen where life was taking me and had rejoiced. My mother came on frequent visits, and every other summer we took the kids to England. Sometimes we saw Stephen, Susan, and Craigy, who seemed a happy threesome. The past no longer dwelled with me, or so I thought.

At Livy's fifth birthday party—we had a magician dressed as a clown —a friend gave her the book *Madeline*. I was so pleased, because I remembered Miss Taylor giving Christa and me that book and how we had done what we called a dramatic reading for my mother and Mrs. Cookson. This had prompted Mrs. Cookson to say she saw two sixth formers in the making, which was code for us being university bound. Of course, in my case there had been unfortunate events along the way, but that was a different story.

Livy had also gotten *The Red Balloon*, and we read that first. It was charming. The next night at bedtime, continuing the Parisian theme, we settled down to *Madeline*.

I contentedly read about the old house covered with vines and then went into the part about the twelve little girls. "See, they are dressed all alike," I pointed out to Livy in a last second of innocence.

Uniforms! That was what suddenly occurred to me. The next line was "in two straight lines they broke their bread," and I had it figured out. Madeline, that slip of a girl, was in boarding school, or at least in some boarding place, since, as the ensuing pages made clear, there was zero emphasis on academics. We had still been in London when I had read the book. I had known nothing about kids being sent to these types of institutions, so the context had sailed right over my head.

I looked at Livy. She seemed absorbed. What could I do but go on with the book, and I did. I faltered only at the line "and sometimes they were very sad." Well, I could tell you what they were sad about, and it was not the man on crutches who had probably managed to evade the plight of these emotional waifs. Jory had, after all, derived some benefits from having had polio.

As a mother, I needed to be mature about this, so at the end, I tried to discuss *Madeline* with Livy.

"What did you think about the kids being in two straight lines?" I asked.

"That was how they did everything, even brushed their teeth," Livy giggled.

"You think we could get Jan to do that?"

"No, but maybe me," she said.

I decided not to tell her that the two straight lines was a paramilitary technique designed to enable one authority figure to keep a whole group of numb individuals under control. My guess was that *Madeline* was probably the one western book read in China during the Cultural Revolution. I shoved the book between two bigger books in Livy's bookshelf. Two weeks later, after we had finished the nice book *Charlotte's Web*, Livy wanted to be read *Madeline* again. I felt I had to comply. This time I choked on the reference to "the dollhouse from Papa" in Madeline's hospital room. The kid has had surgery, and her father can't be bothered to rush to her side. He merely throws a dollhouse at her. He might as well be Samantha Mary's coldhearted father. As for the other little girls, they were so miserable, they thought having their appendix out was an enviable way to kill time. I was queasy by the time I finished the demented little tale.

I said to Livy, "Don't worry, the twelve will be sprung eventually."

"Huh?" Livy said.

We had a twenty-day breather while we read *Little House in the Big Woods*, where everyone fortunately lived at home. Then Livy got *Madeline* down from the shelf. I couldn't understand the attraction.

There was a picture of Madeline being measured for her uniform in her underwear. At least nothing like that had ever happened to me. My mother had always measured me for my dreary uniform while I was wearing ordinary clothes. Then I remembered a posture test at

Longwood, which I had repressed. I also found the aura of excitement around the scar on Madeline's stomach to be strange. Was it meant to symbolize a witch's brand?

Livy took a hankering to Miss Clavel, but I thought she was just plain creepy, waltzing around in a nun's outfit when she wasn't a nun. Actually, the whole situation was kinky. Had the book been banned in Boston?

Jan wanted to learn how to use scissors. I almost said, "Let's start with Livy's book." Exercising the utmost restraint, I got out construction paper.

We read plenty of books. Indeed, we were starting the children's classics, but somehow Livy always came back to *Madeline*.

Mike often read to Livy as well, so I asked him if he thought Livy was obsessed with *Madeline*.

"No, why?" he said. "She suggests it about once a month. The illustrations are neat."

He probably hadn't noticed the picture of Madeline standing on the edge of a bridge. The text implied she was just frightening Miss Clavel, but I thought there might be more to it than that. The child was distraught.

I came to dread Livy's bedtime. Would this be the evening she would ask me to read *Madeline*? And I couldn't deny her. I had once liked the story myself.

One night, I had a dream.

"Mommy," said Livy. "I hate the name Madeline. It sounds very wrong."

"I agree, my darling daughter," I responded. "We'll never read the book again."

"Oh, I like the book," Livy said. "It's just the name I don't like, but we can fix it. Whenever you see the name Madeline, you must say Amelia. You must always say Amelia. Remember, Mommy, remember!"

"Oh, Livy, no," I said, and I wailed.

Livy sat on my lap and looked up at me with her big brown eyes. Putting her thumb in her mouth, she shrank. She was now a one-year-old baby. That meant Jan wasn't even born. My family was receding!

Janet walked by. "Well, I best be running on, dear. Many thanks for giving my son a cultural experience," she said.

"Yes, toodles!" Pam said, surrounded by her own happy family.

I looked down to my lap, and where Livy had been was just my panda bear.

I woke up in a cold sweat. In the morning, I told Mike.

He exploded. "Good God, Amy," he shouted. "How long has this been going on?"

"Over three months. I know it's silly, but I cannot bear to read that book."

Mike said the solution was simple. *Madeline* was Daddy's and Livy's special book. Whenever Livy wanted it read, Mike would read it to her.

A weight lifted from me.

It was now high summer of that year, so the girls and I, along with Pam and her two, were up at the Kleins' pool every afternoon. Livy and Robbie were independent swimmers, and Jan and Rebecca, wearing bubbles, were dog paddling. All could play a version of Marco Polo, which was the successor to the water tag I had played as a child. Janet, Pam, and I were usually right there with them, but we still had time for poolside chats.

I didn't tell Janet and Pam about the *Madeline* thing. I didn't want them to think I was totally nuts. Once, though, I tried to explain how going to Africa had changed everything. I said, "It was as if a hourglass was knocked on its side, causing our time as a family to dwindle. We all were affected, except maybe Stephen, good English boy."

"Must not have been easy," Pam said. "Can't imagine having my kids live away from home."

Janet thought and said, "Of course, I don't know Stephen the way you do, Amy, but sometimes I think you underestimate him."

Thus, Janet, the wise one, helped me to realize that our being so hurt by the experience did not reflect our weakness as a family but our strength.

Without meaning to, and there being no direct connection, I suddenly blurted out, "I've always wondered why you left the Catholic Church, Janet. Mike says it had something to do with whether he and Pam would go to parochial school."

Pam gave her mother a glance.

"Oh, I'm sorry," I apologized. "That's inappropriate of me. You don't have to answer that."

"No, it's fine," Janet said.

She continued, "My parents instinctively knew Alan was a man among men, so as devout as they were, they rejoiced in our marriage. I guessed it helped that my father had been part of the labor movement, where Catholics and Jews collaborated every day. Wouldn't have gotten very far if they hadn't. However, the institutional church was not as accepting. A cadre of priests did everything they could to talk me out of it. They worked on Alan, too. Even after we were civilly married, they dragged their feet on getting the dispensations I needed for a church ceremony. Finally I said to one of them, 'Father, you need to hurry up. There's only so far my mother can let out my wedding dress.'"

Janet paused, and I thought about their two wedding pictures.

She went on, "Eventually, I got the dispensations, and things seem to recede into the background. The war started, and the chaplains on the naval base had many pressing needs to attend to. They had no time to get excited by the respectful nonbeliever who accompanied his wife and babies to Mass every Sunday. In 1946, we moved back to this area. Mike was of an age to begin school, and as part of the quid pro quo for getting dispensations, I had had to promise to give my children a Catholic education. I interpreted that broadly to mean that we'd bring them up in the Catholic faith. My new priest, though, said we were obligated to send the kids to Catholic school. This dismayed us. We preferred the public schools for a number of reasons, but we decided to give the parish school a go. Dutifully, I took Mike for the admittance interview. The nun put a pencil into his right hand and told him to write his name."

"Mike's left-handed," I interrupted Janet to say.

"Yes," she answered. "That's what I told Sister, but she said he would learn to be right-handed like everyone else, that being right-handed was necessary for success. I said, 'His father's a leftie, and he's an architect.' She replied, 'We can do better.'"

Janet went on: "I looked at her dumbfounded. Meanwhile, Mike had put the pencil in his left hand and had made a very good *M*. 'Right hand, Michael!' she yelled, getting out her ruler. Well, that ended the idea of parochial school. Over the priest's objections, I enrolled him in public school, but I also sent him to CCD class, for religious instruction. I figured that with only one hour a week, they'd concentrate on basic Christian teaching, as opposed to peripherals. Unfortunately, Mike came home asking me why the unbaptized went to hell and what made the Jews kill Christ. Alan took it in his stride, but I didn't. I withdrew Mike from CCD. My plan was to have religious conversations with the kids at home, and of course we'd still go to Mass. Deep down, though, I knew I had crossed a line.

"The priests—and now I was talking to a group—asked me how I could see myself as a Catholic mother when I tried to deny my children instruction in Catholicism. I told them that I could not have anyone telling Mike and Pam that something was wrong with their father. I added that now that the atrocities of the Nazis were fully revealed, I was upset that the church was not zealously rooting out any vestige of antisemitism. Jesus as a man had been a Jew, after all.

"The priests were furious at me. They were not used to laywomen talking back to them, and in fact it crossed my mind that I might be endangering my soul. Anyway, one of them said, 'This is not about ethnicity! We have former Jews in our fold, but your husband refuses to believe in the divinity of Christ.'

"I replied, 'I'd rather a man who lives by the precepts of Christ, as enunciated in the Gospels, than a man who merely believes in Christ.'

"They gave me a long look. It came to me then that I was spending so much time fighting the prejudices of the clergy that I was forgetting about the miracle of redemption. My spiritual life was suffering. The priests told me I was risking excommunication, but I said it was too late for that."

Janet stopped, and Pam said, "You left the church to keep your faith."

"That's what I told myself," Janet said, "but I wonder if that was pride on my part."

Listening to Janet, I had been mesmerized. My family had had to contend with many things, but the force of religion hadn't been one of them, or perhaps it had been, dressed up as something else.

I said, reprising an early discussion I had had with Mike, "You can see how strong the pull of culture is when someone thinks he's doing wrong by doing the right thing. Consider *Huckleberry Finn*. The moral climax of the book for me is when Huck decides to help Jim escape slavery, even if it means going to hell."

"Yes," Janet said, "but maybe I should have tried harder to distinguish the church—the transcendent church—from its culture. Anyway, we settled in at Central Presbyterian. They valued Alan as a person, their Sunday school program was thoughtful, and I could practice a version of Christianity."

I looked at Janet. Slight in build, she was clearheaded, strong, and principled. Over a decade into this enterprise, I still was totally amazed and grateful that I had married into the Kleins. "Janet, you're something," I said.

"Mommy, come into the water so I can splash you," Jan called, never being one to spring surprises.

"Oops, we've been neglecting the kids!" Pam said.

"That's soon remedied," I replied, as I slid into the pool so Jan could splash me.

That fall, Livy started kindergarten. I could hardly believe that my first baby was old enough for real school, but I was heartily grateful that there was no agonizing choice over where to send her, as there had been for my parents when we went to Africa and for Mike's parents. There was no fraught weighing of competing interests. She merely went to the good school we knew she was going to go to when we bought the house. "Just a hop, skip, and jump across the park," I told Livy. It was free, too, if you didn't count taxes.

Livy wanted to go right into the first grade so she could be in her cousin Robbie's class, but I said that even though it was certain she could do the work, it would be better for her socially if she stayed with her age group. I reminded her that she'd be with Ricky, and that Lynne and I would be the class mothers.

It seemed to me that one of the problems in my family had been a lack of information sharing. Things had just happened to Stephen and me. I didn't want Livy to be caught off guard by anything. In addition to kindergarten registration, we went to all the optional activities, kindergarten roundup, kindergarten jamboree, and calling all kindergarteners. I then got to know the Edgemont School janitor, and after giving him some of Mike's ginger snaps, he gave Livy and me a secret tour of the whole school so Livy could see each of the rooms she might be in later on. I drove her by the middle school she would attend, assuming there was no redistricting due to changing town demographics, and lastly, I drove her by the high school and reminded her that she had already been in the auditorium twice for youth concerts.

"What about college?" Livy asked.

"Darling," I said, "we don't need to think of college for a number of years. That's why we live in America, not England."

"Oh, all right," Livy said.

That was also the fall that the Montclair Operetta Club put on *The Sound of Music*. It was a family affair for us. Mike played Captain von Trapp, Livy was Martina, the littlest girl, and Jan was assistant to the stage manager, who was Alan. Molly hung out with the lighting crew. I was cast as the baroness. I didn't relish playing a woman whose philosophy was "Compromise and be wise, be wise, compromise." (The song had not been carried over into the movie version, and I felt there was a good reason for that.) Besides, her proposed solution to acquiring seven stepchildren was boarding school. I was on the verge of a Madeline relapse.

"I think she's evil," I whispered to Mike.

"Undoubtedly," he replied matter-of-factly. "Just make that clear." Without Mike, of course, my career in amateur musicals wouldn't have got out of the starting gate. I told him over and over, he should be a director.

Anyway, the review in the *Montclair Times* said "Mike Klein always gives a commanding performance, and his portrayal of the Captain as a stern and principled man with a slightly suppressed sense of humor is no exception. It is Amy Klein, though, in a supporting role, who steals the show. When she says 'boarding school' with a voice full of ice, all the moral duplicity of the Baroness who is willing to collaborate with the Nazis is revealed. Winsome Livy Klein says her several lines with aplomb."

So life went on.

Along the way, we acquired a second sheltie. I don't know why, but I think it was Jan's idea. She said that since Livy had a sister, Molly should have one, too. The Tilsons' sheltie had had another litter, so one thing led to another. Heather, named for heather on the moor, was a lovely dog, sweet and eager to please, with a somewhat fey quality. Like Molly, she was tricolor, but where Molly's fur was predominately tawny, Heather's coat was mainly black, so they made a striking as well as frolicsome pair when we took them for walks. Mike and I did tell the girls that the price of a second dog was no cats, no hamsters, no gerbils, no rabbits, no parakeets, no fish, no turtles, no snakes, and goodness gracious, no horses! There was just one species not prohibited.

When Livy was six and Jan was four, I again became pregnant, as Mike and I had once again reverted to laissez-faire. We were delighted, but I was disconcerted by the change in obstetrical culture in just a few years. When I had Livy, if a couple was happily expecting, it was full steam ahead and hope for the best! Now there were these tests and, in particular for older mothers—I was going on thirty-nine—amniocentesis. I said I wasn't interested. I saw no reason to expose the baby and myself to an invasive procedure just for a chance of getting information that would not change anything.

The doctor said, "With anyone else, I'd remonstrate, but I know you won't be budged."

"Correct," I replied.

My next-door neighbor Deena made a point of asking me if I knew the sex of the fetus, and I said, "Livy tells me it's a girl named Zelda, but Jan insists it's Montgomery, a boy."

Since this was my consistent answer, she figured out that I hadn't had what she breezily called amnio. She decided my refusal either was due to my mother-in-law having formerly been a Catholic or to my being used to problem kids, from being a speech therapist. I took issue with the term "problem kids"—I wouldn't even call her uncontrollable children that—but didn't reveal my rationale to her.

In any event, she was wrong on both counts. Janet and I never discussed my medical appointments, and as for my professional background—if you wanted to call it that—it counted for nothing. Providing services and parenting were such vastly different things.

Mike and I were united. We'd tell no one else what to do, but once the two of us started a child, we would not contemplate sending her away. Besides, whatever the attributes of my baby, she'd still be an Ord, she's still be a Klein. That meant she would never be alone.

On September 25, 1978, Timmy, like his sisters, was born with the lusty cry of health. Timothy had been my father's middle name and was Stephen's and his son Craigy's middle name. Coincidentally, it was also Mike's middle name. With Timothy Alan, we covered all the bases.

Timmy was sunny and mischievous, a blend of Livy and Jan. Very adaptable, he never protested being affixed to my hip as we raced from activity to activity with the girls. In occasional quiets moments, though, I would say to him, "You're my *numero uno* too, Timmy, my *numero uno* too." Indeed, I nursed him much longer than either Livy or Jan. I just didn't want to deal with baby bottles at that stage.

Timmy was our bonus baby. While Livy and Jan bounded through elementary school, we still had a toddler. When Livy left Edgemont School, Timmy started there. Timmy was in junior soccer when Livy led the Montclair High swim team to the state championship twice. Both girls aced the SATs while Timmy learned fractions. Because of Timmy, we could form a quincunx when we played family catch, Mike in the middle and the kids and I each holding down a corner. Equally delightful, Timmy was my one child with a green thumb. In the spring, we'd plant violets, dahlias, petunias, begonias, marigolds, and more, in an ever-increasing assortment of annuals and perennials. People walking by our house tended to compliment us on our flowers, with their grand colors, even before they saw our roses, and I always would reply, "Thank you. My son and I enjoy gardening together."

My mother always enriched our household when she came for her three or four visits a year. The kids called her "Grandma O," and as Jan put it, she was their grandmother who sometimes lived in. She had a unique relationship with each of the three kids. Livy was special because she was the oldest and the link with Grandpa Craig. One of our holiday traditions was to show our growing cache of family videos, and we'd always start with Livy and Grandpa blissfully playing together on the beach in Cornwall. Mum thought Jan was a hoot, a perpetual riot, and was always helping her to concoct funny schemes. I would say, "Let's pick up where we left off in *Little Women*," and Jan, after secretly consulting with Grandma O in front of me, would run and get me *Little Men*, shouting "Try and find your place, Mom!" (*Little Men* was unfortunately about a residential school, but I was trying to take a philosophical view of these things now.)

As for Timmy, she would give him constant hugs and treats, calling him "my baby." I liked that, but it also gave me pause, because I realized that if my parents had had a third child—a baby boomer—instead of deciding to go to Africa, my mother would have been the same age I was when I had Timmy, and the age difference between me and that baby would have been akin to the age difference between Livy and him.

The kids were always pumping my mother for information about me. Once they asked how I came by the name Amelia. It was summer, and we were sitting in the light, airy family room that Mike and I had added on to the house after Timmy arrived. Although this was years before open floor plans became the rage, we had extended the kitchen to include a good-size semicircle so that I could cook supper and still interact with the kids as they played. Yes, I had taken over dinner preparation, although Mike did breakfasts and helped with lunch sandwiches so I wouldn't feel that fixing meals was a major part of my day. That wasn't why I was home, after all!

Anyway, Livy, sitting on the window seat in the bay window, said, "Tell us, Grandma, or we'll think you named Mom after Amelia Earhart."

My mother hesitated and said, "Well."

Jan, who was next to Mum on the loveseat, said, "Yeah, Grandma, we'd think you named her after Amelia Earhart."

Looking a little uncomfortable, my mother said, "Actually, we did!"

"You named me after an aviator?!" I exclaimed in surprise. I was on the floor with Timmy, who was building stuff with Legos.

"Well, you know how your father was very interested in aviation for a while, although that changed a bit after what he saw in the war."

I hadn't known Dad had been particularly interested in aviation, and I should have followed up on that, but my mother continued. "Besides, we didn't like the name Beryl, and we weren't enamored about the way Beryl Markham lived her personal life."

I conceded that I greatly preferred Amelia to Beryl but thought to myself there would have been some irony in naming me after a flyer who had been part of the Happy Valley set in Africa.

"So, how did she get the nickname Amy?" Jan asked. She had a way of talking to Grandma as if I wasn't there.

"Yeah, Amy is a nickname," Timmy commented. "Timmy is a nickname, too."

I told him he was right and then said. "I guess it was just a logical offshoot of Amelia. I think I got the idea from my friend Charlotte, who began to be called Lottie when she changed environments and met new folks."

My mother said, turning to me, "I agree, but I've always thought too that perhaps you were anglicizing the name Aumi."

Amy? Aumi? Was there a faint echo of Africa in the name I had chosen for myself in the new world? Talk about past, present, and future! I looked at my mother for six straight seconds.

"Well, who's Aumi?" Jan demanded.

"Just someone in Tanzania whom we all liked very much," I said. Then I changed the subject by asking Livy if she knew what Churchill had said to Lady Astor.

Livy was a well-read twelve-year-old, so she replied, "Well, Lady Astor was a vain shrew with bad politics, and she told him that if he was her husband, she'd poison his soup, and he answered—"

My mother and I chorused with her, "Madam, if I was your husband, I'd drink it!"

Jan got it and laughed with us, and then Tim said, "I only like chicken noodle," causing us to laugh some more.

Coincidentally, we had our semiannual night of games about a week later while Mum was still visiting. Mike and I were not overtly social people, preferring to spend most of our time with the children, our extended family, and the Gibbses. However, partly to make up for the fact I nixed kid sleepovers (because I thought kids should be in their own beds every night), we hosted two events a year for the whole neighborhood, Timmy and I delivering thirty or so invitations exhorting people to "come to the Kleins"! The winter one featured Twister and Bonanza, a knockoff on poker that Mike had played as a kid. The summer night of games was outdoors, and we played "capture the flag."

This time, it was the best night of games we ever had. Pam and Ben, Janet and Alan, and the Gibbses all arrived with folks to add to the Erwin Park Road crowd. Mum's old friend Honora came with her family. Most people brought salads or sides, and Mike grilled chicken, as well as providing the cookies. Drink choices were lemonade, cider, milk, and water, although Deena did sneak in soda for her kids. The Chartreuse Canines, co-captained by Deena and Jan, faced off against the Magenta Buffalos, headed by my mother and Ricky. Molly and Heather were supposed to be on the Chartreuse Canines but raced from one side to the other. Indeed, once Molly got a flag, she was loath to give it up to anyone, despite the pleas.

The Magenta Buffalos won, thanks largely to my mother, who despite her image of a demure older women, was a master of feints and Hail Marys. Ricky was no slouch, either. Besides, I was on their team and an adept jailbreaker, so what would you expect? Everyone stayed and stayed. It was a grand evening.

My mother, laughing as much as anyone else, had really seemed to enjoy it, but the next morning she acted preoccupied and glum. I tried to think of what might be wrong. Had there been too much noise? Was it all too American for her, the way kids had argued with adults about strategy? Jan had really gotten going with Deena at one point. Alan had had to mediate.

Mike said, "Olivia, if I wasn't the patriarch of Kids World Central, I'd be disconcerted myself!"

My mother laughed at that, and then she was quiet again.

Finally, my mother said to me, "I wished your father and I had given more parties."

"What!" I said in surprise. "You and Dad were constantly giving parties in the compound. Drove me crazy!"

"Drove me crazy, too," my mother replied. "They were just alcohol-fueled functions we were obligated to give, just like we were supposed to frequent the club. Everything was so mechanical, just a never-ending pretense of conviviality."

She lowered her voice, even though there was no one but us in the family room now. "Grace Hobson was really my only friend in the compound."

"I know," I said, because it occurred to me that I did know that.

Then my mother said, "It's funny, because when I first met the Hobsons, I couldn't stand them. There we were out for a walk the night before you and Stephen were going away to school for the first time, and we were all so upset we didn't know what was up and what was down, and she comes tripping along in her high heels and told me that it was my liberation day."

"That couple was the Hobsons?" I shouted, thinking back to that dismal evening in 1947. Then I remembered that they had spoken of their son Jory as a fair to middling student interested only in rugby. This was the same Jory who would become a political science professor. "Why, I never made the connection!" I said.

"They changed dramatically after Jory got polio," my mother said.

"Sometimes a child's disability will bring out a parent's latent strengths," I remarked. "Not always, but sometimes."

"They stepped back from the frivolity of the compound and seized a second chance with him." There was almost a tone of awe in Mum's voice.

I suddenly figured out whom Jory's wife reminded me of, other than Kate Hepburn. With her stylishly impractical shoes and her self-absorbed chatter, she reminded me of Jory's mother the way she was before Jory became disabled.

The phone rang, but I let someone else answer it.

"Things were just so topsy-turvy in the compound," I said. "It was awful bad luck that Jory got polio, and just six years before the vaccine, but it also opened doors for them all."

"Yes, it all was so topsy-turvy," my mother answered sadly, and I knew she was talking about what had happened to us as well.

Right after that, she said, "Your father had lost so much time in the war, and I was so grateful that he had come home to us more or less intact that I didn't see how I could deny him any opportunities. We had discussed going to East Africa a lot when we were younger and just two of us. However, what he really wanted to do after the war was to settle back into ordinary family life in London. He was looking for me to put the kibosh on the idea, just like Val Cookson said no to Saudi Arabia for her husband. I overlooked that the circumstances had changed. I misread the signals."

"Dad could have said no for himself," I gently pointed out.

Just then Livy rushed in. "The rough and readies want us to go hiking in the reservation after lunch. Grandma O, will you come?" The rough and readies were what the kids called their Klein grandparents, because they were always ready to do things.

"Double sure!"

"You, Mom?" Livy asked. "Dad's going, and Aunt Pam and those guys."

"Let me check my busy schedule."

"That's yes!" Mum and Livy replied in unison.

Livy raced off to call Janet back.

"Mum," I started back hesitantly. "Part of the reason Mike and I have the family life we have is that we've had advice and support from extended family every single step of the way. You and Dad never had that, being only children, and your parents not living long enough to be our grandparents. You, Dad, Stephen, and I were an unshakable unit of four, but it must have been hard for you never having sounding boards, having to make all family decisions on your own."

"Yes, perhaps," Mum replied softly. "I had help—Devon would

have been much less manageable without Jenny—and I was very close to Val Cookson; our two families did so much together in London. She did encourage me to think carefully about what we were doing, but she felt limited in what she could say, not having the moral authority of family."

Jan and Timmy, running a race with Molly and Heather at their heels, came rushing in, and we were pulled back into the here and now. Kids and dogs have a way of doing that.

I thought about this conversation with my mother years later when Timmy decided to be a comedian for the middle school talent show. He told me that he had done research and that comedy was best when it struck responsive chords in the audience.

"Double sure, Tim!" I said, quite impressed.

He would begin with jokes about mothers-in-laws. "Everyone hates their mother-in-law," he explained.

"News to me," I replied. "Gram Janet is one of my top ten people. I have no idea what I'd do without her! You know what else? Dad's wild about Grandma O."

Timmy frowned and said slowly, "I really wasn't thinking about Gram or Grandma."

"Well, Timmy, maybe you should. Many mothers-in-law are also someone's grandmother. When you generalize about a whole group of people, you cut a wide swath. It reflects prejudice, dear." I prided myself on not whitewashing things for my kids (except when I did).

Timmy conceded that mother-in-law jokes might not be the right thing. Instead, he would start with some amusing remarks about the British. They sent their children away to school but kept their dogs at home. His own mother was proof of that! Wasn't that funny, Mom?

Actually, Folly had spent six weeks in quarantine.

I didn't want to be known as the Mother Who Kills All Comedy, so I merely suggested that his dad might have some constructive ideas.

Of course, Mike did. He showed Timmy a book of classic comedy routines that he had had since his Yale days. After poring over the book, Timmy decided to team up with his best friend, his cousin Christopher, to do Abbott and Costello's "Who's on First." Timmy, wearing a Yankees baseball cap backward, would be the newcomer to the ballpark who wanted to know who played what position. Christopher, wearing a 1950s businessman's hat provided by Alan, would be the team manager trying to give the names of the players. They billed themselves as T. Klein and C. Klein.

We somewhat abbreviated the dialogue, focusing on who, what, and I don't know, with a nod towards naturally. Even so, it was a very ambitious thing for two eighth graders to do. Mike worked with them, I worked with them, and Pam worked with them. Jan got into the act, so to speak, by telling Tim he should sound more and more exasperated as the only answer he got to his repeated question "Who's on first?" was "Who!" Perhaps he should stamp his feet.

"What?" Timmy said.

"What's on second!" affirmed Jan, without missing a beat.

The boys were splendid, delivering the routine with flair and verve and comic timing. They missed very few words, and the audience loved it. Derek Gibbs whispered to Mike, "No offense, bro, but this beats disappearing milk!" referring to the fact that Mike had done magic tricks for his talent show in the 1950s.

Timmy and Chris won first prize, provoking cheers and applause and a few sour grapes.

Deena, whose daughter had tap-danced to "Rock-a-Bye, Baby" was heard to say, "No one ever has a chance against the Klein juggernaut!"

I was a member of the Klein juggernaut! Twenty years in now, I was still impressed and grateful.

At our celebratory dinner the next night, Janet told the boys that the genius of "Who's on first?" was that it struck responsive chords. People often talked at cross-purposes because they were using the same words to mean different things. That was part of the human predicament.

"Did you ever do 'Who's on first' with the speech kids, Mom?" Jan asked.

"Don't recall that she did," said Livy, who always claimed to have remembered all the sessions she observed as a baby.

"I didn't," I said, "but I should have, if only to show that the production of speech is the superficial aspect of communication. Understanding the other person's frame of reference is much more important."

In the midst of this happy dinner, one corner of my mind was thinking about my family going to Africa. We had mistaken who was on first. We hadn't known what would be on second. Thus, the Colonial Office witch wives had cast their unnatural spell.

Mike brought in the boys' cake. It was a marble cake with white icing, and Mike had etched a baseball diamond in chocolate on the cake. We clapped for the boys, and we clapped for the cake.

Even the most cherished children, whose parents luxuriate in almost every minute of their childhood, grow up. By 1991, when Timmy was in the talent show, Livy was a Harvard sophomore. In 1992, Jan started Yale. Then, in the fall of 1996, Mike and I drove Tim down to the University of Virginia and helped him set up his room in an eighteenth-century dorm. Two days later, we drove home, just the two of us.

Like Pam and Ben and Derek and Lynne, we now had a sort of empty nest. We joked that this was almost like the old fancy-free days in New York, except this was Montclair. Certainly Mike and I still had razzle-dazzle.

My neighbor Deena assumed (or perhaps hoped) that I would fall apart, having oriented my life around my kids for a quarter of a century. She was wrong. All through their growing up years, I had kept my children close. Mike and I had been helicopter parents before the term was coined, but the intent had never been to bind Livy, Jan, and Timmy to us indefinitely. Our goal had always been to help them to become independent-thinking, confident adults who would follow their dreams. After all, I had been more naïve and less secure than they, and yet I had still left my parents to go with my love to the new world, and wonders had awaited me.

As for me, I had never wavered from wanting to have it all, although consecutively. I was taking a few graduate courses and mulling over options.

Of course, Timmy was back for vacations, and Livy and Jan were both in the metropolitan area and popping in and out, so we weren't totally without the fruits of our union.

There had been some surprises with the girls. We had figured that Livy would go into a caring profession. She always wanted to make people feel included, always was the first to propose a social service project. Jan always pushed back and always had zingers. We expected her to be a lawyer.

It was Livy who enrolled in law school. Jan decided to get a master's degree in speech therapy—or, I should say, speech pathology.

"I like to communicate, Mom," she told me. "I want to help other people do the same thing."

She added, "At least I'm not becoming a physical therapist. That would be absolutely disgusting!"

I just laughed, remembering a similar conversation I once had with Jory.

Livy and Derek junior (who had been Ricky and was now called Rick) had been inseparable since the word go and had gone to Harvard together, where they had seemed to be a couple; after graduation, however, they announced that they were just good friends. This caused sadness among some, because a different decision had been unexpected.

Deena tried to comfort me. "At least you won't have biracial grandchildren," she said. Her son Brian had given Livy and Rick some flack in high school until Jan had told him she had a black belt in karate (when she really had only a white belt).

"Oh, I'll have biracial grandchildren," I reassured her. "Don't fret about that!"

Lynne wasn't worried either. Call it mothers' intuition.

A month into law school at Columbia, Livy met a graduate student in history named Ethan Curran while they were both working on a food drive. Ethan was thoughtful and had a sunniness about him. He had sung in musicals, gotten medals in swimming. All right, apart from his carrot-colored hair, he seemed rather like a Klein. We knew things were serious when he started baking with Alan and Mike.

It was not just the kids' expanding lives and my new interests that caused me to reflect that time was quickly passing. There were other things, too. I would call the dogs for their walk, and it would not be Molly and Heather who bounced towards me, Heather squeaking with glee. They had succumbed peacefully to old age, and so it would be Polly and Daisy, racing to the door, quite excited about the outing.

Mike and I both had perfect vision when we married. Now we both used reading glasses. We had stayed trim, but I had to work at it, while he didn't. Perhaps that was why in the 1997 Montclair Operetta Club's production of *The Music Man* Mike reprised his starring role while I was Marian the Librarian's mother! Actually, that was more due to the ways of the world than anything else.

On our biannual trips to England, it seemed the more things changed, the more it stayed the same. Christa, who was now renowned in the antiquarian books realm, had gray hair and was increasingly concerned with her ailing parents. Yet she was still as kind and enthusiastic as she had always been.

I wondered why Christa had never married. Certainly, if anyone had compared the two of us in our late teens, they would have said that I was the one destined for the single life. Christa told me with a shrug that she had just never met a guy who was both the right person and eligible. I thought about it, and that made sense to me. I only knew about four men who were suitable husband material, and two of them were Mike and Alan.

Children were a different story. To my mind, they enhanced life itself. How could Christa deal with not having them?

"Why, Amelia," she exclaimed, "I had children! I had them very early on and didn't even have to go through pregnancy I helped Mum and Dad raise the Booms. They would have had a pretty hard time if they had to do it on their own, what with having to manage Ian and Jon, too."

I remembered going over to the Cooksons after we came back from Africa for the home year and Christa saying, "the girl's the unpaid help"—meaning herself—and she had been laughing.

"Amelia," she pressed. "Don't you think that when I go to the London Symphony and see Ken in the percussion section that I feel immense maternal pride?"

I nodded, because I knew that it was so.

As for Jory, he had taught for fifteen years at UCLA after he and Kate had moved to Southern California so she could try her hand at TV and movies. We had seen them four times during that interval, twice when they were in New York, once when we took the kids on a trip up the California coast, and once when visits to England coincided. I had been aware of the growing gulf between them. As Kate became more and more successful, regularly getting supporting roles, the more she did publicity work, drank and went to parties. Her friends had no interests in common with Jory. Indeed he said that sometimes he felt as if it was the compound all over again. Perhaps if they had had a family that would have anchored them, but Kate had rebuffed all Jory's suggestions in that line. There had been little shouting, few recriminations. They just eventually decided that they were done. They divorced. Kate kept the house in Encino, and Jory went back to Cambridge University.

One plus for him was that he seemed to have evaded post-polio syndrome, a topic that was much in the news. It was his unconfirmed hunch that it was because his parents had gotten him out of the hospital as soon as he was medically stable and had opted for water exercise over invasive treatment on his muscles.

"They let me stay myself," Jory said simply.

I replied slowly, "I think that somehow my parents let me stay myself, too."

Throughout her eighties, my mother also stayed herself. Indeed, she was a spry ninety at Livy's and Ethan's wedding in July 1998. What a glorious day that was for us all. Livy chose to be married at home in the quincunx of roses. In keeping with Ord and Klein custom, she gave wedding traditions her own spin. Her bridesmaids were Jan and her cousin Rebecca, and she had three matrons of honor, her two grandmothers and me. Livy wore white chiffon, and the rest of us wore lemon silk, which harked back to Mike's and my wedding, although in reverse. My mother, standing straight, glowed with pride.

In the next year or so, though, my mother grew noticeably frail. I could tell it even in her voice, when we talked long distance, which we were doing much more frequently. Part of it, perhaps, was that Mrs. Cookson had died after a long struggle with cancer. Dear Mrs. Cookson had lived her life with such flair, insight, and generosity, always quick with her matter-of-fact support of the Ord family. We were all bereft. Why, I never would have met the love of my life if Mrs. Cookson hadn't encouraged me to join GLOCO! However, for my mother, Val's death went to the bone. It symbolized to her that the people she had been young with were blowing away like leaves. She told me that sometimes she went to the little park with Jersey (her current Yorkie) just so she could remember the hours that two quite different women had spent there chatting about all matter of things as their children and a cocker spaniel played.

Once more, I urged my mother to live with us in Montclair. Stephen and Susan implored her to move in with them in Toronto. "Jersey, too!" we all made clear. She always said no. She loved being with us and seeing her grandchildren, but she was a Londoner. She wasn't going to change now.

We would have worried about her to distraction if it hadn't been for Henri Gold and his daughter Rachel.

Even after my mother's friend Ruth had died, Mum still kept in touch with Henri, who had become a businessman in Basel. In the mid-1980s, he had lost his wife in a car accident, and believing that a change in environment would be best for his then thirteen-year-old daughter, he had had his company transfer him to London for a year. My mother had helped him find a flat in Belgravia and had suggested Regency Day for Rachel. She had taken Rachel on shopping excursions and to the ballet. She had recommended doctors and dentists. When Henri decided they would stay in London permanently, my mother gave him house-hunting tips. Henri had smoked, but he gave it right up when Mum asked him to.

Rachel was a lovely, serious girl and a brilliant student. Whereas once I had been the pride of Regency Day, now Rachel was

By 1990, not only were Henri and Rachel on my holiday card list, they were somehow on Janet's.

Henri was extremely grateful for everything my mother had done for him and Rachel when they had been new to London, so now, as it became harder for her to do physical things, he was returning all her favors.

He helped her with grocery shopping week after week. He gave Jersey extra walks. With my mother sitting in a lawn chair and giving him directions, he tended her garden in three seasons, doing things that the paid gardener wouldn't think to do. He and Rachel, who was married now, took her to plays and concerts. I thanked him repeatedly, both in person and by letter, and he always said the same thing. "It's nothing. Your mother helped save my life." He really was terribly grateful for the kindness she had shown.

My mother lived to be part of the digital age. Where long ago, my only communication with her had been the exchange of one letter per week, now e-mail flew between us almost daily. We would write about ordinary things, about the first robin Mike saw in April, or all the caterpillars Mum saw in Hyde Park. "I told Jersey that they'd transform into butterflies but I doubt that she believes me." We would write about the noteworthy, such as Ethan and Livy deciding to live in Montclair. Hooray! Politics was fair game. "Gracious, your election seems to be in a muddle," my mother wrote. "Gore got more!" I e-mailed right back.

On that horrible day in September 2001, as the Kleins who were not in New York huddled together waiting for word of the Kleins who had left for New York that morning as usual, I would e-mail my mother twenty times. The last time was at 10:20 p.m. "Rebecca has made it home. She walked thirty blocks to Port Authority with a coworker, both of them in heels. A stranger gave them water and some granola bars. Pam cried when she came in. With her arrival, everyone's accounted for, but there are families in town who cannot say the same thing. Stephen called again to make sure we are all right. Love, Amy."

Everything changed on both sides of the Atlantic. There would come a time when Janet, Meg Tilson, and I, baffled and disturbed, would reconstitute their antiwar group of thirty-five years before to protest torture in interrogation. Yes, everything changed, except for day-to-day life.

September 11 probably had nothing directly to do it with it, but at a family supper six months later, Janet quietly announced she was going back to the Catholic Church.

"Is she ill?" Pam asked, turning to Alan.

"Fit as a fiddle," Alan said cheerfully.

"Well, that's good," said Tim. "Gram, I'd just hate to see you sick." I glanced at him fondly. Timmy was twenty-four and working in the brash ambiance of information technology but had never lost his innate sweetness. He was like his father.

Janet confirmed that she was fine and then explained. "I left the church because I was afraid I would lose my faith, trying to deal with the prejudices and small-mindedness of the institution and the people claiming to represent it. Then, too, I felt I couldn't let the bigotry wash up against my young family. That was over fifty years ago. Circumstances have changed. I have changed. I can now look at the bigger picture, and in a curious way, the horrible sex-abuse cases we are hearing about have played a role in my decision. The clergy should not be the focus, nor the hierarchy. Transcendent faith will always endure, but it is for the laity to take responsibility and determine what future the temporal church has on earth. At the risk of sounding too pretentious, I would like to play part in this endeavor. At least I want to try. It's my heritage."

I looked at Janet as she spoke a little more. I had admired her independence of thought in leaving the church. Now I admired her courage and steadfastness in returning to it.

My mother had no similar religious revelation, but she remained mentally as sharp as a tack as physically she weakened. In the summer of 2003 when Mike, Timmy, and I were over to London for a two-week visit, she told me with uncharacteristic candor that she had been diagnosed with congestive heart problems. I conferred with Stephen, and we agreed that even with Henri and Rachel's tremendous help, Mum should not be without one of us from here on out. After Mike and Tim left, I would stay on for a month more. Stephen, who had recently retired from his company and now had the flexibility of consulting work, would then come over for a month. My sweet Livy, upon hearing of the plan, said she would be next for a couple of weeks. Following that, I'd come back, and so it would go on, in a cycle.

I did feel disconcerted when Mike and Tim went home without me. During our whole marriage, Mike and I had rarely been apart for more than a few days. Indeed, he had refused some promotions because they involved business travel. (I'm sure there was some in his office who had said, "You know his wife.") I had also never been so far away from the kids. To be sure, they were grown, but they still seemed to like to have me in the background. I was especially concerned about Jan, who was back living in the house after a bad breakup. I had invited Rick over several times just to cheer her up. Mike assured me things would be fine; the fort would be held down. We had e-mail and international cell phones. Communication would be constant. He would send us baked goods every week.

Timmy said, "Get in the zone, Mom. Enjoy Grandma O."

His advice was cogent. I did want to be with Mum. I wanted it quite desperately. Now, though, I understood the feeling that she must sometimes have had of being torn, of knowing that being with one person that you loved meant not being with other people that you loved.

My time with my mother was surprisingly reminiscent of the month we had enjoyed in Malta when I was eighteen. It was just the two of us. There was nothing we had to do. We had a routine but no schedule. We practiced French. We read *Girl with a Pearl Earring* out loud on the sunporch. Most days, we managed an excursion, to Hyde Park, to the Tate Gallery, to the British Museum to see the Magna Carta and to remember how much my father had liked to take us to see it. Once we took a boat ride down the Thames. Several times, we went to the gym my mother still belonged to and swam, although we did laps across the width of the pool rather than its length.

Once when we were swimming, my mother said, "I could have done both."

"Both what?" I asked.

"Gone to university and tried out for the Olympics!"

"Yes, of course you could have! Double sure," I replied.

"I prided myself on being an independent-minded person, but there were instances where I was swayed by others, did conform to custom."

"Janet says that it's tremendously difficult to know when you should stand back from the culture."

"Yes, but you have always seemed to know when to do it," my mother persisted.

"Mum," I exclaimed, "as an adult, I've never been tested. Mike and I had to make a few decisions about the kids and other things, but essentially, we've lived on easy street."

The term "easy street" made my mother laugh. "Otherwise known as Erwin Park Road," she laughed.

"Why don't we give a small dinner party?" I suggested as I helped my mother up the pool steps. "Henri, Rachel and her husband, and Christa."

"Yes, let's!" my mother said excitedly.

I was sorry I hadn't told my mother that she had been a hero in Devon. but the moment had passed.

Instead, I started chattering about how perhaps the time was now right for me to teach in college, like Livy's Ethan.

"Well, probably not a professor at this point," I admitted. "An instructor and write, too. First, I'm getting a doctorate in history. Full circle."

"I know," Mum said simply.

The days were pleasant, each one a bit different from the one before, each having its grace. Sometimes at the edges, though, I felt the specter. When my mother talked about the world and other people's lives, she used the present tense, but in talking about herself, she frequently used "was." Then there was Jersey. Several months before, Henri had kindly started taking Jersey every night, so Mum would not have to stay downstairs longer than she wanted in order to let her out and back in for the last time. When we arrived, I wanted to tell Henri this wasn't needed for a while. I could let Jersey out. My mother stopped me. "No, Amelia," she said. "I want Jersey to think of Henri's house as home, too."

"I see," I said slowly.

Sometimes when my mother and I were in the garden or we were doing French, I would gaze at her unwaveringly as I had as a child, and she would notice and say questioningly, "Yes, darling, yes?"

I would answer, "I just like seeing you, Mum." Indeed, I did. She had a million wrinkles, but her features were still distinct and overwhelmingly familiar. I had to memorize her face and memorize it again and again so that I could keep it always with me.

The minutes were running out.

Stephen came the day before I was to leave, so we had time together, the three of us. He and I teamed up to make dinner, and it turned out he knew how to make stuffed baked tomatoes, which went quite well with chicken breasts, mushrooms, and new potatoes. My mother had lit candles, and they flickered eerily against the beige walls of the dining room, just as the candles had in our Tanganyikan dining room the night before Stephen and I were first sent to Kenya. Stephen and Mum drank wine, while I had water. We had lemon squares just received in the mail from Mike for desert, and we chatted leisurely, as if we had all the time in the world. And why not? We had been to Africa, but we were also the three who had shared Devon.

After we finally washed the dishes, my mother bade Stephen and me to go into the sitting room. There were things to be divided up between us. We looked at each other apprehensively. We wanted to wait a lifetime to apportion the silver.

What Mum had for us were our old badminton racquets, frames slightly warped, strings brittle but our names still indelible on the handles. She gave each of us the one that bore our name and put the other two on the tea table, telling us to pick what we wanted. Stephen and I both made an instinctive choice. Suddenly, we looked at each other, and without a word I handed him the one I had taken, and he handed me the one he had taken. So it was that I got the racquets that said AMELIA and DADDY, and he took STEPHEN and MUMMY, because that was the way we had always played, just to mix things up.

"There!" my mother said, sounding satisfied. She smiled the smile she had bestowed on us all our lives.

The Devon three. The London four, and a little dog, too. Survivors of adventure! We were quite a family, always had been.

The next day, Stephen went with me to Heathrow. At the security checkpoint we said good-bye. "Stephen," I told him. "Stephen, if Mum worsens in any way, or even if you just get a funny feeling, call me, call me right away. I'll be over in a New York minute!"

He did not frown the way he usually did when I used American slang with him. Instead, he clasped my hand. "Of course I will, sis," he replied.

CHAPTER II

The Third Child

London, and Montclair, New Jersey, 2003–2004

IT WAS A raw windy October Sunday afternoon. Bad things always seemed to happen to the Ords in October. The Colonial Office witch wives had come to our house in October. My father had died in October.

Livy had come over because Ethan was at a ball game with some of his buddies, so the girls and I were chatting in the family room. We had a fire going. Mike was in the kitchen making everyone's weekly supply of cookies. Deena would have called it a typical Klein tableau.

Jan had changed from working in a clinical setting to being a school speech therapist because she thought there would be fewer strictures. It hadn't turned out that way.

"I'm criticized for not making kids have notebooks, but I don't want them to think this is just so much extra work," she said.

"I never had the kids carry notebooks either, but in my case it was because I didn't want them to think they were in school," I laughed.

"Wish this wasn't school!" Jan exclaimed. "The individualized education plan is God. I have this eighth-grade girl, and the only time they can schedule her for speech is when Spanish class meets, and she really, really wants to take Spanish."

"How serious is her speech problem?" Livy asked.

"Significant, but that's not the point," Jan said. "She'd rather do Spanish. So I said I could stay later and give her speech therapy after school. That was nixed. All services must be given during the school day! So I suggest that she take a break from speech therapy this year and resume it next year when scheduling might be easier. This way, she won't be behind in Spanish. Her parents are agreeable, but the school said no, speech therapy is written into her IEP. All bow to the IEP! I don't know what to do. The girl's miserable."

"Um," I said. "You're fluent in Spanish, Jan. Why not give her speech therapy in Spanish? It's all transferrable. Get the book the class is using. Do the same drills and oral conversations. Have her do the written work surreptitiously. Grade it. She will probably end up ahead of the class."

Jan said, "Mom, you're so smart, you should have been twins!"

Then, in the midst of the afternoon, in the midst of life, the phone rang. Mike answered it and said, "Yes, she's here. I'll get her."

"Amy, it's Stephen." Mike's voice was lead.

I ran to the kitchen, grabbed the phone. Mike held my waist. "Stephen," I said, talking fast, "If I don't get the seven plane, I'll get the eight-thirty. Tell Mum that in either case, I'll be there by the time she starts her day tomorrow. Tell her, Stephen, tell her." Even as I spoke, I knew what he would say.

"Sis, she's gone." He continued, "Let me tell you about the day."

OK, Stephen, I thought, tell me about the day. I said nothing.

He said that Mum had been feeling much stronger that morning, and they had decided to take an excursion. He had borrowed Henri's car. They had talked briefly and somewhat improbably of going to Devon but had decided it was too far, so they had driven through the outskirts of London in the direction of Hampton Court—beyond it, in fact—and had lunch in a country inn of a type she loved so much.

I hadn't known that my mother liked country inns. Whenever I was with her, we had done city things or beach things. Of course, whenever we had a holiday when Stephen and I were growing up and we were in England, we had gone to a country inn in the Lake District. Genius here had never made the connection—although I must have in some way, since that was the place I had chosen for my family honeymoon.

Stephen went on. "The inn has a nice garden, some of it still in bloom. What do you call those little white and blue flowers?"

"Asters," I said shortly. I was under control, though. "You silly, you dummy" was on the tip of my tongue, but I closed my mouth. When the situation called for it, I could really behave. Jan could do the same thing. She had gotten it from me.

"Chrysanthemums, too?" I asked, feeling I should make an extra effort to be convivial.

"Chrysanthemums as well. After lunch, we sat in the garden for a while. We had the place to ourselves. Mum said that all her life, she had liked being outdoors best."

I did too. I had gotten it from her. I bit my lip.

"We went home," Stephen said. "Mum said she was going to lie down and rest. I returned the car. I did paperwork."

Just like Stephen, I thought. It was a good thing that Mike was standing next to me. His hand was pressing into the small of my back. I didn't want him to think he had spent the best years of his life with an insensitive loony tune, so by sheer force of will, I changed a sudden laugh into a sudden cough.

"Two hours later, when I went in to ask what I should fix for supper, she was gone. She looked peaceful and merely asleep, her head tilted towards the pictures of all of us on her night table, but there was no breath. She was gone, gone just like that. Jersey was lying against her, licking her hand." Stephen's voice had no affect. Now, there's a word —affect.

He appeared to rally. "Amelia, she had a wonderful day, the best she —we, actually—had in weeks. If she was going to die, it was best that she slip away after such a day. That is what I think."

For once in my life, I had to give a thought to Stephen. "Listen, Stephen, Mike and I will catch an evening plane and will be there tomorrow. What are you doing tonight? At least, I'm with family now," and indeed I was. Mike was right next to me. He would catch me if started to fall. Livy and Jan were fifteen feet away. Pam was a half mile away. Janet and Alan were less than two miles away. Timmy was the farthest. He was in Clifton, four miles away. Oh, there were the Gibbses. They were nearly family, probably would be family. They were on Midland, the street behind us.

Stephen replied, "Susan will be here by morning. Craigie, too. Henri has invited me for dinner. I can even spend the night at his place."

"Like Jersey?" I nearly said. Sometimes I thought something was quite wrong with me.

"That's good, Stephen," I said instead. "Henri will be our friend forever."

"You bet!" Stephen said. "Also, Jon Cookson said I should have breakfast with him and his family."

Being the mature person I was, I decided not to get into a snit because Stephen had apparently called half the world before he had called me.

"That's good, Stephen," I repeated.

[315]

Then I added, "Thank you, Stephen. Thank you for being with Mum today. Thank you for going with her for one last family excursion. I wish that I could have been there. Stephen, Stephen, Stephen! You have always been our family's rock. Ever since Devon, Stephen!" I meant it with my whole heart.

"Not really, sis," he said shakily.

"Well, I'll be there in the morning. We'll be together, Stephen."

When I hung up the phone, Mike called Timmy and then Janet and Alan while I went back to the girls. Jan was looking downcast. Livy was biting her lip and frantically pushing buttons on her cell phone.

She said, "Ethan and I got these things for emergencies, but it does not occur to him that everyone other than him might have an emergency." She snapped the phone shut.

I said, "Darling, this is not an emergency. Grandma O has died. She was ninety-five. There's nothing we can do about it. She had a—

I paused. I was about to say a good life, but had that been wholly true, with all the separations? "She had an interesting life," I amended.

Jan asked, "Are you going to deal with this OK, Mom?"

I replied slowly, "Yes, I think so. It's just that—"

Mike came in, and I ran into his arms. "Oh, Mike," I cried. "I have never been able to be with my mother when I wanted to be."

"I know, love," he said.

It was then that Livy wailed.

I flew to her. Here I was thinking of myself when my children were in grief. Some mother I was! "Oh Livy, dearest, my sweet girl. It will be all right. It's just that there were things I would like to have told her."

Livy wailed louder.

"Livy, what's wrong?" Mike's voice was steady.

"I'm pregnant!" Livy cried.

"Oh Livy, how utterly glorious," I said, kissing her.

"Absolutely wonderful!" Mike said, also kissing her.

"Well Liv, aren't you scene stealer!" Jan said. "Grandma O breathes her last, and what do you say, 'I'm pregnant'! So what's the problem? Isn't Ethan the father? Geez, I hope it's not Rick. That would be a little obvious, Livy."

"Jan," I said.

"Of course, the baby is Ethan's!" said Livy angrily. "The problem is we could have been telling people for weeks now, but we decided to wait a bit. I'm starting my second trimester." She put her face in her hands.

"Honey, that's all right," Mike said.

"We waited until the end of my first trimester to share the news about both you and Timmy," I added.

"With me," Jan said, "they probably waited eight months and then decided they had no choice but to warn folks of the impending disaster."

"No, with you, we blurted it out to everyone the minute we knew for sure. Grandpa Craig had just died, and we needed cheer," I said. Oh great, I had brought up another death.

Livy was now completely undone. "The plan was," she cried, "the plan was I would tell you and Dad the day before I left for England and then tell Grandma O the minute I got there."

"Well, when were you going to tell me?" Jan asked. "I'll be the aunt. From my own personal perspective, I'm the most important one!"

Livy ignored her. "We had a plan!" she wept.

Mike was holding her. "Dearest, not everything works out as we expect."

"Isn't that the truth?" Jan said. "I had every intention of being disco queen of America by now."

Livy turned to me, and I took her hand, "Mom, I knew Grandma O probably would not see the baby, but I wanted her to know that her first great-grandchild was on the way! That was why I was so eager to go over there. My child would be the link with Grandma, just as I am the link with Grandpa Craig. But she didn't know!"

Jan said, "Livy, if it's any comfort to you, I told Grandma at your wedding that you'd have at least six kids, given that you had gotten all of the domesticity genes Mom had inherited from Dad's side of the family."

"Jan, you didn't," I exclaimed.

"I did. Grandma laughed. She thought I was a hoot." Jan rocked back on her heels.

"Livy, there's a link. She was alive when your baby was conceived and during the first trimester," I said.

Livy just cried.

Jan told her, "Oh Livy, please stop. You're raining on Mom's parade. You would think she's the one who would be flat out on the floor."

I laughed but quickly stopped because Livy was in such distress.

Jan sought to reassure me. "Pregnant women get emotional. It's due to hormones."

"So I've heard," I said.

No matter what I said and no matter how outrageous Jan was, Livy would not stop crying. Mike took an intentionally loud breath and said, "I will reveal the secret ingredient. It's bourbon. I put a splash of bourbon in the ginger snap mix. I do it straight from the bottle, never with a spoon."

"No kidding!" Jan said. "After all the lectures I got about alcohol in high school, Dad here was spiking the cookies for our lunchboxes!"

Still Livy was in a paroxysm of tears. I was beginning to get scared, so I said, "We need a grandmother!"

Livy wailed and said, "But grandma's dead, and I didn't tell her."

"No, your Montclair grandmother!"

"Well, there you go, Liv," Jan put forth, "we've got a spare. You can tell Gram about the little one."

So Mike called Janet and explained why Livy was so devastated. He came back and said, "Gram's coming right over, and she said—and I quote—tell Livy not to despair, I've got mail!"

"Now, that's enigmatic," I said, and even Livy smiled.

It was as if everything was choreographed. Timmy suddenly pulled up in his Honda and came rushing in.

"I wanted be with you guys," he explained.

"And we with you, Tim," I said, kissing him.

"How come I'm the only one not getting kissed today?" asked Jan, who was twenty-nine. Mike and I both kissed her.

Then Ethan, who Livy had finally reached, walked in.

All hands were on deck when Janet hurried over with Alan.

We all settled around her as she sat down on the couch and pulled a piece of paper from her purse.

She said, "This is the e-mail exchange I had with Olivia yesterday. Sorry Livy, I hope you can forgive two grandmothers for being presumptuous."

Livy curled in Ethan's arm and nodded.

Janet said, "The first is from me: 'Dear Olivia—Thought I'd tell you something on the QT. There have been no announcements or anything like that. It's just that Livy has had such a glow recently that

I suspect she is pregnant. No, let me amend that. Livy is pregnant. We went out to lunch last week, and when I asked her if she would like a bit of wine, she demurred. What more proof do we need? I just say, thank goodness she's not a teetotaler like her mother! I'll close now. I see Amy and Pam coming up the sidewalk to get me for a tennis game. We play Canadian doubles. What this means is that they play singles and I stand on one side or the other, managing to hit a few balls. Hope you are feeling strong. Love ever, Janet.'

"Here is the reply: 'My dearest Janet—Thank you so much for your e-mail and I'm sure you're right. Let's call it Grandmother's intuition. Livy's having a baby! Don't worry. I'll act suitably surprised when Livy comes next week and tells me the news. There will be no pretense about my delight surely. Janet, you may not realize it being only in your eighties, but time is so fleeting. Livy is about to be a mother, and it seems like only yesterday that she was a baby and Craig and I were meeting her at JFK for the first time and Amy was just so joyful. She kept saying you don't know how much I love her, Mum, you just don't know. Well, of course, I did, having had the same experience. Indeed, it seems like only the day before yesterday when I was walking on the moor in Devon with tiny Amelia and her slightly older brother. I was fearful and anxious, but we had taken refuge in a beautiful part of the country, and my little ones made me so incredibly happy that I almost felt I should keep it secret. Well enough. Stephen has invited our friend Henri for tea, so I must rest up for that. It's simply glorious about Livy, and applause goes to Ethan, too! Love, Olivia."

"Livy, she knew!" I cried ecstatically. "Thank you, Janet. Oh, Janet, thank you!"

Then I asked, "Janet, how did you know to suddenly write to her?"

"Amy," she said, as if she was explaining the obvious, "your mother and I started our correspondence in 1966!"

My mother and I started our correspondence in 1947, when I unfortunately went away to school. The hourglass had been knocked to its side, but she wrote me, she wrote me faithfully. There were 403 letters by the time I got out of the sixth form, and more when I was in university, and many more after I came to America, and in the later years e-mail, too. Perhaps my mother had sent me her greatest love three thousand times.

Janet was reading the postscript my mother had added to her message, "Can you imagine our Amy a grandmother? As Jan would put it, watch out!"

Under cover of laughter, I raced to the den. I had not been on the computer since early that morning, but yes, my mother had written me one last time.

"Dearest," she wrote. "Stephen and I went on a grand outing in the country today. After a nice lunch at an inn, we passed an hour or so in a garden within a garden where the flowers sang and the sky was blue for everyone. It would have been perfection itself if only you had been there. There was a light breeze and the leaves rustled, so perhaps you were there. Remember how we did that to know we were close in spirit? I am going to take a bit of a nap now but will write more tonight. My greatest love, Mum."

I read her note five times on the screen and then printed it out. I kissed the paper and imagined the scent of jasmine. The wind had picked up, and the leaves strongly rustled. My mother was passing through.

Mike called out, "Love, the kids all want to come with us. Jan called Rick, and he'll come too. They won't be dissuaded."

So there were seven of us at the airport that night. I could not help but remember the evening thirty years ago when Mike and I had forlornly set out to England with our little girl after my father died. This time the mood was different. We were all sad and talked quietly, but there was no sense that there had been a twist of fate.

Stephen and I both spoke at our mother's service. We had divided up the territory. He spoke about what Mum did in the world. I spoke about what she did for us.

Stephen went first. He said our mother Olivia had been such a modest person, always believing that one should do what one was capable of and not brag about it, that almost no one knew the full range of extraordinary things that she had done in everyday life and in various circumstances.

He began the litany. She had swum well enough to have been considered an Olympic hopeful. She had been one of the few women of her time to go to university. She had traveled on her own in France and Switzerland. In our village in Devon, where the people had been initially suspicious of her because they had never met anyone of her background, she had won respect and admiration by rolling bandages and saving grease and generally doing what everyone else did. She learned Kiswahili when we went to East Africa, although this was not expected of her, and she had done what she could to fight racism. In later years back in London, she had headed the education committee of the London East African Club.

She had? Somehow, genius hadn't known. I guess that explained why about one-third of the people at her service were black. (Rick had whispered when we walked in, "You all arranged old home week for me? A little off on the geography, but I'm not choosey.")

"In fact," Stephen elaborated, "she was the liaison between the London East African community and the Regency Day School and helped students who needed it find the financial resources to attend."

What? My mother had sometimes spoken of the fund she and my father had set up after Lottie had given back the money they had contributed to her education. I had known that the fund had continued to grow, and Lottie had helped her to administer it. However, I had never asked questions about who the fund was helping. I wanted to smack my head but I felt I should continue to listen to what Stephen was saying. I might learn other things.

Stephen wanted to also mention a personal thing that he thought illustrated our mother's essence. He said that in her sixties, Mum had become a numismatist! She had known how much he and our father had loved working on their coin collections together. Stephen said, "I didn't know if I could proceed on my own after he died, so she jumped into the fray and learned everything, and together we got my own son Craig interested. Every time she visited us in Toronto and even when Craigy became a rough, tough football player, the three of us spent many happy hours discussing both coins and Craigy's grandfather. With my father dead and Susan's parents never in a position to visit, my mother had to carry water for four grandparents, and so she did."

There were such scores of things that hadn't registered on me that I might as well have been living in a parallel universe! Of course, the personal was supposed to be my territory, so I guess he had just stolen some of my thunder. But what the heck, she was his mother, too, and there was enough of the personal to go around.

Stephen ended by saying, "In this day of noisy self-aggrandizement, our mother's reticence might seem out of step. A simple fact remains —she did everything that she did."

Then it was my turn. I started with, "Mum was one of the finest people I have ever known. She is the reason I went one way when so many girls I was in school with went the other, although Dad helped tremendously, of course. She communicated love to me so well that she made it possible for me to be a mother too."

I took a breath and continued, "My first memory is of Devon and of our tiny rented house where the morning sun came through the bay windows of the sitting room and made patterns on the rug. It was here, while war raged in the outside world and with my father gone to fight in it, that my mother created serenity for Stephen and me. She made circumstances bow to childhood."

I told the story of Devon, not informed by adult reflections, but as I first remembered it. I told of how she had read to us, how she had taught us and talked to us, how she had always been with us in the afternoon, how we had walked on the moor among the wildflowers and the heather, our little dog Folly who meant so much to us running ahead and circling back.

I said, "In high summer and at other times when the weather was very fair, we walked in the other direction down a trail lined with roses to the beach where the Atlantic came in with a whoosh and out with a whoosh, surf and spray bouncing towards the gulls overhead and then sailing to our feet. Stephen and I would play in the rock pools, and my mother, taking pictures of us—snaps, as they were called—to send to my father on the battlefront, would tell us to pretend we were on holiday. There was no need to pretend, though. Every day that we were with my mother was a holiday."

The map with the pins was up next, but I suddenly digressed. "I have spoken Americanese for almost forty years, but there's one word in English English that outshines its American counterpart. Americans speak of going on vacation. The root is vacate. You leave your routine and do something different. Everyone needs a break. The English on the other hand refer to going on holiday. You do something sparkling, something uplifting to be treasured and remembered. Every day we spent with my mother was a holiday. When my father could be with the three of us, that was even better. That was truly a holy day."

I was going wildly off script. "My mother once said that London was where she had the happiest times with her love. My father said London was where it all happened for them. What that means is London was where my brother Stephen and I had the happiest times of our childhood. That was where it all happened for us."

Strange it was that I would have this realization not at my father's death but with my mother's. Extraordinary as things had been in Devon, the zenith for us as a family had been in London. The war was over, my father was home safe, Stephen and I went out to school every day, my parents had a social life again, we all had friends. In London, we had lived the life!

For some reason, I felt cheered finally figuring that out. I guess I had not realized that before, because of where we went after London. This was, of course, supposed to be my mother's eulogy, though, and not Amelia's epiphany, so with sheer force of will, I reined myself in and talked about how she helped my father resume his role in our household so seamlessly I could not recall it occurring.

Then, taking another deep breath, I spoke about how my mother had kept us close knit as a family all through the long and difficult years in Africa when Stephen and I were away three months out of four. "We wrote at the same hour," I said. "We thought about each other every time the leaves rustled. So it was fifty years ago, and so it was just the other day when she died. Time and distance are no match for love."

I ended by reciting a stanza from Wordsworth's "Intimations of Immortality," which both my parents had loved and which Mr. Cookson had quoted at Dad's service. My voice did tremble a little bit on "the glory of the flowers," but looking at Livy, who was carrying our line into the next generation, I had resonance when I said, "the strength in what remains behind."

I sat down, and Stephen whispered, "Sis, you did great!" as we watched Henri and Rachel get up to speak.

We had a lunch reception, and I was glad. There were so many people there that it was easier for us to go from table to table greeting everyone than to have a long receiving line. Along with persons I didn't know or only vaguely knew, there were the usual suspects. Christa was there with all five of her brothers. I wondered if there was anyone but Christa, Stephen, and me who still called the middle-aged Lawrence, Dennis, and Kenny—um, Ken—Cookson the Booms. Lottie had come along with the ever-loyal Ted Sanders, who had once again undergone a transformation. Now a fitness buff, he almost looked better in his sixties than in his thirties. Jory was there with the elderly Mrs.

Hobson—Grace—who had so earned her name and who had been Mum's only friend in Africa, just as Jory had been mine. On impulse and thinking it was better late than never, I suggested that the Hobsons sit with the Cooksons. Once I looked over and saw Christa and Jory talking animatedly.

Sitting quietly in one corner was an older lady who looked slightly familiar, but I had to ask who she was. It was Alice, our Alice. She had seen Mum's obituary, and so she came.

People stayed and stayed, and that was what we wanted.

That night, at a last family supper—everyone but Stephen and me were going home the next day, and Jersey would permanently become Henri's dog—the kids remarked that as sad as it had been, the day had had a glow.

Livy said, "You should have heard Jory go on and on about Grandma. He doesn't know what his family would have done if you guys hadn't been in the compound with them. He said she swam with him, tutored him, played games with him when you, Mom, were unavailable. What's more, she kept his mother in one piece."

"Yes," Jan remarked. "I thought I was going to a memorial service, but so many folks came up to me wanting to talk about the major things Grandma O had done for them, it seemed like a remake of *It's a Wonderful Life*!"

"Well, she did have a wonderful life," I said. "I misspoke when I said she just had an interesting life. She had a wonderful, wonderful life."

"She did what she was capable of doing and didn't brag about it," said Susan, who with Henri and Rachel had quietly managed all the logistics of the reception.

"And she was a fallible person too," Mike put in.

That was the ultimate compliment. My mother accomplished so much good and had been a fallible person, too. "Here, here!" Stephen and I chorused, and then everyone did, too.

Most of us wanted to take it easy after supper. Livy especially wanted to rest, but suddenly Jan asked, "Hey, Mom, I want to show Rick London at night. Would it be inappropriate if we went out?"

"Not at all," I replied. "Grandma O would like that."

"I'll go with you," Timmy said.

Livy, her feet on a hassock, cut him a look.

Then Craigy, whom I had not deemed to be terribly intuitive, said,

"Tim, let's do some male cousin bonding, go to a couple of pubs, hear some music."

I never was so glad to have someone invite my son out drinking.

As Mike and I were going to bed, I said, "Life among the Ords and the Kleins will go on."

"That it will, my love," Mike replied.

I intertwined myself with him.

In the year after my mother's death, life among the Ords and the Kleins not only went on, it speeded up.

Jan and Derek announced their engagement on Christmas Eve, right after Janet and I finished our reading of "The Gift of the Magi."

Jan later whispered to me, "We first did it, Mom, the night of Grandma O's service. Was that wrong?"

"No, darling," I answered. "There's some symmetry here. You were conceived the night of Grandpa Craig's service." Jan laughed delightedly.

They were married in late May on Martha's Vineyard, a place where both we and the Gibbses had vacationed. It was thought to be outlandish when Mike and I had had a family honeymoon, but it seemed to me that a destination wedding was not so very different, only in reverse order. The sky was blue for everyone, and the surf pounded in the background as Rick and Jan said their vows on the wide lawn at the Spinnaker Hotel. Livy, as matron of honor, watched them wed with a beatific smile, her and Ethan's son Michael Oliver, baby of honor and the new king of Kleinland, cooing in her arms.

There was sadness, too, that my mother wasn't there, but I assured Jan that she had known that this was in the offing.

"How, Mom?" Jan asked.

"I told her when all of you were in high school that Rick and Livy had the stuff of great friendship but that the razzle-dazzle was between him and you."

"Guess you knew before me," Jan said.

"Perhaps," I admitted. "Call it moms' intuition." It suddenly occurred to me that even when I was at my most arrested, my mother had suspected that I would be all right. That cheered me.

Two months after the wedding, we had the first annual Ord summer holiday in Lake Placid, New York. We were essentially having, in 2004, the holiday that my father had planned for 1974 but that we had never had because he had died and I was having Jan. Stephen and

I had laid the plan right after Mum's service, when I told him how sorry I was that we had pretty much gone our separate ways after we started raising families, that I had made very little effort to get to know Craigy. I had not been much of a sister-in-law to Susan, who was so kind and strong and who made so little of having survived a problematic childhood with a volatile, war-damaged father and a timid, passive mother.

I told him, "You and Susan even let me share your apartment so I could be weaned away from living with Mum and Dad after university. I mean, you guys needed me for a roommate like you needed a hole in your heads."

Stephen had said "Lake Placid is still about equidistant from Montclair and Toronto, and by then we'll have three Ord generations again."

So we shook on it.

The house we rented was on Mirror Lake, the quieter lake in town. Although not a huge dwelling, it had two full stories and an attic under the eaves and was designed to sleep a growing number of people. The living room had windows on three sides and a glass slider that opened onto a flower-ringed deck, beyond which was a wide lawn—ideal for croquet and badminton—leading down to a strip of a sand and then the lapping water. There was a dock, and we had a rowboat, a kayak, and a pontoon boat (very good for a baby) for our use.

Livy, Ethan, and Mikey O stayed the whole two weeks with us, and Craigy and his girlfriend Cara a week and a half. The other kids were there for a shorter period, but for a glorious five days there were fully twelve of us, plus our two dogs.

We swam, we boated, we hiked, we cuddled Mikey O, and in the evening after supper we played board games and charades. No electronics were allowed!

Perhaps it was the Adirondack Mountains surrounding the lakes or the nip of cold before the sun was high in the morning, but the whole area reminded Stephen and me of the Lake District in England. We wondered if my father had guessed that. We wondered if he had been giving us a sign. We were just so sorry we hadn't figured it out when Mum was alive. The evergreens murmured in the breeze. How she would have loved this holiday!

On our last day, Stephen and I brought the real estate agent a box of ginger snaps that Mike, Timmy, and Craigy had baked, and while she was nibbling, we inquired about renting the house for the same interval next summer.

"Sorry, guys, it's being converted to a time share."

"Perfect," we exclaimed. "We want to share time!"

Without my consulting Mike, or Stephen consulting Susan (because we knew they would be enthusiastic), we each signed up to purchase back-to-back periods. This would give us a month every year forever.

As I told Stephen, this was an investment in the future. "This is on the QT, but Jan told me that she and Rick are trying to get pregnant."

He said, "This is on the QT, but Cara and Craigy are pregnant."

"This family gets on!" I exclaimed.

We whooped and hollered, a brother and sister who went way back, walking down the main street of Lake Placid, New York. "You'll be getting a wedding invitation soon," Stephen told me.

When we got back to the house, I celebrated by joining Livy for a swim across the lake, Mike rowing the boat beside us.

That fall in Montclair was busy. I was an active grandparent. Livy, working part time at a local firm, and Ethan, with a flexible schedule as a professor, had arranged things so that most to the time one of them could be with Mikey; but for odd hours that weren't covered, Janet and I were joyously available, and we tended to stay for a while even after a parent had returned.

Jan had switched from being a school speech pathologist to private practice because she didn't like people telling her what to do, and I was in a loose partnership with her. Jan was just as intuitive with clients as I was, but she was also absorbed in the science of speech in a way that I had never been. While it was a hoot working with her, we both saw the arrangement as temporary. She was bringing in a colleague her age, and I had other fish to fry. I was in a doctoral program at Columbia now and expanding my master's thesis, "The Bonds of Sex: Woman Power on the Underground Railroad," into a book.

Finally, Mike and I were acting in yet another production of *The Music Man*. Once again, Mike reprised his role as the Music Man. Unfortunately, the ways of the world hadn't changed. I was judged too old to be even Marian's mother, who after all had a young son, so I was cast as a Pick-a-Little lady. That was the role I had originally been given when it had all begun for Mike and me.

My plate was full enough, but I kept puzzling about why my mother and Henri had seemed to have such a bond. He had been more than a son of a friend.

I reached back to when memory was mystical and time indivisible. In Devon, where the morning sun came through the bay window of the sitting room and made patterns on the rug, my mother joyously had told her ladies group that the woman and the boy had gotten to Switzerland. They had helped save two. Two, they had helped saved. Two! Two! I held up two fingers for two, and the ladies clapped and cheered again. They all wanted to help save more. My mother sang "Tea for two, and two for tea" as she poured tea, and everyone clapped and cheered again. Had the woman and the boy been Ruth Gold and Henri?

As luck would have it, Henri came to Manhattan for a brief business trip. He didn't have time to come out to Montclair for a night, so I met him in the city for lunch at a café in Greenwich Village. It had been one of Mike's and my favorite places when we had lived in the Village, and I told Henri I was pleased to see that they still used red-and-white-checked tablecloths.

After we ordered, I told him that he had done so much for my mother, and now I had one more favor to ask him. Since my mother's death, Lottie had been running the Regency Day scholarship fund more or less on her own, quite well and cheerfully, but she thought that someone close to Mum should also be involved. Stephen and I thought any advice we could give from across the Atlantic would be too limited. It seemed to us that Henri, with his caring and business acumen, was the right person, especially since that would let Rachel, a fairly recent graduate of Regency Day, also provide input, and so we'd get two for the price of one.

Henri said yes with alacrity.

We talked a little about Rachel, who was expecting, and then about how Jersey was. Henri said, "She's just fine. She's my buddy, and we have our routines. However, every time our walks take us past your mother's house, she pauses and looks at the door as if she expects Olivia to come out and call to her."

"We're so glad a young family brought the house," I said. "Thank you for handling that for us, Henri."

"It's nothing," Henri said.

We had finished our main course, and the waitress had brought apple cobbler for me and espresso for Henri. It was now or never.

"Henri," I asked, "what's the link between you and my mother?"

His jaw tightened. He looked surprised. Mike had suggested that I leave it alone. I should have listened.

"Oh, I'm sorry, Henri," I said. "You don't need to say anything."

"No, it's all right," he said. "Olivia was such a quiet unassuming person, but you should know what she did for my mother and me in 1944."

"We were in Devon in 1944," I said, "and that was when you fled to Switzerland."

"You know your mother's cousin Céline and her husband André were in the French underground."

I nodded.

"Through intermediaries, they were in contact with a man known as Louis the Buyer, who repeatedly slipped out of France to purchase supplies in London and New York for the Resistance. Through intermediaries, your mother was also in contact with this man. What this meant was—"

"My mother and cousin Céline could be in contact with each other!" I said. "I think I knew that."

"Yes. Your mother organized a small group of reliable local women to help her fulfill requests. They collected clothes and dropped them off at certain places. They mailed needles, buttons, and thread to designated addresses. There was an account in Bideford they made deposits to. They did other things."

"I do remember her ladies' group," I said. They had been quiet, unassuming women, too, the antithesis of the Colonial Office witch wives.

He continued, "Now, my father had been an ophthalmologist in Paris, but when the roundups were about to start, we moved to an outer suburb east of the city. *Mon père* worked as a mason. I think we took an assumed name. I went to a Lutheran kindergarten. We were all right for a while. People were getting poorer, though. There was a reward for turning in Jews. My mother and I were visiting her friend —your cousin Céline—in the next town when the police arrested my father. André found out, alerted Céline, and so we hid at their house in a small attic room."

We both looked down.

After a minute, Henri resumed speaking. "We couldn't stay with Céline and André indefinitely. It wouldn't have been safe for anyone. It would have jeopardized their other work. We had relatives in Switzerland. It was disturbing to think of fleeing east, especially when the Allied invasion, when it came, would come from the west, but the adults could think of no other way. Céline knew people who would move and shelter us through central France, but her network didn't extend to the French-Swiss border. The person who knew or, more accurately, had known persons in the area was Olivia."

"But that had been in 1931," I said.

"Exactly! It had been a different time, under different circumstances. Approached through Louis the Buyer's contacts, she could only go on her instincts as to who was trustworthy, who could be quick-witted, who was brave, and who would be least likely to be Nazi sympathizers. She picked three families, agonizing the most over the last one, since it would be for them to get us across the line. She wrote us letters of introduction to give to each family, writing them in such a way that if we were caught, the persons they were addressed to would not be revealed. She had a Swiss bank account. She said it would be ours when we got there. Two days after Céline received everything, my mother and I started. We went from village to village, house to house, barn to stable. It was a little like the American underground railroad."

"My mother wanted me to be frightened enough to follow instructions without questions but not terrified. She said that although people were after us, Mrs. Ord's letters had magical powers. On the border, Olivia's sense proved unerring. All three families come through. They all risked their lives for us. Sixteen days after we had said good-bye to Céline, we were in Basel."

"That's good," I said faintly.

Letters, neat script filling sheets of thin paper, were flying before my eyes—my father's letters to my mother during the war, my mother's letters to me to school, her letters for and to Henri and his mother, Janet's and my mother's letters to each other. They all had been magical talismans.

"I was in my third year at the local university in 1958 when your mother visited us, and it was so grand for my mother to see her again and for my stepfather and me to finally meet her. She was just so gracious. We thanked her over and over, but she always replied by expressing gratitude to us. She said she was so grateful to have the opportunity to do something in the face of so much horror."

"I know she was very glad to help save two people, even if she couldn't help save more," I said.

"Two?" Henri exclaimed. "Two? If my mother and I had not survived, my half brothers and their children never would never have been. Rachel would not exist, and I would not be expecting a grandchild. Amy, your mother helped saved our whole family line!"

"Oh, Henri," I murmured. "Oh, Henri, you have given me such a wondrous gift."

He replied, "Olivia didn't just help save me once, she helped saved me twice. When Rachel and I arrived in London, so distraught and bewildered after my wife's sudden death, Olivia was there for us. She helped us live a manageable life again. I think of her as my second mother. Is that presumptuous of me?"

"No, Henri, goodness no," I replied. "When Stephen and I became adults, we journeyed away from my mother to make our homes where we were supposed to have them. You were the one who came to be with her in England. Thank you, Henri, so very much!"

Joy rose in me. I had always thought Timmy stood for the child my mother might have had if we had not gone to Africa, or the child she might have lost in miscarriage—and in a way he did. It was also Henri, though. Henri was the third child!

"Life is miraculous," I said to Henri.

"Agreed!" he replied.

Lunch was over. Henri had to get back to his business meeting, and I wanted to be part of Mikey O's first swimming lesson later in the afternoon. There was some haggling over who would get to pay the bill, but finally I snatched it.

We said good-bye on the sidewalk outside the café. I hugged Henri, my head momentarily resting on the lapels of his tweed jacket, which covered his shirt and vest. I laughed a little. Henri, a man of various nationalities, looked supremely British in Greenwich Village.

"Henri," I all but pleaded, "please come visit us at Mirror Lake next summer—Rachel and her family, too. Stephen and I want it to be a gathering place for kith and kin. If you are there, it will be a holiday!"

"If not next summer, then the summer after," Henri promised. "We'd be enchanted!"

This was enchantment, as my father used to say. That was what I thought as I drove back to Montclair to meet my firstborn and my grandson at the Y. The Colonial Office witch wives had not prevailed. The hourglass had been righted! Henri had righted it for us.

The time we lost as a family when we so heedlessly went to East Africa in 1947 had been made up in infinite degree later on for three of us. For me, it was through my marriage with Mike and our raising children exactly the way we wanted to in the swirl of extended family. For Stephen, it was through his equally happy, if different, life with Susan and Craigy in Toronto. For my mother, it had been through her three decades of being a grandmother who sometimes lived in, and by having Henri, the child she had helped saved, come to Britain and be her mainstay in her old age.

As I swung off the highway, drove a few blocks through Clifton, and turned onto Valley Road, joy continued to rise within me, but it was tempered and would always be tempered by the bittersweet. On the ghastly, terrifying day that Stephen and I were sent off to Nairobi for the first time, my father had told the indifferent pilot, "This is tough on all of us." The salient words were "all of us." Bloody hell, he wanted to be with his kids, too!

My dutiful, well-meaning, loving father had lost the most time and gained back the least. The war had taken him from us for five years. We had thought we were going to Africa for his sake, but he had had to endure long separations from the children he had been united with less than two years before. Then he had fallen down dead at sixty-six. What a gyp, what a measly gyp! He had had only a glimpse, the merest tease through Livy and from Craigy's expected arrival, of what was to come. Yet perhaps he and I had a different measure of time. He looked for the glory in the flowers. In fleeting moments, he found enchantment.

I pulled up at the Y. Livy had just parked and was lifting Mikey O out of his car seat. She did it in one deft swoop. One second he was in the car, the next, he was in her arms. She looked as if she had been doing this all her life.

"Hey, Mikey O," I called.

He smiled a smile that looked like sunrise.

"You can be the first to know," Livy said. "Ethan and I decided that Mikey O sounded too much like an old-style gangster, or as some would say, a gangsta. We're switching to calling him Michael."

The appellation Grandma O had worked, Mikey O hadn't. I was so glad I had followed Janet's advice and had not ventured any opinions.

"Wonderful," I said, kissing Michael and kissing Livy. I was pulled back into the here and now.

A few days later, at the Klein family Sunday supper, I told the crew what my mother had done for Henri and his mother. They already knew the other things she had done, so, as Jan put it, this wasn't just icing on the cake, this was a whole other cake, fully frosted. Mike, my baker lover, lit up at that analogy.

"Did Uncle Stephen know?" Timmy asked.

"Not specifically," I replied. "He was two years older than me, though, over seven on VE Day. He did have a concept of what the war was, that it was why we were separated from our father, that my mother and the women she had organized were doing things in the shadows. Later, he sort of connected the dots."

"But why didn't Grandma tell anyone?" Livy wanted to know.

"I've pondered that," I answered slowly. "It's not like she went to lengths to keep anything secret. I heard about Ruth and Henri now and again when she was growing up. We set up the Swiss village each Christmas. She merely didn't speak of how she had helped them. I think there was some heroic part of her that she wished to keep to herself, although surely my father knew. Perhaps it was her way of remaining her own person."

I paused and then spoke again. "My family did have difficulty with information sharing. If we had an Achilles heel, I think it was only that. Things just seemed to happen to us without much explanation. This may be partly a reflection of that. Then too, during the war, people had their ordinary lives placed into suspended animation. They did unheard of things in a temporary existence driven by overwhelming circumstance, and then afterwards, there was some sort of bifurcation as people grabbed for the lives they expected to have. We never saw Jenny again after the war, for example."

No one noticed I had mixed metaphors or had thrown Jenny in for some reason. Instead, Janet said, "I'm sure you're right, Amy, but remember too that your mother was considerate to a fault. When you met Henri, she undoubtedly wanted you to see him as Henri and not as someone she had helped save. She may have thought that if anyone was to tell the story, it should be him."

Mike added, "She did what she was capable of doing and didn't brag about it."

"And she was fallible too," all my kids chorused.

Suddenly, Jan threw her napkin up in the air and then joined hands with Rick. She said, "Now is as good time as any."

Her slender creamed-colored hand looked so right and natural against his large mahogany-colored one.

"We're expecting," she said. "I'm fifteen weeks."

"We had an ultrasound Friday," Rick said. "And drum roll, please."

"Her name is Amelia Lynne Klein-Gibbs!" Jan and Rick said together.

There was pandemonium.

My heart swelled to know that the first biracial child born in our family would have my name as well as that of her other grandmother.

I looked first at Mike and then at everyone around the table, settling last on Janet, whose eyes were alight. Everything was full circle. Respectful nonbeliever that I was, I had an inkling of redemption.

CHAPTER 12

The Fullness of Time

Mirror Lake, New York, July 25, 2014

THINGS CAME FULL CIRCLE for me again, although in a different way, the next year when Christa, a radiant bride at age sixty-five, married Jory. The pairing of my best childhood friend in London with my best childhood friend in Africa was so natural and obvious that I wanted to smack my head that I hadn't introduced Christa and Jory when we were all at university, Kate Hepburn notwithstanding. Christa assured me though that it happened when it was supposed to happen, in the fullness of time. Indeed, the theme of the wedding was it's never too late to live happily ever after. She and I did share a bittersweet laugh, though, over the fact that I wouldn't have connected with Mike if her mother had not suggested I join GLOCO, and she would not have finally gotten to know Jory if my mother hadn't died and had a memorial service.

"Here's to the other mother!" we shouted.

I have not been back to England since Christa's and Jory's marriage. My life is fully on the western side of the Atlantic, and when Mike and I travel, there are other places we want to go. Last year, we accompanied Stephen and Susan to Singapore, where an international numismatist convention was being held. It was the first trip with only the four of us, and we had an absolutely lovely time. Stephen, who picks up his grandson from school most days and coaches his soccer team, has fortunately evaded the widow maker.

We lost our sweet Alan in 2008, but not before he met Livy's second son, his namesake Alan. Janet continues strong, ever a blend of energy and serenity. She is treasurer of the League of Women Voters, on the board of the library, and local chairperson of Pax Christi, a Catholic peace group. She gave up her driver's license at ninety-two, but Pam and I drive her anywhere she wants to go, and yes, we still manage games of Canadian doubles!

Janet shares the Highland Avenue house now with Jan, Rick, and their three daughters Amelia Lynne, Olivia, and Emma. Jan constantly tells her girls how lucky they are to have a great grandmother who always lives in. It's family assisted living all the way around, and Amelia Lynne says that having the family pool in the backyard is nice too. The two older girls both intend to be president of the United States (consecutively), because, raised in the Obama era, they believe that all children with a black father and a white mother must grow up to lead their countries.

Timmy and his wife Greta don't have children yet and may not even plan to, but they have plants. They met on the internet, their common link being that they were both working at tech companies. However, when they became a couple they left that world and, to my delight, opened up a greenhouse and nursery in Cedar Grove. It is to Mike's delight as well, since in the corner of Klein Flower and Vine there is a shop-within-a-shop called Kith, Klein, and Cookies where Mike, retired as an actuary, sells baked goods.

I think Mike still has one more rendition of *The Music Man* in him, but he has largely given up leading-man roles since Livy, the one child of ours who inherited our love of amateur musical theater, now usually gets leading lady roles. Instead, he does directing, which is what he always had a natural flair for. I still do bit parts. The plays get rave reviews.

"Grandma Amy, you're a rock star!" Little Alan tells me whenever he sees *The Ties of Sex: Woman Power on the Underground Railroad* in the window of the Montclair Barnes and Noble.

I am not a rock star. It is more like adopted hometown girl makes good. My book is on the back shelves of the Verona and West Orange branches and not stocked at the Paramus one. (Online sales are doing reasonably well, though.) I couldn't even prevent alteration of the title. I had referred to "Bonds of Sex" for a reason, but the publisher thought readers would enjoy the pun provided by using "ties," as in railroad ties. Pam, from her years in editing, says that such things are not to be fought. Oh, well!

No, I am far from a rock star, but in my older years I am pleased to be adjunct professor of history Amelia Ord Klein at Montclair State University, and I do thank Ethan for so graciously sharing his department with his mother-in-law. My area is American and British social history, 1850–1970. My students, many of whom are commuters and juggling many responsibilities, are seeking a glimpse of how the strange past flows into their perplexing present and mercurial future, and I do my best to be a guide.

As I told Mum, it is coming full circle here as well, because at sixteen, I did tell my favorite teacher Miss Linfield I wanted to be a history teacher. The aspiration did not get loss in the shuffle so much as it got overlaid with other things I needed to do to be who I wanted to be. My mother knew that I would choose to go into academia when the time was right, even if that was at retirement age, and I guess I did, too.

One of the advantages of teaching is that you ostensibly get summers off, and it is summer now, high summer. My family and Stephen's family are all up at Mirror Lake at our time share. Henri, Rachel, and her family are here for their biannual visit and have rented the house next door, so it's a holiday!

Today it is warmish. The sky is blue for everyone, and there is a light breeze, causing the leaves to gently rustle. The lake sparkles in the sun! Mike and Stephen are out on the pontoon boat with one contingent of family and friends. Livy and Ethan have organized a game of badminton with their boys, and everyone else but me is playing in the lake or by its edge. I am sitting on the flower-fringed deck in an Adirondack chair, alternately surveying the scene and roughing out a book proposal.

For my new book, I am shifting gears. Reams have been written about the baby boomers, but what about that sliver of a generation who came just before them, the war babies? Regardless of how safe some of us were, World War II enveloped our dawning consciousness in so many ways that people like me have never called that war anything but "the war" (as my speech kid Tricia, now a psychologist, pointed out years ago). The war separated us from our fathers for years and sometimes permanently. Our mothers did unheard of things; they ran the show, and then slipped back into traditional roles. The war babies were the first to answer President Kennedy's call to service and were at the forefront of the civil rights and feminist movements, movements that were the paradigm for the other movements for social justice that came afterwards. All that the baby boomers, that large and noisy cohort, did was steal our thunder. Perhaps I will title the book "Stolen

Thunder." The publisher, though, will probably have me change it to "Silent Thunder" so as to make a pun about the silent generation, of which the war babies were supposedly a part. Then again, I like the title "War Babies." I will start with my experience in Devon.

A small hand taps my knee. It is Emma. Named only after herself, she is the family's youngest, three and a half and still with a touch of baby fat. Her neon-blue bathing suit is dripping.

"Grandma Amy, come into the water so I can splash you" she says, sounding just like Jan used to.

Oops, I've been neglecting the kids! Well, that's soon remedied.

"Double sure!" I reply, closing my laptop. I dash into the water with Emma so she can splash me.

I have come to understand that time need not always be linear. It doesn't even have to be finite, to be hoarded, contained in an hour-glass. Time, if you experience that love that Mike and I have had from our families and with each other, is never ending, swirling, melding color, as in a kaleidoscope.

ABOUT THE AUTHOR

Lisa Blumberg was born in Montclair, New Jersey. She is a graduate of Wellesley College, with a major in political science, and Harvard Law School. Her main career has been as an in-house corporate counsel, but she has also written numerous pieces on medical ethics and disability rights topics, as well as an article on the historical basis of the *Little House* books by Laura Ingalls Wilder. A childhood letter that she wrote to Jacqueline Kennedy after President Kennedy's assassination was included in the best seller *Letters to Jackie* edited by Ellen Fitzpatrick. *Righting the Hourglass* is her first novel. She lives in Connecticut.

Made in the USA
Coppell, TX
12 December 2020

44353657R00204